Ellen Bray

JANE JULIAN

William Morrow and Company, Inc.   *New York*

Library of Congress Cataloging-in-Publication Data

Julian, Jane.
Ellen Bray.

I. Title.
PR6060.U39E4   1986   823'.914   85-31975
ISBN 0-688-06471-X

Printed in the United States of America

First U.S. Edition

1 2 3 4 5 6 7 8 9 10

BOOK DESIGN BY JAYE ZIMET

To Cicely
without whom none of this
would have been possible

Acknowledgments

Thanks are due to many people but especially to F. L. Harris of Redruth who, in a different context, showed me what rich seams remain untapped in Cornish history; and to the staff of the Cornish Local History Archives section of Redruth Library who provided many of the tools —the *West Britons* of the 1860s and the 1870s—for working the seams; to June Hall who worked hard to bring the ore to grass; and to Victoria Petrie-Hay, my editor, who knocked it into shape.

—J.J.

Ellen Bray

Chapter One

I

WORKING in the heat was oppressive, sweat soaked even their thick aprons. Their arms were reluctant to lift their cobbing hammers, and they had become indolent. The man in charge of them was no more lively: he had fallen asleep and lay, head to one side, snoring peacefully.

The bal maidens joked coarsely about him. Here, in the cobbing sheds, women ruled. Had the overseer dared to rebuke them they would have been quick to resent his interference, for the sheds were *their* world. It was only with the newer, younger, girls that his words ever held sway.

The bal maidens were a neatly dressed band of women, though by now, at the end of a hot and sticky day, their crisp bonnets were limp and dust-stained. They were proud women too, independently minded; in conversation, they were coarse and unbridled, and now, with a man asleep and at their mercy, they taunted him, speculating on his physical attributes, bringing blushes to the more tender souls among them, the Methodists and Bible Christians, and the new young maids.

Ellen Bray laughed with her comrades, though she did not

join in their comments. She was vaguely embarrassed by their bawdiness. She was not ignorant of man and his form—living at home was too intimate and close for that—but her upbringing had made her reticent about sex. It was something private, she felt, too serious a matter for jest.

Her friend, Jane Rowse, looked differently on it. She enjoyed talking about men, and their performance; she took pleasure in recounting her adventures with them, and especially when those stories revealed male shortcomings.

Ellen looked at Jane now. She was less affected by the heat than the others; her hammer still swung steadily, pounding the rock, reducing it to manageable size. Her arms were well muscled, her shoulders strong, and her figure full. She had loosened her hessian apron and her bare shoulders ran with sweat and glistened in the heat. Her face, always cheerful and ruddy with health, was touched by the sun in spite of her bonnet's shade. She smiled, showing white even teeth, when she saw Ellen looking at her.

Ellen was seventeen, two years younger than her friend, but nevertheless she was much the taller. Where Jane was round and full, Ellen was tall and slender; where Jane was fair, Ellen was dark; where Jane was light-hearted and frivolous, Ellen was thoughtful and serious. But in spite of the difference in their temperament they were close, and Ellen thought of Jane as a friend in a way she thought of no one else. She knew her father disapproved of Jane's manner with men, of her "loose morals." But Ellen could not accept his judgment; he did not know her friend's true worth, could not, as a man.

Ellen felt disloyal to her father for her fondness for Jane, but when the afternoon shift ended and they left the dust and heat of the cobbing sheds, she wished for no one better to walk home with. The air was sultry, the sun still high and hot. Even at the top of the hill there was little breeze. Across the downs the gorse shone golden bright and even at this distance, its scent, heavy with honey, came to them. They stood for a moment leaning on a stone wall looking out over the countryside. Below them, beyond the village of Carharrack, a long line of mine buildings, chimneys of engine houses, smithies, wagon sheds and powder stores stretched along the seam running from Wheal Pink to Wheal Jane marking the great copper field of Gwennap.

"Burrowed with holes, 'tis," said Jane. "Just think of it, someday 'twill be so riddled with shafts and levels, 'twill collapse beneath the weight of the buildings atop of 'em."

Ellen smiled. "What was it like before, I wonder, before they started to dig for copper and tin? I do suppose it was pretty then?"

" 'Tis not so pretty now," said Jane. Over the mines a pall of smoke hung. " 'Tis pretty even so," said Ellen. Just below them, under the brow of the hill, nestled an old farmhouse, set in a clump of trees. There was a murmur of insects, a soft mournful low from a single cow, the grunt of pigs seeking shelter within the copse. Beyond that, she could see the village of Carharrack, its Methodist chapel frowning over the long rows of humble cottages. There was no movement in the streets. Even for the children it was too hot and they would be sheltering within the thick cob-walled houses.

Then she heard the sound of voices, men's voices, singing a miners' song, or was it a hymn? Either way it was an unfamiliar tune, its air deep with passion. With it came the sound of marching feet. Where could men find such energy on so lazy a day?

Jane raised her head at the sound. "Look," she said, her voice showing surprise and curiosity.

Round the corner of the road, past the village inn and the church, came a treble line of men—miners still clad in working clothes, red-stained, and with their hard hats on their heads, some still with candles affixed. They marched with purposeful stride, keeping ranks and singing lustily. One deep voice led the men, a voice Ellen knew. It was her father there at the head of the column, with her brother Edward beside him, her father raising the voice that lent body to the Stithians chapel choir. The tune had changed now and she recognized the Wesley hymn, "Christ Whose Glory Fills The Skies." It was one of her father's favorites. Most of the men behind knew it and those who did not quickly picked up the air. The notes came up the hill toward them, now clear, now faint, but always with her father's bass beneath the rest.

"What are they about do you reckon?" said Jane. Ellen could not think, but she was moved by the sight and the sound, and she was proud that, whatever the reason for the men's marching, it was her father at their head.

"Come on," said Jane. "Let's go down to see where they're going."

They raced along the dusty lane down the hillside, but when they reached the bottom the lines of men had vanished. Ahead was a swirl of dust and the lingering echoes of the hymn. They ran on in spite of the heat, and caught up with the last of the marchers at the entrance to Wheal Clifford. Jane caught hold of one of the miners by the arm. He turned and grinned.

"Not now," he said. "Any other time, but not now."

"You flatter yourself," Jane haughtily replied, but Ellen noticed how she clung closely to the man.

"What's it all about, Jos?" Jane asked.

"Man's work," he said dismissively. "What's it to you?"

She jostled him and he stumbled. "Man's work!" she snorted and stood, strong arms on broad hips. "I'll give you man's work."

"Strike, that's what 'tis." Jos grinned at her and looked admiringly at Jane. "I'll see you after."

"You'll tell me now," she said and held him so that he could not follow his comrades into the mine workings.

"Strike, like I said. We're trying to persuade Clifford men to strike with us. We want the end of the five-week month, that's what."

Ellen knew how indignant her father waxed about this and other injustices suffered by the miners. She saw Jos looking at her.

"You're George Bray's maid?"

She nodded.

"He's a brave fighter, is George. It's him as is going to speak to the men at Clifford. He's all right, is George."

Ellen was proud her father should be spoken of like this. She had heard him at home talking about the mines and knew how important it was to him that the miners should stand up for their rights.

Jos seemed to have given up his struggle to follow his comrades and seemed satisfied to stay with the girls. He put his arms around Jane and drew her to him but she thrust him away.

"If 'tis man's work," she said, "hadn't you better join 'em?"

He grinned at her and went into the mine, past the great gates, over the workings toward the crowd of men standing at the heads of the shafts, waiting for the Clifford miners to come to grass at the end of their core.

"Man's work!" said Jane. She was still irritated. "What sort of work do they think we do? We dress ore! Are we any softer than them?" She clenched her fists and raised her arms to show her muscles. "Wait till I get Jos Paynter on his own."

"What'll you do?" Ellen asked.

"I'll show him what man's work really is, and woman's too. He's all right, is Jos. They're all all right in their place." She sniggered as if remembering something secret and pleasurable. She glanced at Ellen. "You're a deep one," she said.

"What do you mean?" Ellen wanted to go into the mine workings to find out what was happening, but Jane took hold of her arm and led her away.

"You're a deep one," she repeated. "You never say what you get up to."

"I don't get up to anything," Ellen said, but she remembered, with mild guilt, a walk in the woods with a farmer's boy from the village when they had held hands, then kissed. Reuben had tried to persuade her to lie with him in the bracken but some instinct held her back.

"I don't know what you mean," she said, but was aware of the blush spreading up her cheeks.

Jane sniggered again and then said defiantly, as if Ellen had accused her, "I enjoy it anyway."

They had left the mines behind them and were coming to the farm fields that ran beside the stream to Gwennap Church. Trees, giving welcome shade, hung over the lane. The bramble bushes, white with blossom, promised a fruitful autumn. Ellen breathed deeply. She was filled with a satisfying content: it was the warmth, she thought, and the country air, the leafiness and lush growth that abounded here, and the soft murmur of the stream over its granite bed. Here it was peaceful, quiet, somnolent. There, beyond the hedge, where the parish burial ground lay, the peace was of a different kind. She turned her head away from the sight of the gravestones, so many of them to men of the mines, young men killed below ground. That had no place in her thoughts now. There were other more lively, hopeful, things to occupy her.

Jane was humming a tune, and soon the hum changed to

a low throaty contralto. Jane's voice was seductive. The songs she sang in the cobbing shed were popular ballads but now the song was a sweet sad country air, telling of love betrayed. Ellen joined in, softly, and so, singing in harmony, they came to the road up the hill and had to save their breath for the steep rise.

At the top their ways parted, but they stood for a moment, unwilling to break their warm companionship. It was Ellen who broke the silence, reluctantly, for the news she had to tell, though exciting to her, would bring sadness to Jane.

"We shall be going to Australia."

Jane turned sharply. "When?"

Ellen did not know. They had talked about it at home for as long as she could remember, ever since they had heard of the opening of mines in South Australia. Many of their friends and neighbors had gone and sent back tales of plenty. Her father was cautious and unbelieving, but the enthusiasm of Edward, her brother, had finally convinced George Bray. " 'Tis likely to be better than here," he had admitted. "However rough it be."

They had saved and scrimped and though they had not yet enough for the passage, the pitch that George and his son were working now was so promising, Edward claimed, that at the end of another two months, with luck, they would have plenty and to spare.

"I don't know when," Ellen said to her friend. "Not for some time yet." They looked at each other and Jane smiled. "I'll miss you," she said. "You're the only one . . ."

Ellen did not ask her what she meant. She thought she knew. She and Jane had begun in the cobbing sheds of Wheal Prosper at the same time, when Ellen was twelve and raw and innocent. Jane, worldly-wise and already a bal maiden of experience, though not yet fifteen, had sheltered her from the harshnesses of the work as much as she could until Ellen could stand up for herself.

"I'll miss you too," said Ellen.

"I've thought of going myself," said Jane. "They do say there's twenty men for every woman. That would suit me, don't you think?" But she was not serious.

Ellen turned for home with the echoes of the song they had sung still ringing in her ears. She began to sing it to herself softly, not wishing to disturb the peace of the lanes. She crossed the main Falmouth road. Below, in the village of Ponsanooth, she could see wagons at the gunpowder works. Large draught horses stood swishing their tails against the flies; beyond, a mill wheel lazily turned in the sluggish leat from the Kennal River. She would miss this when they got to South Australia. It wasn't only people like Jane she would miss. It was the beauty of the Cornish countryside, the gently rolling hills, the green fields, the valleys that shyly disclosed themselves, the banks of black-thorn, the clumps of thrift, but above all, the golden gorse.

Would there be gorse in South Australia? What would this new world hold for her? She did not mind so long as her father and brother were there with her, and her sister Julia.

She should hurry home, to help Julia. Her sister was in charge of the household now, though she was only twelve. Ellen smiled to herself and hurried on. Julia was too proud to ask for help but there were times when she was grateful for Ellen's strength.

She heard a call and saw her sister ahead, waiting for her at Matthew's Meadow, sitting astride the stile, her dress spread about her. She was a rosy-cheeked child; no, child no more, thought Ellen, for she had to behave like a young woman, managing the house, cooking, washing, cleaning, while the rest of them went out to work. She seemed happy with her fate. When their mother had died, two years earlier, she had im-mediately made herself mistress of the kitchen, and Ellen, who had no wish to leave the cobbing sheds to become a household drudge, was grateful that Julia was happy to take over.

"You're bright and cheerful," she said.

Julia, for answer, jumped from the stile and from behind her back took a large daisy chain she had been hiding and, reaching up, put it around her sister's neck.

"There," she said. "You're a princess. It's a magic necklace. It will bring you good fortune."

"It'll break."

"You must be careful with it then." She danced away across the field, and the cows, lying contentedly in the shade of the hedge, raised their heads in mild curiosity at the girl's move-ments. Ellen followed more slowly, still conscious of the heat and the sweat which, with the dust of the sheds, had congealed about her skin. She wished there might be water enough at home for her to have a proper body wash, with Julia to sluice her down, but the village pump was running low and there would only be enough for her to sponge herself.

She stood at the sink when she got home and stripped to the waist, glad to shed the shirt and shift that clung wetly to her. Julia brought her a dipper of cold water and she soaked a cloth in it and cooled herself, under her arms, about her neck and under her breasts. Julia took the cloth and reached up to wipe her back. Ellen stretched and luxuriated in her sister's attention. She loosened her skirt and stepped out of it and bathed her legs and thighs with what was left of the water. If she had thought in time she would have gone to Kennal Vale and plunged in the pool below Clymo's Mill.

Refreshed, she put on a cotton dress, one that had been her mother's, and set about helping Julia prepare the meal for the men's return.

"They're late," said Julia. "Has anything happened?"

"I saw them going to Wheal Clifford to meet the men there. I expect they're talking. You know what men are like," Ellen said in a superior manner. But she wished she might have been able to be with the men to know how things were faring. It wasn't only men's work, she thought, whatever Jos Paynter might argue. Women too had a say in what went on in the mines. Without their work it wouldn't matter how much rock men brought to grass. It was the women who rendered it fit for smelting.

Edward was full of the matter when at length he and his father returned; but George Bray was more reticent.

"We told 'em," said Edward. "You should have seen us."

"I did see you," said Ellen.

"What did you think?" said Edward.

"You looked as if you meant business," she answered and turned to her father. "What was it about? We saw Jos Paynter and he said it was about the five-week month."

"Not only that," said George Bray. " 'Tis time we formed a miners' society, combined together, matched the mine captain's strength with strength of our own, time we got together and chose men to speak for us."

"What did the Clifford men say?"

"Bloody cowards," said Edward.

George Bray looked at his son reprovingly.

"Well," said Edward. "That's what they are. Afraid of being

blacklisted. They'll not stand up for themselves," he said, turning to Ellen. "They're afraid."

"They know copper's in a bad way," said his father. "And tin. They think now's no time to ask for better conditions or more money, when mines are closing."

"It'll be better in South Australia, anyway," said Edward, his voice brightening at the thought.

"Maybe, maybe not," said his father. But he too was buoyed up by the thought that perhaps in a few months' time they would be on their way to a world where the skill of the Cornish miner was valued, and where, if the tales were true, meat was to be had every day of the week.

"Yes," he said, and began to say grace before Edward could start eating the pilchards and turnips Julia had brought to table. "Maybe, God willing, things will be better there."

II

THE sultriness yielded to thunder and Sunday, their blessed day of rest from the mine, was fragrant with scents sweetened by the rain. It seemed to Ellen sinful to spend any part of the day indoors and she resented the need to go to chapel, but she kept her thoughts to herself. Her father would have disapproved and she could not bear that. She suffered in silence, listened to the long, droning sermon of the minister, a visitor from Redruth, sang willingly enough with the rest of the congregation, but breathed with relief when the service was over and she could go again into the open. The chapel had held the heat of summer within its walls; its varnished pine pews had been sticky, its air musty.

As they walked back along the village street toward home, she thought that her father guessed her feelings, but he said nothing, merely smiled and, like her, breathed deeply of the soft country air.

" 'Tis sweet here above ground," he said and took hold of her arm to link it with his. "Well, Ellen my love, what do you want to be doing this lovely day?"

She was surprised at his question. What would she want to do but what they always did after chapel? They would go for a walk along Kennal Vale, beside the river where they could and climbing up into the woods when the river plunged into channels too steep to follow.

"Why," she said, "walk of course, as usual. With you." She clasped his hand affectionately. "What else do I belong to do?"

"I'm expecting visitors, Richard Bryant and his son James. You won't want to be bothered with us. We'll be talking tin and copper, talking about forming a miners' society. You won't want to be concerned with that. Miner's talk. Man's work."

There was that phrase again that had so annoyed Jane and that angered her in the same way.

"Well?" her father said. "What'll you do?"

"Stay and listen," she said. "Do you mind?"

George Bray laughed. "How could I mind, my love? But don't blame me if you get bored. It'll be wearisome business, bound to be."

Ellen knew the Bryants were miners, tributers with her father and brother. She had never met them, though she had heard of them. They lived at Cusgarne, near neighbors to her grandmother, Granny Pascoe, but she knew little else of them. She felt little curiosity about them and when they arrived she sat quietly in the background, almost out of sight in the shadow, to listen to their "man's talk."

"What's the news from Clifford?" asked George Bray. "Have they agreed to support us?"

Richard Bryant shook his grizzled head. His hair was cut short, as most miners wore their hair, to fit beneath the skull caps they wore under their hard hats. His features were firm, unscarred, his eyes a light gray. He had looked at Ellen with interest and smiled at her with the sort of smile her father gave her, one which curled the mouth and lit up his eyes. His son James, on the other hand, had barely noticed her, as if she was too young for his attention, and had turned to his friend Edward to chatter with him. Ellen had noticed him though, and when the men had begun to talk about their business, she studied him furtively. He was unlike his father in that he was tall, narrow in the hips, broad at the shoulders but without the heaviness of them that usually went with the miner. He had the same firm features as his father, though, the same set of the jaw, but there was a restlessness about his eyes, an impatience in his manner as they discussed the reaction of the men at Clifford to the appeal to them to strike.

"What did they have to say?" asked George again, when Richard Bryant hesitated.

"They be afraid to talk to us," said Richard. "Cap'n Vincent has given them warning. Anyone who joins a miners' society will find no work at Clifford, nor anywhere else, he says."

" 'Tis time to teach 'em a lesson," said James, his eyes narrowing.

"Who?" said George. "Teach who?"

"Cap'n Vincent," replied James. "And those lily-livered tinners at Clifford. Time to put the fear of God in them." He became angry as he spoke, as if he could see the faint-hearted Clifford men there before him.

Richard Bryant looked at his son in reproof. " 'Tis not proper to talk of fear. The Lord Himself will pass judgment in His own good time."

"So," said George Bray. "The Clifford men will put up with the hardships and do nothing but grouse. Is that the whole of it?"

"No, there's more. It's said we're known to be ringleaders hereabouts, you and me, George." Richard Bryant laughed and seemed to find amusement in being so called. "What do you think of that?"

" 'Tis no laughing matter, Richard," said George. "Where would we earn our living if we were blacklisted?"

"Are you drawing back?" said his friend.

Ellen looked at her father. She could not think that he would lack the courage to fight for what he believed in. She wanted to speak out to urge him not to give way, but she saw the men were indifferent to her and she had sense enough to recognize they would resent any intrusion by her. Besides, the decision was her father's.

"No," said George Bray. "I'll not be drawing back, save to choose better ground for our struggle, to bide our time."

James Bryant opened his mouth to protest but his father put out a restraining hand as George went on.

"No. I can see why the men of Clifford think twice about joining us. There's talk of Clifford closing anyway. And where is work to be found?"

"America," said James.

"Australia," said Edward.

" 'Tis a counsel of despair to leave our homes here and seek another world," said Richard Bryant.

"It's hope, not despair, it offers us, Richard," said George Bray. "Hope." His voice lifted as he spoke and Ellen was moved, with him, to think of the future, rosy and comfortable, in the new rich copper fields of Australia.

" 'Tis not Gwennap," said Richard, and Ellen wondered why he was so stubborn. It seemed to her that half the parish of Gwennap had moved away. What was so marvelous about Gwennap that it held this man so strongly to it? She looked at him again and watched as his eyes moved to look at James, his son. James was shaking his head at his father as if he only half understood him. Then James turned to look at her, and seemed to see her for the first time, for his eyes opened wider and the ends of his mouth rose in a smile. She lowered her head and then got up from her chair and moved through the kitchen to the back door.

She had become impatient with them. She had wanted to join in their discussion but they had ignored her. She was annoyed with herself, piqued she had accepted without protest their judgment that she had no part to play in such a serious matter.

She stood for a moment outside the cottage, wondering vaguely if the young man James Bryant might follow her out. But of course he did not, so, shrugging her shoulders at their indifference to her and her opinions, she went into the village street and turned to walk in the direction of the river. She soon left the dusty lane to move into the shade of a grove of oak trees, twisted, hung with ivy, ancient and neglected. It was a place where her imagination took flight, wondering what manner of folk had planted trees here, and under the influence of the mystery, her mood changed and lightened. For a moment she allowed her thoughts to linger on the young man, James Bryant, who had come to their house and who, when he finally noticed her, had smiled.

She wondered if she should have swallowed her resentment at the men and stayed. They might have spoken together then, she and the young man. A jay, starting from a near branch and flashing blue before her, broke into her reverie and brought her back to the moment, and the woodland and the life about her. There was a rustle in the undergrowth and this time a blackbird flew up and away from her a few feet then half-turned to look stonily at her. She heard another rustle behind her, louder, no bird this time, but human. She turned to see Reuben Menear, the boy she had once kissed; he was no longer a mere boy, but was broad and burly, dressed in Sunday chapel-going best, hair smoothed, face ruddy.

"I saw you," he said in his slow way. "I followed you."

"What for?"

"Well, I told myself, that's Ellen on her own. Now's the time, I said."

"Time for what?" She was amused at his earnest manner.

"Time to take up again where we left off." He winked broadly. "Where are you going?"

"Down Kennal Vale."

"Can I come?"

She was flattered by his humility and took his arm in response. Above the smell of camphor that clung to his clothes there was an odor of the farmyard, not unpleasant, and a taste of male sweat too.

"You're all dressed up," she said.

"Chapel," he answered briefly. "That's the worst thing about it. I don't feel comfortable in these things." His collar was tight and his thick neck bulged redly over it. He grinned at her. "But I do look smart, eh?"

She did not answer but held to his arm. They walked along in silence, through the woodland and down to the river bank. He stumbled against her every now and again on the uneven ground. She did not object; he was an old friend and there was something comforting about his closeness.

The paths beside the Kennal River were favorite places for Sunday strolls; families came out together to take their ease; courting couples held hands or linked arms, or snatched sudden kisses where the shade was deepest. Today there were families but no courting couples, no lovers swiftly embracing. Ellen felt Reuben's arm tighten about her and draw her toward him, so that she was held firmly to him. He bent his head to kiss her but at that moment a child ran along the path and stopped as he came upon them. He was seven or eight and full of curiosity at their behavior, eyes wide, mouth agape, unabashed at Reuben's angry gesture.

Ellen laughed and the boy laughed too. Ellen could hear the voices of his family behind him on the patch and was glad. She had no wish for Reuben to hold her and court her. They were friends, nothing more, and friendship did not mean they should fondle and caress each other. They stood aside to let the family party pass and as soon as they had gone Reuben tried to draw her to him again, but she resisted and when he sought to use his strength to compel her to yield, she pushed at him and showed him her own strength was not less than his.

"Bal maidens!" he said. "They're all the same. Teasers, that's what."

"Oh," she said. "What other bal maidens have you known?"

"Never you mind," he answered. "Come on, Ellen. It's all right. They've gone. Nobody can see us. I know somewhere private, like."

She turned back along the path in the direction of home.

"Hey, Ellen," he called as she strode rapidly away, "I'll not waste time on thee in future."

"That's all right by me," she replied, but she was sorry their meeting had ended like this. It had been pleasant to walk with him, holding hands. Why had he wanted to spoil it? She paused and looked back. He was standing, downcast and sullen, his red face set in a scowl.

"Come on," she said. "You're not going to leave me to walk back on my own, are you?" His face brightened and he came toward her. She held out her hand and he took it.

"No funny business, mind," she said but with a smile in her voice which must have left him, she realized, room to hope.

"You're all right," he said. "Really, I don't know any other bal maidens. I don't want to. Just you."

Ellen stopped and, facing him, kissed him lightly on the lips but drew away before he could make the contact linger.

"Oh, Ellen," he said and meekly followed her back to the village.

The Bryants had gone when she reached home and she felt annoyed she had not seen more of them. She had liked her father's comrade, Richard Bryant, and would have liked to get to know his son James, but there was little chance of that for the mine where she worked was distant from Wheal Jenny, where the Brays and the Bryants dug for copper. Only if they visited Granny Pascoe might she see the Bryants again, and that, thought Ellen, was too large a price to pay, loathing the old woman as she did.

"Well," she said to Edward, "did you settle your man's work? Did you sort out the problems?" Then she added, "What did your friend James Bryant have to say?"

Edward looked closely at her until she felt herself blushing at his scrutiny.

"So," he said. "That's the way it is."

"I don't know what you mean," she said. "What did he have to say about a miners' society? That's all I wanted to know."

"The same as me, that we'll have to do it sooner or later, and the sooner the better. It's no use waiting till everything's set fair. It never will be. The mine captains and the adventurers and the mine lords have their own society. They know it pays to combine. Why shouldn't we? We should do something now. Or get out."

"To Australia?"

"To Australia."

They both sighed. They had begun to use the name Australia as a spell to banish all anxieties. Their father joined them and took up their thoughts.

"Australia," he said, in the same sanguine tone. "We'll be there come this time next year, earlier maybe, for we've struck a good vein, I'm certain. Two months and we'll be ready I do believe." He turned away and looked from the window onto the village street. "There'll be nothing like this," he said, gesturing to the houses and the chapel beyond. " 'Twill be rough living but worth it to get away from the Cap'n Vincents with their driving ways. The voyage will be desperate hard, too, I do hear."

"Two months," said Ellen. It was hard to believe, for the prospect of leaving had somehow seemed unreal, a vague hope and, like so many hopes, unlikely to be fulfilled. "Two months," she repeated, and began to feel qualms at the thought of losing friends and changing familiar scenes for the huge unknown. She looked around the small room, almost as if to store the memory of it to comfort her overseas; it was small and humble, but it held for her a warmth of love, a belonging that nowhere else could ever do.

"And the miners' society?" she said. "What of that?"

Her father was silent. There seemed a conflict within him, between the lure of the colonies with their hopes of greater freedom and prosperity, and the pull of his conscience here, loyalty to his comrades, attachment to an idea of justice.

He shook his head. "There'll be others to fight for that. We've to think of ourselves sometimes, of our loved ones." He turned to Julia who had come from the kitchen and said, "And what do you think of it all, my lover?"

"Tea's ready," answered Julia in a matter-of-fact tone.

III

THE cobbing shed rang with laughter as Jane recounted her triumphs of the day before. She described in detail her encounter with a miner home from America and hungering for a Cornish maid, as Jane put it.

"Maid?" said Becky Opie in disbelief. " 'Tis long since you've been a maid."

"In a manner of speaking," said Jane. "He wasn't too particular." She sighed heavily in mock rapture at the recollection. "He was tall and handsome, and rich."

"Come to find a Cornish bride, I do suppose, to take back with him," said Becky. "Did you say yes?"

"I sent him packing. Rich!" said Jane scornfully. She wielded her hammer as if the rock she was striking was the man she had spoken of. "Rich but mean, mean as a Methodist brewer."

Ellen gave only half her attention to the conversation around. Her mind was still full of thoughts of Australia. She had talked far into the night with Edward, and this morning, as her father and brother had gone cheerfully off to work, they had spoken again of their hopes.

"We're within a few feet of the tin. I feel it in my bones," her father had said and she had been surprised at his optimism, for usually he was a cautious man, knowing how often hopes voiced above ground turned to despair below. She shuddered as she thought of the ever-present dangers, but recovered her spirits as she remembered Edward and his irrepressible good humor of the morning. She had wakened with their rising and had gone downstairs to help Julia get their croust ready. It had barely been dawn, but she had watched as they had walked along the village street. They had turned and waved before rounding the corner, steps light with hope.

Ellen looked around her at the benches and her comrades, clad in their aprons, heads shrouded under their bonnets, bending to their work. Conversation had ceased as the day lengthened, and the steady rise and fall of the hammers, the thudding of steel on rock, the sorting of dross from tin-bearing ore occupied the fifty or so women and girls. She would miss these friends of hers, and especially Jane. She would miss the gossip; she would even miss the work, though perhaps in South Australia too they had bal maidens. How else would the rock be broken to workable proportion?

She had no idea what they might find on the other side of the world. Friends wrote of the life there, but it was not easy to imagine what it was like. Little Cornwall. How could anywhere else repeat the beauties she found here? She thought of her walk yesterday along Kennal Vale, the river tumbling along beneath the shady banks of willows. She thought of Reuben and smiled at the memory of his clumsy attempts to persuade her to kiss him. And she thought, without intention, of James Bryant, the young man who had visited her home, and she saw him suddenly, tall and slender, with the strength of a miner about his shoulders, and his eyes, no longer flashing with anger as she had seen them the day before, but with a look of concern in them.

She saw him. And he was there, standing hesitantly at the entrance to the cobbing shed, standing as if seeking someone, uneasy at the curious looks of the women. He stood looking around before coming further into the shed.

A voice called, the voice of Jane, warm, intimate, enticing. "A man," she said. "A real man. Don't wait there. We're all willing."

Ellen wanted to protest, to protect James from the taunts of the bal maidens. It was a brave man who would venture in among them, but James seemed indifferent to the others. He had seen Ellen and he walked over to her. There was something in his face that silenced Jane and cut short the comments the other women were about to make.

"Ellen," he said, uncertainly, and she realized that he had not spoken to her before. "Ellen Bray?" as if he did not recognize her from yesterday.

She stood from the bench and drew back her bonnet so that he could see her clearly. She smiled at him, but he did not smile in return, and in that moment she knew that he had come to see her, not for her sake, but as the bringer of news from Wheal Jenny. He had come to see her with a message from her father. Or with a message about her father. She could tell from his silence and from the eyes. He looked intently at her, seeking to find in her some understanding that would make it unnecessary for him to speak.

She took off her apron and removed her bonnet, shook her hair free, and moved away from the bench. She heard Jane come toward her and knew that her friend, like her, had divined the news. She felt Jane's hand reach for hers and clasp it strongly. She returned the grasp. The shed was silent. The women had stopped their work. Distantly wagons rumbled.

"Ellen," James said again, and could not go on.

"Tell me."

James glanced at Jane as if he hoped she would be able to tell Ellen and spare him the task.

"Tell me," Ellen repeated.

"They're both . . ." He hesitated, and then quickly added, "Both, George and Edward, dead, killed by bad air. They're . . ."

Ellen interrupted. "Where are they?"

"I came to tell you. They'll be bringing them home."

Home. What and where is that without father and brother? But she remembered Julia and knew she must spare her sister the pain of seeing her father brought lifeless from the mine.

She could not move. She did not want to move. She wanted to go back in her mind to the thoughts that had occupied her before, the country walk, the Sunday walk that they always took together, she and her father. She saw the river flowing between its banks, she heard the birds fluttering in the trees, saw the swallows swooping after insects and she saw, so clearly that they seemed to be with her here and now, the serious eyes of her father; she heard his gentle voice. But it was not her father; it was the man James Bryant and she wondered what right he had to usurp her father's place. She heard Jane's voice and felt her hand at her elbow, supporting her. "Ellen."

"I'm all right," she said, but she was not all right, for there was an emptiness within her. She was drained of feeling, incapable of expressing the hollowness of living: living, and her father and her brother Edward dead.

"Ellen," Jane spoke again.

"Yes," Ellen said, "I must go. I must tell Julia. Get things ready for them." There was something to do and that would fill the emptiness.

She turned to Jane, appealing to her to understand, though she herself could not. "Come with me, Jane."

IV

ELLEN thrust the window open and let clean air flood into the room. She wanted to shout at the line of miners as they trooped behind the coffins, the pine boxes which the mine had provided. She wanted to shout, not in rage at the miners shuffling sadly along, but reviling fate. The numbness which had seized her before was going, and she wanted to let her emotions run free. She opened her mouth, but no sound came. She felt herself trembling so violently that at first she was afraid she would sink to the floor in a fit. But strength and control returned. There was so much to do that she could not indulge herself in pretended sickness. She was not sick; she was strong, strong in body, and must be equally so in spirit.

She watched the procession make its way out of the village to the burial ground below the churchyard. She wondered who all these men were who had come to mourn her father and Edward, to follow them to the grave. They were miners, of course, but not only from Wheal Jenny, she knew. Her father's name had been respected throughout the parish and beyond. She recognized Richard Bryant, but did not see his son James and wondered why he had not thought it needful to come.

As she stood she felt Julia's hand reach for hers and she put out her arm to hold her sister to her. They stood together and watched the procession until it had gone from view and was only with them as a distant sound, a drifting echo of the burial hymn, "Sing From The Chamber To The Grave."

"Come," she said to Julia, her voice calm, subduing the turmoil that ran through her. "We've work to do." She looked down at her sister, small, fair-haired, old enough at twelve to work with Ellen in the sheds at the mine, cobbing ore.

"No!" Ellen said aloud, feeling a sudden loathing for the mines. Her whole life had been caught up in them, in the production of tin, in cobbing the ore men like her father had brought to grass.

And this was their reward she thought as she looked around the cottage, with its bare walls, its earth floor, its open stairs leading to the bedroom above, the bedroom shared till now with Edward and her father. She thrust the thought from her, refusing to give way to sorrow.

"Come along, Julia," she said. "Granny Pascoe will be angry if we're not ready when she comes." She busied herself removing traces of the day. There were a few tired sprigs of greenery left from the funeral trappings at the door. She brushed them out into the village street where a sudden breath of wind caught them and carried them away. If only memories could be so dislodged she thought, the memories of the last days.

She would not like to lose all memories, of course. There had been so many gentle happy days. She had not known it while they were with her but now, thinking back, she recalled the richness of their life even after the death of her mother; she recalled the love her father gave her, and that of her brother with his teasing ways. She had not known then how precious the days were, but she knew now as she looked forward to the emptiness of days to come.

She busied herself with the besom, sweeping into corners, needlessly going over ground, twice, thrice-swept, but she could no more clear her mind of gloom than she could rid the room of the scent of death. She went outside and stood in the morning sun, looking down the long village street, not in the direction of the graveyard, but in the other, toward the open moor, to the gorse. She imagined she could smell the honey flavor of it wafted by the breeze and drank deeply of it. But with the honey scent came a bitter flavor from the mines which dotted the moor, the acrid smell of fumes from the engine houses. She could hear now the thud and rattle of the mine machines. She could see smoke rising from the tall chimneys and, on the engine houses, she could see the swing and bob of the beams rising and dipping in their task of draining the deep shafts.

"Are you ready, girl? Or are you dreaming as usual?" She

heard the harsh voice of her grandmother and turned resentfully to confront the old lady.

They stared at each other. Granny Pascoe saw a girl, tall, shapely, dark-haired, black-browed, frowning now with displeasure, but still with a disturbing beauty. Ellen saw a woman, short and spare, sharp-featured, black-robed, a shawl gathered over her white hair, eyes piercing and suspicious.

They stared at each other until Julia rushed from the cottage and flung herself, weeping, into the older woman's arms.

"There, there, my lover," Alice Pascoe comforted her granddaughter, her voice soft with concern.

Ellen watched, unsurprised at her grandmother's sympathy for Julia. Who could fail to respond to the child's open nature? But she knew her grandmother would offer no consolation to herself, for between Ellen and Granny Pascoe there was nothing but hostility, kept in check only for Julia's sake.

"Well, Ellen?" said Granny Pascoe, voice cold now, brisk. "You're ready? Everything packed? I've arranged for Bryant's boy to come. He'll not be long now." She turned to Julia and her manner changed. "Come along, Julia. Let's see if you've got everything ready. You'll like it with me."

Ellen turned into the house. Julia might like living in Cusgarne, but she would not. She would not allow herself to like it. Her friends were here.

"Must we?" she said, impulsively speaking her mind.

Granny Pascoe turned sharply to her. "Must you what?"

"Leave home." Ellen looked out to the village street. Here and there women stood, talking at their doors, looking with interest at the house, not troubling to conceal their curiosity.

"There's no home here. The lease is up with Edward gone. You know that." Granny Pascoe spoke unfeelingly, and Ellen resented it. "So don't waste time talking about it."

No, thought Ellen, I shan't. I shan't speak of it again. I shan't show my feelings to her. She tossed her hair and brushed past her grandmother to go upstairs, from where she dragged a bundle of linen, wrapped in a blanket tied together at the corners. She went back for the bed, the truckle bed which she and Julia shared. The other had been sold, and she was glad of it, for that was the one her father and brother had slept in till the last moment, and she had no wish to see it again.

"Leave it," said her grandmother impatiently.

Ellen ignored her and moved the bed downstairs.

"Leave it," repeated her grandmother. "Leave it to James Bryant."

"And why should I leave it to him?"

"You can't do it on your own."

She could and did. James would be no stronger than her. A bal maiden's shoulders and arms were as muscled as any miner's. She would not admit weakness of any sort to her grand-mother and soon the bed was piled outside on the village street, with the linen, the kitchen table and chairs, and the few other possessions of the Bray family.

"What's in there?" said Granny Pascoe suspiciously, as Ellen set a cane basket aside from the other goods. It was tattered at its corners but from Ellen's handling of it it was clear that the contents were precious to her.

"Things," replied Ellen curtly.

"What things?"

"My things," replied Ellen.

"There's no room for nonsense in my house," said her grandmother. "What've you got there?" She moved over to the basket as if to lift the lid and pry.

Ellen stood, defiantly glaring at her grandmother.

"Books," she said.

"Books!" snorted the old woman, but she seemed satisfied. "Your father and his books!" But the contempt she pretended was unconvincing. She could read and write herself and was proud of the accomplishment.

"I'll look around," she said, "and make sure the place is tidy." She put out her hand to Julia and led her upstairs with her while Ellen stood on the pavement outside the house and took a last look at the village.

V

JAMES Bryant was whistling, improvising melodies freely. It was a day to enjoy, the sky was clear, the air fresh, and on the Downs the gorse was rich with golden bloom. And here he was, above ground to enjoy it, no longer in his accustomed element—the hard rock face, the hewed gunnis, the shafts and levels of Wheal

Jenny—but above ground, breathing dust-free air, smelling the cattle clustered at the farm gates for milking. Was there ever so lovely a country as this? he thought, and then looked back to the Downs, past the gorse and across to the line of engine houses silhouetted on the horizon.

The donkey, Rosie, paused with him and stood contentedly grazing beside the path. James's conscience stirred him. The Bray girls would be wondering what had happened to him, and he did not want to incur the anger of Mrs. Pascoe. He was more than a little afraid of her.

He gave a tug on Rosie's bridle and she followed him meekly as he walked steadily on, silent now as he thought of George and Edward Bray. It was he who had found them and dragged them from the pitch where they had been working. They were beyond saving then; their dreams of striking it rich and of making their way to Australia were beyond them too. He thought back to the narrow stope where the bad air had caught and killed them. In his mind's eye he saw the jagged walls reflecting the thin light of his candle and he knew, as surely as a tinner could, that the Brays had only failed by inches. The "sturt" they had hoped for, the striking it rich, had only just escaped them. They had failed, but someone to follow might succeed.

He began whistling again, cheerful at the dreams which possessed him, but then, as he passed the churchyard, he was reminded of the day and his own purpose there. His father had come earlier to the funeral and James would have been with him but for his promise to borrow a donkey and cart and help the Bray girls to shift. He wondered how the occasion had gone. Tinners liked to make a ceremony of a burying.

He looked along the village street and saw Mrs. Pascoe standing at the door of the Brays' cottage. She nodded to him as he pulled up the cart in front of the door.

"Well?" she said, as if she expected an explanation of his being late.

James did not answer, but stooped to lift the bundles of possessions outside the house. They were few enough, but they would be too many for Rosie for the way was hilly and rough. Ellen came to help him load the cart and he smiled at her, but she seemed hardly to see him, had no interest in him.

"I'll have to come back," said James in apology when they had loaded the cart almost beyond Rosie's strength. "This was the best I could manage."

"You bide here, Ellen. Look after what's left." Mrs. Pascoe spoke sharply. James watched as Ellen, without answering her grandmother, turned into the house. James followed her.

"I'll not be long," he said to the girl's back. He hoped she would turn to look at him, but she merely gave a slight shrug to her shoulders that sent her black hair floating gently about her neck. "I'll be back as soon as I can."

"I heard you," she said, still with her back to him.

"Right," said James, defeated, and went to lead the donkey and its load to Cusgarne, accompanied by a grim and silent Mrs. Pascoe, and Julia, wide-eyed and uncertain.

Ellen heard the door close behind her and the sound of the cart wheels dying in the distance. She went to the window and peered into the street; they had gone and she was alone with her thoughts.

Till now the pattern of life had been regular, uncompli-cated, governed by routine. Now certainty had gone. No more, at the end of the day, would they sit together, she and her father and Edward, to the meal Julia put before them; no more would she respond angrily, impatiently, to Edward's teasing. She recalled how she had lost her temper with them, and she remembered how tolerantly they had dealt with her tantrums. She wondered why she behaved so; she loved them, but could not hide her impatience with them. Why? And why, to her irritability had they always returned understanding?

She was filled with remorse at the thought of her behavior. How rarely had she shown her father and Edward the depth of her love for them; she could not show them now. She turned from the window and gazed at the bare room; a flood of mem-ories invaded her and brought her almost to tears. She could weep when she was alone; that she would permit herself, but no tears would come.

She went to the cottage door, for she felt she wanted now to leave the house behind, to start on her new life, free of memories. She was impatient for James to return so that she could close the door on her past. But she knew she could not help taking it with her; that although her impatience, her pas-

sion, were her own, her values and her beliefs were drawn from
the family she had grown with, from her father most of all,
from Edward, from her mother while she was with them, and,
she reluctantly admitted, even from Granny Pascoe. Somehow
these people had fashioned her. She was dimly aware that,
though she was herself, Ellen Bray, what she was owed so much
to others.

She heard a gay whistling at the end of the village street
and the noise of the donkey cart on the granite setts. There
was the young man, James. She had paid little attention to him
before, her thoughts being too full of her own misery to admit
him. Now she watched him as he approached. He had not seen
her standing on the shadowy threshold; his face and manner
were cheerful, lively, irresponsible. His dark hair curled untidily
about his head and was longer than was customary for a miner;
his mouth was well shaped and lifted at the ends as if formed
into a lasting smile; his chin was square, his neck firm, so that
his head was held proudly alert. He was taller than her brother
Edward had been but he had the same toughness of form that
came from his work as a miner. He had been shaped from
childhood to work at the rock face, and, tall though he was,
there was no mistaking his trade in the set of his shoulders. Yet
his walk, as he led Rosie along the street, was easy and graceful.
She stepped back into the cottage but he had seen her and
waved as he drew the donkey to a halt.

"There. I kept my word, didn't I? I wasn't long, was I?"
His voice was light, casual, friendly.

"You needn't have hurried." Ellen tried to show indifference, but could not help looking at him. He was Edward's age,
she guessed, maybe older, nineteen perhaps.

"I didn't," he said. " 'Twas Rosie that did."

"Poor thing." She sounded concerned for the animal.

He laughed. "She's fat and lazy."

Together they stacked the cart with the few remaining
things, and while James tied ropes to keep the load steady Ellen
went into the cottage and gazed again upon its bare walls and
floors. It had been home, but now held nothing of the family
it had sheltered. It was stone, and cob, and thatch; nothing
more.

Nothing of me is here, Ellen said to herself. Nothing of
me or mine. She closed the door behind her and joined James

Bryant. He reached out a hand to hers and she knew that he had seen in her what she felt, a great unease at the uncertain future stretching before her.

She let him hold her hand as they moved away down the village street. Neighbors came to their doors and nodded as they passed. She smiled at them but she could say nothing; she could not trust herself to speak.

As they left the last cottage behind and the cobbles changed to dirt, Ellen halted. She felt sick and wanted to turn aside, but she suppressed the feeling. The hand still clasped hers. She looked up at the young man and seemed to see him clearly for the first time. His eyes met hers and she saw in them his anxiety for her. She gazed back at him, unable to hide her grief. He took her other hand. His eyes held pity for her, a pity she wanted to reject. He had seen what she had hidden from others, the reality of her grief, and he was moved by it.

She was moved by his understanding and emotion seized her. It was not only the loss of her father and her brother, not only the parting from her childhood home, not only the concern about what lay ahead for her. It was all that, and more, and at the center of it was the young man who was holding her by the hands, who was looking into her eyes as if searching within her for the meaning of it all. At the center of it all was this James Bryant.

She slowly unclasped her hands from his and walked with him toward her new home as his neighbor.

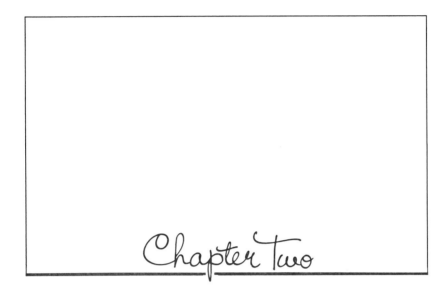

Chapter Two

I

DROPLETS of mist gathered on the dead brambles and thorns clutched at Richard Bryant's coat as he turned out of Pitti-Patti Lane up the stony track of Cusgarne Hill. Behind them the sun tried to break through to light their way to work but night was slow to yield to day. As they drew nearer the brow of the hill and the spread of the Downs, with its engine houses, whims and shafts, other sounds came to them—of the machinery in the mines, the plunging of pumps, the hiss of steam in the mighty engines, and the steps of other miners on their way to work.

This was their country; it belonged to them, the Bryants and their like. Here they had worked for generations; here they had met danger and disease; and for every Bryant who had yielded to one or the other, there was another to take his place. For the Bryants survived, and Richard himself seemed to bear a charmed life. At forty-three he was a veteran. There were few older working at Wheal Jenny, few who could equal his thirty-four years underground. He maybe had little to show for those years but a rare skill and, what counted much, the respect of his fellows.

Richard's thoughts turned to George Bray. George too had seemed to bear a charmed life until. . . . It did not do to let the mind dwell long on such gloomy matters. But he could not forget his friend for his daughters were now neighbors and, more than that, close to his family. He let his thoughts linger on Ellen for a moment. If he had been blessed to have a daughter it would have been such a girl as she he would have wished for—brave, independent, proud. And beautiful with it too, he thought, as in his mind's eye he captured an image of her.

He should not grumble. He had three fine sons and a loving wife. He regarded James, his oldest son, with special pride. He had learned his craft well and if he could temper his impetuosity he might one day, if fortune smiled, make a fine mine captain. He remembered James's first day underground, how he had linked the boy to himself with rope as they descended the ladderway. He had taught him everything he knew and he had learned well. It was time now to initiate his youngest boy. Mark was ripe for work and impatient to join his brothers. Richard decided he must end Jessica's cosseting of the boy. He would have a word with the mine captain today and have Mark join his "pare" after next setting day.

Richard heard William beside him, running to catch up with a boy in a group ahead.

"Save your breath," he called after him. "And mind your croust," he added as William dropped the small canvas bag he was carrying. "It's all you'll get."

Through the swirling mist he could see, looming near, the great building of the Wheal Chance engine house, with the idle bob of the beam engine peering like a huge bird of prey through the slow Cornish dawn. No sound came from the workings, no movement from the whims or pumps. The stamps were silent, their clacking and thumping stilled.

" 'Tis knacked for sure, Wheal Chance," said James at his father's shoulder. "They all are—knacked, finished, hereabouts anyway."

" 'Twill never be finished," said Richard. "There's as much down there still as we've ever brought to grass."

"And for what?" said James. "What did we have at last month's gettings? Barely four pounds for us all. And one pun ten to candles, powder and fuse. And a shilling for club and barber. And what was left?" He paused and added indignantly, "Two pounds ten shillings, for two months' work."

" 'Twill get better," answered Richard, unwilling to admit his own sense of defeat at their poor earnings.

"It couldn't get worse," said James.

"Don't challenge fate," said Richard, but James had walked on ahead.

Richard followed. He was proud of James, yes, but he wished the boy were not so impatient, not so willing to cut corners, not so irritated when progress was slow. And progress had to be slow in hard-rock mining; it was in the nature of the work. So Richard watched James uneasily, sought to guide him into a methodical approach and was careful to provide example by his own thoroughness.

The mist was thickening and Richard could only guess at the shapes of the miners ahead. He thought the small figure was that of William, but there were boys in other pares, some as young as ten, younger even than Mark. Yes, he must make sure Mark joined them after the next setting. It was never too young to learn.

He caught up with his sons at the entrance to a barnlike building which served as their changing shed, the miners' "dry." He sat on the rough bench and put on his underground clothes, his red-stained jacket, his hard miner's hat. He gathered his candles and tied the wicks together to the buttonhole of his jacket. The mist had given way to a steady rain and the Bryants scampered from the dry to the shaft head, clutching their candles, hammers and picks to them. The rain drove at them over the moors and, wet though they were, when they got into the shelter of the shaft and began to climb down the rungs of the ladderway, their spirits had been cheered, the remnants of sleep dispelled.

When they reached the platform at the two hundred and forty fathom level—almost the deepest point of Wheal Jenny —they still had a walk of three hundred yards along the level to their pitch. They paused for a few moments at the foot of the ladderway to gather their tools about them and then set off, scrambling over piles of useless rock left here and there along the drive, stumbling from time to time in the uncertain light of their candles, and wary of the rocks jutting from walls and roof. Water dripped from the stone above and there were times when they had to stoop almost to kneeling before they came to their working place.

They knew well what work lay in store for them. For most of the core they would be boring into rock, a slow, wearisome job in the hard country they had struck. But, though only two men and a boy, they were a skilled team, working steadily together, boryer held by William driving into rock, as Richard and James in alternate rhythm struck hammer blows upon it. William, though barely out of boyhood at fifteen, did a man's job, his arms muscled, his hands roughened and hard, nails chipped, fingers scarred and bruised.

As they worked the sooty candle smoke curled to the darkness above. Tallow trails dripped over the clay sockets on their hats. Sweat glistened on their shoulders and ran down their arms, for the air was close and the rock walls hot to the touch. The boryer blunted against the hard rock and they were disheartened at the rock's reluctance to yield to the drill. Richard had supposed as much when they had bid for this pitch at the last setting day, but hard and discouraging though it was it was familiar work, and reassuring in its familiarity. Gradually the hole they were driving deepened until Richard thought it sufficient for powder to be tamped home for the "shooting."

"Ho-old, boys," he called. The hammering stopped and William withdrew the boryer. By now the hole was driven some two feet deep. William straightened and stretched, clenching and unclenching his hands. James and his father stood back and rested their hammers on the dead rock behind.

"William," said Richard, when he had rested awhile, his voice a hollow echo along the stope. "Come along now." He would see how well William had learned to lay a charge, though he would make sure the boy was well out of the way before shooting took place. Richard had known too many miners lose fingers, or sight even, through carelessness at this stage. Maybe the loss of a finger or two could be borne easily enough, but loss of sight was a horror too dreadful to imagine. He had survived until now, whole and largely unharmed, from a combination of skill, caution and good fortune. He could not guarantee good fortune, but he could make sure his sons inherited his craft.

He scrutinized William's work carefully as, with a long

wooden swab stick, he cleaned the hole of dust and chippings. The hole they had driven was a back hole rising upward at an angle into the rock. The charge of powder would have to be wrapped in paper and this homemade cartridge tamped home. William, with scrupulous care under his father's watchful eye, formed the cartridge, poured powder into it from the powder can and handed the wad to his father.

"Pass me the tamping bar," said Richard. William stooped, picked up a metal bar and passed it to his father.

Richard looked at his younger son and quietly, without rebuke, said, "The tamping bar." William hesitated and looked to his brother for help. James ignored the appeal. "The tamping bar," repeated Richard. "Copper, not iron, copper. Mind that, boy. Why?"

William's head dropped in shame.

"Why, boy? Tell me."

"The iron might strike a spark," said William.

"And give a misfire," said his father, still quietly, without blame in his voice for his son's mistake.

"Get thee along now," he said and William retreated along the drive, leaving James and his father to complete the charge and fuse, and fire it.

James had shaped a fuse of rushes, each fed into the other to make a long tube. Richard first tamped the cartridge home with the copper bar William had given him, then with the needle, a long pointed rod, he reached to the wad. Around the needle he packed clay, firmly bedding it in.

"The fuse, James," he said as he slowly withdrew the needle, leaving a channel to the powder. He fed the fuse gently into the hole and cupped his hand around the top of the tube while James trickled the black dust into it until it was full. Richard twisted the end, signaled to James to leave and glanced after him to make sure the way along the drive was clear.

For Richard this was always a lonely moment. He took the candle from his hat, touched it to the fuse, turned, and ran. The first few seconds after the fuse was lit were frightening. For all his experience, and indeed because of it, Richard had a deep respect for explosives. He was always astonished at the way in which a small charge of powder could wreak such change on a wall of rock.

He heard behind him, too soon for his liking but safe

enough nevertheless, the twin sound of the successful firing, the knock of the explosion throbbing through the rock, and then a deep boom filling the air with a sudden rush. He stumbled with the force of the blast and almost fell over a heap of stone. The flame of his candle was doused in the sweep of air and dust from the explosion, but ahead, through the black swirl, he could see a light. The boys had taken shelter in a side channel, an abandoned stope. He stumbled toward them and crouched with them. The boom echoed and reechoed, its force dwindling until almost imperceptibly stillness arrived. Richard expelled a long breath. His sons smiled at him and James leaned over to relight his father's candle.

"Croust time, boys," said Richard with a satisfied smile. He turned to William. "You've not dropped your croust bag again along the way?"

William grinned and showed the canvas bag on which his mother had embroidered "WLLM BRYANT." From it he drew a hard flat cake, his hoggan, his croust.

The dust began to settle and with a sharp smell of powder biting at their nostrils the Bryants sat together, Richard, James, and the young miner, William.

II

ELLEN, who had resented the move to this hamlet of Sunny Corner, became enraptured by it. It was not so much a hamlet as a dotting of cottages along a lane. Sunny Corner began at the crossroads near the long-exhausted mine of Ale and Cakes. From the crossroads you could look north to the still-active mines of Poldory and United and a dozen more, west to the trees that hid Pendarves House, south to Pulla Farm, its huddle of haystacks and its granite-built byres. And east led along Sunny Corner itself, past the chapel built by miners for themselves, past Sunny Corner Farm, past the carpenter and coffin maker's and a terrace of three cottages to the Bryants' home and Granny Pascoe's.

And the people of Sunny Corner, they too gave her pleasure, from old Mother Minson, with her happy toothless smile of recognition, to George Penrose, the carpenter, coffin maker and lay preacher. All alike welcomed her and turned their heads to follow her passing along the lane. "All right?" they would call, and she would reply with the same greeting, "All right?" And they would smile and nod and bend to their work.

Ellen loved the walk along here. She could imagine, as she went, that there were no mines near, for there were none to be seen along Sunny Corner. They were only a few hundred yards away but they were hidden behind the ridge on Cusgarne Downs. Here at Sunny Corner was a world different from her everyday working world; here cattle grazed, sleek and satisfied from the fecund pastures of the Manor Farm. Down in the valley, sheltered by rook-busy elms, was the Manor, the "big house." Ellen had never seen it close to, but she had heard tell of its grandeurs and, if she stood on top of the Cornish hedge, the bank that bordered the lane, she could catch a glimpse of the twisted chimney stacks.

Ellen and Julia often walked together along Sunny Corner but usually before they reached the crossroads, they would turn to follow the footpath that led behind the chapel and along a bramble-fringed path back to the Bryants' cottage. Here Sunny Corner narrowed and the hedges grew head-high. Here there was barely room for a horse and trap to pass; certainly no mine wagons could move here. For some reason, lost even beyond the memory of Mother Minson, the crone who lived at Sunny Corner Farm, this part was called Pitti-Patti Lane. Granny Pascoe's cottage was built along here, a yard or so back from the lane with a patch of unkempt grass leading to the door. This door opened directly onto one of the downstairs rooms of the house—the other was a tiny lean-to room where pilchards were salted, turnips prepared. From the living room open-tread stairs led up to Granny Pascoe's bedroom, a room private to herself from which Ellen and even Julia were excluded. The two girls were confined to the living room—their truckle bed occupied one corner—and the linny, the lean-to, where there was a sink.

The cottage was too small for her and Granny Pascoe to share. But then even Cusgarne Manor, with its reputed fifteen bedrooms, would have been too small to house two women like them. Ellen admitted to herself that the fault was as much hers as her grandmother's. They struck sparks simply by being in the same room, and had Julia not been there to douse their anger, it would have erupted into flame. For Julia loved them both and each of them loved Julia.

Ellen's work at Pednandrea took her away from the cottage and gave her relief from the close attention of her grandmother. And the money was needful too, for Granny's small allowance from the mine where her husband had been killed could not support them. Julia had tried to persuade Granny to let her go to work with Ellen, but on that at least Ellen and the old lady were agreed. The time might one day come when Julia too should become a bal maiden, but that time was not yet.

But she loved Sunny Corner most of all because here the Bryants lived, only a few yards away, and when the walls of her grandmother's presence closed too hard upon her she would find freedom there, with Richard and his wife Jessica, and friendship. She went to the Bryants, she told herself, not because she might meet James there, but because Richard Bryant provided something she had missed since the death of her father. In the long winter evenings she had sat with her father listening to his talk, and talked with him, not casual gossip about village matters, but discussion of the mines and mining, of politics and religion, of the matters of the day. Her father, though penny-pinching in many ways because of the need to save for the voyage to Australia, bought a newspaper every week and read it keenly from the first column to the last. Among his fellows he had earned a reputation for learning; they came to him for advice when they fell foul of the law or their employers; he listened patiently and talked wisely, and Ellen drew some of his wisdom and experience to her.

Richard Bryant was a man very like her father. Like him he had been brought up from the age of nine, when he first went below ground, to respect the craft that belonged to the Cornish miner. Like him he had a deep interest in mining and resented the indifference of the mine lord and the mine adventurers to the welfare of the working miner. When Richard saw her interest he began to speak, in the way that her father had, of conditions in the mines, of the need for miners to organize. He told her of the times in the past when men had tried to combine together, when parties of tinners had marched from working to working seeking to rouse their fellows to action. Something had always frustrated their efforts—fear of being blacklisted by the mine companies, the lingering hope of striking it rich, and, what angered Richard most, the belief that "cap'n knows best."

And from the first Richard Bryant had read Ellen aright. He had recognized the gap in her life left by the death of her father and brother, he had understood her grief and, with his gentle manner, had put her at ease and given her strength to face her changed life. No one could replace her father, but Richard Bryant came near. She turned constantly to him, and more and more her evenings were spent at his side, listening to him and responding to his encouragement to voice her feelings.

She told herself it was for this she was such a frequent visitor to the Bryants, but she knew it was also in the hope that James would notice her, pay her some attention, perhaps even hold her hand and look at her in the way he had that long time since.

He was there often in the room with his father sitting by the hearth, listening, as Ellen did, to Richard's reminiscences. Sometimes he would speak, to ask a question in that dark rich voice of his which stirred her so that she would lose the thread of the argument and have to force herself to listen to the sense and ignore the sound. He was there, but he seemed indifferent to her. She had become, she thought, too much a part of the household. Familiarity breeds contempt, she remembered, and she tried to stay away from them. But she could not. She was drawn to them, for they were a complete and loving family who recognized her need for affection and gave it unstintingly. She could not deny herself this. She longed for a chance to be alone with James, away from Mark and William his younger brothers, away from his mother, and even from his father. She wondered if for some reason James was avoiding her.

One evening, many months after the move to Sunny Corner, she turned to James and asked, "You brought them to grass, Edward and my father?"

"I was there. Yes," he answered.

"It was you went in the stope for them?"

"Yes."

"How were they?" Ellen asked, unsure of what she wanted to be told, but needing to know.

"I don't want to talk of it," he said.

"Answer her," said his father. "She's a right to know."

James hesitated, seeming unwilling to call the scene to mind. Ellen waited, grief renewing itself. Why had she asked?

"I need to know," she said, so softly that it might have been only to herself that she spoke.

"They were lying there, in the narrow way. 'Twas thin and bad, the air. We all knew it." His voice fell as he recalled the scene. He looked into the fire, where the burning furze threw sudden sparks aloft. "Edward was furthest in, face down." He looked up at her as if hoping she would permit him to stop, but she gazed intently at him, compelling him to tell all. "Your father. He was behind Edward, with his arms clasped around his legs, trying to drag him out to safety, I reckon, when the bad air got him too."

Ellen sat for a moment, seeing nothing there of James or the crackling blaze in the hearth, seeing only the body of her father as it had been brought from the mine, washed clean of the dust, eyes closed, face unmarked, serene. She rose and left the cottage, and was aware that James rose too and followed her into the lane. She walked slowly in the dusk between the high hedges. She heard James's footsteps as he caught up with her, she felt his arm about her shoulder as he drew her to him. She shook herself free impatiently, angry at his pity, his intrusion upon her sorrow.

Then to free herself of gloom she called over her shoulder, "Race you to the chapel," and was ten yards ahead of him before he could take up the challenge.

She reached the little building a step ahead of him, breathless. He stood behind her and rested his hands lightly on her hips. She felt his breath at her neck and could not move. She wanted to turn to face him but was afraid that by moving she would lose the touch of him upon her. She leaned back against him, her heart pounding from the swift race along the lane— or was it beating so for some other reason? His hands moved from her hips to clasp her about the waist.

Would he not say something?

She wanted to speak but dare not.

"Race you back," he said and loosed his hold of her.

Annoyed, she turned and saw him a few yards in front of her, waiting for her to race with him.

"James," she said and knew she had expressed longing.

"Ellen," he answered and came back to her. Then again, as he had done on that first day, he took hold of her hands and stood facing her.

She looked at him but dark had gathered and she could not see into his eyes. They were shadowed and impenetrable and she could not find in them the secret that was there before. He drew her gently toward him. She was almost as tall as him and only needed to turn her face slightly upward for their lips to meet. But they did not.

"Poor Ellen," he said. "I didn't mean to remind you. You made me. I didn't want to."

"I shan't mention it again," she said. She did not know what she wanted from him, only that the brief touch of him had reawakened in her that strange, confusing, engulfing emotion of that other day, the day of the burying.

They did not race back but walked, hand in hand, slowly to the Bryants' cottage. Neither spoke and when she left him to walk the few yards further to her home he made no effort to detain her, made no move to hold her. He cares nothing for me really, she told herself, not for me as me, not for Ellen Bray, but when she got to her door she turned to see if he was still there.

It was dark now and the wind was rising. He was standing there where they had parted and she could just make out the light blur of his face. He raised his hand and waved before turning away and, as he did, a sudden spatter of rain gave warning of the breaking storm.

III

THE tall thick-set man stood looking over the scarred landscape, past the heaps of dead rock which disfigured the foreground to the buildings beyond, the granite engine houses, built to resist time, as if the ore they existed to mine would be there to be dug forever.

This was not the picture he had been promised. "Our cliffs, our beaches, our rolling seas—that's what will bring fresh heart to you," his friend Rowland Blamey had said. "The good Cornish air," he had promised, "will see you to rights."

Robert Buchan smiled. His friend Blamey was beside

him but looking in the opposite direction, to the south, where a different pattern showed of irregular fields grazed by lazy cattle.

He wondered how he had allowed himself to be persuaded to come so far from home. He had needed to get away, and had not been sorry to give up his practice in Edinburgh but he could have recuperated as well in the Highlands as here in the soft southwest. That would have been more to his taste. He turned to his friend.

"It's time I went back to work, took another practice."

"In Scotland?" said Blamey.

"Where else?"

"You're not fit. Besides we had hopes you'd stay and take a practice here."

"We?"

"My family. They've taken to you. Especially my aunt."

Buchan thought back to his first meeting with Rowland's aunt, the powerful Rebecca Langarth. Rowland had warned him before they met of his aunt's overbearing nature. But they had got on well, he, the Scots doctor and she, the influential wife of the "mine lord" Langarth.

Buchan had been puzzled at the term "mine lord." He had expected to meet someone of noble and ancient lineage. The lineage was ancient enough, he learned, but not noble in any accepted sense. The Langarths were a mining family and in the distant past had been working miners. Now, through careful marriage and prudent management, they held land throughout the county, land dug for copper and tin, and producing for every pound sterling of ore brought to surface, one shilling for the Langarth fortune.

"And with the fortune," Rowland had said, "has come influence. Uncle Langarth is listened to, respected, kowtowed to. And behind him is Aunt Rebecca, the power behind the throne. I wouldn't like to cross her." He paused, pursed his lips and added, "Nor cousin Veronica either. She's as bad as her mother—worse, I sometimes think."

Buchan did not know if that was so. He had not met Veronica, but he had been impressed with Rebecca Langarth. She had questioned him relentlessly about his background. She seemed satisfied with his antecedents when she learned his father was a propertied gentleman, but she was less certain about his own decision to follow the practice of medicine.

"What made you do that?" she had barked.

"Duty to my fellow men," he had smugly replied.

"Ah!" she had said, as if satisfied with his answer, and had looked searchingly at him. She seemed pleased with what she found, tapped him with a gloved finger and said, "I can see we shall get on." There had been a thoughtful look in her eyes, and Buchan was not sure what it portended, but he knew she had made some decision which concerned him.

So now he knew. She had decided he should remain in Cornwall, to practice medicine there.

"I shall go back to Scotland," he said to his friend, "whatever your aunt wants."

"You're not fit yet. You need a few more weeks recuperation."

Buchan admitted he was still easily tired. He had worked in the teeming tenements of Edinburgh until even his robust physique had protested. Blamey had appeared in Edinburgh on a journey back from touring the Highlands bearing a letter of introduction to Buchan's father. They had met and, to Buchan's surprise, for Blamey's irresponsible carefree manner was the opposite of Buchan's own, they had become friends.

"Come to Cornwall," Blamey had said. "It's a place to relax in."

"Go to Cornwall," his father had urged. "You deserve a rest."

He had come to Cornwall and had found here something in the air, some elixir that tranquilized and charmed. He was falling victim to it and must resist, he told himself.

"I must go back," he said, and added, "in time."

They remounted their horses and rode slowly back to Cusgarne Manor, but Rowland, impatient as ever, grew weary of the plodding pace, dug his heels in his horse and made it gallop down the lane. Buchan saw a figure press back against the hedge to avoid being trampled. Mud spattered the woman's skirt, for woman—or girl—it was. He slowed his horse to a walk and raised his hat in apology for Rowland's behavior.

The woman's dark eyes met his. They were defiant eyes and her whole attitude was one of pride; she held her head

high, indignantly. He saw, as he paused, her features had a
classic beauty. The sight brought him up sharp so that his
good manners deserted him and he stared, but she turned
away, ignoring him, and strode up the hill.

He rode after Rowland and dismissed the woman from
his mind.

IV

ELLEN sometimes explored the valley below Sunny Corner. Signs
of mining were absent here; another style of life prevailed: there
was a corn mill, farm buildings, pastures, and an old manor
house, the "big house." Here the Blameys lived, Ellen was told,
a family once modest farmers, now, like their powerful relatives
the Langarths, waxing rich on mining dues.

Once, wanting to see more of the house, she walked down
the lane from the Bryants toward the valley. She came to the
walls that bounded the gardens of the Manor and sought to
look over. She turned away when she heard the sound of horses
at the top of the lane. She did not wish to be seen prying. She
had to stand against the hedge, for the leading horse was being
ridden carelessly, the young man in the saddle "Hallooing"
when he saw Ellen. He laughed when the mud spattered up at
her and galloped on. Behind, a second man drew his horse to
a halt beside Ellen, raised his hat and revealed bright golden-
reddish hair. His eyes were of an intense blue as he looked
down at her. She turned away, angry at his rudeness, and walked
back up the hill.

As she passed the Bryants' cottage she hesitated a moment,
wondering whether to call in the hope of seeing James, and
then, impatient with herself for her weakness, walked on home.

In the quiet of the night Ellen often lay sleepless in spite
of physical exhaustion, restless with longing. She was not sure
at first what it was she longed for, but gradually she became
convinced it was of James she thought. She would try to bring
his features to mind and there were times when they came easily
to her, but there were other times when it was her brother
Edward's face that surfaced, her brother Edward's sparkling
eyes, his teasing smile. She would catch her breath then and
hold back the sob that threatened. Sometimes she was so restless

that she had to leave Julia's side and go to the window to look out on the dark lane. She would look up at the sky, bright with its stars, and slowly peace would return to her.

She thought of James at other times than at night. She did not speak of him to Julia nor to Jane. Her imaginings about him were too precious for that. She kept him to herself. She was not sure what it was about him that she admired, nor was she sure admiration was the right word for her feeling. It was a longing to touch him, to clasp his hand, to reach up her fingers to his cheeks, to fondle him; it was a longing to be touched by him, to have him bend his head to hers, to have his lips pressed to hers, his eyes search hers; a longing to be his.

She magnified the feeling by holding it to her, nursing it in her secret moments, until it seemed to her that she was incomplete without him, that she needed to be with him to be herself, that only part of her—a dull, meaningless empty part—could exist separate from him. It was a feeling strange to her and disturbing in the intensity of it. It came over her unbidden at times when James was far from her thoughts, or so she had imagined. At the bench in the cobbing shed she would suddenly recall his long easy loping walk, or see the alert tilt of his head, or, what moved her most, his smiling lips. She would bend then to her task with a smile on her own lips and a warmth within her.

Yet when she saw him she would be disappointed. The smile was there, but it seemed not to be for her. He would walk with her but as a neighbor might, for casual company. It seemed he barely noticed her when she visited them to talk with Richard his father. She could not understand how he could be unaware of her feeling for him. How could such intensity of emotion as she persuaded herself she felt for him go unnoticed? How could he be so indifferent to her?

V

JAMES Bryant was not indifferent to Ellen Bray. He had noticed her; he could not fail to, for she had an air about her that commanded attention. She was unlike her sister bal maidens in her height, the slenderness of her hips, the length of her stride: she was unlike most of the Cornish girls he knew; they were short and broad, heavily built and strong. She too had strength—her work demanded that—but the gracefulness of her movement gave no hint of it.

James noticed her and admired her. He even allowed himself, from time to time, to think tenderly of her, to imagine himself in love with her. It was easy to be attracted to her for she had a beauty that marked her out, her raven-dark hair framed an oval face, high brow, wide-set dark and thoughtful eyes, straight nose (slightly large for the rest of her features) above firm and full lips. He let his mind linger on her lips for a moment and wondered why he had not kissed them; he had no hesitation with other girls. If lips were meant for kissing he kissed.

Ellen Bray was not to be treated like other girls. For one thing he had known and respected her father. This set her apart. He could not regard her in the same light as the girls he had taken into Unity Wood to fondle and be fondled by. He even felt guilty imagining such behavior with her. She was untouched and untouchable.

But there was an even stronger influence holding him back from admitting to himself his feelings about Ellen. For the moment women were unimportant in his reckoning. His thoughts were elsewhere. He looked around him at the mining scene and saw the closing of familiar workings. He saw the engines of one mine after another sold as mines failed, copper seams were worked out, and the price of tin dropped. He saw friends laid off and then heard they had gone elsewhere to work, up country to Lancashire to hew for coal, to the Colonies to dig again for tin, or to the far west of America following the lure of gold. And he was tempted to go after them. Though he loved the place where he had been brought up, its charms did not compensate for the slow strangling of hope that was here. Elsewhere fortune beckoned, and freedom, freedom to band together in unions, freedom and opportunity, the chance to use his craft as a hard-rock miner. Others from Cusgarne—Verrans and Michells—had gone and prospered.

He had spoken of this with Ellen's brother Edward and shared his hopes with his friend. Since Edward's death he had told no one of his ambitions. They were precious to him, to declare them would be to risk destroying them. Nor did he want to disturb his parents by raising the subject of his emigrating.

He had hopes of earning enough to pay his passage over-seas, hopes based on the pitch which had killed George and Edward Bray. In the year following their deaths it had remained unworked. The promise of tin he had seen there had gone unrecognized, for about Bray's Pitch there hung a pall of ill fortune.

He worked hard to persuade his father that they must bid for Bray's Pitch at the next setting day. Richard Bryant, mindful of the dangers which had killed George Bray, hesitated to agree, but as the pitch they were working became less and less pro-ductive and the country they were working in harder and harder he yielded, but not without a show of resistance.

"Bray's Pitch," he argued, " 'tis bad fortune. Like a scarlet woman, tempting from afar off, but dross when you get close, and dangerous too."

"There's tin there. I went along, crawled right in. 'Tis there all right, for the picking."

"Plain for all to see?" said Richard, thinking of Captain Vincent and his shrewd eye for rock.

"Only if you do look close. Cap'n Vincent'll not risk his neck."

"You risked yours," said Richard, but James smiled, for he could tell his father was won over. "I'll come too," his father went on. "Quiet like, so's not to warn the Cap'n."

James went outside to hide his self-satisfaction. He had prayed for this, the key to fortune, to his passage overseas. He smiled to himself. If his instinct was right, there would be money enough to leave his parents in some ease while he went to make his mark on the other side of the world.

"You look pleased with yourself," said a voice, the soft throaty voice of Ellen. "What's the secret?" She took his hand naturally, as a sister would, he thought, but there was something in the quality of the touch which was more than sisterly.

"Ah," he said teasingly.

"Tell me," she urged.

"Wouldn't you like to know?"

"That's why I'm asking."

Without thinking he said "Come setting day we're going to bid for Bray's Pitch." He felt her hold of him tighten and heard her sudden intake of breath.

"No!" she said fiercely. "Why?"

" 'Tis safe enough," he said.

She did not answer and he saw he had opened the old wound.

"I'm sorry," he said. He had to explain. "We've been driving into hard country for nothing for months. We need to find a new pitch, one where we may hope to strike it rich."

"I've heard that before." She was still standing in front of him, holding his hand, looking up at him, searching for an understanding of his willingness to risk his life. She shook her head. "No!" she repeated vehemently.

"I need to get out from here. I need to earn enough to pay for my passage."

"To Australia?" she said bitterly.

"Yes." He was stubbornly determined. "Or Ameriky. Anywhere away from here."

"Do you hate it so?" she asked.

"Hate it?" He looked over her shoulder to the valley of Trehaddle. "Hate it? No. I do love it. But where's the hope here? And what can a man do without hope?"

"Or a woman?" she said, but so softly that he was not sure he had heard aright. She gripped his hand and he felt the strength of her. "Don't," she said. " 'Tis not safe." She looked away from him, like him staring over the valley to the fields beyond. "It's already taken two men I loved." She turned suddenly to him so that she could look directly into his eyes.

"Is it so great a matter," she said, "this going oversea? Is that all that counts? Is there no reason for you to stay here? Why risk your life for that?" She compelled him to face her and look at her. "Why?" she said and added, softly, "Why, James? Why?"

He was held by her gaze until he seemed drawn into her eyes. He found himself leaning toward her and taking hold of her by the shoulders to press her to him. She flung her arms about his neck with a sudden laugh of sheer delight and began to kiss him, first on the nose, then on the chin, and then on the lips, fiercely almost, demanding he share her joy. He opened his mouth to hers and for a moment felt intoxicated, heady, at the mingling of their breaths. Then she drew away slightly.

"Don't," she whispered. "Not Bray's Pitch. Please, not Bray's Pitch."

The spell was broken. He had forgotten Bray's Pitch and

his ambitions in the fever of their kiss. There had been nothing then but Ellen and himself. Now he was reminded again he felt betrayed. He let his hands fall from her, so that they stood, still close, but no longer touching.

"I must," he said.

She turned sharply away from him and he knew she did not understand, would not. How could she? It was man's nature, not woman's, to venture abroad, to seek new lands, explore and conquer them. She was thinking still of the dangers of the pitch that had killed her father, was blind to the hopes of fortune it held, and he was angry that she would not share his dream.

"James," she said pleadingly, and held out her hands to him, but though he took them between his the mood was broken. He tried to avoid looking at her, but could not. He saw she was near to tears. She waited for him to speak but when he was silent she thrust him away and walked from him. He wanted to follow her, to catch up to her and hold her, assure her Bray's Pitch was safe enough for him, but pride forbade him to humble himself by explanation and he watched as, without looking back, she was lost to sight.

Chapter Three

I

SETTING day came and Richard and James, in their Sunday-best clothes, went together to Wheal Jenny and, with other soberly dressed miners, assembled before the count house. Here were the offices of the mine purser, here the men were paid out, here the adventurers met when dividends were shared, here the merchants came, and the mine hangers-on, the bal surgeons and others, to partake of the famed count-house dinners.

The stones marking the roadways of the mine land would at one time have been whitewashed, the heaps of buddle tidied, but Wheal Jenny's days were no longer glorious and the four-square majesty of the count house belied its present fortunes. Copper prices had tumbled and tin was faring little better. The adventurers, whose money had financed the mine, were restive, for dividends were poor and calls upon them to meet the cost of further exploration were met unwillingly or refused.

The miners who assembled to share in the allocation of work knew the days of the mine were numbered. They did not expect Captain Vincent to tell them so; he would keep them in ignorance as long as he could, and they would be last to hear the "bal was knacked" and would, without warning, be out of work.

Thoughts of this gloomy kind passed through Richard's mind as he nodded to his comrades, Joe Beskeen, Matthew Paynter and the rest. Since the last setting day there were many familiar faces missing.

"What's happened to Ira Davey?" he asked.

Paynter answered, "Gone up-country—to Wales, to work in the mines there."

"He'll not like that. Why didn't he join his brother in America?" Richard asked.

"His wife wouldn't let him," came the answer.

"Catch my old woman telling me what to do," roared Joe Beskeen, a squat hulk of a man.

The crowd was silenced as the tall-hatted, frock-coated figure of Captain Vincent appeared at the count-house door. The clerk, young John Oliver, was seated at a table at the top of the steps; there was a large book and an inkstand in front of him.

The ceremony began, a traditional ritual disappearing from some newer mines but still cherished by the older mine managers. Not so by the miners. They were becoming aware that the setting auction—the selling of the right to work a pitch to the miner willing to work for the least reward—put power in the hands of the mine captain by playing off miner against miner.

The details of the pitches to be offered were announced in turn. There was no exploratory work to be done, no new shafts to be sunk; work at the mine was confined to the setts already familiar to the men. The first was the pitch worked previously by the "pare" of which Joe Beskeen was the spokesman.

"You willing to work it again, Beskeen?" Vincent asked.

"Same terms," said Beskeen gruffly. "Five shillings and fourpence."

"Anyone work it for less?" Vincent surveyed the group, confident another bid would lower the price. He waited. The men looked ahead.

"Five shillings," came a voice from the rear. The men turned and Beskeen stood on tiptoe to see who had bid against him.

"Beskeen?" Vincent asked.

"Four shillings and eightpence." Beskeen spat to the dust.

Vincent nodded and glanced at the book in front of the clerk.

"Well," he said. "What else am I bid?"

"Four shillings and sixpence," came another voice.

Captain Vincent gave a slight smile and from the table took a round white pebble. He weighed it for a moment in his hand, and looked at Beskeen as he did. The miner looked stolidly back, giving no sign of his intentions.

"Stands at four shillings and sixpence," said Captain Vincent. He tossed the pebble a little way into the air, caught it again and then, with deliberation, took the pebble between his fingers and threw it aloft.

The white stone glinted in the sun.

"Four shillings and fourpence," Joe Beskeen called, and before his bid could be challenged by a lower one, the pebble struck the ground.

"Four shillings and fourpence, Joe Beskeen and pare," Vincent announced and John Oliver wrote in his book the details of the pitch and the price to be paid to Joe Beskeen "for each ton of what is fit to stamp when brought to surface."

Beskeen turned angrily away. "Crafty bugger," he said to Richard. "We had poor gettings last two months for a shilling more. We should stick together but there's always some selfish sod ready to bid lower."

The pitches were knocked down, usually at a price favorable to the mine and less than that fixed at the last setting day, until it came to the pitch worked till now by the Bryants.

"A good price, ten shillings," said Vincent, turning to Richard. "Richard Bryant and his pare."

Richard shook his head.

"Can't go higher," said Vincent.

"Not interested," said Richard.

Vincent looked around. There were no takers. Everyone knew the hard country to be worked there. Vincent seemed unconcerned. He had surveyed the stope thoroughly and knew its nature.

"It's hard country certainly," he said to Richard. "I'm sorry to lose you."

He closed the setting by having John Oliver read the conditions and rules of work and moved away as the miners dispersed.

"Cap'n Vincent," said Richard.

"Well Bryant?"

"There's one pitch you didn't put up."

"What's that?"

"Bray's Pitch."

"You'd work that?"

"If the price be right."

Vincent turned to the clerk. "What was Bray working it for?"

"Thirteen and fourpence."

"Then it's fair at twelve shillings now, since they opened it up," Vincent said.

"It's killed two men since. Thirteen and fourpence it should be still."

Vincent looked closely at Richard Bryant and at his son.

"Do you know something I don't?"

"How could we?" said Bryant.

"Thirteen and fourpence. So be it. But God help you. You'll need Him by you to come well out of that. It's taken its toll already. You're sure, Bryant? Your old pitch is still to be had."

"We're sure," said Richard and hoped his voice carried more conviction than he felt.

II

JAMES left his father at the mine entrance. He had decided to use the rest of the day—a rare freedom from the close air of the levels below—to walk to Redruth. It was four miles through Crofthandy and St. Day, a walk which would take him past the mines, past the gunpowder factory in Unity Wood, past the places where he had dallied with girls. The day was bright and James was exhilarated by the bite of the clean air and more by the success of the bid for Bray's Pitch. He had no doubts about it, it carried tin, it carried hope, it carried with it the prospect of America.

That excited him. He loved this land, the gorse which

touched the lanes with gold wherever you looked, the heather which carpeted the old men's workings on the Downs through summer and autumn, the jackdaws, the magpies, all this he loved. There was so much to love, but there was also so much to shun here. As he passed the closed gates of Wheal Prosper he saw posted on them a notice of sale. It was like that so often. "For Sale by Auction," he read, "one 60 in Pumping Engine, with two 10 in Boilers" and the rest, chains, ropes, kibbles and kieves, all to go. Wheal Prosper was knacked. However rich the green growth, however golden the gorse, there was no wealth to be dug here. His fortune lay overseas.

The gloom which oppressed him at the sight of the dead mine and of the others dying about it was brief and was finally dispelled when he came to the top of the hill out of Vogue. From here he had a view over to the sea, to the bright blue-green water of the Atlantic, the gleam of St. Ives Bay, the little island of Godrevy, and the sharp white of the new lighthouse there. He knew then, as he looked, that the world beyond called.

Bray's Pitch would make it possible. Bray's Pitch would bring him luck. He was certain of it. Bray's Pitch.

He said the name aloud, and as he did an image of Ellen Bray rose in his mind. He tried to shake himself free of the thought of her, for he did not want to be distracted from his dream of a future overseas. But try as he would there was no moving her. She was there, smiling at him, lifting her face to his, and he could see her dark eyes laughing into his, could see her mouth, lips parted.

Thoughts of America were swept aside. Ellen Bray occupied him. It was a sudden revelation and he could not understand why he was unable to free himself of the image of her. He tried with conscious effort to switch his mind to other things, the underground levels at Wheal Jenny, the descent down the ladderway, but at every pause on the way he met Ellen. Finally he gave up the struggle. He stopped by the roadside, climbed to the top of a bank, and gave himself over to thoughts of her and dreamily gazed out to sea.

He saw her clearly when they had kissed, and recalled the joy with which she had flung her arms around him; and he remembered how she had turned from him. He had been willing then to let her go. He had been afraid to say he wanted her. What had held him back then? He did not know—fear of himself and his fickleness? But he was not fickle, or would not be so with Ellen. His feelings for her were not of the fading kind. He could see her now, feel her warm passionate embrace and he knew he wanted her as he had wanted no one before.

He jumped down and unaware that he was singing aloud turned away from Redruth and began to retrace his steps to Sunny Corner. He would see her now.

James Bryant knew he was good-looking; the attentions of the girls who worked on the surface of Wheal Jenny assured him of that. He had walked out with several of them, never with any serious intent, and had enjoyed it. He thought he was sexually experienced; he remembered the girl who had initiated him; he remembered her well, with a mixture of pleasure tinged with guilt—Jane Rowse. The recollection of her now and of their lovemaking stirred him physically and he was angry with himself that it should. It was Ellen Bray not Jane Rowse who held him.

He had walked quickly, unobservant of the hedges, the gorse, the heather. He had come to the crossroads where Sunny Corner met the road across Cusgarne Downs, and there talking together were two young women, the two who had only now occupied his mind, Ellen Bray and Jane Rowse.

He paused and would have turned away to avoid meeting them together, but they had seen him so he had to walk on and join them. He knew he was reddening as Jane surveyed him.

"We were just talking about you," she said.

James looked anxiously at her. He wanted to plead she should not reveal her knowledge of him.

"I told Ellen that I'd seen you about, that we'd passed a word or two together," Jane said, smiling. He was reassured and looked at Ellen.

It was she who was reddening now.

"Don't flatter yourself," said Jane. "I was only asking after Ellen's neighbors. She just mentioned you in passing." She grinned from one to the other, but James was uncomfortably aware of the amusement in her eyes. He looked away. She bade good-bye to Ellen and, with a jaunty wave to James, walked away.

"Ellen," he said, expecting she would turn to him and take his arm as he offered it to her. She did not move but stood looking after her friend.

"Ellen," he repeated.

"Well?" she said, and he found no encouragement in her voice.

" 'Twas setting day, this day," he said.

"I know."

"We got it." She did not reply.

"Bray's Pitch," he said. It had become so familiar a term to him and fellow miners that he had forgotten the meaning it had for her, until he saw her face darken.

"And what do you want me to say to that? Halloo for joy?"

"I . . ." He could say no more. What had he meant to say to her? Why had he hurried to find her?

"You don't understand," he said.

She looked at him then, but he could not read her thoughts. This was not the young girl he had teased, treated as a family friend. This was a woman, and he was lost before her.

"I understand," she said and turned to walk away.

He reached out and seized her by the shoulders. She shrugged him off, but stopped where she was and turned to face him.

"What is it?"

He grew suspicious. "Has Jane been talking? What has she told you?"

"What has Jane to do with it?"

He tried to cover his indiscretion. "I meant to say . . ." He looked at her for some encouragement. "Please, Ellen," he begged.

She seemed to relent for a slight smile touched her lips. "What is it?" Her voice was softer now.

"I have to," he said.

"You told me. You have to get away. I see. But why that pitch?" He could see she could not bear to repeat the name. "What good can that bring?"

"Trust me, Ellen. I know my rock."

"So did my father."

"He was right."

"What does it serve him now, that he was right?" Her anger was mounting again and he hurried to explain.

"Come with me," he said.

She looked at him in surprise. "Where? Where are we going?"

"When I go overseas, I mean. Come with me. To America, Ellen."

She did not speak. Wind rustled through the trees that bordered the lane. In the distance there was a rumble of cart wheels and a child called to another.

She reached out to him and allowed him to enfold her in his arms. They stood for a moment, close, neither wanting to break the silence between them; words confused, touch was safer. The sound of footsteps came along Sunny Corner and James drew Ellen through a gap in the hedge into the field beyond, so that they were out of sight of passers-by.

They stood, bodies touching, but without sound until the footsteps had faded. Then Ellen sighed, but still said nothing, content to rest her head on his shoulder. He nuzzled her ear and then let his hands wander about her impatiently, with mounting excitement and desire. He could feel the whole length of her against him, and as he held his hand to her back she moved herself nearer to him and raised her face to be kissed.

He was lost, submerged in feelings of a depth beyond his understanding or control. His senses seemed alive to everything about him, and everything about him was Ellen. There was nothing more. He felt at once passion and tenderness, so that his body urged him to make love to her, violently, while a second, gentle, impulse held him back. He wanted to fondle and caress her; he wanted to bestride her. He wanted to soothe and calm her; he wanted to arouse her. He wanted to tame her, to be tamed by her.

He thrust her against the hedge and as her desire showed itself in the probing of her tongue at his and in the movement of her hands about his face, he wanted to take her, there, against the hedge, a yard only from the road. He felt Ellen pushing her hands against him to hold him back but he ignored her and tried to force her to the ground.

"Listen!" she said and, through the pounding of his blood, he tried to do as she said. He heard the voices of his brothers, William and Mark, and a laugh from Ellen's sister Julia.

"In here," said Mark.

James let his arms fall from Ellen. She straightened her clothes and smiled at him. He was angry, somehow humiliated at the interruption, but she seemed content, as if the fervor of their embrace had been enough to satisfy her.

"Hello," said Mark. "What are you doing here?"

"What are *you* doing here?" said James gruffly. He found it difficult to control his voice. He felt Ellen reach for his hand and took it gratefully.

"Are you two walking out together?" said Julia.

"Are we?" said Ellen.

For reply he linked her arm into his and strode past his brothers along the lane to home.

III

ELLEN could not suppress the dread that came over her at the thought of James working Bray's Pitch. It held no promise, only threat. She tried to tell herself that his father was a miner of long experience and a man of caution—but so had her father been and it had not saved him. She hid her fears and, in spite of her weariness from her day's work she would rouse herself when she heard the mine bell tolling the end of the late core —at ten o'clock—and would go to the entrance of Wheal Jenny and wait to see James safely come to grass. She would hold back then, though she longed to rush to him and fling her arms about him in gratitude for his return.

He would smile when he saw her and hug her, while his father beamed upon them and his two brothers watched and smirked. But she had chance of little other contact with him and as day followed day and tiredness overwhelmed him, James grew less effusive in his greeting. Bray's Pitch was not about to yield its riches without a struggle.

Ellen kept silent but at night she clung to her sister Julia and whispered to her her worries and her love. Julia would clasp her comfortingly, but it gave Ellen no solace.

Granny Pascoe was impatient with her. "Stop mooning about, girl," she would say. "No good will come of that," and she drove her granddaughter to complete the household tasks allotted to her until Ellen, resentful of her grandmother's tyranny, would storm out in a rage and would later be surprised that anger, for a time, had freed her of fear. But fear returned whenever she thought of the dangers of the pitch that had killed her father and Edward. That she could not forget. The pain of it was with her always and was now made agony by her care for James.

It was not only Ellen who felt concern. Though James was confident, Richard was still uneasy and wondered why he had allowed himself to be persuaded. He had been driven by despair, he realized—or hope, the same urge that drove other men away in search of work. Here, in Gwennap, the mines seemed to be dying, and with their death, poverty struck the area. Men went overseas and left behind them families to wait upon their fortune: families without resource, families surviving only through the friendship of neighbors or the charity of the Distress Fund that was set up to help. Richard felt he had at least some hope. There was Bray's Pitch, and if James was to be believed it would save them.

Perhaps James's judgment would be vindicated. The boy had flair and Richard had taught him all his craft; what he had not been able to teach him was something that only years of experience gave—awareness of the presence of death alongside them when they worked below ground. Richard felt this keenly as they worked at Bray's Pitch. Danger was palpable; the corpses of George and Edward Bray had left a presence that Richard could not ignore. He worked cautiously, more so because Mark, his youngest son, had joined them, and needed to be given proper respect for the rock surrounding them.

James began to show impatience at their slow progress, and Richard was short with him.

"We'll not prosper by haste," he said.

"We've not much time," James argued.

"We'll not buy time with lives," Richard was firm and kept his sons rigorously to his practices: short bursts of work, two together at the end of the drive, while one waited, with Mark, preparing fuses or cleaning tools in clearer air, ears pricked for sounds of danger. At croust time they would walk to the foot of Johnson's shaft where the air flowed more freely.

Each day, though, as they faced the descent to their level, Richard found himself turning back along the drive with mounting reluctance. Even from his long experience he could not recall as disheartening a lie. At the end of the fourth week of work at their new pitch, Richard sat in his cottage, taciturn, spirits wearied.

"We shall need more powder and candles come Monday," James said, interrupting his father's gloomy thoughts.

"We're in debt enough," said his father curtly.

"We need powder and candles, or we can't go on," said James and added, "There's tin there, I know it."

"And it will take a fortune to get it. We'd best give up now."

Jessica came from the kitchen and looked with surprise at her husband.

"There's no point in throwing good money after bad," he said.

"All that work for nothing!" his wife commented.

"No copper or tin, no gettings, love. That's the way. Wheal Jenny's spent, knacked; and so, near enough, am I."

"One more week, please," urged James.

Richard gazed into the flames. "We'll see, come Monday."

On the Sunday Ellen was determined to see James and keep him to herself. She waited until Granny Pascoe and Julia had gone to the chapel at Hick's Mill where the Bible Christians met.

Her grandmother had shown her displeasure that Ellen was not going with them. " 'Tis the Lord's Day," she said.

"I'm going to Sunny Corner Chapel with the Bryants," Ellen replied.

"Wesleyan Methodys," said Granny with ill-concealed contempt, but she was half satisfied. Worship was worship after all, even in a Wesleyan Methodist building.

Ellen stood at the door of the cottage until she saw the Bryant family gathering to walk together the few hundred yards along the lane. She hurried to catch them up. James turned and saw her, and when she stood still he came back to her. The rest of the family walked on.

"Are you coming to chapel?" he said with surprise.

"I came to see you," she said.

She could see how tired he was. There were deep lines about his eyes, an unfamiliar stoop to his shoulders, and his walk was stiff-legged as if he had difficulty putting one foot in front of the other. The spring had gone from him.

" 'Tis the working double core makes you so," she accused.

"Aye," he said. " 'Tis not so easy as I'd thought. But we must drive. 'Tis rumored Wheal Jenny'll soon be knacked. There's not much time." His voice lifted a little. "If bal's to be knacked we'll pick the eyes out of her first."

He took her arm and led her toward the chapel.

"No," she said. "Let's go alone somewhere."

He grinned at her and for a moment the tiredness lifted and he was the same James as a month before.

"Where?" he said. "America?"

"To the valley."

But it was too late. The Bryants were waiting for them at the chapel door and reluctantly Ellen joined them, holding tight to James's arm. She sat through the service and prayed for the safety of James. She had no thought for anything or anyone else. She heard little of the sermon until the word "America" caught her ear. The preacher, by his voice a local man, was saying good-bye to some members of the congregation who were emigrating. "They are going to that wild country," he was saying, "to dig there for copper, and to bring to grass not only the precious ore from below, but to mine for God's truth, God's word, and His gracious love."

He prayed for a safe journey across the "storm-tossed oceans" and the congregation sang "For Those in Peril on the Sea."

That peril, thought Ellen, was nothing to the dangers that surrounded James here, and she prayed again for him, ignoring all others in her supplication.

When they left the chapel and came out into the crisp clear air she held onto James again and did not want to let him join the others. She wanted to take him down to the valley, to be alone with him, to tell him of her anxieties and her love.

But they walked along as a family to the cottage, and it was taken for granted she would come with them. Richard took her hand and led her to the bench before the hearth.

"You look pale," he commented. "What ails you?"

"I'm all right," she answered.

Richard turned to his wife. She too looked white and drawn, and Ellen saw her own worry in the face of the older woman. Ellen realized the selfishness of her own anxiety and wanted to say something to comfort Jessica, but she knew, from her own suffering, it was useless to offer sympathy.

"You noticed how many were gone?" said Richard to James. "Chasing illusions. What likelihood is there life will be better there than here?"

"There?" said James.

"Australia. America. Up-country. Where you will."

James was silent. He caught Ellen's eye, briefly, and she smiled her secret understanding.

"A Jack o'lantern," said Richard, and dismissed the subject.

IV

ROBERT Buchan, the Scottish doctor visiting the Blameys, had been persuaded to consider a medical practice in Redruth, but he had not found it difficult to reject the proposal. The house going with the practice was substantial enough, in a new part of the town, but the town itself—at least when he visited it— had an air of defeat.

"It's only temporary," said Rowland Blamey. "It will pick up. Mining is like that, up one year, down another. But it survives."

Buchan was not convinced. He read in the local newspapers of the closing of mines, many of them formerly prosperous enterprises; he heard of the large numbers of Cornish men who were leaving their homes to seek their fortune elsewhere. The place is dying, he thought, but kept the thought to himself.

There were compensations to be found here, he admitted. He rode out with a party of the Blamey family to spend a lazy weekend with friends of Rowland at Falmouth, rowing on the river, visiting the castle, acting like the tourist he supposed he was. But idleness did not suit him. He wanted work, the challenge of problems to be faced and solved, of sickness to be diagnosed and cured. Moreover he was impatient with the complacency of the Blameys, their acceptance of the status quo. Buchan was for change: he had made radical friends at University; he had radical instincts. He felt stifled here and considered he had made a sufficient recovery to leave Cornwall. He announced to Rowland that he intended soon to return north and seek a practice in some Scottish town, among his own folk.

"Don't be so hasty," his friend urged. "You're welcome here as long as you care to stay."

"I'm getting lazy," said Robert, "and it doesn't suit me."

"At least wait until Thursday of next week," said Rowland.

"You've not met cousin Veronica yet. Mamma has arranged a dinner party then. For several local worthies as well as the Langarths."

"Another week won't make so much difference, I suppose," admitted Buchan, and agreed to wait.

"But," said Rowland, "watch out for Veronica. She's more frightening even than her mother."

V

RICHARD Bryant yielded to his son's request for powder and candles. In any case it was not in his nature to give up on a task once begun, and under the influence of his son he felt the smallest of hopes. Without hope, however slight, no one would ever dig for metal. So they had drawn powder and candles from the mine store and put themselves further into debt.

Each day's work was so hard, the driving through rock so wearisome, that at the end of the day they rested at the bottom of the shaft before beginning their long climb up the ladderway to the biting damp above. Richard and his sons were aware that time was against them. It was rumored that the adventurers were likely to close the mine at the next setting day so they had only a couple of weeks to strike it rich. Their work became infected with desperate urgency. Richard had yielded to working double core with reluctance. He knew how working to exhaustion blunted judgment and destroyed habits of craftsmanship. He would not allow Mark to remain for the second shift, but he and his two older sons, bone-weary though they were, continued below, driving slowly forward.

It was on the Thursday, with another fifteen days to go before the next setting (if there should be another) that the three of them sat at the foot of the pumping shaft listening to the rhythmic plunge of the pistons, the opening and shutting of the clack valve. They sat in the dark, candles snuffed to save money, each full of his private thoughts.

James's mind was full of Ellen. He tried to hide it from himself as he had sought to hide it from her. He felt an angry sense of guilt at his thinking of her, anger that she was distracting him from his planned future, that she had become involved in his dreams, and guilt that physical desire stirred him to a point where he was afraid of losing control when with her. He had tried to avoid being alone with her, but the abstinence he forced on himself was working to intensify his longing for her so that now, if he closed his eyes, he could see her, could hear her voice, soft, low, rich with meaning. He knew he must try to clear his mind of her now and give his attention to the work before them, but he could not. Wherever he turned he saw her, felt her as she had pressed herself against him, wanting him, he thought, as much as he wanted her.

His father spoke and James reluctantly came back to sweltering reality. He stretched, flexing his hands. They lit their candles and moved back along the level to the stope. Their labor of the last weeks had widened access and the danger of bad air was lessened. Richard's caution had not forsaken him, but his muscles were tired, his bones ached, and his mind was working more slowly than usual.

They cleared the rock from their last shooting and prepared to drill a hole for the next, and it was not until almost the end of their second core, when they had been underground for thirteen hours, that they had finished driving it and were ready for the firing. They had all three stripped to near-nakedness for the heat; the sooty flames of the tallow candles reflected from their sweat-glistening bodies. The contrast between them was largely hidden in the gloom, but Richard, wiry, tough and spare, looked frail beside his sons. Even William seemed more robust.

Richard leaned on his pick and watched while James, with long sensitive fingers, worked at shaping a fuse. He bruised the powder on his shovel and poured it into the paper cartridge. Until now it had been Richard who had tamped the powder home, set and lit the fuse, but he motioned to James to carry on and light the charge himself. He and William retreated along the drive while James, with no less care than his father, prepared the shooting. He took the candle from his hat and set the flame to the paper. It caught and he turned and sped back along until he reached his father and William. They waited for the explosion.

There was silence, save for the steady drip of water and the raspy breathing of the three of them as they waited. The stillness of the deep working settled upon them. Even the plunging of the pump in the shaft was too distant to be other than a faint throb. They waited.

"A misfire," said Richard.

James rose to his feet, but Richard put out a hand to stop him.

"I'll see to it," he said and before James could protest he had scrambled out into the drive and approached the shooting hole. James saw his father stoop to pick up a tool, an iron bar, and reach to thrust it in the hole to pick it out. As he did so—and James's shrill warning was drowned in the blast—the powder fired, a spurt of rock burst forth, a series of booms echoed and reechoed along the drive and dust, black and choking, fell about them.

VI

ELLEN was tired and kept awake with difficulty. It was hard to bear the thought of James coming weary to grass without her arm to comfort him. She worried that he was working double core, from six in the morning to ten at night. It was folly, surely.

"Is Granny sleeping?" she asked as Julia came downstairs. Granny had been troubled with a cough and they had been plying her with spoonfuls of Chlorodyne.

Julia, her usual smile absent in the worry about her grandmother, nodded. "She seems a bit better," she said uneasily.

"Do you mind?" said Ellen as she reached for her shawl. She did not need to explain further. A smile at last appeared on Julia's lips. "Go to bed," said Ellen. "I'll not be long, just see that James is safe."

"I'll be all right," said Julia and Ellen watched as her sister lay down and wrapped the blankets around her.

The night air was cool, with a light breath of wind. She turned along Pitti-Patti Lane and then up Cusgarne Hill. There was rustling in the hedgerows as she passed; the night animals were prowling and she wondered if she would glimpse the badgers whose sett was in the patch of woodland near the chapel. But she saw nothing other than a gray fleeting cat. As she walked up the hill she caught the lingering scent of a fox, sharp and pungent. Her senses seemed unusually keen so that sounds and scents flooded into her from the nearby banks and the distant hills.

The buildings of the mines were silhouetted against the sky, tall elegant chimneys reaching up, here and there mere gaunt relics abandoned to ivy and to rooks. From an engine house fire flared and the boilerman shoveled churks out to a glowing heap outside the house. That was Poldory, still active.

When she came to Wheal Jenny she paused at the entrance. All was calm and peaceful, the only sign of life being the lanterns that swung at points about the workings. There were yet thirty minutes or so to the end of the core and she settled, with the granite pillar at the entrance at her back, to wait for the Bryants, gazing toward the shaft head at which they would appear.

She saw a figure at the mouth of the shaft, slowly emerging, a half-naked figure whose skin caught the light as he stumbled forth. She ran toward him, recognizing in his movement a desperation fighting with weariness, an urgency that drove him on. She ran to him and turned him to her. He tried to shake himself free but as she enfolded him in her arms he yielded to her. He opened his mouth to speak but it was no words that came forth, but a sob, uncontrollable, a burst of anguish that tore at Ellen's heart.

"James," she said, and again, "James," seeking to calm the painful tremors that convulsed him, stroking his head and holding him close.

"Father," he said. "A misfire. Bray's Pitch. It's blinded him. The bal surgeon." He looked around him as if he would find the doctor there waiting on need. "I must find Cap'n Vincent. Get him to call the bal surgeon."

A voice came from the shadowed door of the count house. "Who is it? What's to do?"

"Bryant," called James. "There's been an accident below. Where's Cap'n Vincent?" He was in control of himself now.

"Over to Cusgarne Manor you'll find him," said the voice, that of John Oliver, the clerk, working late.

"I'll go," said Ellen. "I'll go," and before anyone could deny her she had turned back to Cusgarne and was running, leaping over the heaps of rock to find the mine captain and summon the bal surgeon.

He is safe, she thought, as she ran. James is safe. It has happened. Bray's Pitch has another victim, but it is not James.

Then she remembered Richard Bryant, the man who had befriended her on her father's death, who had welcomed her to his hearth, had taken her to his own family, and as she ran, she found her relief changed to dismay and sorrow and, as she neared Cusgarne Manor, to horror as she thought again of the dangers of that awful part of the mine, that sett that lured men to sacrifice.

She was gasping breathlessly when at last she reached Cusgarne Manor. A bewigged footman answered her knock. He barred her way.

"The other entrance. The kitchens. Round along."

"Cap'n Vincent," she panted.

The man seemed to understand her urgency. "From the mine?" he said.

"An accident."

"Come in along," the footman said.

He led Ellen through a long hall hung with sober-colored tapestries and gestured to her to wait. He knocked on a door and entered, half-closing the door behind him. Ellen heard him cough, deferentially, to interrupt the conversation.

"What is it?" She heard a woman's impatient voice.

"A young woman, ma'am, with a message from the mine for Captain Vincent."

There was a moment's silence.

"All right, then. Let her come in."

The door opened and Ellen saw into the room. It was alight with candles, they shimmered from wall and ceiling and table. She had never seen so much waste of light before. Silver and glassware on the table sparkled and she hesitated on the threshold, sharply aware of her own shabbiness, the sweat that made her clothes cling to her, the dust that covered her skirt.

"Well?" It was a woman talking to her, hair set almost as artificially as the footman's wig. Her cheeks were rouged, her eyes dark, her voice haughty, her whole manner arrogant. Ellen met her gaze for a moment then, indifferent to her, turned her head to seek Captain Vincent, sweeping her eyes around the table. She would know him, she thought, for she had seen him at the mine.

Her eyes moved from face to face. They looked at her, the five men and three women sitting there, with curiosity, and most with the same arrogance as the mistress of the house. It was she who spoke again.

"Well? What have you to say for yourself?" she said, with even more hauteur than before. "Get on with it, girl."

" 'Tis Cap'n Vincent I be seeking," Ellen said, unconsciously exaggerating the Cornishness of her speech. "I've a message for 'un." She had not recognized Vincent among the frock-coated men at the table. He should have been wearing the uniform of his trade—a high stove hat and a white coat—then she would have known him.

"I'm Cap'n Vincent," said a man's voice. "What's the trouble?" He fingered the glass in front of him.

"There's been an accident. At Bray's Pitch." She dropped her voice.

"Go on, girl," said the man. "Much damage?"

She hesitated. "Damage?" she echoed. "There's a man hurt, blinded maybe. Richard Bryant."

"Pity. A good man. A good miner." He looked at his hostess as if ready to dismiss the messenger and return to his glass.

"The bal surgeon, sir. They want the surgeon."

"He's over to Truro. It'll not do much good to send for him now."

"A doctor, sir," Ellen said stubbornly.

"Come along, m'dear," she heard the footman say quietly as he put a hand to her arm. She would not move.

"You'll send for him, sir." She tried to sound humble but her voice came as a demand rather than a plea.

"There's no need." A large man at the end of the table pushed his chair back. "I'm not the bal surgeon, but maybe I can be of help."

Ellen looked at him, frock-coated and smartly turned out like the rest, but younger than them, with a broad face, eyes of a piercing blue and fair hair, which in the lighted splendor of this room showed golden. She had seen him before, riding in the lane, she recalled.

"I'm a doctor. I'll come." He turned to Vincent. "You've no objection, I take it?"

"None at all, my dear Buchan. But there's no need you know. The miners are well used to this sort of thing. They know the ropes. They'll manage very well. There's no call for you to disturb yourself."

The doctor turned from Vincent to his hostess.

"You'll excuse me, Mrs. Blamey, I'm sure. I may be able to do something."

He turned to Ellen. She saw the concern in his eyes, concern not only for the miner who had been hurt, but concern for her. He had seen her distress and sought to allay it. He led her from the room and she heard the buzz of conversation resume as the door closed behind them.

He seemed to be familiar with the household and to be known to them. He gave orders to a servant to bring his doctor's bag and in a short while a pony and trap were brought from the stables.

"You know the way," he said, taking the reins. "Guide me."

His accent was unfamiliar to her. Certainly it was not local. There was a lilt to it, a breathiness that made her wonder if he was foreign.

"And who are you?" he said as they drove along. "Wife, daughter to the man who's injured?"

"Neither. A neighbor."

"And what do they call you?" He half-turned to look at her.

"Ellen Bray."

"Ellen Bray," he repeated softly as if he wanted to remember.

"Turn here," she said and they drew near to Wheal Jenny. Ahead she could see lanterns held aloft at the shaft head, men grouped, waiting. She could not see James, but he must, surely, be there; he could not have returned below. The man beside her, the doctor, pulled on the reins and leaped to the ground.

"Hold it here," he said and left Ellen sitting in the trap, staring into the dark.

Above ground, word had spread rapidly from store to blacksmith's shed, from office to boiler house, and underground along levels, rises, winzes, wherever men were at work. By the time William had supported his father to the foot of the ladderway there were men at every platform, eager to help. Richard Bryant was a miner's miner, known for his loyalty to his comrades. At each sollar strong hands gripped his shoulders to help him up. At each one Richard, through his pain, heard voices encouraging him. He recognized each; he knew William was beside him.

"James?" he said. "Where's James? James, are you there?"

"He's gone for the surgeon." His young son tried to be reassuring but his anxiety showed.

Richard's joints ached and though a blanket and his coat had been wrapped around him, he was shivering. As he climbed the ladderway the miners reaching to help saw the telltale pitting on his cheeks, the blood caked around his eye sockets.

At the top of the shaft James waited and as he saw his father slowly struggling up the last section of the ladder, face turned up, torn, raw flesh burned and dark-stained with blood and powder, a sob burst from him.

"James!" his father said. "Thank God! I didn't know if I could believe them. All right boy?"

"All right, father."

James gripped his father's arm and helped him up. A tall, heavily built man came forward.

"Dr. Buchan," someone explained. "He's come to help."

The doctor put out a hand to Richard. "Sit you down here. Are you his kin?"

James nodded. "His son."

"You look gone yourself. Tell me what happened. A misfire?" He swabbed gently at Richard's cheeks and temples. "We'd best lie him down. I'll need to get him to hospital. Where do accident cases go?"

A voice from the group of men answered bitterly. "The Infirmary at Truro—if you're lucky. But they'll not take him. They say they've no room for miners. If they let them in there'd be no space for anyone else."

"Is there no miners' hospital then?"

"We'll take him home," said William.

"You're another son?" asked Buchan, but he knew the answer from the trembling anxiety in the boy's voice as he knelt beside the injured man.

"Get some clothes on, both of you, or you'll catch pneumonia and be no use to your father or anyone else. I've a trap here. We'll take him home in that." He began to organize the men and before long Richard was gently lifted to the trap where Ellen, overcome at the sight of his helplessness, put her arms around the shoulders of the injured man, cradled him to her breast.

"Who?" he asked at the touch of a woman.

"Ellen," she replied. "Ellen Bray."

Above them the vast velvet dome of the sky was spangled with a myriad of stars, pinpoints of light in a dark, dark world.

Doctor Robert Buchan admired the stoical acceptance of the examination he made when they had got the miner home and to his bed. He admired the wife also. Though distressed, she had worked speedily to prepare the bed for her husband. She had roused her younger son, who was asleep, and bustled him downstairs where he was to sleep with his older brothers.

Buchan stooped into the bedroom. The roof was unceilinged and, holding the candle aloft, he could see the bare rafters and the underside of the slates. There were two beds in the room; Richard lay in the smaller, narrower bed, and soon slept, heavy from the morphia Buchan had administered. Buchan, satisfied the miner was as comfortable as he could be made, returned downstairs.

The sons had washed most of the dust and sweat from themselves. The older was white with shock, his black wet curls contrasting with his pale face. Beside him stood the girl who had brought Buchan to the mine. She too was pale, young eyes tired. Buchan studied her with interest; there was something, even here, in this dark room, that marked her out. There was a dignity to her, a composure, more than a hint of strength. Hers would be an arm to lean on in need, he thought, and he saw how the older son was drawn to her in his distress. Buchan wondered who and what she was. She was called Ellen, he recalled, Ellen Bray, but that meant nothing to him.

Suddenly Buchan felt weary and sat on a chair beside the hearth. The older brother, his voice uneasy and faltering, spoke. "Thank you, sir," he said. "Tell us. Is he . . . ?" He could not complete the question.

Buchan stared at him. "He's blinded, I fear. . . . No, he'll not see again. I'll have to examine him closer in the daylight, but I'll not be wrong. He'll not see again. He should be in hospital," he added.

"You're new hereabouts," said the miner. "Maybe that's why you were so quick to come."

"What do you mean?" said Buchan.

"We're grateful to you, but bal surgeons are not always so helpful. When a miner's hurt below ground, the doctor won't go down. We've to drag the man up, however badly hurt he is. And there's no hospital because they'd rather put up monuments to mine lords than spend money on a miners' hospital."

"James!" protested his mother.

" 'Tis true," the girl Ellen broke in. "We all know it. It's the miner who faces the danger, who drags the copper from below, but it's not the miner who gets the rewards; he gets the knocks and bruises, he gets the shattered bones." She paused and it was the older of the two sons who added, brokenly, " 'Tis he who's blinded." It seemed that he was ready to weep but he strode from the cottage into the dark outside. The girl followed.

Buchan rose and bade them good night. He had no place there now.

VII

ROBERT Buchan, driving the trap back to the Blameys, felt bemused. The day—and the events of the last hour or so—had worked strangely on him. He had previously come to a decision against taking a practice in Redruth. He had resolved to go home.

Now his resolution was weakening and he was not sure why. Perhaps he had been won to admiration of the Cornish nature by the courage of the miner, Richard Bryant; perhaps his brief insight into mining conditions had stirred his radical spirit, made him angry enough to want to attack the injustices he had heard of. He tried to rationalize his feelings. He had been offended by Captain Vincent, a fellow guest at the Blamey's dinner party. Perhaps it was a desire to oppose Vincent and men like him that now led him to consider staying. Whatever the reason the more he thought about it, the less certain he was. There were good reasons for staying here. He would seriously consider the Redruth practice after all.

He negotiated the entrance to the Blameys' drive. He could not presume on his friendship with Rowland any longer; there was a house attached to the Redruth practice and he could occupy it as soon as he reached a decision. The company Rowland's mother kept was not his kind.

As he handed the reins to the stableboy who had waited up for him, he thought back to the men and women he had met earlier that evening. Captain Vincent he dismissed as an illiberal bigot. He recalled an incident during the meal. An incautious remark of his had set the Captain aflame. Vincent had mentioned with approval an association of miners that had just been formed. Robert misunderstood him; the association, it later turned out, was of mine agents and owners.

"Miners?" Robert had said. "You mean the working men, the tinners?"

"God forbid!" spluttered Vincent. "We'll not have that. There'll be no unions here, no miners' societies. We do all that's necessary for them."

"I . . ." began Robert, but was not allowed to speak.

"The curse of the nation, you'll see," Vincent stormed. "Thank God it's not reached here, never seriously. We've stamped hard on it, cut if off at source."

"What?" said Buchan, only half understanding.

"Unionism, strikes, combinations. Look what misery they've brought up-country! The Cornishman will have none of it, you'll see. He knows which side his bread is buttered. Common sense." Spittle spattered across the table as his voice rose. "Common sense—that's the mark of the Cornish miner. Respect for the mine captains. You ask 'em. Any one. A good living they get."

Robert recalled now the cottage of the blinded miner, the bare walls, the rough furniture, the earth floor.

The Manor House was almost in darkness. The guests had left, the household retired, save for a young woman servant who was waiting for him with a lighted candle.

"Mistress says I'm to get whatever you do want from the kitchen, sir." Her brown eyes were sleepy and he wondered how long a day she had had.

"No thank you," he said and went quietly upstairs to his room.

He remembered the dinner again. The women had been much more interesting than the men: Rebecca Langarth of course. He had been conscious of her watchfulness of him. He remembered one of Rowland's comments about his aunt: "She rides roughshod over any opposition. Sets her mind to a thing and that's that. No use trying to stop her. And," he had added, "Veronica's even worse. A fire-eater. Better to avoid her."

But he had not avoided her. They had sat next to each other and he had found her conversation stimulating. He recalled her appearance now, as he lay in bed and snuffed the candle; not so plain as her mother—who was almost ugly, with her jutting chin and beetling brows—but no beauty, except for the flashing challenge of her eyes.

And then, as he was drifting into sleep, he saw another woman, the girl who had led him to the Bryants, the woman with the dark compassionate eyes, Ellen Bray. And he wondered, in the moment before sleep finally came, if it was the thought of her that had decided him to set up a practice here in Cornwall.

VIII

ELLEN called daily following the accident to inquire after Richard. She saw nothing of James. It seemed he was working all hours at the mine, desperately striving to tear something out of the sett before Wheal Jenny was closed. At night she could not sleep until she heard his footsteps along the lane, his and William's. Then she would sigh and sleep heavily until at first light she had to rouse herself and go off to the cobbing sheds at Pednandrea. She could no longer meet James at the end of his core, for Granny Pascoe's fractious demands were too much for Julia to bear alone. Ellen had to share the burden, though she found it difficult to give the old woman her sympathy.

She felt no such reservation about Richard Bryant. She admired his stoical courage; she recognized his need for independence, which made him refuse help in moving about the house. She wanted to put out a hand to guide him to his chair by the fire, but she withheld and, with Jessica, watched his stumbling efforts to find his way. They quietly moved obstacles out of his path but he heard and smiled painfully, for his scars were not yet healed.

Ellen was present one evening when Doctor Buchan called to see Richard. She watched him from the shadows as he delicately removed the bandage from Richard's eyes; she admired his gentleness, the concern in his voice when he spoke to Richard, confirming his fears that he would not see again.

"Healing nicely," he said as he applied clean bandages. "There'll be no complications—but I expect you think it's complication enough to be deprived of sight."

"I'm not the first miner to have this happen. There's many an ex-miner tapping his way about the streets of Redruth. There'll be more yet."

Ellen watched the doctor's firm and stubby fingers gripping Richard's shoulder as if to transfer strength to him by the touch. He came from Scotland, she had been told, and that explained his strange, and strangely attractive, accent. She had barely noticed him on the night of the accident in her concern for James and Richard. Now she studied him. He was tall and bulky so that his shadow darkened half the room. His strength and size were tempered by a tranquil manner that went, she supposed, with his profession; his voice was soft and deep, his gaze thoughtful.

He was thinking now. "We must find things you can do," he said at last.

"What sort of thing?" Richard spoke dismissively, with more than a tinge of bitterness.

"We'll give our minds to it," the doctor said. "The world's an interesting place. And there's a world of ideas waiting to be discovered. You enjoyed reading," he said, "judging from that shelf of books."

Richard put out a hand and fumbled among them.

"When I had eyes, I hadn't time for much. Now . . . Yes, I enjoyed reading."

"Someone can read to you," said Buchan, looking across at Richard's wife.

Jessica shook her head. "I can't read, doctor, but . . ."

"There's Ellen," said Richard, and turned to where some instinct told him she was. The doctor turned too and looked at her.

"She reads handsome," said Richard, "but she'll have better things to do, a young maid. A beautiful young maid," he added, as if recalling, in his mind's eye, the way she looked.

The Scot looked inquiringly at her.

"I'll read," said Ellen, coming forward to kneel beside Richard. "I'll read and enjoy to."

"I'll bring books and papers," said the Scot. "The *West Briton*, the *Mining Journal*." He looked at Ellen. "They'll be solid matter, I'm thinking."

Richard reached a hand to take hold of Ellen's. "Not too much for us, I do believe," said the miner. "She'll lend me her eyes, and I'll lend her my years, my life."

In that way began an enrichment of the two minds, of the old miner and the young bal maiden, as together they explored the issues of the day and the ideas of the time. Ellen did not see it that way then, for the pleasure she got came from the act of reading itself and was enough for her. There was something of the actress in her.

IX

ELLEN was at the Bryants' on the following Saturday, reading to Richard, when James returned from the mine. He was hot and angry and stormed into the cottage, slamming the door behind him, so that Mark, following, had to leap aside to avoid it.

"There," James said, flinging some coins on the table. "There's our gettings for the past two months. And that's all. It's knacked." His voice rose savagely. "Knacked, I tell you, with our sett ready to pick."

Richard stretched out a hand to the table to feel the coins. "How much?" he said.

"Six pounds," James said scornfully. "Six pounds and there's sixty locked down there, or six hundred. Who knows? But not for us. The adventurers have closed it. And that's that."

There was silence.

It was Jessica who broke it. "The club money?" Ellen knew she had been hoping the club—money subscribed by the miners for help in need—would pay something weekly to Richard.

"Club money!" said James. "What's that? Cap'n Vincent says the adventurers claim it all. It belongs to the mine, to them, not us. There'll be nothing from there, mam. Here," he said and pushed the sovereigns over to her. " 'Tis not much, but 'tis yours."

"It's closed?" said Richard unbelievingly. "Wheal Jenny?"

"Closed, and everyone laid off," James said. "Closed and

for what? They say the price of tin's so low the mines can't pay their way. The adventurers! Those men have drawn enough from us in the past. They should be willing to answer calls on them now."

"There'll be other jobs," said his mother.

James did not speak. Ellen moved to the door, anxious not to intrude on a family crisis. James followed her.

"Well?" she said. "What now?"

He seized her roughly by the arm and led her away from the cottage.

"What now?" he echoed. "There'll be no bloody America for a start. There's not enough for that. My God, when I think of it. There's tin there enough to pay passage to America and I'm kept from it. Tin enough to leave the old folks in comfort for the rest of their lives and it's locked below. It'll stay there forever. The bastards!" he said and repeated, "The bastards!" Ellen was silent. His hands still gripped her fiercely, as if he had to have something to hurt to ease his resentment.

"America! Freedom, fortune, a future! What a stupid dream. Gone, like a dream." He let go of her so sharply that she stumbled. She was angry with him for his petulance. It was true that fate had dealt ill with him, but what of his father? Fate had dealt him a harsher blow, but he did not yell and shout and whine.

"Are you the only one who counts?" she said. "Listen to me." She took hold of his arms and raised her voice so that he could not ignore her.

He looked at her in astonishment and shook himself free of her.

"What have you to say?" he asked. "What can you do to help? There's nothing to be said."

"James, my love, I understand," she said. "But it's not the end of the world."

"Understand? How can you understand? It's my dream that's shattered, not yours."

He's already forgotten his promise to take me, she thought, and her own anger began to mount to match his.

"Your dream! There's reality here, all about you. Why should you have to cross the ocean to find what you want?"

"Because there's nothing here."

"Nothing!" She felt fury rising within her that even her

love for him could not control. "Nothing! Am I nothing then? And your father!"

He looked at her and she could see he was listening to her now.

"What about my father?" he said coldly. Ellen was now deaf herself to the meaning in his voice.

"You've forgotten. You're not the only victim of Wheal Jenny, are you?" And she gestured toward the cottage where they had left Richard, eyes bandaged, fumbling at his books.

He raised his hand as if to strike her, but she did not yield ground and he let his hand fall to his side.

"You don't understand," he said again, with hopelessness in his voice.

Her anger was softened.

"Try me," she said and put her hand out to him, but he turned away.

"How can a girl like you have any idea?"

He left her there and went back into the cottage and she, hurt most of all by his last words, went angrily home to another confrontation, with her grandmother who, well again, displayed her customary ferocious animosity.

X

ELLEN was glad she had work to go to, and work as a bal maiden; it was physically demanding but somehow the very exertion released her tensions. And Jane was a good comrade, cheerful whatever the conditions.

She wondered about James. She had not seen him since their quarrel. No doubt he would be going from mine to mine, seeking a job. She looked about her at the sheds and shafts of Pednandrea. This old mine somehow survived. Perhaps there would be work for him here.

They had taken on two more girls in the cobbing shed. One, a robust tough girl from Stithians, she recognized; she was thirteen or so, and already seemed to know her way about. She settled at the bench and was soon raising her raucous voice with the other bal maidens. The other was a slight, dark-haired wisp of a girl, barely twelve, with wide wondering eyes and a hesitant manner. Ellen remembered her own first terrifying day in the shed, terrifying till Jane had befriended her. She beckoned the newcomer to take her place beside her.

"What's your name?" she inquired.

"Jenny," came the answer, with tears only just suppressed.

"Come by me, Jenny. I'll look after you," Ellen said and the girl, smiling her thanks, nervously came to sit beside Ellen.

Jenny was too frail to be a bal maiden but she was willing enough. Following the movements of the others, she began to sort rock and lift the cobbing hammer. She tired quickly, and though she tried not to show it her movements were slow and clumsy; she paused frequently to rest. It was in one of these pauses that Ralph Carkeek, the overseer, came behind the bench, observed Jenny for some moments, then, offended by her idleness, raised his cane and with a vicious energy brought it down across the girl's shoulders. She crumpled in tears over the bench and Carkeek raised his stick again, but Ellen was quicker. She stood in front of the girl, eyes blazing, and said, "Hit me, then, go on, hit me if you dare!"

Carkeek, astonished at this, struck at Jenny behind her, but Ellen, hammer still in hand, raised it threateningly. The overseer paled and retreated a step, with Ellen, brandishing her hammer, advancing toward him. The other women stopped their work and watched in silent approval as Ellen strode after the retreating overseer. Jenny's sobs broke the quiet and seemed to rouse Ellen to greater fury. She threw her hammer to the ground at Carkeek's feet. He stopped and looked at it and she reached forward, took hold of him by his white coat and shook him back and forth. He tried to resist but she was too strong for him. His head lolled this way and that as she became more violent, then, with a gesture of disgust, she thrust him from her. He stumbled and fell, struck his head on the stones, and lay still.

"By God, you've done for him," said Jane at her elbow.

Carkeek warily opened his eyes and peered up at Ellen.

"Get away from me, you . . . harridan," he said. "Get away from me and get away from here." He got to his hands and knees and shuffled away until he could stand up out of Ellen's reach. "You're finished here," he said. "And you." He gestured at Jenny who had ceased her sobbing and was gazing with awe at Ellen.

"And me," said Jane, and spat, copiously, at Carkeek's feet.

"And you!" he shouted. "Go on. Don't wait. Get out, all three of you then. We'll have no trouble finding others to take your place."

Ellen took hold of Jenny's hand. "Come along, my lover," she said, and with a wave to the other bal maidens she swept out of the shed.

"Wait for me," called Jane and ran after her.

They walked, heads held high, aprons of their trade still around their waists, bonnets on their head, out of Pednandrea workings into the streets of Redruth.

"Well, Jenny m'dear," said Jane, "that's the shortest job you'll ever have. '

"I'll get the belt when I get home," the child said, in a matter-of-fact way. "Me mam'll leather me."

"What about your Dad?"

"He's over to Californy," she said. "To dig for gold."

"He'll find it," said Jane.

The wind blustered along Redruth Fore Street, snatching Ellen's bonnet from her head, up the hill, across the street, to land in the porch of the Red Lion Hotel. She scampered after it, black hair flowing free and stooped to pick it up, when another hand reached down to collect it. She straightened up and was surprised to see Doctor Buchan. He stared at her costume and looked curiously at the bonnet a moment before holding it out to her.

"It's my gook," she said in explanation.

He seemed none the wiser.

"To cover my hair against the dust."

He still looked puzzled.

"I'm a bal maiden," she said. "At least I was till ten minutes ago. You know what a bal maiden is, I suppose?" She found it difficult to believe anyone could be ignorant of that.

He shook his head. "You must tell me sometime," he said and raised his hat to her as he was joined by another young man coming from inside the inn. They went together to the cab rank.

Jane came up and whistled softly. "You shouldn't have let them get away," she said. "They'd have done us proud. D'you know 'em?"

Ellen explained her acquaintance with Buchan.

"He's a proper gentleman, you can tell." Jane gazed after

the men as they were driven away. "You'd better get off home, Jenny."

The child looked to Ellen for guidance.

"Where d'you live?" she asked.

"Down along." She pointed to the bottom of the hill.

"Good-bye," said Jane firmly. "You're too young for what we're about." Ellen looked at her friend, only half-guessing her intent.

Jenny turned and skipped down the road, leaping over puddles, apparently unconcerned at the beating waiting for her.

"What are we about?" Ellen asked.

"Don't ask questions," Jane said, linking her arm into Ellen's. "Look over there."

Ellen looked and saw two flamboyantly dressed men standing under the clock tower. Each wore a broad-brimmed hat; their faces were brown, their eyes roving; one had a cigar between his lips, and the other chewed endlessly and then spat a brown stream of saliva into the street. They stared over at Jane and Ellen and the cigar smoker beckoned with a raised finger. Jane turned to Ellen and winked.

"Here goes," she said and, holding her skirts high to avoid the mud, stepped into the road.

"No!" said Ellen in protest. "No, Jane, I'll not . . ." but Jane, dodging between the carts, had crossed to the men.

How could she respond to so arrogant a gesture as that raised finger? Ellen wondered. She would be ashamed to. When Jane waved to her, however, she crossed over.

"Come away, Jane," she whispered, but her friend ignored her.

"They're from America," Jane said. She had already marked the cigar smoker for herself. "They belong to Redruth really, and have come back. Made your fortune, eh?" she said to her man.

"Charley," he said. "That's me. He's Wally," pointing to his interminably chewing friend. "We've made enough and to spare." He winked and spread his hands out before them. Gold rings adorned three fingers on his right hand and two on the left.

"What have you come back for?" Jane asked in a coaxing voice.

"A good time. What d'you think? And I've struck lucky,

have I?" He pulled Jane to him and, with a flourish, threw his half-finished cigar into the gutter and leaned down to kiss her. Jane held him away.

"Not so fast," she said.

Ellen looked away. She hoped Doctor Buchan was nowhere near to see, nor anyone else she knew. Wally edged up to her and nudged her. She looked down at him. In spite of his high hat, and his high-heeled boots, he was three or four inches shorter than her. He spat again and then reached to her as if to draw himself up—and her down—to kiss. She turned her face away, but not before she had smelled his breath, a compound of tobacco and rum.

"Come on, girls," said Charley. "We've a room down at the Rose." He took it for granted they would go with him. Jane did not hesitate. She linked her arm in his and set off. Ellen did not move. Wally looked at her, chewed, gestured to her to come, took her arm and went after the others. Ellen allowed herself to be drawn along, but had no intention of staying. She could not pretend she did not know Jane's purpose. She had listened to her tales often enough to know. But she could not behave so herself. She looked at Wally. He swaggered as he walked, as if he had money enough to buy this miserable town. Perhaps he had—there were tales of miners returning from America with fabulous wealth—but it would make no difference to her. She was true to James, however he behaved toward her; it was only James she wanted, no casual flirtation with another.

She suddenly freed herself from Wally's hold and, without a word, started back up the hill.

"Hey!" she heard him call after her. She went on, ignoring his shouts.

"Good riddance!" followed after her, but she paid no attention and strode away, swinging her bonnet beside her.

I'm out of a job, she thought. Like James. The fact suddenly hit her with dismay. She felt no regret at her set-to with Carkeek. He had deserved it. She could not have stood by and seen that child unjustly treated. She wished now she had struck the man with her hammer. It would have been worth losing her job for that. But how would they fare at home without her income? Perhaps another job would not be hard to find. She was a strong and willing worker. Even though tin and copper were going through hard times, there were mines still in production. There was always need of a bal maiden's skill.

She dreaded telling the news to her grandmother and, as she drew near the house, her steps faltered. She turned aside. She would visit Richard and hope too to see James; perhaps he would speak to her at last, forget their quarrel. She put her hand to the latch of the Bryants' door. She could hear James's voice raised cheerfully. She hesitated, uncertain how he would greet her, but then, persuading herself it was Richard she had come to see, she opened the door.

James turned to her and she saw there was no need to fear his ill will, for he greeted her with a smile.

"I've found work," he said. "At Wheal Busy." He put out his hands to hers and swung her around. "There's hope yet."

"I'm pleased," she answered.

James was deaf to the anxiety which her voice betrayed, but Richard, in his chair by the hearth, said quickly, "There's something wrong, my love, I can tell."

She went to sit on the bench facing him, wondering how he could know, from a mere word or two, that she was worried.

She told him what had happened, describing as she remembered it the astonishment on Carkeek's face as she had shaken him. Anger still seized her as she recalled Carkeek's treatment of the girl Jenny.

James burst into laughter. She turned sharply on him. " 'Tis not funny," she said. "I'm out of a job."

"I do wish I'd seen it," he said.

"I don't know how I'll tell Granny."

"Don't tell her," said James. "Come with me to Wheal Busy. There's work there. They're opening new shafts. There's hope abroad." His mood was no longer dark and lowering as it had been when they had quarreled, but gay and easy, filled with a confidence that work was to be had and life was good.

"They'll have need of bal maidens?" she asked.

"Where would the mines be without they?" said Richard.

Chapter Four

I

ELLEN, arm in arm with Jane, came from the mine. There were
still a couple of hours of daylight to be enjoyed and in spite of
her day's work she felt exhilarated. The heat of the summer
had passed and the gentle warmth of September made even
work at the bench tolerable.

She hoped that James would be waiting for her. She was
disappointed. She looked over to where a group of young men
stood, laughing and jostling each other, waiting for their girls.
She could not see James among them. She knew these miners.
One or two had asked her to walk out with them, but she had
rejected their advances. Now they whistled as she and Jane
walked past them down the hill.

"They do fancy you," said Jane.

" 'Tis you more like," Ellen replied.

" 'Tis any maid, maybe. That's men all over."

Not James, Ellen reassured herself, but she was not sure.
Why had he not been waiting for her? There had been many-
times recently when he had disappointed her. Perhaps she disappointed him, perhaps it was her fault he blew hot and cold

in his attentions. Perhaps she did not let him see clearly enough how much she loved him.

She glanced at her friend. Jane would have no such problem; she wore her heart on her sleeve; she seemed to have an abundance of affection, and to spare. She wondered if she should confide in Jane, tell her how unsatisfied James was at the kisses and caresses Ellen permitted.

She found herself reddening at the recollection. James had walked with her down to the valley, and leading her into a tumbledown building beside the road had spread his jacket for them to lie on. She had, at first, no inkling of his intentions, but as his kisses became more passionate and his hands more active she had become alarmed. She had not wished to refuse him for her own passions were aroused, but a strange reticence had curbed her desire so that she had taken hold of his hands and held them away from her. She had returned his kisses until afraid her will would weaken but somehow, in spite of his urging, she had withheld herself from him.

"What is it?" Jane asked.

" 'Tis James," said Ellen but, sorry she had spoken, said no more. Why had he not been waiting for her? Had he found another bal maiden, one more willing to give herself? She did not care, she told herself, but she did. Perhaps he was already at home, hoping to see her there.

She remembered then that there was a new supply of papers and broadsheets that Doctor Buchan had brought for Richard, and at the thought her anxieties about James receded. It was always exciting to have something new to read, to see glimpses of another world beyond Sunny Corner, beyond the valley of Trehaddle, beyond Cornwall even; to read of the events of the day in London and overseas, in Paris and America. One day maybe she would see that world for herself. But now it was enough to read of it and to share the excitement with her dear friend Richard.

Unconsciously her step had quickened and Jane had had to let go her arm, saying, "I can't keep up with you." She waved Ellen to go on. Ellen paused for a moment but then hurried home. She would have tea first and then join Richard.

The young men stood together across from the entrance to Wheal Busy. The bal maidens would soon be appearing. James

Bryant sat on a granite boulder at the rear of the group, idly listening to the gossip of his friends, his attention wandering, thinking of the mine where he worked and that had provided him and his brothers with a living for almost twelve months. There had been rumors that the mine was facing hard times, but there were no signs yet of that.

"That there Cap'n Hosking do mean trouble," he heard Jos Pascoe say.

James gave his mind to their talk. Captain "Brimstone" Hosking, as he was known, had come to the mine within the last weeks; he had a reputation as a hard man; perhaps bringing him to take charge of the mine was a sign that the rumors were true, that the mine was in difficulties.

"They do say he's going to make us pay for bringing the ore to grass," Jos went on.

His mates derided the idea. " 'Twas never so."

James raised his voice. " 'Tis time we formed a society."

"You and your society," said Jos. "What good'll that do?"

James snorted with irritation. That was always the answer. Only one or two of his fellows thought like him that a miners' society would help protect them. He shrugged his shoulders; he was tired of arguing with them. And they were not interested. Their conversation had turned from the mine to the girls who were issuing from the gates.

"There she be, James," said Jos. "She's too good for 'e, right enough."

James knew they were talking of Ellen. He kept hidden behind the men. He had no wish to see her or be seen by her. It was Annie Rowe he had arranged to meet. She would wait for him in Unity Wood, where they had met last night.

"You'm a lucky bugger," said Jos. "But I do tell 'e, she's too good for 'e by a long way. She's a proper beauty. Go on, James. She's waiting."

James, from where he was sitting, could see Ellen standing at the gate looking toward the young men. It was true she was beautiful; he had always seen it; but beauty alone was not enough. She was cold, ice-cold, or how could she have resisted his pleadings? There was no such reluctance from Annie. He felt a slight stirring of unease for his deception of Ellen, but she only had herself to blame. He could not bear the frustration that her self-control brought him.

"There's Annie Rowe," said Jos meaningfully. "Slipping off toward Unity Wood. I wonder who she's got her hooks into now?" He glanced down at James, who pretended indifference.

One or two of the men whistled as two bal maidens passed by down the hill. James waited a moment and then turned up the hill in the steps of Annie Rowe.

"She's too good for 'e, is Ellen Bray," Jos called after him.

Maybe 'tis true, thought James, but the sight of Annie's swaying hips as she walked ahead of him toward the trees drove Ellen from his mind.

II

As Ellen's beauty had matured, so had her mind. Her association with Richard sharpened her intellect and opened her further to ideas, for Richard had a curiosity about the world that made her own interest active in the effort to satisfy him. She read from the papers Doctor Buchan brought regularly for Richard, of the progress, or decline, of mining, of events in the wider world, like the Civil War in America, and of the efforts of J. S. Mill to introduce votes for women into the Suffrage Bill. But it was not only ideas that were in ferment when she read to Richard, for emotions were also stirred when she took up a copy of *Nicholas Nickleby*, which Richard proudly owned. She read vibrantly, at first without artifice, but as she gained confidence giving a deliberate intensity to her reading. Her voice, always low and attractive, became flexible and sensitive, moving from serenity to passion, from joy to tragedy, with a change of tone, a subtle inflexion. Her audience—the whole Bryant family more often than not—was captivated.

This evening when she went to Richard she picked up a broadsheet poem among the papers Buchan had brought. She read it aloud; it was a poem crying out against the denial of justice to the working man. The last stanza came to her lips before she realized its significance to Richard. She halted a moment but then read on, in a voice rich with compassion.

Ye have shorn and bound the Samson and robbed
   him of learning's light,

But his sluggish brain is moving, his sinews have all
   their might.
Look well to your gates of Gaza, your privilege,
   pride and caste.
The Giant is blind and thinking, and his locks are
   growing fast.

Richard's voice burst out, " 'Tis true, 'tis true. The Giant is blind and thinking. 'Tis like me. I have no eyes to see, but, blind though I be in that, I begin to see the cruelties of man to man; and to see some of the beauties too. You have become my eyes, my dear. Through you I begin to see, more clearly than ever before. The Giant is blind and thinking. 'Tis true, not just of me, but more, many more."

The silence that followed was broken by a movement behind Richard, and Ellen saw Robert Buchan. She was embarrassed that he had heard her read and rose to go.

"No, stay," Richard said, hearing her move. "The evening's young."

"Doctor Buchan is here," she explained.

"No cause for you to take flight," Richard said. "He's only come to talk, I do suppose."

"Aye," said the doctor. "I was this way." He gestured to Ellen to sit again and took his place on the bench beside her.

The fire was low and Ellen stooped to pick up a log. Buchan bent forward, took it from her and placed it carefully to catch the dying flame. She handed him another and again, with care, he laid it across the other. They sat in silence, waiting for the flame to take.

She thought he looked tired. His face was lined, serious, the look in his eyes distant. He glanced up at her and smiled, as if her face had suddenly come into focus and he was seeing her for the first time.

"You read with rare feeling," he said. "I had been told so. I'm glad to have had the privilege of hearing you."

Ellen hoped the glow from the fire would disguise her blushes.

"The Giant is blind and thinking," he repeated. "Aye, it's a fine thought." He paused then, as if to himself, he said, "God, what a wearisome time it is, though!"

"What is it?" said Ellen, sensitive to his despair.

"I don't want to burden others with it." He looked at Ellen and she saw the need for him to speak.

"It will help," she said.

He looked in surprise at her, as if unused to having others care for him.

"It's gloomy telling, but it weighs heavily. It's the waste. . . ." He paused for a moment. "I was visiting a patient near Wheal Granville. Nothing out of the ordinary. I was just leaving when I heard . . ." His eyes clouded at the recollection. "I'm used to misery and blood, and violence. I've seen plenty."

She waited.

"I'm not the bal surgeon there, but someone knew I was near. They called me to help. Three boys—children, ten, eleven, thereabouts—caught in an explosion, a powder blast, God knows what. Miners they called them! Children." He closed his eyes as if to blot out the sight of the burned bodies. "One was alive—just. He could even talk, a little. He went too. I could do nothing. Nothing. They were naked, their rags torn from them. What could I do?"

Ellen wanted to reach out to him to offer some comfort, but she did not dare. She sat, silent, her eyes alone expressing her concern. He slowly looked up.

"What could I do?" he said again.

Ellen had thought such men as he, used to sickness and death, might be immune to feeling. He was not. There was anger as well as weariness and sadness in him at the deaths he had witnessed.

"Children," he repeated, "and I was helpless."

"We know," said Ellen. "We understand."

III

ROBERT Buchan had been on his way to the Blameys when the impulse to visit his miner friend had seized him. At the Blameys he thought he might find a gaiety to dispel the gloom which the morning's accident had brought, but he was glad he had gone to see Richard Bryant instead. There he had found an understanding and sympathy which he would not have met at the Blameys. He stayed talking with the Bryants and gradually the clouds of despair lifted. He enjoyed having political discussions with Richard, and as he had become a frequent visitor to the Langarths and Rebecca Langarth's political salons he was able to retail the latest gossip. The blind miner was greatly interested in the Government's intentions on electoral reform. Buchan explained that it seemed certain some working men would get the right to vote.

"What about women?" the bal maiden Ellen asked.

He was taken aback by her question. "Women?"

"Yes," she answered. "Women. Aren't women to have a say?"

"Where did you get that idea, my love?" Jessica Bryant said. "It's never been so in the past."

"I don't think it's likely," Robert said.

"So Mr. Mill's arguments won't come to anything?"

Mr. Mill's arguments? What could this mere bal maiden know of the pleas for women's suffrage made by J. S. Mill? His silence must have conveyed his surprise, for she added, with a touch of annoyance, "I can read. It's been in the papers, the papers you've brought for Mr. Bryant."

Robert looked at her more closely. He had been taken by her voice as she read, and comforted by the concern in her eyes; now he was caught by her lively interest in politics and as he looked at her he saw again what he had noticed before: the firm lines of her chin, the high cheek bones, the full lips, the wide dark eyes. She was beautiful, this woman.

He answered her questions as well as he could. He talked about the issues of the day and especially, at Ellen's prompting, about the organization of trade unions. He mentioned the case of the Sheffield sawgrinders who, it was said, had used violence against workers unwilling to join their union. " 'The Sheffield Outrages' they've been called." He talked about that and other matters. The girl, no less than Richard Bryant, was interested in everything and was shrewd and quick in her understanding. James Bryant, the miner's son, he noticed, had come in halfway through the evening and had stood in the background, broodingly silent.

He had arrived at Richard's cottage with a mind filled with the tragic deaths of the children at Wheal Granville. He left bearing with him the image of a bright and beautiful young woman. Gloom and despair were banished.

IV

As they walked home from Wheal Busy the following day James was unusually taciturn. A black mood held him. He told his brothers to go on ahead. Ellen, walking beside him, tried to link her arm into his, but he ignored her.

He stopped at one point where they could look back to the workings. From here they could also see down to the village of Chacewater, the cluster of houses and inns that depended so closely on the welfare of Wheal Busy. When Busy prospered, so did Chacewater; when the mine ceased to flourish, the village declined. It was now in limbo; one or two shops were boarded up, empty; the inn at the top of the village looked ill-cared-for; a row of cottages, long since abandoned, was collapsing, roofs gap-toothed, cob walls disintegrating. Yet further along the village street there was sign of new building, a chapel maybe.

James did not move. Brow furrowed, he stood staring at the mine buildings. They could see them laid out below, as on a builder's plan: count house, blacksmith's shed, the building which housed the seventy-inch engine, the pattern woven by paths from one shaft to another, they could see it all.

"That's it," said James, as if he had suddenly resolved a question in his mind.

"What?" Ellen asked.

He did not answer at first, but at length he said, "Your Doctor Buchan."

"My Doctor Buchan? He's not mine. What do you mean?"

"You were mighty thick with him."

"Someone had to be kind to the man. He was in distress. Couldn't you see that?"

"Doctor Buchan," he repeated, deaf to her indignation.

"What of him?"

"Those Sheffield Outrages he talked about. What do you know?"

Ellen tried to recall what she had read of them. She had found the story depressing. "The sawgrinders in Sheffield—they formed a union—and those men who wouldn't join were dealt with, it seems."

"How?"

"The union men threw a can of gunpowder down the chimney of the home of one man, so they say."

"What happened?"

She could not remember.

James said again "That's it. That's the way." He smiled at her, his sullenness vanishing, and he took hold of her arm and led her away. "We've been trying to start a miners' society," he said.

"I know. Everybody knows."

"Oh," he said. "I didn't think you bal maidens cared for anything but yourselves."

She was annoyed, but kept her temper. "What's happened to your society? Are you going to blow up the cottages of those who won't join?"

"Nothing so foolish as that. 'Tis not the men, 'tis the masters need blowing up. 'Tis not the miners, but the mine cap'ns who need to be taught a lesson."

She stopped and turned him to face her. "You're talking nonsense."

"I am, am I? How far do you think we'll get with the society unless we show we mean business?"

"Blowing up someone's home's no answer."

"Not their homes, woman, their mines. That's where it'll hurt 'em most."

"I don't understand you."

"Then let me tell you. Brimstone Hosking. You've seen him about?"

Of course she had seen him, he was the mine captain. Abel Hosking's broad figure was familiar to everyone at Busy since he had been brought in to rescue the failing mine. He had been everywhere, poking his grizzled beard into every part of the mine, watching the men with his shrewd and calculating eyes, thrusting his broad shoulders past the cobbing benches, glaring fiercely at the women so that the most humble stopped their work to curtsy at him.

"I know Cap'n Hosking. Who doesn't?"

"They brought him over from Clifford to beat us down. His soul's as black as the deepest level below, though he's a Methodist and a preacher. You know what he's doing? Charging us for the dressing of the ore we bring to grass. 'Tis never been heard of. He needs to be taught a lesson."

"Then organize, in a society. There's strength in numbers."
He looked dismissively at her.

"What do you know? Strength can be in a few, if they're brave and willing. When we show we mean business, then maybe the rest will follow and join."

"What do you plan to do?"

He did not answer, but whistling a cheerful air he walked on, his arm linked to hers.

She did not understand him, with his sudden changes of mood; she could understand his urge to get back at Brimstone Hosking, but she could not see the point of violence. She had heard lots of wild talk at the mine—from Malachy Trenow and the other scatterbrains; she had discounted it as mere talk, but if James was involved, there was more to it than that. She shuddered.

"What's the matter?" he asked.

She did not answer. She would try to dissuade him, but now was not the time.

"Why did you say 'my Doctor Buchan'?"

"You're sweet on him," said James, teasingly. "I can see."

"I'm nothing of the kind. He's a doctor. That's all he is."
It was true that was all the Scot was to her, a doctor; she had not noticed him as a man, not until now at any rate, but at James's teasing she began to consider Robert Buchan in a different light. "Sweet on him! You talk nonsense sometimes," and she held tightly to James.

V

REBECCA Langarth, Rowland Blamey's aunt, saw in Robert Buchan many qualities to admire. His earnestness, his evident concern for others, and his devotion to his work matched her own seriousness. She was a keen student of politics; indeed, more than that, she exercised political influence through the patronage and preferment her husband's wealth gave. Buchan had qualities absent in men of her circle. Many of these were dilettante politicians, faded gentry, absentee landlords, men of breeding and charm, but weak and vacillating.

The mining men she knew—the smelters, merchants, mine engineers—were altogether more to her liking than these mountebanks. They were men of vigor and purpose, men who proclaimed a firm moral code which she admired, though she recognized it was shaped to their own ends and she suspected their public attitudes often concealed private peccadilloes. She knew, too, that many of them were opinionated tyrants, as authoritarian by the family hearth as at the mine; wedded to traditional habits and values, they found no cause for self-doubt in the troubles of mining; others were at fault, not they.

She sometimes felt contempt for these men but hid her feelings. When she met Robert Buchan she was glad, for he was different. He had radical instincts, she judged, and a fervor which could be useful if harnessed to the right sort of political activity. She took him under her wing though she did not reveal to him the hopes she had for him. It would take time to groom him but she was a determined woman, used to getting her way in however devious a manner was necessary. She confided in her daughter, Veronica.

"He has a great deal of promise."

"But is frightfully earnest," her daughter interrupted.

"Believe me, he has promise. He only lacks polish."

"I thought you liked rough-hewn men," Veronica said.

"Don't be pert."

The relationship between mother and daughter was easy and warm. Veronica's views were, like her mother's, radical. At times, thought her mother, extravagantly so.

"He needs the rough edges taken off. I hope you will help me to see to that," she said.

"What have you in mind, Mamma? To marry me off to him?"

Rebecca Langarth looked at her daughter in disbelief. "Don't let such an idea enter your head," she said sharply. "What an extraordinary notion! He's a doctor, girl. You can aim higher than that."

"I thought you said he had promise," retorted Veronica, with a smile.

"Political, not social."

"I'll be pleasant to him," said Veronica.

Her mother looked at her with suspicion, but seemed satisfied with what she saw.

The men and women who assembled at Rebecca Langarth's invitation on that occasion were, for the most part, practical miners, with experience drawn from around the world—Mexico, Portugal, California, Australia, Malaya, and other exotic places. They had prospected for gold, tin, copper, silver; they had had modest success and were content to enjoy its results in their own beloved county. They were united in believing it the most beautiful corner of the world, its mines the richest, its miners the most skilled.

"Things are like to change, though," said a heavy-jowled, stoutly-built man, holding the center of one group. "These are hard times."

" 'Tis always so. Hard times come, and they go." The man who spoke was a grave-faced man with a self-important manner, one William Andrew, a leading mine captain from the west of the county. "They'll go. There's only one thing worrying me."

The group around him maintained a respectful silence. Andrew's manner was, as always, portentous.

He looked around him. " 'Tis the unions. These miners who go up-country or overseas come back infected with ideas that bode no good, no good at all." He shook his head mournfully.

The solid, broad-shouldered, bearded man, known to most as "Brimstone" Hosking (from the Hell and Damnation sermons he preached on Sundays) snorted in dismissal. " 'Tis nothing but nonsense. The Cornish miner will have none of it. He's too independent. His interests lie with ours. He'll have no truck with unions or combinations. Let a union man put his nose in my Wheal Busy, he'll be run out never to come back. Don't 'ee fear that. My tinners wouldn't stand for that foolishness. They'd scat 'un good and proper, I tell 'ee."

"Like years back over to Carn Brea," said one.

"And St. Just," said another.

"And Caradon," said another. "It's never come to aught. There's no union remaining now."

They took heart from each other and dismissed as fantastical any possibility of union organization among the tin and copper miners of Cornwall.

Veronica drew Robert Buchan aside.

"And what do you think?" she asked.

Buchan was slightly flushed. She could not tell if it was from annoyance at the talk, or from embarrassment at her approach.

"What do you think?" she repeated. "You can say. I shan't give you away."

"Look at them, sleek and fat and prosperous! Have you been into Redruth lately? Do you know it?"

"Why should I go into Redruth?" she asked.

"To see for yourself the distress there, written on every face. Do you think they see it, these smelters, the merchants, the mine adventurers, the mine lords? Do they see it?" His voice dropped, as if it were pointless here, in the house of the largest of the mine lords, to talk about distress among the working population.

"He's a very intense young man," commented Veronica to her mother later, and paused.

Rebecca looked at her daughter. She was not sure she liked the look in Veronica's eye.

"Yes?" she said.

Veronica smiled.

Chapter Five

I

WHEAL Busy abounded with rumors of its closing. However ill-based they were, it was an unhappier place since Abel Hosking had arrived to manage it. The tinners resented him and reviled him for his rapacity on behalf of the company. They watched him as he walked about the mine workings, white-jacketed and wearing his high stove hat, and cursed impotently. He was indifferent to their black looks.

He was a broad man in the Cornish stamp, heavy about the shoulders so that he looked shorter than his five feet eight. He wore a full beard, dark, streaked with gray. In Camborne, where he preached, he was well regarded; in Wheal Busy he was loathed. Even his fellow mine captains walked in awe of him. Wherever miners met there was talk against him, angry, bitter talk, but futile. Some began to show their resentment in minor damage to company property, at first the result of mere carelessness, and then of petty destructiveness.

The anger which ran below ground, along the levels, at the stope was fed by tales of injustice to one man and another, was fostered by the poverty of the men and their families, and grew in the long, dark hours of unrewarding labor.

" 'Tis time we did something," said Moses Tregunna to James.

James smiled. "I've been thinking. We've talked about combining into unions and such. That's not worked. Mere talk. We should combine to smash the mine. Give Hosking some of the fires of his own hell and damnation. Set fire to his bloody count house."

Moses Tregunna looked around, to see who was near enough to hear them. He seemed satisfied. "Go on," he said.

"That'll show him we're not afeared. Show him we mean business."

Word quickly spread among the men below ground and above, among the smiths and carpenters as well as the tinners. James argued for careful planning, anxious not to involve too many men and to avoid those who, careless of their own safety, would put the whole enterprise at risk, but it was impossible to curb the indignation of the men.

"Burn the bloody place down," said Malachy Trenow, a huge man, blacksmith by trade, violent of nature, unpredictable in behavior.

They planned together, Moses and James, and Malachy too, talking, hesitating, until the smith, intolerant of delay, said, "Hosking won't be worried by this . . . talking. 'Tis action we want. No second thoughts. We belong to do something, now."

"This weekend," agreed James.

They smiled. "This weekend."

Ellen waited for James to come to grass and saw him go over to the blacksmith's shop where Malachy stood, black-aproned, hammer at his side. They nodded to each other as James passed without speaking.

"Well?" Ellen said, aware from the talk about the workings that some madcap scheme had been formed.

James said nothing.

"You've settled it then," she said accusingly. "I can tell."

"You don't know anything." He spoke warningly. "Remember that. You don't know what's happening."

"You're mad, I know that."

"We have to do something."

"Combine in a society, that's what you should be doing. Present your grievances openly. There's men over to Pendeen and Caradon trying to form societies. That's the answer, not powder, not burning the mine. That's criminal."

"So's a union, so what good's that?"

"Please," Ellen said. "Don't do it. Besides, Hosking will know. 'Tis all over the mine, your madness. Some of the girls even want to join in."

"It's man's work," said James.

"It's fool's work, more like. 'Twill end in disaster."

"It's got to be done and I've got to be there doing it. They look to me."

"It's tonight, isn't it?"

"You don't know. You mustn't know."

"It's tonight. I can tell from the excitement. Hosking will know. He'll be ready for you. You're all mad."

"We're desperate," said James. "It's that makes us mad."

Ellen found it difficult to sleep but at last, even though her heart was tortured with fear for James, her eyes closed in a disturbed nightmare of a sleep broken with crazy images and wild silent cries in her mind. Once, a sudden shriek of a soul in pain woke her and she sat up, startled, nerves jangling. Julia stirred beside her but did not wake. She told herself the cry was that of a screech owl and tried to get to sleep again, having forgotten for the moment the events planned for that night. Then outside in the lane she heard footsteps, and was reminded. She rose from her bed and went to the window. In the moon's light she saw two figures, and creeping stealthily behind them another, smaller shape. It was the brothers James and William in front, unaware, she thought, of Mark following behind.

She wanted to cry out to warn them all, to shout to them to come back, to keep away from Wheal Busy, for she was sure the night was ill-omened. They had planned the venture without thought to the moon. A deed as dangerous as theirs needed dark to assist it, dark to hide them, keep them safe. Moonlight was an enemy. They were blind not to see it.

They had disappeared from view. She closed the curtain to shut out the moon's beams. Julia, smiling in her sleep, had not stirred, nor was there any sound from above, from Granny

Pascoe. Ellen, not knowing quite what she could do, dressed hurriedly and went to the door. The hinges grated as she opened it an inch or two, but the household remained undisturbed. She slipped out into the lane and ran in pursuit of James and his brothers. She would catch up to them and hold them back, keep them from their folly, protect them from danger.

But they had vanished. She paused at the end of the lane to catch a whisper of them.

There was nothing, save, far off in the valley, the sharp bark of a fox.

She ran on, following her usual route to Wheal Busy, through Crofthandy, but saw no sign of them. They must have fixed a meeting place with the other men, perhaps at the lower end of Chacewater; perhaps it was there they had hidden the powder and fuses; perhaps they planned to attack the mine from the north where the workings were bounded by scrub and woodland.

As she ran, the fears which had haunted her sleep leaped to her conscious mind and she had to pause at a field gate to stop the choking clutch at her heart that came with every breath. So driven had she been by her anxiety that she had run further than she realized and now, looking across the field, she saw in the distance below her at the bottom of the village a line of figures, gray and furtive, moving into the shadows.

She could not recognize anyone at this distance and dare not shout to them for fear of waking the village. Then as the leading man came into the brief light of the moon in a gap between the houses she saw the unmistakeable shape of Brimstone Hosking. Those were not the miners stealthily approaching the workings; it was Hosking and his men, forewarned and, she saw, armed. There were men with cudgels and she thought she caught the glint of moonlight on steel. Guns.

She wondered desperately how she could warn her man. "James," she whispered into the night. "James." But of course there was no answering whisper, no reassurance from the silence.

Then pandemonium broke the peace of the night. A flare, a blast of powder, a clamor of shouts, a gunshot, another, and throughout the workings of Wheal Busy torches were lit, fires swiftly blazed and against the flames she saw black shapes of men leaping upon each other, cudgels raised and lashing.

She hesitated no longer. Heedless of what lay in her path, she ran across the field, scrambled over a hedge, through another gate and headed for the mine. She came out in the workings by the arsenic labyrinths, a place unfamiliar to her. She picked up her skirts and ran toward the miners' dry, which seemed at the center of the disturbance, then, stumbling over the heaps of dead rock, she missed her footing and fell.

She lay breathless for a moment and watched, disbelieving, a group of men some yards away surrounding a figure on the ground, belaboring him unmercifully.

She heard a movement beside her and saw a boy, stooping as he ran.

"Mark," she called.

He turned, astonished. "Ellen." She thought he was going to break into tears, but he recovered and crouched down beside her.

"James?" she asked.

"He's . . . I don't know." She shook him.

"Tell me," she said. "What's happened?"

"He's . . . I don't know. He's hurt. William's with him. They sent me." Now he did, suddenly, burst into tears and as he wiped his tears away she saw that his arm was bleeding. A bruise discolored his cheek.

"They sent me home. Said I shouldn't have been there anyway and it was no use me getting caught as well."

"They're caught?"

"Not yet. William's hiding James."

"Take me." Mark looked at her with dismay. "Take me. Then you can go home."

"They're by the old vanning house, hiding."

"Come on."

Reluctantly he guided Ellen through the maze of buildings. The fighting had died down; Hosking's men had beaten off the miners and were now concentrating on dousing the flames by the count house and the pump engine house. Mark's confidence seemed to grow as he led Ellen along.

"He's around to here," he said and pointed to a derelict building by the side of the new vanning shed.

"James," she whispered, hoping her voice would carry to him.

"Ellen." It was William. "What are you doing here?"

"Where is he?" she said, ignoring his question.

"I dragged him in here," William answered. "He's badly."

Ellen's heart plunged with terror but she tried to hide her alarm as she went into the ruined building, calming herself, saying with soft deliberation, "James, it's me, Ellen."

There was no answer but she could make out, in one corner, James lying where his brother had dragged him. There was no movement from him, merely a slow gasp of breath that both reassured and alarmed. She knelt beside him and took his head in her hands. His cheek was rough and bristly but she bent down so that her skin met his. He moved his head slightly so that their lips met, but the effort seemed to hurt him for he drew in his breath and a low moan escaped him.

"James," she said, but there was no answer. Unconsciousness had shielded him from further pain.

"It's his leg," said William. " 'Tis broke, I fear."

"Stay here," she said. "I'll be back, with a doctor."

"A doctor? Who'd come here to help?" said William.

"I know one who might," she said. "I'll try."

My Doctor Buchan, she thought wryly. We'll see what he's made of. He talks about the miners as if he understands them, sympathizes with them. We'll see if his words match his deeds.

II

ROBERT Buchan wearily replaced his instruments in his bag. His skill had been of little use after all. As he had expected, the confinement had been difficult. Poor Mrs. Rodda had little strength left. Perhaps it was a blessing that he had been unable to save the infant. The Roddas had little enough to feed another mouth.

He rode up the hill, glad of the moon to light his way. He wondered what time it was, but was too indifferent to pull out his watch to see. It was late—or early—whichever way you cared to look at it. Either way he was ready for his bed. He had earlier spent a couple of hours with the Langarths—how distant it seemed now, though it was only a few hours since. The Roddas' home was a world away from the Langarths' stately mansion. He thought of the contrasts he saw, from the backlets and alleyways of Redruth where poverty stalked, to the house of the Langarths with its broad acres and its sweeping lawns. He thought of the Roddas and their like, with the men going to their long spells underground (when they had work to go to) with little in their bellies but coarse bread and skimmed milk, and coming home to a meal of turnips, and a few pilchards if they were lucky. He thought of the salmon and capon and baron of beef he had partaken of at the Langarths.

He had spoken to Rebecca Langarth of the distress he saw and she had commended the efforts of the County Distress Committee, supported by so many of her class. He had argued with her about its purpose. "Charity only covers up the distress and, in so doing, does the poor a disservice."

She had not agreed. "If one mother is made easier in her mind, one child has its hunger staved, one man has boots provided so he can get to work, if only one family is helped, is that not better than standing back and wringing your hands?" she had said.

"It soothes the giver more than the one who receives," Robert had countered. "They feel absolved from responsibility—these dispensers of charity—and how can they not be responsible? It is the way we organize our lives, the way we live, it's that that brings misery to the lives of others."

He had observed her tolerant smile; she was amused at his seriousness, but not displeased at his views. Veronica's eyes had shown her approval of them. He would have liked to talk with her about them, but her mother had diverted the conversation to gossip about the London theater.

How remote that—and Trevorrow itself—was from the reality surrounding him. The streets were silent and he found himself nodding, soothed by the steady clip-clop of his horse's hooves on the granite setts. There was a light at his porch. No doubt Mrs. Honeychurch, his housekeeper, would have dutifully set his whisky out for him, and left a fire burning.

He stabled his horse and went into the house. He had meant to take his nightcap to his bedroom, but the warmth of the fire tempted him to sit beside it. He stretched out his legs and sipped his drink, staring into the flames, dreaming idly. At last, relaxed, he put the empty glass down and stood up. He was glad at the thought that tomorrow, since it was Sunday, he had no surgery to attend to, and might be spared too many calls.

He stretched, yawned and moved to the stairs.

A knock came at the door, so soft that at first he believed he had imagined it. Then it was repeated, more loudly, urgent.

Oh, no, he thought, not at this time of the morning. There was a movement on the stairs above and he looked up to see Mrs. Honeychurch, a woolen gown clutched about her.

"It's all right, Mrs. Honeychurch," he said. "I'll see to it. No call for you to disturb yourself."

"At this time of the night," muttered the housekeeper resentfully. "Some folk!" but she turned and went back to bed.

The knocking came again and, with irritation, Robert strode to the door, flung it open and thrust his candle forward to cast light on the caller. He recognized her, the young woman Ellen Bray, the girl with the passionate voice, the questioning mind, the dark and caring eyes. The flame from his candle shone in them now; there was concern, anxiety, uncertainty there.

"What is it?" he said, his resentment banished, his weariness put aside.

She looked around as if afraid to speak.

"Come in," he said and led her into the drawing room. She stood before him, dusty and disheveled, dark hair awry, plucking nervously at a button on her blouse. The thread snapped and the button fell to the carpet. Robert picked it up and gave it to her and felt the hard calluses on her fingers and noticed the strong wrists of her.

She seemed hesitant to explain her presence.

"Well?" he prompted. "What is it?"

"There's been trouble . . . at Wheal Busy."

"I'm not the bal surgeon there," he said, puzzled. "That's Dr. Gray in Chacewater."

"Not an accident."

She still seemed uncertain whether or not to confide in him.

"What can I do?" Her black hair had come loose from its comb and strands of it straggled across her face. She swept them back and looked at him as if weighing him up.

"This trouble—what sort of trouble?"

"The men—some of them—most of them—they plotted to attack the mine, blow up the count house, destroy the pumps, burn. . . ."

"In God's name, why?" he interrupted.

"To get their own back on the mine, on Cap'n Hosking. I know 'twas foolish," she said hurriedly. "But they were desperate. They didn't know which way to turn." She paused and caught her breath.

He was struck by the beauty of her as he waited for her to continue.

"James," she said. "James Bryant."

"He was part of it?" he commented dryly. So that explained her anxiety. He was dismayed at the sharp feeling of annoyance that came to him.

"Yes. He was part of it. I tried to stop him but . . . He's hurt . . . badly, I fear."

"Where is he?"

"In hiding, on the mine."

"In hiding?"

"The men were caught, attacked. There were constables there. I saw them when I left him, searching the woods for the men." She looked at him and when he said nothing she repeated, "He's badly hurt. He needs your help."

"You know what you're asking?"

"I'm asking your help for a sick man." She looked directly at him, challenging.

"A man at odds with the law, being sought by the police, according to you."

"A miner, injured, in need." There was a quiet determination in her. He envied the man who was at the heart of it. But he felt stubbornly unwilling to respond.

"You'll come?" she said and there was a plea in her voice that he could not refuse, however little he relished helping a lawbreaker.

"The police," he said thoughtfully. "You said they're on the prowl?"

She smiled, knowing she had persuaded him to help.

"We can give them the slip." She was impatient for him to move and he was willing enough now, but tiredness made him slow to respond.

"Are you all right?" she asked and he was pleased to hear concern in her voice for him too—or was it, after all, only that she wanted him fit to tend this young firebrand, James Bryant?

They drove by pony and trap as far as Scorrier Station. From there Ellen insisted they went on foot so that they could choose ways to avoid the search parties. Buchan was uneasy, half-regretting the impulse that had made him yield to the girl. Why should he risk his position for James Bryant? What did the man mean to him? He had no sympathy for people who stepped outside the law, however unjust the laws were. He heard a sudden burst of birdsong from the woods below Scorrier and realized it was almost day. He was conscious that they must present a strange—and to searching police, a suspicious —picture, the doctor with his case, the shabbily dressed young woman, hurrying through the lanes, keeping stealthily in the shelter of the hedgerows.

They were not seen. The mine workings seemed deserted. A wisp of smoke rose from a heap of timbers but there was little other sign of the miners' sabotage. What a fruitless exercise, he thought, to risk life and limb in such destruction, and how desperate they must have been to attempt it. He felt sympathy, in general terms, for the men who had been reduced to this, but he felt little sympathy for James Bryant.

When he saw him, lying in the corner of the shed, with his brother William kneeling beside him, it was not sympathy that was needed but his professional skill. In spite of his tiredness, his brain and his hands came to life. He stooped down to examine him.

Chapter Six

I

THE futility of the miners' protest was soon evident. Captain Hosking strode about the workings more masterful than ever. The malcontents had been identified and got rid of. Those— like Malachy Trenow and Moses Tregunna—against whom hard evidence could be brought were in Bodmin Jail awaiting trial. There was smug satisfaction in Brimstone's manner, soured only by the escape of James Bryant, the known ringleader. He had vanished and it was rumored he had fled abroad. The police, with other crime on their hands, seemed inclined to believe this. Nevertheless, Ellen was cautious in her visits to James's hiding place. With the help of Jane she had taken blankets, food, a basin for washing, and soap to the hut on the outskirts of the mine where James was hidden. She confided to Richard that James was in hiding, but thought it safer not to disclose the place to him. And she forbade William and Mark to come near. Together she and Jane nursed James through the next days, when his pain was greatest and his spells of unconsciousness frequent.

Granny Pascoe's suspicions she could not allay except by the truth, and to her surprise the old lady did not oppose her actions, only urging her peremptorily to be careful.

Buchan came twice in that first week and Ellen was grateful. She watched as the doctor examined James's leg. It had been broken but, the Scot assured her, "He's a healthy young man. It'll mend without problems." He seemed less certain about internal injuries James might have suffered, which were difficult to deal with in the rough circumstances of the hut.

Ellen, unworried for her own safety, was nevertheless alive to the risk Buchan was taking and made her gratitude plain. She could not tell him how much she admired his sureness of touch, or how moved she was by his gentleness, the sensitivity of his hands, the calm assurance of his voice, but she hoped he would know how she felt.

On his second visit Buchan noticed the blankets spread alongside James and looked at Ellen inquiringly.

"He needs nursing through the night," she explained. She did not think it necessary to say more.

"Aye," said Buchan. "That's true, I suppose."

She wondered at the tone in his voice and the way he turned away out of the shed and left without a further word.

She lay by James at night sleeping, but sensitive in her sleep to his every movement. She had water and a cloth beside her so that she could alleviate the fever of the first nights. He was unaware of her, she thought, and did not know how tenderly she wiped his brow. She would kiss him lightly each time he stirred and whisper endearments to him, hoping he might sense her presence.

Then the time came when as she kissed him he turned to her, opened his eyes and saw her. The pain, for the moment at any rate, had gone and his eyes showed the spark that had first touched her heart, the hint of laughter beneath the serious gaze.

"Oh, James," she said. "You're back."

"I've not been away," he answered slowly. He tried to lift himself, but the effort seemed to pain him. He touched his chin and felt the beard that had begun.

"How long?" he said. "How long's it been?"

"Seven, eight days."

His hand moved down to his leg and felt the splints bound there.

"You?" he said, wondering.

"Doctor Buchan," she explained. "He's been to see you."

"Your Doctor Buchan," he said, and she was glad at the teasing in his voice.

She brought him some oatmeal porridge. It was cold for she dare not light a fire, but James, in his hunger, did not seem to mind. When he had finished she washed his face. He took hold of her fingers and kissed them gently. He had never before dealt so tenderly with her. She hoped it was love and not mere physical weakness that made him so.

"You're sleeping here?" he said in surprise when he saw the blankets and pillow on the floor beside him.

"Until you're better."

"What will Granny Pascoe say?"

"She understands."

In the night she felt his hand move to her under the blankets. She took it and held it to her. She had stripped off her blouse and skirt and was wearing only her camisole. She unloosed it so that his hand lay touching her flesh. It was warm and comforting and she turned to face him, to be near to him, but he was asleep again, though his hand, held by hers, still cupped her breast.

II

ROBERT Buchan visited the derelict building in the evening, after nightfall. He told himself that it was safer then; but he recognized, with growing force, that he went then because Ellen would be present. James Bryant no longer seriously needed him; it was for Ellen he went. He had slowly come to see his obsession with the young woman. He persuaded himself at first that his admiration for her was dispassionate, but he could not blind himself for long to his real feelings for throughout the day he would think of her until, toward the evening, the need to see her became irresistible.

He hid from her, successfully he thought, his desire to be with her; after a cursory examination of Bryant, he would stand for a moment filling his mind with her before leaving, feeling anger that it was for Bryant she was sacrificing herself, risking her freedom.

"You must get away from here," he said one evening. "You will do yourself and Bryant no good by exhausting yourself in service of him." She did indeed look tired, though she tried to conceal it. "Is there no one who can take over for a night or two—though he does not really need constant nursing now," Buchan said.

James was apparently uninterested in the discussion going on above him.

"I beg you," Buchan said. "For your own sake, your own health. Is there no one you can trust?"

She thought for a moment then conceded. "There's Jane, Jane Rowse. She can be trusted. She's helped already, but . . ."

"Believe me, it's needful," said Buchan. "Or I'll be having you as a patient."

So, though she felt guilt at surrendering responsibility for James to another, Ellen agreed. Jane insisted she was happy to spend the nights with James until Ellen was sufficiently rested to resume charge, and Ellen returned home and crept into bed with Julia.

Jane's first night in the hut indicated that James had already recovered enough to fend for himself. She had thought him asleep when she had prepared herself for bed. She had undressed to her camisole, ignoring his presence, but when she got down to her bed beside him, she caught the flicker of his eyes. He had been watching her and seemed to have been amused by her indifference to him.

She pretended she had not noticed his awareness of her and settled to her bed. She longed to put out a hand to him; she remembered with particular fondness her adventure with him years before when they had met in Unity Wood and she had seduced him. He had been willing enough, but inexperienced. She had treated him gently at first—the memory of it was vivid with her now—and then passion had overcome them both. Her desire for him stirred and she moved a hand toward him but withdrew it in shame at her disloyalty to her friend. But, she thought as she went to sleep, he is a handsome young fellow, and full of love.

On the second night she was more aware of his interest in

her movements and as she began to prepare for bed she could not help lingering over her undressing. But she felt a sudden shame at the betrayal of her friend that threatened with every languorous gesture. She got under the blankets and stripped off her outer garments there, hotly aware of the nearness of James.

She felt his hand move to her and she wished she had put the blankets down farther away. She turned her back to him and pretended to be asleep, but when she felt his fingers reach to her neck and begin to stroke her gently, playing at her hair, she leaned back toward him, unable to resist the sensations that spread from her neck, flowing through her. She wanted to turn to face him and answer his own urgings with hers, but she compelled herself to think of Ellen: Ellen, her friend, her support, who would never betray her; how could she betray Ellen? It was unthinkable.

But she moved slightly, half-turning toward James, to lie on her back. Her body was challenging her will and responding to James's touch. His hand, as she turned, moved from the back of her neck to her shoulder and then slowly, insidiously, to her breast and held it gently, lovingly, caressingly, so that she wanted to reach to him and take him to her.

She heard him shift his position and wince as the movement caused him pain. She came to her senses at that, slid away from him and then threw the blankets away from her and stood up.

"No," she whispered. "No."

He laughed. "You do want me."

"No."

"I can tell it."

It is true, she thought. I do want him. But I will not. I will not.

She bent down and dragged her blankets away from him, so that there was a wide space between them. She looked out from the building to the lights twinkling distantly on the workings. Men would be active below ground. The mine captains would be walking the drives. Tomorrow Captain Hosking and his hirelings might be continuing their search for James.

"Be careful," she urged.

"Come here," he said, seeming indifferent to his danger. "Come here, my lover."

But she lay on her bed away from him, despising herself for the weakness which had almost overcome her.

In the morning at first light, Ellen arrived with a basket of food. "How is he?" she asked.

"Wanting you."

III

THE hue and cry for James Bryant seemed to have died down but when the mine agents and captains met they showed their annoyance at the failure to apprehend him.

"Someone must be sheltering the man," said Hosking at one of the Langarth's receptions, when the conversation turned to the sabotage at Wheal Busy.

"He's escaped up-country, or overseas," said John Daniell, a local magistrate. "What do you think, Buchan?"

Robert Buchan was startled at the question. He'd tried to avoid being drawn into the conversation.

"Eh, Buchan? What do you think's happened to the man?" Daniell repeated.

"I should think if he's any sense he'll have got away," he answered. Perhaps, he thought, that is the answer. Perhaps I could arrange for him to take ship to America.

"That's it," said Daniell. "Some of those fishermen over to St. Ives would help a murderer escape justice if the price were right."

Veronica Langarth drew Robert away from the group.

"What do you think has happened to him?" she inquired.

"How should I know?" he said uneasily.

"You work among these people, the miners. They must have some idea."

"They'd not confide in me," he said, but he was sharply conscious of his vulnerability. He would not be made so welcome here if his activities were suspected. He deeply regretted, for his own sake, having helped James Bryant, but in that it had brought him closer to Ellen he was glad of it.

"You know your standing with the mining interest is high," said Veronica, and he wondered if somehow she had guessed his secret and was discreetly warning him of the dangers.

"Is it?"

"Mamma has high hopes of you."

"What hopes?"

"She is planning a political future for you." She turned him around so that they looked back along the gallery where the guests were moving to and fro. "She's singing your praises." She indicated her mother in lively conversation with Josiah Thomas, the influential chairman of the Dolcoath mining companies.

"You'll have to keep your fingers clean if you're to be the next Member of Parliament for the Mining Division."

"A Member of Parliament! How could I afford that? I've no private income."

"There are ways. You could marry money." She touched him playfully on the cheek. "Have you thought of that?"

He laughed, pretending to dismiss her notion, but it had its attractions and as he rode home he began to wonder about the future. Reid, the present MP, was a sick man and rumored to be unlikely to stand for election again. Robert Buchan knew the Langarths' influence. If Veronica were to be believed, it might happen. But it seemed unreal to him. He had no money other than that earned from his practice. Members of Parliament were expected to support themselves. Where could he find money enough? A marriage of convenience? He shook his head in disbelief.

His way home took him near Wheal Busy and he realized that pressure of work had kept him for many days from seeing how James Bryant was, and from seeing Ellen. He would go now, he decided, but then, as he turned into the lane leading to the rear of the workings, he began to have second thoughts. It was dangerous, this association with Bryant—and unnecessary; healing was only a matter of time now.

And, he told himself, this obsession with the woman Ellen Bray was dangerous too. He heard again Veronica's teasing tone, "You could marry money. Have you thought of that?"

He had not thought of marriage at all—for money or anything else. His feelings for Ellen had not reached that point, but now he began to wonder. Marriage? He was lonely. Returning from his visits to the sick he was frequently depressed. His house offered shelter, but no affection. It needed another presence to make it home.

It needed—he refused at first to admit it—it needed, as he needed, Ellen.

"Ellen," he said aloud and repeated it, whispering the name into the night. What did money matter? Or political ambition? They faded from his mind.

As usual when visiting the hut he left his horse in the lane a few hundred yards away and walked, with caution, the remainder of the way. It was dark and he stumbled once or twice.

"Who's that?" He heard Ellen's startled voice.

"Robert," he said. "Robert Buchan."

He saw her at the door of the hut. Her face was in shadow but his heart leaped at the mere shape of her. He imagined she was smiling but he could not tell until she spoke and, in her voice, there was a welcome, a sound of joy that he took at first for his.

It was not. When she spoke he knew her delight was in the man Bryant.

"He's so much better," she said. "I'm so glad."

He was jealous of her regard for the miner.

"I'm glad too," he said. "Perhaps there's no need for me to come here again." He could not conceal the bitterness in his comment, but she did not seem to notice. She held out her hands to him and said, "You've been so good. We can never thank you enough."

"We," he heard, "we," and felt again an angry jealousy.

The miner was sitting against the wall of the hut. He had by now a crisp black beard.

"Well," said Robert. "Ellen tells me you're much improved."

"I am," Bryant said. "I can move." He demonstrated by raising himself to his feet and standing awkwardly. "I could get away from here."

"Where?" said Buchan and then thought of the rumors that the man had already escaped overseas. "To America, maybe," he added.

"No," said Ellen in swift rejection. "No."

"He'll be out of harm's way," said Buchan.

"He's not fit."

"By the time it can be arranged he may be," said Buchan. They were ignoring the miner.

"I'll not go," said Bryant. "I've a score to settle here."

"What?" Ellen said. "Don't think like that."

"Brimstone Hosking for one."

"Have you learned nothing?" said Buchan, with contempt. "Your friends are in jail. You're hunted, an outlaw, and you talk of petty revenge. Grow up, man. Learn political sense." His jealousy was finding an outlet. "And think of others, for once. Think of the risks Ellen has taken to help you. And me too— if that's of any account."

He could not, in the dark, see James's expression, and there was silence for a moment. Then it was Ellen who spoke. "He's grateful to you, Doctor. You don't need to come again. He's well enough now to spare you the danger of coming."

"And you?" Buchan asked.

She drew nearer to the miner.

"There's nothing I wouldn't do to save him."

Buchan turned impatiently away. "Then I'll be leaving and I'll be saying farewell to you both." He moved to the door and he stood for a moment outside looking up at the stars. Why was he wasting time here? He had a practice to attend to, influential friends to cultivate, ambition to serve.

"Doctor Buchan," he heard and felt Ellen near to him.

"Yes?"

"You have been so good. I'll never forget you," she said.

"Nor I you," he replied and wondered if she would see the truth of it.

IV

JAMES Bryant, as he grew stronger, became impatient, longing for the freedom which lay beyond the confines of his bare and gloomy hiding place. He had been disturbed by Buchan's outburst and in the lonely hours brooded over it. At the time he had resented it, but now he began to see the justice of the accusations. The doctor, for some unknown reason, had taken risks to help him, and James was genuinely grateful. He took Ellen's willingness to endanger herself for granted, for he would have done the same for her if need be, he believed.

He wondered about his situation, how he could avoid being taken. He felt he had to leave the hut; it depressed him; it encouraged self-examination and he found no pleasure in that.

He had behaved like a fool in his anxiety to get back at Brimstone Hosking. He should have recruited three or four men he could trust, not allowed all and sundry to join him in his enterprise. He had been reckless and paid for it by failure. And perhaps, after all, Hosking was not the real enemy. If Hosking were not there, his place would be filled by some other mine captain, no less willing to serve the company interests.

His mind wandered here and there and often he thought of his father. Then he felt a double guilt—guilt at the accident which had blinded Richard—for James felt the misfire must have been due to some error of his—and guilt at his wild act of sabotage which ran counter to all Richard's beliefs and practice. He recalled his father's attempts to interest his fellows in forming a miners' society. Perhaps that was the way, but he knew he could have done no other than he had done; violent protest against the mine and its indifference to the men who served it had been inevitable.

James Bryant was not used to such introspection; loneliness and idleness forced him to it and he did not like the feeling.

He hobbled to the door and stood looking out to the mine. He longed to be back at work, deep in the levels, following his craft. He was tempted to walk over to the miners' dry and join his comrades.

He dare not, of course. He was doomed to be a fugitive, hiding where he could, disguising himself, running always.

He had not noticed Ellen's approach and was startled when she spoke, with anxiety in her voice.

"You'll be seen. Come inside, please."

He wanted to stay there but knew it was folly to show himself, remote though the hut was from the center of the mine.

"I've been thinking," he said as he allowed Ellen to lead him inside, "about escaping overseas."

She was silent. He eased himself down onto his blankets and she knelt beside him and kissed him. All his frustrations welled up and he responded fiercely. Ellen moved to him, stretching herself beside him, her hands clasped around his neck, her body pressed against his. His leg made his position awkward, forced him to lie passively, save that his hands wandered about her searching for a way through her clothes. His fingers were clumsy so Ellen loosed her hold of him, sat up and began to unbutton her blouse.

His hands moved to her breasts and he closed his eyes. Her skin was soft, her breasts firm. He heard Ellen speaking, whispering, but did not know what she was saying, only that the sounds were full of a depth of meaning he had not known in a woman before. The world vanished. He became deaf and blind to all but the nearness of Ellen, the feel of her skin, the touch of her lips. He forgot the clumsiness of his leg and moved to bestride her.

"No," she said. "Listen."

He heard nothing but the pounding of his blood.

"Quiet," she whispered and drew back from him. She began to button her blouse and, though he tried to hold her back, she rose from him and cautiously moved to the door of the hut.

"James," she said. "They're coming, Hosking and his men. James." She turned to him in alarm.

He stumbled to his feet. He could not believe her. How had they known?

"Someone saw you standing at the door, that's it," said Ellen.

James looked around for a means of escape, but there was none. He limped to the door and peered out. They were there—Brimstone Hosking and five men, armed with picks, only four hundred yards away, striding purposefully toward the hut.

Ellen turned and held James to her. "I'll not let them have you," she said.

He took her arms from him. "There's no way out," he said. "You mustn't be seen. Stay here. Stay here, please."

He kissed her swiftly and turned to the door, moving stiffly, so that she thought he might fall, but he held to the door jamb. He would meet them standing.

He stepped from the shelter of the hut and moved slowly toward the advancing posse.

"We've got him," shouted one of the men with a hoot of elation and ran forward, pick upraised.

"Hold it," came Hosking's voice. "We want him fit to face trial. We'll make an example of this one."

James advanced slowly, dragging his leg, barely able to remain upright but determined to do so. He stopped a yard or two in front of Hosking.

"You've found me," he said. "Now take me away."

He hoped they would be satisfied with his capture. He hoped Ellen would be wise enough to remain hidden.

"Well, Brimstone," he said, looking down on the stocky mine captain. "You've caught me. What are you going to do with me?"

The men gathered around him, keeping a wary distance as if they had learned to fear this man, this outlaw, who, only weeks before, had worked in the drives with them.

"Caught, Bryant. I knew we'd get you. You're for trial, boy. You'll not escape me now." He gestured to the men and two of them seized James by the arms and dragged him along.

So Brimstone Hosking and the five men brought James Bryant back to Wheal Busy, and Ellen, in tears, watched from the shadow of the hut.

Chapter Seven

I

THE five years' sentence passed on James was longer than expected and the Bryants were plunged into despair by it. Ellen tried to comfort James's parents but, though Richard responded to her and welcomed her visits, nothing could help Jessica. The thought of her son languishing in the jail at Bodmin aggravated the illness which was already dragging at her, and when William, in despair at being unable to find work in Cornwall, went to the Lancashire coalfields, she took to her bed. The courage which until then had enabled her to bear her pain with fortitude was used up. Gradually her will weakened and six months after the sentence on James she died.

The Bryants, who had seemed to Ellen a warm and secure family, were suddenly a family no longer: James was in prison, William up-country and only Mark, the youngest son, remained.

Julia took it upon herself to look after the two men and gave as much practical comfort to Richard as Ellen gave spiritual. She washed clothes, prepared food and cleaned the cottage. Ellen was proud of her; she still thought of her as a child but in domestic matters she was womanly and adult. She thought of her less as a child when once, bursting into Richard's cottage one evening, she saw Julia in the arms of Mark. They separated at Ellen's entrance but there had been an intimacy in their embrace which made Ellen realize they were children no longer but young people of marriageable age. Ellen's own mother had been no older than Julia when she married.

Ellen had turned away, embarrassed for Richard's sake. He had been sitting at the hearthside while Julia and Mark had been fondling each other a few feet away. Ellen had rebuked Julia afterward but Julia had smiled, her feelings for Mark making her invulnerable to criticism.

Granny Pascoe resented the attention which Julia paid to their neighbors.

"Is my need less than theirs?" she asked in a quavering voice of Ellen one evening when they were alone together.

To her surprise Ellen understood her grandmother's feeling of neglect. Julia still provided for Granny Pascoe's material needs but in the evenings, where formerly she had kept her grandmother company, she now had little time to spare. Ellen, in pity for her, began to pay attention to her grandmother. She was no longer hurt by the old lady's sharp tongue. (Ellen did not think anything could hurt her now, since the capture of James.) She recognized the indomitable spirit which had sustained her grandmother through the loss of her husband and two sons—and her son-in-law and grandson—to the mines. It was a strength which she wished were hers too.

And Granny Pascoe seemed to understand something about James. She did not condemn his behavior at Wheal Busy as folly.

"He's got more fight in him than most of those cowardly laggards," she said and she added, with the only words of praise Ellen had ever earned from her, "And you were a brave, if foolish, maid to help him."

Though increasingly infirm she insisted on spending her days downstairs. She would sit, shawl huddled around her, trying to keep warm.

"You'd be better off in bed," Ellen would say when she returned from work.

Her grandmother's reply was to say, "Bed's to die in, when you're as old as me, and when there's no one to share it." She glanced at Ellen as if to say more but shook her head and was silent.

Slowly there grew respect between them and, even more slowly, affection—on Ellen's part at least. She admired the old lady's determination to be independent, her refusal to accept support toward the stairs, her stubborn insistence she could do things for herself, her resolve to hide her frailty. In the end she had to accept Ellen's arm to her bed, but did it as if it were more for Ellen's sake than her own.

So Ellen began to divide what time she had after work between her grandmother and Richard. She tried to lift his spirits by questioning him about the past and work in the mines, but that served only to depress him further. She tried to distract him by reading from the papers Doctor Buchan had brought but they were out of date, for the doctor had kept away since James's capture and imprisonment.

There was little news of James. Once, long months after the trial, a Methodist minister who had visited Bodmin Jail called at Sunny Corner to see Richard and to tell him about his son, but there had been no word of comfort for Ellen. She secretly saved enough money for a journey to Bodmin. It was a dreadful experience which ended in her standing staring at the prison walls after she had been refused permission to visit James. It had been a cold day, and, as she stood despondent on the pavement outside the jail, snow had begun to fall. As it swirled about her, she had turned away, face into it, to make her way back to Bodmin Road Station. There were others, women mostly, who had been more fortunate than her and had seen their sons or husbands. Their visits seemed to have given them even less comfort than Ellen's wait outside the jail.

She did not try again. She sought consolation by picturing James to herself, not as he had been when he had been taken, leg in splints, dragged across the mine workings, but as he had been on that day of their first meeting when he had appeared along the street in Stithians, dark hair curling about his brow, eyes smiling, mouth—those curving lips—pursed in a cheerful whistle. She could not remember what they had said to each other, but she recalled how she felt, how grief then had suddenly become supportable.

As the months passed it became more difficult to recall his appearance; she would try to draw his portrait in her mind but as she pictured one feature, another would become indistinct and she would find it impossible to capture the whole. At night, lying beside Julia, she hoped to dream of James and see him then, but he never came to her. She wanted to weep; when no tears came she began to wonder if she were unfeeling. Yet there were times when, unbidden, the image of James, clear and penetrating, flashed before her. This happened especially at the bench in the cobbing sheds and she would become, for a moment, incapable of movement and would let her hammer fall from her hand. She would hear Jane's voice and, surprised, would return to her surroundings, pick up her hammer and attack the rock.

Jane was a constant comfort and understood Ellen's anxieties. She was irrepressibly cheerful and for this Ellen envied her. She also envied Julia, for her sister was now clearly in love with Mark, and a satisfying love it seemed. She envied the fulfilment Julia seemed to get from Mark's love and, because of Mark's physical resemblance to James, she felt her own deprivation the more. The resemblance was only superficial but at times in the dim candle-lit cottage Mark's slender hips and slim grace would remind Ellen strongly of his brother. At that she would turn away, trying to suppress the fear that came at the thought of James in confinement in a damp, dark cell.

She wrote to James but had no means of knowing if he ever got her letters. There was never any sign that he was aware of her existence.

"My beloved James," she wrote, for she had no difficulty in expressing her love in writing.

> I miss you. Every morning I wake thinking of you and you are with me through the day. At night when I visit your father I feel you are about me in the cottage and know that, somehow, you are with us. We do not talk about you, we do not need to.
>
> I would like to see you but they tell me I am not related so I have no right. I have a right I know. I love you and who has a greater right than me? I am your sweetheart. Is that not enough?
>
> Can you write to me, my love?

No answer came and gradually her own letters grew less open in her declaration of love. There came a time when she wrote but did not post the letter and then she even ceased to write, so futile did it seem. Justice was punishing not only James, but those who had loved him.

At first Ellen accepted the inevitability of it, but as she thought forward to the long years of separation she began to question the rightness of it all. She had disapproved of James's wild act of sabotage and she still condemned it, but she understood the desperation which had led to it; she felt the law should have understood that too, but it had been blind to all but the need to protect property. There had been no threat to life in the miners' actions, only to buildings, to engines, to pumps. The injuries that resulted had been inflicted on the miners; James had not been the only one to suffer; Malachy Trenow had lost an eye in the fracas. The law exacted no retribution for that.

Ellen bridled at the injustice and expressed her feelings to her comrades in the sheds. They listened, sympathized with her for the loss of her man, but "That's the way of the world," they said, shaking their heads and bowed themselves to their tasks.

Only Jane expressed herself as strongly as Ellen but Jane seemed to have an inner contentment that reconciled her to events.

Ellen felt in conflict with the world around her, solitary and impotent. She remembered she had once said to James "There's strength in numbers" and she wondered, as she looked around at the bal maidens bent to their work, where she would find the numbers. She recalled seeing her father at the head of a line of striking miners and, in the remembrance, gained encouragement. She was not alone. There were others; there were always others ready to fight against wrong; it was only difficult to know them.

II

ROBERT Buchan had followed Bryant's trial with apprehension, afraid of drawing police attention to himself. And for some time afterward he kept away from the Bryants, though he longed to see the woman Ellen Bray. Questions had been asked as to who had tended Bryant's leg, fed and nursed him. Bryant, thank God, had remained silent and no suspicion had attached itself to Robert. The police at length decided that some miner (tinners often had to treat broken limbs) had ministered to his wounded comrade.

Eventually desire to see Ellen Bray drew him back to the Bryants. It was Ellen herself who opened the door to him. He held out the newspapers he had brought.

"For Richard," he said. "I hope you're still reading to him." He looked beyond her to where the blind miner sat and was dismayed at his appearance. He looked an old man, gazing sightlessly at the hearth.

"You're looking tired, old friend," he said.

"With hearing nothing," said Richard. "We do hear naught of James. We have no inkling of what's befallen him."

Ellen went to Richard's side and rested her hand on his shoulder.

"Is there nothing we can do?" said Richard. "Is he lost to us forever in that black dungeon?"

"Maybe I could discover something," said Robert, but he was uneasy. It would be unwise to show too close an interest, even after this time, in the young firebrand's fate.

" 'Twould be manna to the soul to have word," said Richard.

Robert could not refuse the appeal in his friend's voice.

"I know the doctor who visits the jail. I might get to see him, I suppose."

Richard raised his head in hope and Ellen lifted her eyes to his and smiled. Buchan's heart trembled at the sight.

"I'll do what I can." He hesitated. "It will take time. Don't hope for news too soon."

"See him," pleaded Richard. "Some time. Any time. Tell him I do think of him day by day. Bring me news."

Robert looked beyond Richard to Ellen. She was watching him with her dark eyes. She understood his unease and was concerned perhaps for him. Or was it concern for the man Bryant that showed there? Was she not yet free of him?

"Bring us news of him," she begged.

III

THE cell was below ground, the stone walls ran with damp, a narrow barred window, out of reach, admitted a weak light. It was, James had thought when he was first imprisoned there, not much different from the underground levels where he had worked.

Now he no longer thought of the levels and drives of the mine; he no longer thought of himself as a tinner. There were times when he even doubted his own name, when he woke to cries from a cell along the corridor, and wondered who and where he was. At those times, in the shuddering dark, he almost lost reason. He would struggle for breath, alarmed at the vast emptiness around, as if the world had receded into the black distance, leaving him alone, puny and defenseless, at the center of the void. In panic he would reach out and be grateful to touch the wet walls that held him prisoner. That was reality, the touch of stone.

He grew fond of the walls, marked out the stones as individuals confined like him, gave each one a fanciful name. The big one, pitted by the scrawls of prisoners past, immediately above his bed, was the friendliest; it was comforting to feel its scars, to hold his hand against it, let his fingers measure it in the dark. This one, for no reason that he could fathom, he called Methuselah. The next one to it he named Samson, and there was one in the opposite wall he called Noah.

He talked to them, oftener as the months passed, and with each he had a different conversation. He could say to Methuselah things Samson would not understand, and Samson knew secrets he kept from Methuselah. To Noah he would gossip about old friends, men he had worked with somewhere, or imagined he had known.

James felt he would have gone mad but for his conversations with the stones. He never doubted his sanity; the only way to retain reason here was to abandon it knowingly, and this he did. He had ceased to hope for contact with his old world, or even to desire it. This was his world for now—the cell, the walk to the treadmill and its ceaseless round, the walk back, the clang of the cell door and the long long hours of darkness. That was reality, that and Methuselah and the others.

He resented interference with this reality and when he was told one day he was to be visited by a doctor he felt angry and morose. He sat with his face to the wall, looking at Methuselah, caressing the stone, whispering confidences to it. It reassured him and the anger faded, for it was too demanding an emotion to survive long here.

He became aware he was not alone. He did not immediately face his visitor but, inch by inch, shifted on his bed until he had turned around. The light was indistinct but his eyes were accustomed to it and he had no difficulty recognizing the man standing before him.

What did he want, this Doctor Buchan? Why was he here reminding him of that unreal world outside? James dared not let hope enter his thoughts, for hope was fragile.

"Bryant?" The man seemed unsure and James wondered if he had so changed that he was no longer recognizable.

"Aye," he said. "James Bryant." He remembered his name and spoke it with pride though he knew, as he uttered it, that his voice was hesitant, uncertain.

"Buchan. Doctor Buchan. I've come to see how you are."

"Oh?" James was not interested.

"I've a message from your father," the man said.

James was silent. He reached out to Methuselah and felt the stone. It was there, solid, permanent, a friend.

"My father?" he echoed, as if he had forgotten he had ever had a father.

"He wants to know how you are."

"How I am?" Why must this man persist in this way? Can he not see I am what I am, a convict, imprisoned here, a different self from any I've been before. "My father," he said again, as if recalling an image to mind.

"He would like to know how you are faring," the Scotsman said.

James spread his arms to point the confines of the cell.

"This," he said, "is how I'm faring."

The Scot looked back at the grating in the cell door as if afraid he might be under observation.

"Your leg. How is it?"

James patted it. "It's a leg," he said and smiled to himself. When would this man take himself away to his own world?

"Your father—have you no message for him?"

"Tell him," said James and paused. What could he say? "Tell him," he pleaded, but added no more.

"Do you want to send a message to anyone else?"

"Who is there?" said James and turned again to talk to Methuselah. "Who is there?" he said to the stone. "Who is there?"

IV

ROBERT Buchan had never liked James Bryant, but he had seen him as a tough young miner, brave in the way his craft demanded. Now he was a trembling shadow of a man, a cowering wretch muttering incoherently; he was destroyed and unmanned, pitiful. How would he be at the end of his term? Buchan shrugged the thought away. He would give Richard Bryant an anodyne report of his son's condition, and he would report to Ellen, truthfully he felt, that James no longer had thought for her.

As he traveled back to Redruth he let his thoughts linger on Ellen Bray. He was drawn powerfully to her; the long interval that had passed without his seeing her had merely increased his obsession. He had realized that when he saw her at Richard's side. His dislike of James Bryant rose solely—he recognized now—from the position that the man held in Ellen's mind. Well, James Bryant was out of contention and he could allow his impulse to see her free rein without risk of disappointment or humiliation. He could not doubt she was drawn to him. He thought he had read in her eyes a liking for him, he had heard in her voice a concern that was surely not all for Bryant.

From the train he caught a glimpse of the tops of the towers of Trevorrow's new wing above the trees, and was reminded of Rebecca Langarth's remarks to him the previous day. She had told him of the illness of Reid, the sitting Member of Parliament for the Mining Division.

"I wonder if you're ready yet?" she had said to him.

"For what?" he had ingenuously replied.

"To succeed him as Member of Parliament, of course."

He had pretended awed rejection of the notion.

"You need a wife, a woman of substance," she had said. "We must see what we can do."

A wife? A woman of substance? He supposed one might be found but there was none such to whom he was attracted, except maybe the Langarths' own daughter. But even if such a union were possible, he did not think he would like a lifetime wedded to her earnest radicalism.

He thought again of Ellen Bray. She was excluded as a

wife, he had to recognize that. His political ambitions (and he could not suppress them) could only be fulfilled through a marriage of convenience. Ellen could not be his wife, not openly at any rate, but there were other ways of keeping her to him. He had heard rumors that Captain Abel Hosking, of Fire and Brimstone sermon fame, kept a mistress in Plymouth. No one seemed to think less of him for it. Perhaps the same tolerance would be extended to him.

Thoughts of Ellen Bray dominated him as he was driven from the station home. Some sort of union with her, if discreet, was an attractive idea; she was a woman of real passions—in beliefs, and likely to be so in love; she was independent of mind, unspoiled by the conventions of the artificial society of most of the women he knew; she was a woman hardened by labor but not destroyed by it. She was a fit companion for him, fit to be a lover, a mistress, if not a wife: some complaisant, empty-headed heiress would answer that.

He rejected the idea as unworthy. If he loved Ellen—and the obsession with her indicated that—surely he should accept her as his companion in all things, public as well as private? But in his mind he could still hear the echo of Rebecca Langarth's "You need a woman of substance to marry you."

The image of Ellen Bray occupied him to the exclusion of all this and he hurried through his surgery so he had time to go to Sunny Corner.

He found Richard impatient for news of James. Ellen was beside him, having put her book down on Buchan's entrance.

"He's well then?" said Richard when Buchan had finished an imagined account of his conversation with his son.

"As well as can be under the circumstances."

"He's a brave young man, foolish but brave."

Robert saw Ellen eyeing him as if she doubted his report. He spoke to Richard but it was for her he said, "He sent a message to you, Richard, but to no one else. It's as if he's finished with his old life for good. As if he wants to forget it and all that goes with it."

She did not move from her seat when he turned to go. He beckoned to her to follow him out to the garden and, reluctantly it seemed, she did.

"He had no word for me?" she asked.

"No thought of you, it appeared."

She shook her head as if it could not be believed.

"He's not of your world now," Buchan said but he knew, in her disappointment, he dare not yet move to her. She would need time to put James away from her altogether.

V

BUCHAN was now a frequent visitor to Trevorrow and was flattered by the attention the Langarths paid to him. His dour manner softened and he began to cultivate a deliberate charm. Where before he would have argued abrasively with the men from the mining companies, he now listened attentively and prefaced any opposite opinion with a mild "We should try to see the other point of view." Imperceptibly he was developing the ability to seem all things to all men. The mining interest approved him. And Rebecca Langarth, observing him, smiled her Sibylline smile.

Her daughter, Veronica, was not so mysterious, nor so approving.

"You're trying too hard," she accused.

"I don't understand," said Robert.

"We admire you for your thoughtfulness, your bluntness of speech, your honesty," Veronica said.

"Well?"

"You're in danger of surrendering all that to ambition."

"Ambition?" He was tempted to deny it. "I'm a doctor. In a mining community. I tend the sick, alleviate pain, or try to. I've no ambition beyond that. How can I have?"

She turned her large eyes to him searchingly. There was a moment between them when he almost confided in her, but the moment passed.

She sighed, then with a businesslike change of tone said, "You once invited me to see this community of yours, to see for myself what life is really like for these people."

"You'd not take kindly to such an experience."

"Try me."

Before he could answer they were joined by Captain Hosking.

"I want you to do something for me, Buchan," he said. "I want Miss Langarth to see over Wheal Busy. I'm told she's never been nearer a mine than her father's bank account. 'Tis time she saw where it came from—all this." With a sweep of the hand he gestured at the damask curtains, the paneled walls, the elaborately plastered ceiling.

Veronica laughed. "And what has Doctor Buchan to do with that?"

"I'm inviting you both to dinner at the count house at Wheal Busy, Wednesday next week, midday. I'll take you over the mine in the afternoon. You'll learn something, Miss Langarth."

"I'm sure I shall," said Veronica with a demureness that Robert thought hid some secret amusement. "You'll take me, Doctor Buchan?"

"With pleasure," Robert replied, but he recalled his last visit to Wheal Busy and its purpose, and with the recollection came the picture of Ellen Bray standing at the door of the old hut, thanking him and saying, "I'll never forget you."

"I'll take you with pleasure," he repeated.

VI

THOUGH Wheal Busy was in many ways a well-organized mine, the sheds where the ore was dressed were exposed to the elements. The bal maidens tolerated with little complaint the mild days of autumn and the Cornish mists. They even found them refreshing and the soft raindrift brought a glow to their complexions. But autumn went and winter descended suddenly upon them as November and December brought hard driving winds and drenching rains. Cold swept unmercifully through the sheds, making the skin pucker and hands chap and become clumsy at their work. Ninepence a day began to seem poor recompense for their labor's hard discomfort.

Ellen was conscious of the smoldering discontent among her comrades, the resentment that the present prosperity of the mine was not being shared by the workers on it. There had been a rumbling among the men, with threats of strike, but that had come to naught. Over the cobbing benches conversation which, in kinder times, consisted of bawdy and convivial gossip turned to grumbling about their conditions, the open shed, the strict management, the paltry facilities for them to heat their pasties at mossel time, and, inevitably, their poor pay.

The women turned to Ellen as their spokeswoman. They remembered her anger at the imprisonment of her man and they recognized in her the leadership they needed. It was over a minor incident that they burst into action. Jane Rowse had, for some reason, found it difficult to maintain the normal rate of work. Her breath was short and she often paused to rest. In one such pause Captain Tregurra had looked in at the women. He peered into the shed and called, "Idling again, you lazy whore!" Before Jane could retort he had disappeared beyond earshot and her words were lost in the wind. She stood, arms akimbo, and said, "That's that. I'll not work for these bastards if that's what they think. Who's with me?"

The women, without hesitation, put down their tools and looked to Ellen.

"Right," said Ellen. "Let's tell them." With Jane beside her and the other women following they marched from the shed. They had not premeditated action; their dissatisfaction had slumbered; now, awakened, it rose explosively.

Ellen heard behind her the steps of her comrades, sixty furious determined bal maidens and pride surged within her, and with the pride went a feeling of power. She led the women with deliberation the few hundred yards across the mine workings toward the office, past the men's dry, where the tributers above ground at the end of their core were hanging their underground clothes. The tinners watched with silent astonishment at first and then a cheer arose, and another, as the men came out to watch their women. Ellen smiled, held up her head and strode purposefully on.

The rain had ceased and, though the afternoon light was dim, as they drew near the count house they could see on the steps a group of men and women drawn from inside by the cheering. Ellen barely noticed them. It was toward the office she made her way, but Jane whispered, "Your Doctor Buchan's there, at the count house, watching you."

Ellen ignored her. Doctor Buchan was an irrelevance. Only

one thing was of importance now, to demonstrate to authority the combined strength of the bal maidens. And behind her, at last, the others felt this too; she could tell from the firm sound of their feet on the stones. At the office a startled clerk raised a wavering hand to bar their entry but as they advanced he retreated step by step into the outer office. The women crowded after him but there was only room for six or seven inside. The remainder gathered at the door. They were silent now, threateningly so, it must have seemed to the clerk.

He began, "I don't know . . ."

"You soon will," said Ellen, any lingering nervousness vanishing as she spoke. "We want to see the purser here and now."

"I don't know," repeated John Vernon, and for a second she was sorry for him.

"I'm telling you," said Ellen. "You don't need to know. Go and tell Coad now that we're here to see him."

The clerk looked at the tall young woman facing him. He had never before seen an angry group of sober women. In the streets of Redruth he had seen fights between drunken women, abusive and violent affrays, but this was altogether different—and exciting. He recovered his composure and looked with admiration at the spokeswoman.

"Hang on. I'll go and let him know." He winked at Ellen.

"You tell 'em, Ellen," called one of the women in the crowd outside.

What? thought Ellen in a moment of doubt. What shall I tell them?

John Vernon returned. "Mr. Coad says he's no time to see you. He's busy with one of the adventurers." Then, in a whisper, he added, "It's not true. He's on his own. He's scared as a rabbit."

"Right," said Ellen. "In we go."

The clerk took refuge behind his high desk while Ellen, with Jane close behind her, thrust open the broad oak door into the purser's office. At its opening the purser, a dumpy man with florid, heavy-jowled face, half-rose from his chair behind the large leather-topped table.

"I told him I couldn't see you. Off you go. I've no time for this nonsense. Vernon!" he shouted to the clerk. "Go and get Cap'n Hosking."

"That's right," said Ellen. "We'd better have him too."

"Don't stand there," went on the purser. "We can't have this. Get back to work."

"Not until we've sorted this out," said Ellen.

Jane, eyes sparkling with enjoyment of the situation, intervened. "Don't you offer a chair to ladies who come visiting?"

Coad's irritation at the irregularity of the proceedings flared to anger. "Ladies!" he spluttered with indignation. "*You!* Ladies? You come bursting in here without a by-your-leave! Get back to work." Then, as he saw his words were having no effect, he took a different tone. "Now, if you've anything to say, just tell my clerk in the outer office and we'll see what we can do." He came from behind the table and approached Ellen, his arms widespread to usher her out.

Ellen folded her arms in front of her. "We'll wait for Cap'n Hosking," she said.

The purser retreated behind his table again and sat, acute anxiety on his face, until the voice of the mine captain was heard outside, berating John Vernon for letting the women through the office. Hosking came in, pushed his way past the women and turned to face them. Under his white jacket he had a dark suit. His face was flushed, his eyes narrowed.

He looked at Ellen and then past her to Jane. He turned to Coad and said, "Get these women out of here."

Ellen smiled. "That's what he sent for you for." Hosking looked closely at her.

"I'll remember you," he said. "All right. Say what you've got to say and get back to work."

There was silence for a moment. They had not stopped to prepare a case. Their complaints were many, some of them small, some not easy to put right, but in the end it all amounted to one thing, they were paid too little for the job they did. Ellen realized the others were waiting for her to speak.

"There's lots we've got to say. And we'll not go back to work till we get promises from you."

"Go on, girl, go on. I'm listening," said Hosking. He sat on the edge of the table and began to pick his teeth with a sliver of wood, noisily opening his lips and, wide-mouthed, prizing debris out. His half-closed eyes were fixed shrewdly on Ellen.

She gathered her courage. "It's Cap'n Tregurra. His language."

Hosking snorted with sudden laughter. "Bal maidens complaining about bad language! I've heard the lot now!" He continued to chuckle with calculated offense.

Ellen said sharply. "We want your apology. Cap'n Tregurra called Jane here a lazy whore."

"Did he?" Hosking replied looking at Jane. "Well, she may be a lazy bal maiden, but we all know she's not lazy when it comes to whoring. I apologize for him." Ellen heard Jane catch her breath and hurried on before her friend's anger could explode.

"That's not all. Our pay. It's not enough. In this weather and those dressing sheds, ninepence a day's too little. We want elevenpence a day. We'll not work for less."

"That's right," called one of the women from behind.

Hosking looked beyond Ellen to the others. "You all think that?"

"Yes, we do!" they answered. "Ellen speaks for us all."

"We'll not go back to the sheds till we get some word from you," said Ellen. "You'll get no work from us till then."

The mine captain raised his eyebrows and turned to the purser. "Well, Mr. Coad, what will the adventurers think? Is the mine earning enough to pay sixty bal maidens an extra twopence a day?"

Mr. Coad shook his head. "They'll not like it. The mine's only just getting back. They'll not like it."

"Tenpence a day?" Hosking looked at Ellen.

"Elevenpence," she said in answer.

"And soon," said Jane.

"I can't promise anything," said the purser.

"Then we'll not work," said Ellen. "No promises, no work."

"What Mr. Coad means," interrupted Hosking, "is that he can't promise what the adventurers will do. They might choose to close the mine. They can't go on losing money, you know."

"They're not losing money," said Ellen, remembering she had read in the *West Briton* a report on Busy's profits.

"They soon would if they gave in to everyone who asked for more. After you it'll be the boys, then the men. Where would that leave us?"

"No promises, no work," repeated Ellen.

"There's plenty of women to be got for ninepence a day," said Hosking.

"You try," said Ellen. "There's none around here will work for you if we stop."

Hosking smiled. He seemed to be enjoying the confrontation, but Coad, beside him, ostentatiously took out his pocket watch.

"Right. Back to work and we'll promise to let you know in a few days." Hosking got up from the table, slapped his hands together then put out a hand to Ellen's shoulder to turn her to the door. She stood her ground and resisted. He gripped her by the arm and thrust her around so that she stumbled into Jane.

"You bullying bastard," Jane angrily cried. "I'd buck you if I'd my hammer with me."

Hosking bustled them through the door and closed it against them. The women, angry at the unceremonious dismissal, rejoined the crowd outside and reformed into a straggly procession and, this time with Jane in the lead and a white-faced Ellen beside her, they marched, singing and shouting, from building to building on the mine grounds. As they came to the office again some of the women shook their fists and shouted abuse at the windows. Behind the glass cowered the purser. At the mine gates Ellen and Jane parted from the other women and walked away together, Jane still buoyant from the excitement of the protest.

"Your father would have been proud of you," she said.

So Jane remembered too, thought Ellen, and was pleased. But her exhilaration had died, replaced with a cold anger brought upon her by Hosking's dismissive gesture. She could still feel the imprint of his hand upon her arm and her flesh recoiled at the sensation. She could have struck him and now did not understand why she had held back.

She was hardly aware of Jane until her friend said pleadingly, "Don't walk so fast. What's got into you?"

It was indignation that stirred her, she knew, and fury. She waited for Jane to catch up with her.

"You're getting soft," she said to Jane, then looked more closely at her friend. Her cheeks, usually ruddy with health, had lost their color.

"You're ill," said Ellen and took hold of her friend's arm.

" 'Tis nothing," said Jane. She paused at the corner of the lane where their ways parted. "You do rush on so," she said.

Ellen watched her friend till she was out of sight. It was this harsh weather, she thought, the sweat of the work and the cold wet blast of the winter winds. Spring would restore her health. Spring would bring comfort for them all.

VII

ROBERT Buchan led Veronica Langarth up the granite steps into the count house at Wheal Busy. It was pleasing to be in her company. She was lively and entertaining, and association with her added to his own standing. He noted with interest the other guests—Daniell, the smelter from Truro, Captain William Teague of Illogan, Harris the lawyer from Redruth, and others—all men of influence in the community. If he were to take seriously the idea of going into politics these would be men to cultivate. They all, he noted with pleased pride, treated Veronica with deference.

The large banqueting room of the count house was furnished with an enormous sideboard, a massive dining table and solid chairs, all designed to suggest stability and permanence in an enterprise that was, of all things, uncertain. On the walls were displayed prints, lithographs, engravings of local scenes, and tinted drawings of the mine workings, showing shafts sunk and levels driven.

Daniell drew Veronica's attention to one engraving. It was of the Langarth's home, Trevorrow, a century back, before the Tudor manor house had come to the Langarths and been extravagantly transformed by a London architect into a vast unlovely mansion.

"Not so grand then as it is now," Daniell commented.

Veronica shrugged her shoulders as if to disown connection with the Langarths.

"It would be nice to be welcomed for my own sake," she said aside to Robert.

"A bal maiden?" he laughingly asked.

"How would they treat me then, I wonder?"

The conversation at the table was inevitably about the fortunes of tin, and the bedevilment caused by the interference of government, the prying of mine inspectors.

"We know what's best," said William Teague. "What do they folk in London know of us?"

"Parliament! Royal Commissions and the like!" snorted Hosking derisively. "We need men up along who know us, sympathize with us, work with us." Robert thought the mine captain's remarks were addressed at him. He smiled but did not speak. He was accepted as one of them and was gratified.

Teague spoke of the fears he had of the Education Act and the setting up of School Boards.

"Don't you approve of the Act?" asked Veronica with deceptive mildness.

"Well, now, m'dear," Teague replied. "Who doesn't approve of schooling? But there's schooling and schooling. There are those who need it to take their place in society," he nodded to Robert and to Harris, "the doctors and the lawyers. And then there are others, the working miners and their people. They need a different sort of schooling. You can't deny that. What's needed for a lawyer would be wasted on a miner. The tinner has to grow up with a pick and a gad to his hand, learn to use them from a lad. It's never too soon to start on a craft like mining."

"And," said Hosking in approval, "it's not a craft to be got at a desk with slate and pencil. Down below's the place to learn."

Veronica tapped her fingers on the table, impatiently waiting for the men to finish.

"And the miner's daughters?" she asked. "What of them?"

"Ah!" said Teague. "Needlework will never come amiss. Bal maidens don't need much about them but brawn and sinew and to know their place, but they'll be wives and mothers too. You don't learn that in no school, neither. There's no problem with the schooling of girls. A bit of reading and writing and sewing, good manners, knowing their place, that's enough."

A murmur of approval spread around the table. Veronica looked to Robert expecting him to voice an opinion. He opened his mouth to do so when, into the banqueting hall, there came from outside the sound of tramping feet, steps marching over cobblestones, then the raising of a cheer and a shout, clear and shrill, "Go to it! Let old Brimstone have it!"

Hosking grinned at his guests and said, " 'Tis nothing," but rose and went to the door of the count house to see the cause of the commotion. The rest followed and stood behind him, looking out. Across the workings strode sixty or seventy women, bal maidens, stained hessian aprons covering their black dresses, their card bonnets, the "gooks," swaying back and forth as they marched, two or three still with their short-handled hammers swinging at their sides. Their arms were bare, sleeves rolled up to reveal sturdy muscled forearms. Their faces were grim, their advance purposeful.

Robert felt Veronica's hand grip his arm.

"There," she whispered. "That's what I'd like to be. A bal maiden! If only . . . look at her," she said, indicating the woman at the head. "Is she not a fine figure of a woman? Look at her, the pride in her!"

Robert, in fact, could not take his eyes from the woman leading the march. It was Ellen, an Ellen he had not seen before. He had seen her beauty, felt her compassion, admired her shrewd intelligence; this was different, for here was an energy, a will that moved him more than her other qualities.

"Is she not magnificent?" he heard Veronica say.

"Yes," he answered.

Hosking turned to them. "Don't let's allow that little business to spoil our afternoon. There's a fine French brandy waiting for us." He urged them back into the dining hall. "You get on. I'll sort it out." He left and the others, comfortably reassured, sat again at the table and commented, with amused tolerance, on the women protesting outside.

Robert was deaf to their remarks. The sight of Ellen had disturbed him. He had told himself when he had returned from seeing James that the time would come when she would put thoughts of the man Bryant from her. That time surely had come and he could approach her with his own suit—whatever it was. He had tried unsuccessfully to put her from his mind, but he was as besotted with her as ever, more so. He could not deny it.

"Robert," he heard Veronica say. "Robert," she said again.

"Yes?" He looked at her. Her cheeks were flushed.

"I cannot stay here," she said.

He had been unaware of the discussion around him. It

was obvious Veronica had said something to irritate the other guests. He wondered what it was.

"Come, Robert," she commanded and obediently he rose from his chair and went with her. The other men, half-rising from their seats, nodded to him with, he thought, sympathy.

She stood on the steps of the count house, breathing deeply.

"Why didn't you say something?" she asked.

"I'm sorry. I wasn't aware."

They saw, not far away, the bal maidens gathered at the door of the office, broad bulky women, silently listening to what went on inside.

"There!" she said. "Real women. Not the simpering delicate pampered fawning creatures they want us to be."

The crowd of bal maidens parted to allow two women to come through, Jane Rowse, cocky and triumphant, and with her a white-faced Ellen Bray.

"I want to know her," said Veronica.

"Why?" said Robert.

"Can you not see why?" Veronica replied. "Is she not wholly admirable? Come." She took Robert by the arm and would have led him over to Ellen had he not resisted.

"No," he said. "Now is not the time. I'll arrange for you to meet."

"How? You know her?"

"I know her," he replied.

VIII

ELLEN was restless, disturbed by the excitement of the protest. She helped Granny Pascoe up to bed and left her. She could not stay in the cottage for her mind was in turmoil.

She went into the lane. The rain had ceased though there was still a sense of storm brooding over the valley. Autumn was usually a long season here, blending almost imperceptibly into spring; winter, if it came at all, was confined to a week or two of February. This year it had set in early, harshly, and they had had months of it.

She thought back to the cobbing shed and her work there and, for the first time, began to question its rightness for her.

She was a bal maiden and proud of being so, she told herself; it was honest and fulfilling work. But she now knew it did not fulfill her. There was surely more to life than that. To be a bal maiden, take a man, bear children who would grow to be miners or bal maidens themselves—that was the lot of women here. That had been Granny Pascoe's lot. Why could she not accept it for herself? She knew she could not.

Take a man? What man was there to take? James had no interest in her. He had forgotten her, it seemed. He was out of her life, not merely for the five years of his sentence, but forever. He had rejected her. There was no comfort there.

Ellen moved along toward the Bryants' cottage. She thought the restless activity of her mind would be calmed by talk with Richard. Perhaps he might have words of counsel to give her on her challenge to Hosking and the mine company. She thrust open the gate and was going up to the door when she heard the sounds of a horse behind her. She turned and saw Doctor Buchan dismounting. She waited, hesitant about visiting Richard if the doctor was going there.

"I'll go," she said, "if you've come to see Mr. Bryant."

"It's you I hoped to see."

It was dark and she could not make out his features. He was merely a large dark shape in front of her.

"Me?"

"I was there at Wheal Busy. I saw you."

She remembered Jane had noticed him.

He went on, "I don't think you saw me. I'd been invited to dinner at the count house by Cap'n Hosking. You looked splendid."

"Splendid? What does that mean?" She was angry at what she saw as condescension. "Splendid? It got us nowhere. A fine hope we have of getting justice from your friend Hosking." She put her hand to her arm where Hosking had grabbed her.

"No friend of mine. Tell me what happened." His voice was persuasive and he drew near to her, took her by the arm and led her away from the door of the cottage.

"What happened?" he repeated. Was he really interested? He still had his hand on her arm and there was about his touch a sense of rightness. He held her now where Hosking had grasped her earlier. The doctor's touch was firm but gentle, and conveyed something beyond the mere touch. She did not know what it was she felt but she wanted his hand to remain. She did not move, fearful she would break the contact that had brought such reassurance.

"What happened?" he prompted.

"Why do you want to know?" She could not think it of any importance to him.

He did not answer at first and she thought as he moved he was going to loose her arm, but he did not. Instead he took hold of her other arm and stood facing her. She could see little of his expression but she knew he was looking at her. His face was in shadow, but the moon which slipped from its cover of cloud for an instant lit her face.

She heard him draw in his breath and felt his grip upon her tighten.

"Why do you want to know?"

"I want to know what makes you protest. What stirs you. What moves you. I want to know. Is that not reason enough?"

They were close now, so close that she need only move forward half a step to be touching him, for her body to be against his. For a moment she thought he was going to draw her to him and she might have yielded.

"My" Doctor Buchan, she suddenly thought, that's what Jane called him, and James too, once before. The thought of James made her stiffen and instead of moving half a step forward to be enfolded in Buchan's arms, she moved back and he let one hand fall from her. But the other remained on her arm and she was glad of it.

"Well?" he said.

She told him the circumstances of their protest.

"And what next?" he said.

She shrugged her shoulders. "We'll stay out until we get what we want." But she was not confident and he sensed her uncertainty.

"It's true, I suppose, as Hosking said, that there are plenty of women ready to take your place. Will they back you?"

"I don't know."

"How long can you afford to give up work?"

Ellen laughed shortly. "We can't afford it. We've no money to fall back on."

"And no organization either," said Robert. He let his hand fall from her and turned to the cottage. The moon, free from its shroud once more, lit his face, rugged, intent, serious. She moved to him in an impulse which came too quickly to be suppressed and he took hold of her, this time not with a hand on her arm but with his arms about her. She felt his hand at her back and she looked up at him and felt his lips come to hers, gently, as if surprised, then she let herself respond to him, clinging tightly to him.

"Ellen," he said and she wondered how her name, ordinary and familiar, could take on such magic as when he spoke it.

"Ellen," he said again and kissed her lightly on the brow.

She had no wish to speak, only to remain there, in the night, folded in his arms. She had lost touch with all but him.

"What do they call you?" she asked shyly. "What's your given name?"

"Robert," he said. "Say it."

"Robert," she said and raised her face to kiss him again.

The moon had gone now and the cloud had thickened. She heard the sudden beat of rain and felt it on her hair. Robert turned her toward the cottage and they ran together to the door and burst inside.

Richard was alone, sitting by the hearth. The fire in it was low. He turned at their entrance. "Mark? Julia?" he said uncertainly.

"No," said Robert. "Your friend Robert Buchan, and Ellen."

"Ah," said Richard with a sigh of contentment. "I was hoping you'd come, Ellen. Tell me about it. Mark said something's up at Busy with the women."

Ellen gathered her wits and told her story again.

"I don't know why they chose me to lead them," she said at the end.

"I do," said Robert and reaching to her moved his silk-soft fingers over hers, touching the roughened palms, then gently stroking her arms and wrists so that sensation flowed through her. She closed her eyes, happy to confine her senses to the touch of him.

"James would be proud," said Richard. His voice broke the spell. Ellen opened her eyes and saw the cottage, the bare walls, the simple furniture, the table at which she had sat with James. "It's a beginning," said Richard.

"A beginning?" she echoed. "And maybe the end. We were angry. It brought us together, but the anger will die away and so will our togetherness." She looked at Robert and saw him, in this setting, as he really was: a doctor, a man from another world. What were they doing together? It was unreal.

"You can do it," said Richard. "If anyone can, you can."

"I? A mere bal maiden?" She shook her head. The doctor still held her hand but the magic had gone from his touch. Here, where Richard sat and talked, there were too many memories of another. She stood up and went to the hearth to sit on the floor beside Richard, resting her hand on his knee.

"What can a mere bal maiden hope to do?" she said but was angry with herself at admitting any weakness. "We'll see, shall we?" She put her hand up to Richard's face, moved by sudden tenderness, and let her hand rest on his scarred cheek a moment. "Women have courage too," she said.

She heard Robert Buchan move and turned from Richard to look up at him. He was smiling down at her as if he understood her. How could he? She could not understand herself.

"I'll be away now, Richard," he said. "The storm has eased slightly." He stood for a moment at the door of the cottage as if waiting for Ellen to join him but she stayed by Richard, resting against him, staring into the fire, until the continuing silence compelled her to turn to look at Robert. His eyes held hers briefly and then he went. Outside the rain fell and a peal of thunder rolled along the valley.

IX

THREE days, with the bal maidens refusing to work, went by before a message came from Hosking.

"You're to report to the office," said the clerk. "Just Ellen Bray. He doesn't like crowds of women. There's no dealing with them then, he says. He said he'll talk to Ellen Bray. He takes it she can speak for the rest."

The women had gathered each day at the mine entrance for news. At the message they took their victory for granted and cheered. Ellen, alone and fearful, followed the clerk across to the office. Her knees shook and she wondered what had thrust her forward. She would have been happy to have been one of the women cheering another spokeswoman.

In the office the sour-faced purser sat behind the table. Hosking, back turned to Ellen, stood at the window.

Coad began, "We've thought about what you said. We've been thinking for some time another penny might be possible. Don't imagine your stopping work made any difference."

Hosking turned from the window and impatiently interrupted. "Tenpence a day. That's good pay. You'll get no more. Tell your friends that. And another thing. We'll want more work for it. We're not running a charity. Tenpence a day, that's that." He looked closely at Ellen and, as Coad was again about to speak, intolerantly waved him to silence. "There's something else. We'll have to turn off some women to make it pay. I'm not saying who they'll be just yet, but some of you will have to go—just one or two." He smiled humorlessly. "I think we know who's most likely to be got rid of, don't you?"

Ellen did not answer.

"You understand?" he said.

"Oh yes," Ellen said. "I understand."

"Right. Back to work straightaway and no nonsense." He put out his hand as if to turn her to the door as he had done before, but something in her eye made him think better of it.

"All back to work," he said.

"I can't promise," said Ellen, but she knew that the women felt they had sacrificed enough by the loss of three days' pay. They would take the granting of an extra penny as a victory, though it was still below the rate in some other mines.

She was right. They cheered her for the news she brought.

"We showed 'un," they said. "We made old Brimstone see sense."

A week later Ellen and Jane were called to the office to be told there was no more work for them at Wheal Busy. The other bal maidens shook their heads, said they were sorry, that that was how things were, and bowed themselves to their work.

Ellen and Jane turned their backs on their comrades and walked away from the mine. Ellen was concerned about her friend for her cheeks were flushed and she stopped to cough and draw breath.

" 'Tis nothing," she said. "A cold. 'Twill go with the fine weather."

There was wind and rain still as they walked to Wheal Bush, to Clifford, to Poldory and Wheal Maid, but nowhere was there work. At each mine they were hopeful until, as they gave their names, they saw a wary look come to the eyes of the clerks.

"Sorry," they were told. "No work here."

They even returned to Pednandrea in Redruth, where they had worked before. The overseer was the man Carkeek. He scowled when he saw them, then grinned.

"I thought you might be back," he said. "I heard."

"What?" said Ellen.

"You're blacklisted, you two. I'm not surprised. I said you were troublemakers. You'll not find work around here, let me tell you." He stood before them, arms folded, barring their way. "You're not wanted here—nor nowhere else."

They turned away and had walked a few paces when Jane held to Ellen's arm. "Let's stop," she said. "Just for a minute or two." A spasm of coughing shook her and she leaned back, faint, against the granite wall of the mine boundary. Her eyes were closed; she had drawn her shawl over her head against the rain.

Ellen took hold of her friend, dismayed at the weakness of her. She drew her into the shelter of a shop door, a shop boarded up and closed. She looked about for help to get her the half mile or more to her room behind the Rose Tavern. The street was empty; the rain had driven folk indoors. Then she heard the rumble of wheels on the setts and turned to see a wagon laden with sacks drawn by two large horses coming along the road from the country into the town. Ellen ran into the road to intercept it.

"Please," she said. "Can you help? My friend's sick."

The driver brought his horses to a halt and looked down at her.

"I do know you," he said.

She looked up to see Reuben Menear the farmer's boy from Stithians, but a boy no longer, a solid well-built, prosperous-looking man.

"Reuben," she said. "My friend. I have to get her home. She's . . ."

"I can see." He got down and walked over to Jane. "Now, my lover," he said. "Put your arm around me." He led Jane to the cart, let the backboard down and helped her up among the sacks.

"Comfortable?" he said.

Jane opened her eyes and gazed at Reuben. Her eyes sparkled briefly at the sight of his manly figure.

" 'Tis nothing," she said.

Reuben grinned at her. "A maid like you out in weather like this. 'Tis not proper. I'll get 'ee home." He turned to Ellen for guidance. She got up to sit beside him and pointed the way.

"Here?" he said, when Ellen bade him stop at the rear of the Rose Tavern.

"She lives behind in a linny there."

The door of the lean-to was unlocked. Inside, in the narrow room, was a bed, unmade, against the wall. A small table stood beside it, on it a cracked mirror, a comb and a hairbrush. Reuben helped Jane from the wagon into the linny. He almost filled the doorway as he stood looking down upon Jane.

"Are you all right, my lover? Is there anything I can do for you?" Ellen was surprised at the anxiety in his voice.

"You'd better go," Ellen replied. A spasm of coughing again shook Jane. "You'll tell me?" Reuben said to Ellen.

"Tell you what?"

"How she fares. I'd dearly like to know." He went out to his wagon and she heard his "Gee up there" to his horses and then the clatter of their shoes on the road.

She went to Jane who lay exhausted on her pallet. Her ringlets fell in disorder about her face. She reached for Ellen's hand.

" 'Tis nothing," she said. "Truly," and then she smiled, in recollection of Reuben. "A fine figure of a man," she whispered and then a raw cough seized her again.

X

VERONICA Langarth had looked forward to spending an hour or so with Robert Buchan in Redruth, accompanying him on some of his calls. She was sure it would be "interesting." She had not anticipated how distressing an experience it would prove to be to see for herself the marks of poverty in the people Robert visited. Guilt at her intrusion into their crowded rooms seized her and she tried to keep in the background.

The people whose homes she entered expressed no surprise or resentment at her presence. Distress—and the charity it sometimes brought—seemed to have deadened their curiosity. They knew and respected Doctor Buchan and that was enough for them.

Veronica was most moved by the condition of the women she met: ill-clad, pale, underfed, they showed anxiety about their children and their men. She guessed it was they who bore the major burden, that it was they who were the first to go without, and last to be eased when work returned.

The homes were small, huddled together in backlets off the main street, hidden behind the stores and chapels and public houses, hovels of mean appearance outside and mean provision within. In one court women and children stood with buckets and jugs at one tap, waiting for water to flow. They ignored the filth which blocked the launders waiting for a downpour to sweep it away. Wherever she went she was most conscious of the smell, the overpowering stench of the middens. It was bad enough on Fore Street where horse droppings mingled with the mud, but here, where the people lived, the smell was of another kind, rank, suffocating. She felt she now knew what was meant by "the smell of poverty."

As she gazed around the court her stomach was queasy. Robert had left her for a moment and she was alone. She clutched a handkerchief to her nose, but it was not the stench alone she wanted to suppress, it was her own sense of guilt at the misery about her. She knew nothing of this world. She had read of it, of course, for she was her mother's daughter, and thought it her duty to be informed, but the Reports of Royal Commissions on Housing were mere words; here were people, women, children, wives, mothers, and what poverty meant to them could not be represented in paragraphs and tables of statistics.

She watched a mother gather a child into her arms. He had fallen and grazed his knees on the rough steps about the tap. His mother, an aging woman of fifty, caressed him tenderly and held him to her. She carried him past Veronica and, as she went by, Veronica saw the woman more clearly. Beneath the lines the face was young; she was no older than Veronica herself. Veronica wanted to reach out a hand to help but the woman had gone without a glance at her.

She felt humbled and distressed, conscious of her helplessness. What have I to give here? she asked herself. What use am I with my fine notions, my sympathy, my gentility? She wanted Robert to return. If he didn't come quickly she would leave. She could not bear to stay. She had seen enough, enough to show her own inadequacy, enough to people her sleep with nightmares for weeks to come. When Robert came from the door of the tenement where he had been his face was drawn with tiredness and frustration.

"Have you seen enough?" he said and there was a touch of bitterness in his voice which added to her feeling of guilt at her intrusion here.

She took his arm, wanting to express her admiration for him, her wonder that, day following day, he could work here among these people and still retain his sanity.

They walked together into Fore Street and down to the bottom of the town. There, in the yard of the Rose Tavern, the Langarths' coachman would be waiting for her, to convey her back to Trevorrow. As they paused at the entrance to the yard, a woman, stout and homely, came from the inn and spoke urgently to Robert.

"Thank God you've come, doctor," she burst out. "She's badly, I fear."

"What are you talking about?" Robert was impatient.

" 'Tis a young woman around the back, brought home by her friend." She led Robert around the side to the rear, to a shack built against the inn wall. Within the dark room the figures were shadowy, but as Robert approached the bed Veronica recognized the woman who stood from beside it to turn to Robert. It was the bal maiden, the one she had admired so for the fire of her in leading the women of the mine. Veronica had hoped to meet her in different circumstances. This woman had place in her mind now only for her friend, another woman from the mine, Veronica saw. She looked about her. So this was how bal maidens lived.

She turned away, having no longer any desire to stay. The air was close and unclean, she thought. The rain had ceased and she decided to wait outside until Robert had finished. She left the shack and stood watching the passage of traffic along the Portreath road, the brewery drays, the growlers from the station taking passengers out to their country villas, a hearse drawn by plumed black horses and followed by solemn weepers.

When Buchan came out he seemed weary and a little impatient as he helped her into the carriage and joined her.

"That was the woman, wasn't it? The bal maiden. You promised I could meet her."

"Oh yes," he said. "The bal maiden." He sounded preoccupied.

"You give yourself too much to these people," she said as he looked back toward the door of the shack. "I'm sure you have done all you can," she added with a touch of irritation.

He did not answer.

Chapter Eight

I

ELLEN could not find work. No sooner did she appear at the office of a mine than the door was closed to her. Her name was known, and so too, it seemed, was her face. She met her former workmates in the village and they said it was unfair that she had been blacklisted, but they did not see what they could do to help.

Fortunately Julia had found work in the candle factory at Pulla Cross and that, with their grandmother's small allowance from the mine, was enough for their simple wants. But Ellen missed the companionship of the dressing sheds, the give-and-take, the banter, the rough humor of her friends. Jane, whose recovery from her fever had been slow, was now well but rarely came to see her, for she had her own interests to pursue and her own living to earn.

Ellen did not often leave the cottage, except to visit Richard, for Granny Pascoe had become increasingly frail and, at last admitting her weakness though still not reconciled to it, had taken to her bed.

She had seen Robert three or four times, when he had

called upon Richard, but they had never recovered the intimacy of that day weeks back when they had touched hands and lips and when, she had imagined, he had shown for her some of the affection she felt for him. Every now and then she had thought that he was about to speak to her as before, but he had said nothing.

Then one evening she was in the house with Richard when he arrived with a book and some papers in his hand. She took them from him, and as she did their fingers briefly touched; she wanted to take hold of his hand, but the moment passed. He had turned to talk to Richard. She chided herself for imagining there could be anything between them. They belonged to different worlds. It was only here, in Richard's cottage, that their paths ever crossed. She meant nothing to him. She picked up her shawl in readiness to leave.

He turned to her. "There's an item of news in the *West Briton* which should interest you," he said. He opened the paper and read aloud from a report: " 'Last week upward of three hundred bal maidens and boys in the Caradon district struck for wages. The agitation is spreading throughout the mines in the area. The girls and boys are seen daily congregating on the Downs, discussing their grievances and visiting other mines.' You see," he added. "You are not alone." He smiled at her.

Robert, she wished to say, but dared not. He looked tired and drawn, so that she was concerned for him. She would like to cherish and comfort him. But he had returned again to his conversation with Richard.

She left them to talk and went into the garden intending to go along the lane back home, but she could not leave, not without speaking to Robert, to say good-bye, anything to hear that soft Scots voice in return. She heard the cottage door open and she looked back. Robert was there, watching her and she went toward him, hoping he would hold out his arms to her. He did not move, but stood, silently considering her. When he spoke his words disappointed.

"The agitation in Caradon," he said.

"What of it?"

"You should make contact with the women there, don't you think?"

"What good would that do?" She was hurt by his having forgotten that it was here, at this very spot, that they had kissed.

"You are isolated here. You need to talk with like spirits, consider what might be done to join forces with other women."

For the moment she was not concerned with that. She drew nearer, hoping still that he would hold out a hand to her, but he went on. "Make contact. Talk with them. Someone has to make a move sometime."

"Why me?"

"Who else? Who else can plead as passionately as you? Who else has such power to persuade?"

She smiled at the feeling in his voice. He believed in her and that was something.

"I've no money for such journeys."

"I'll take you to Callington myself. You'll need nothing."

"I don't like being away from my grandmother for long."

"We'll be away the inside of a day, that's all," said Robert persuasively. "We'll catch a train early in the morning and I'll have you back by seven at night. Surely there'll be a friend, someone from the village to keep an eye on her."

"And how shall I make contact with the women?"

"I'll make inquiries. I have friends in Callington who will know."

She smiled. He was eager for her to go and though he did not move to take hold of her now, he was willing to give a day of his time to help her and to be with her.

"I'll be ready to go whenever you say," she agreed.

He mounted his horse and rode away.

II

ELLEN had no illusions about the proposed visit to the bal maidens of Callington; she felt little would come of it, but there would be the chance to travel with Robert and to spend most of the day with him. When, after several days, however, no call came from him she told herself that he had forgotten her. He had mind for her only when he saw her; she had no place otherwise in his thoughts.

Lying in bed, before drowsiness overcame her, her thoughts sometimes turned to James. Perhaps it was the sound of miners returning from their late shift, boots ringing on the path down Cusgarne Hill, perhaps it was the distant murmur from the working mines, but it was a fleeting thought for as she closed her eyes it was the Scot's fair hair and blue eyes that came to her, not James.

She spoke with Richard about the likelihood of the bal maidens banding together in a union. He was skeptical. "It was talked of once, long since," he said.

"What did the men think?"

"You can guess. They pooh-poohed the notion. Babies and bed, that's all maids be fit for, they said."

"And what do you think?"

Richard sighed. "Maybe 'tis so. What do your women think?"

Ellen shrugged. "I do reckon they think the same."

So when, to her delight, the message came from Robert that arrangements for their journey were complete, it was with no expectation of success with the bal maidens of Callington that she set out.

The day began badly when wild wet weather set in and she arrived, damp and bedraggled, at Redruth station. She was conscious of her shabby and unkempt appearance and hoped Robert would not feel ashamed to be seen with her. She saw the other passengers looking furtively at her, no doubt wondering what the smart young Doctor Buchan could be doing with her. Perhaps they've decided I'm a poor relation, she thought, or maybe a family servant, in whom the doctor is taking a kindly interest.

He said little to her on the journey and it occurred to her he was perhaps as nervous as she was.

When they left the train at Liskeard further disappointment met them. The friends Robert had spoken of and who were to provide transport on to Callington had left a message with the station master pleading a family crisis. From then disappointment and delay turned, it seemed, to disaster. Every attempt by Robert to arrange for private hire to Callington was frustrated. Finally they boarded a horse bus to discover, after an hour, that its route was so circuitous that no sooner would they arrive in Callington than they would have to turn around to make sure of getting back to Liskeard for their evening train.

So when they reached the Butcher's Arms, the halfway point between Callington and Liskeard, they decided to alight and wait for the next conveyance back to Liskeard. The weather, which till then had continued gray and wet, brightened with the sudden caprice of the Cornish climate, the clouds thinned and the sun shone.

From that moment the nature of the day changed. They had a belated lunch at the inn and afterward went for a walk down a lane overtopped with gently dripping oaks to a hamlet, hidden, neglected and peaceful. A stream bisected the village and the lanes around it were thick with mud from the trampling of cattle and the passage of farm carts, but Robert and Ellen took no heed. They sat on a stile at the churchyard and looked over the tombs to the ancient church beyond. There was silence between them, no longer the silence of the train with its nervous concern for appearances, but an intimate silence, full of unspoken content, at least on Ellen's part; and she was sure Robert must feel the same. She was glad now that their plan for her to speak with the women at Caradon had miscarried. Thinking of it, she had had moments of terror. Now her bravery in overcoming that fear had been rewarded by this unexpected leisurely day with Robert. She turned to him and saw he was studying her.

"Disappointed?" he asked.

"No."

"Nor I. I couldn't have planned it better," he said, then added, hastening to reassure her, "I didn't plan it this way. But I'm glad it's turned out like this." He put his hands out to help her from the stile. She took hold of them and was glad he kept her hand in his as they walked slowly up the lane toward the inn.

They had not long to wait for the horse bus to Liskeard. For much of the way they were alone. They spoke little, for they were content to enjoy the unfamiliar experience of being together, with no one to see. The horses drew to a halt in the square of the market town and they had to walk the half mile or so to the station. The sky had darkened and as the train steamed in, storm broke with a fierce gust of wind and a sudden squall of large cold raindrops. Ellen and Robert tumbled into a compartment in haste to escape. The door slammed and the train pulled slowly away.

They laughed at each other with a catch of breath. They were alone in the compartment and in their haste to get out of the rain they had fallen on the seat together, so that Robert's head was lying in Ellen's lap. When he looked up at her, she knew that her eyes concealed nothing—the enjoyment of the last hours, the delight of being alone with him, the excitement she felt in the nearness of him. She was filled with a desire unlike any she had experienced before, or, if she had, she had forgotten desire could be so overwhelming. She put a hand to his face and, surprised at her temerity, ran her fingers down his cheeks to his lips. She was brimming with tenderness for him.

All this, she was sure, was reflected in her eyes. She could not hide it, even had she wished. She did not wish to hide it, there was no reason to, for his eyes also showed desire. He straightened up, put his arm around her and drew her head down to his shoulder. So she sat, her senses heightened to an intense awareness of him.

Reluctantly they separated as the train drew into the next station and they were joined by two farmers. From then to Redruth they were not alone, for no sooner did the farmers leave than other travelers took their place.

When they drew into Redruth station it was dark, and the storm still raged. The rain had forced the cabs to abandon their ranks so that they had to run to the doctor's house, Robert trying to fold Ellen under his Inverness cape as they ran down the station approach and along the road. Though the house was barely a quarter of a mile away Ellen was soaked by the time they got there.

They ran, laughing, up the stone steps to Robert's door and stood in the shelter of the portico for a moment to recover breath and dignity. A gas lamp above the door shone onto Robert's face. When the laughter went, a strange speculative look came to his eyes.

"You'll not go back to Sunny Corner in this," he said. "It would not be kind to take a pony out on a night so black and wild. Indeed we might not get through. You'll stay the night."

Ellen could not deny the sense of it, but she was uneasy. "There's Granny Pascoe." Her protest was halfhearted, but she repeated, "There's Granny."

"Isn't your sister there at night to look after her?" He had opened the door and ushered her through.

At the sound of the key the housekeeper, Mrs. Honey-

church, had come from the kitchen. She looked in surprised
distaste at Ellen before controlling her expression to turn to
the doctor.

"This is Miss Bray, the . . . daughter of an old friend of
mine from Cusgarne. She can't get back tonight. Can you get
the front bedroom ready for her and something for both of us
to eat?" He sounded half afraid of the housekeeper's reaction.

Ellen did not think she had heard herself referred to as
"Miss Bray" before, and would have taken pleasure from it had
she not seen the haughty look on the housekeeper's face.

Robert showed her into the drawing room and left her.
She stood awkwardly, wet and cold. There was an oval gilt-
framed mirror over the mantelpiece. She caught sight of a
reflection and was taken aback to recognize herself. The small
cracked mirror that served her in the cottage showed always a
distorted, speckled image. She stared coolly at herself in this,
put up her hand, removed her dripping bonnet and shook her
black hair free, admiring the picture before her. Her cheeks
glowed, her eyes were dark and intense, her lips slightly pale
so that she pinched them between her teeth to redden them
and ran her tongue over them. She thought then she was comely
to look upon. Perhaps Robert would think so too.

She turned guiltily from this self-examination when she
heard him at the door.

"Mrs. Honeychurch will show you the guest room. I've
asked her to find something for you to change into. I don't
suppose it will fit, but you cannot sit in those things. Then we
shall eat."

Ellen followed the housekeeper who led her in silence up
the stairs to a large room at the front of the house. Ellen stopped
at the open door. She could not stay here! The bed which stood
in the center of the room was large, wide enough for herself,
Julia and Granny Pascoe together. An elaborately quilted counterpane covered it, a more luxurious thing than she had ever
seen, unless it was the curtains of rich red velvet hanging at the
windows. All this belonged to a foreign world and she felt at
odds with it.

Mrs. Honeychurch interrupted her thoughts.

"Come along in, girl," her voice betraying her local origins.
"There's things to wear. My old things," she emphasized as if
only old things were suitable for such as Ellen. "They'll be better

than you're used to." She left then, with a quick glance around the room, as if to take an inventory of the furnishings and knickknacks. Ellen wondered if, next morning, she would take another sharp look to check that all was present.

She hesitated to go over to the bed where the clothes were laid out. Her shoes, stockings and skirt were wet and muddy. She took them off where she stood and let her wet top garments fall to her feet. Her chemise was wet too and clung unpleasantly to her. She wondered if Mrs. Honeychurch had provided undergarments and went over to the bed to look. There was a voluminous petticoat and a large dress of shiny, unflattering black.

She took off her chemise then started, for there had seemed to be a movement on the other side of the bed. She thought for a moment she was being watched, but realized there was a mirror there too, a full-length mirror set in a large, ornately-carved wardrobe. She had begun to fasten her underbodice as she turned to the mirror and now, as she loosened it and it fell from her, her naked breasts were reflected there. She stood, lost in the reflection a moment, then, as if amazed at the sight of herself, she cupped her hands to her breasts, and with a finger traced the brown aureole around her nipples, discovering herself. She looked into her own eyes and saw a tremulous, uncertain look there, hurriedly turned away, caught up the housekeeper's petticoat and covered herself in it. It fell in folds about her. Ellen pirouetted around and the hem, which came to her knees, swung billowing about her. She put on the black satin dress. That too hung loosely from her shoulders, but there was a belt to it and by careful pleating and folding, she was able to fit the dress to her figure decently enough. The folds of material which gathered about her bust concealed her shape beyond recognition, she thought, and she was disappointed.

She regarded herself in the long wardrobe mirror. Her black hair hung free and she left it like that. Her legs and feet were bare and her shoes and stockings too wet to put back on. She would have to go down as she was.

As she came downstairs, her feet soundless on the thick carpet, she heard Robert's voice. "We'll have it here by the fire, not in the dining room. Leave it now, Mrs. Honeychurch." The housekeeper's reply was indistinguishable, but Robert's answer sounded conciliatory. Mrs. Honeychurch came out of the room and saw Ellen poised on the landing above. She seemed sur-prized, then, loudly, with mock deference, she said "The doc-tor's in there, madam."

As she went in Robert rose and stood looking at her. The black satin dress, unflattering and concealing though it was, had a certain dignity. Ellen's face, pale with anxiety, dark eyes wide with wonder, was framed by hair black and shining as the satin, so that the firm bone structure that gave her beauty was emphasized. She stood at the door, tall, with her head held alert. Her hands were clasped before her and the loose fall of the sleeves showed her strong wrists and long capable fingers.

Robert was still and silent, as if to fix the moment in his mind.

"I don't look foolish in this?" she inquired.

"Far from it," he replied and beckoned her to him.

The gas lamps in the room were low and most of the light came from the fire, flaming with lavish heat in the great hearth. The rich comfortable furnishings were hidden in the shadows, but she could feel the thick luxurious pile of the carpet at her feet. He held out to her a glass of golden wine. She sipped it cautiously and found it pleasant. Pleasant too was the feel of the thin, fine glass at her lips. She drank, soaked in the warmth, and ate as he bade her until she could eat no more. Somehow food was not what she longed for.

She sat back on the sofa; the whole of her world was now encompassed in this warm, glowing corner of the room, with Robert sitting beside the fire, looking at her, and herself, arms stretched along the back of the sofa, mind blissfully content.

Robert rose and came to her, lifted her feet onto the sofa and sat on the floor, his back against the sofa arm. She put her hand out to touch his head in a fusion of tenderness and desire. But the desire was uppermost and she found it impossible to conceal. The touch of her hand upon his hair became more urgent and, as she let her fingers slip to his neck, she knew they conveyed her longing. He turned to her, his eyes showing an eagerness as great as hers. She reached down and kissed him ardently and probingly. His response was immediate as if a dam had burst, doubt swept away. She, driven by desire, took his head between her hands and kissed eyes, nose, lips, ears. She could smell the sweet, wine-laden scent of his breath as it mingled with hers, and was lost in it. All self was centered at her lips and tongue.

Her hands seemed to have a life all their own, at the back of his neck, then at his waist, and then seeking to find a way through waistcoat and shirt to the bare skin. His hands, she was dimly and happily aware, were running the length of her calf, knee and thigh. She shifted her position slightly, without thinking, so that his hand could more easily reach her. She sighed with pleasure as she felt, through the thick cotton of her drawers, the pressure of his hand upon her. She wanted the feel of him, the touch of him, his bare flesh to hers; she was aware of only one thing, the strong central passion for him.

She had slipped down from the sofa to the carpet. A sudden fall of coal in the fireplace and a shoot of flame as it fell threw a light across Robert's face, under hers. His eyes, pupils enlarged, looked dark. He smiled at her.

"It isn't very comfortable down here," he said.

"Oh," said Ellen in surprise. Comfort was irrelevant.

"We would be better off upstairs," he said.

"Upstairs?" Ellen was not admitting his meaning to her mind.

"In bed."

Ellen was silent. Bed was not for lovemaking until marriage. It was natural to let desire overwhelm you against a hedge, on a sofa, in a barn. There was wickedness in deciding to go to bed to make love out of wedlock.

He misinterpreted her hesitancy. "Mrs. Honeychurch will be asleep. She'll not hear a thing."

Ellen stood. Her enormous dress had bunched about her waist. She smoothed it down. Though uncertain of herself, she was still liquid with desire. She could not resist the urge to touch Robert and put out her hand to him. He took the gesture for agreement. She was anxious to please him but what was happening now was so beyond her experience that her responses were automatic, echo only of his will.

She followed him as he led her up the stairs and into the bedroom which had been set out for her. The large double bed confronted her as she entered the room. The quilted counterpane had been pulled back and the bedding folded so that the sheets and pillows shone startling white in the light of the oil lamp beside the bed.

The foreign world of white sheets, the large bed, the high-ceilinged elegant room, the solid furniture, the soft carpet and the full-length mirror, frightened her almost to the loss of her desire, but it was too strong to be denied. She turned to Robert. He had closed the door and, with his back to it, was looking at her. He smiled, as if at secret thought, and came to her and kissed her, then, with slow deliberation, he unloosed the belt which held in the pleats of her dress. As he threw the belt over a chair he laughed at the enormity of the material revealed. He turned Ellen around and began to unfasten, one by one, the long row of buttons at her back. He left the topmost one to the last and, as he undid it, he put his hands to her bare shoulders and slid the dress down so that it fell around her feet, and stood close against her, his hands caressing. She was helpless to resist, was without will, conscious only of the nearness of him, pressing at her back, his hands exploring her. Then she felt him gather the cloth of the petticoat and lift it over her head. She raised her arms to make it easier for him. She was bare from the waist now, his hands were at her hips moving up along her slowly so that, in spite of her anxiety, she found it exciting, trembling as his fingers reached her breasts and fondled them.

He turned her around to face him and stood for a moment looking at her, not at her face, but at her breasts. He stooped down and she felt him take a nipple between his lips and play his tongue about it. An unfamiliar shiver of pleasure ran down her spine, but at the same time the strangeness of it made her recoil. She looked down at his head, bent to her breast. She wanted to stroke his fair, untidy hair, and yet she wanted to thrust him away. The sensations at her nipple, the feel of his hands as they sought now to push her remaining garment down from her hips, filled her with a helpless craving. She was disturbed and angry with herself at her acquiescence, and pushed his hands away from her. He loosed his hold on her nipple and looked up at her. His eyes were unfathomable, his lips were open, with the tip of his tongue protruding. She moved back from him to sit upon the bed.

She knew now that in spite of her unease in these surroundings, in spite of her self-doubting, there was no going back. Her own feelings were smoldering, curious to know, her own hands longing to discover him for herself, to reach for him. But for a moment she held back, slipped under the sheets and, as he watched with an amused smile on his lips, she wriggled out of her drawers and, with her feet, pushed the clumsy garment from her until it fell from under the blankets to the floor at his feet. Slowly at that he began to undress.

She lay, the sheets pulled to her shoulders, watching him, desire mounting as he lifted his shirt to reveal the bare, pale skin. He was thick-set, though not muscled like Mark or . . . she killed the thought. His skin was smooth, unscarred, clean. She put out a hand to touch him and he smiled down at her and offered himself to her, then, with a sudden movement, he joined her beneath the sheets and their bodies touched.

Ellen lay, motionless at first, rigid, overwhelmed at the enormity of being in bed with Robert, of their nakedness together. She could not imagine what lay before her. The ribald crudities of the bal maidens were of no use to her now; they had no meaning here. This was new, strange, unexplored experience and she was terrified at the unknownness of it.

She felt Robert's hand at her hip, following the flat fall of her stomach to her mound, fingers reaching, curling about her pubic hairs. She put down a hand to stop him and turned her back to him in a sudden startled movement. She felt him close upon her, the whole bare length of him along her back, the hard pressure of his penis in the hollow of her spine. He put his arms around her to hold her tightly to him. His chin rested on her shoulder and he nibbled at the soft lobe of her ear, while his hands, one at a breast, the other again at the curving base of her stomach, were emptying her of control. She was surrendering to his will and was finding pleasure in it. She turned to him, open and eager, pressed her lips to his, breathed of his breath, and took him to her willingly, caressingly, endearingly, passionately, unaware of the pain of his thrust, only knowing that this was all, beyond imagining, beyond reason, beyond herself. She was another person beneath him, holding him to her, feeling the weight of him upon her, the surge of him within, knowing him as she had known no one before.

She opened her eyes to search his face for signs of the tenderness she felt for him. It was there and at the sight she sighed, replete with content.

He moved out of her slowly and she was reluctant to lose

him. He lay beside her and held a hand to her where he had entered her, gently fondling her wet curls until his fingers were still and she knew he slept.

She was somehow disappointed. There were things to say, words of affection, deep satisfying pledges of love. She wanted to say them to him and to have him speak to her, but he was dead to her now, had taken himself from her and was in a world closed to her.

His arm still lay across her. She moved it aside and slowly, so as not to wake him, rose from the bed. The oil lamp still cast its gentle glow about the room. She walked around the bed to it to turn down the wick. As she did she again noticed herself in the mirror. She paused before it to study herself, her long naked body flushed from its first act of love. She could see no difference about her. But the difference was within.

III

ROBERT Buchan stirred, throwing off the heavy cover of sleep, aware of a drumming on a door downstairs. He did not think he had slept more than an hour or two but had no clear idea of the time. He moved from under the bedclothes and recalled as he realized his nakedness the events of the evening before. He turned his head and saw the shape of his companion stretched on the bed, unmoved by the thumping on the door below. He smiled with recollection of their lovemaking. He wanted to put out a hand to her but he refrained and, as quietly as he could, slipped from the bed.

He remembered then his clothes, heaped haphazardly on the carpet where he had shed them. He must collect them together and return with them to his own room. It would not do for Mrs. Honeychurch to know what had happened between Ellen and him.

He picked up his garments anxious to get to his room before the household was wakened. Ellen was still undisturbed. He gathered his clothes to him and put his hand to the door. He heard a bustling movement outside and the slippered footsteps of his housekeeper moving down the stairs to the side door. He quickly opened the bedroom door and, his clothing clutched to cover his nakedness, sped across the landing. He could hear Mrs. Honeychurch's voice raised angrily, and a gruff reply.

Robert hastily donned his quilted dressing gown and appeared on the landing at the door of his room as his housekeeper put her foot on the stairs. She looked up at him. She had a candlestick in her hand and the flame cast long and curious shadows up her face, making it witchlike and repellent.

Her voice was harsh and irritable. " 'Tis a miner," she said. "From Wheal Uny. I've told him you'll see to him in the morning, but he won't go. He says you belong to see him, seeing as you're the bal surgeon."

A figure appeared behind Mrs. Honeychurch, a broad dust-stained man. She turned angrily toward him but before her indignation could discharge upon him he spoke.

" 'Tis not I, doctor. There's been an accident, serious, I do fancy. A rock fall. It's. . . ."

"I'll come," Robert interrupted. "Give me time to get dressed and I'll come down straightaway. Get back to bed, Mrs. Honeychurch. And if I'm not back by morning tell Miss Bray I'm sorry. Tell her I've been called away to a mine accident. She'll understand."

Mrs. Honeychurch paused at the door of the bedroom to light the gas jet for him. "Don't you be going down below," she said, her voice showing concern. "There's no call for you to do that."

Robert dressed hurriedly. He would have liked to return to Ellen to rouse her and explain that duty took him away, but Mrs. Honeychurch was on the landing. She watched him as he joined the miner. He turned at the door.

"Give Miss Bray my message," he reminded her.

Buchan set his foot on the ladderway. As he stepped into the blackness of the shaft, his hands gripping the uprights of the ladder, his feet reaching for the rungs, he felt a surge of fear. The flame of the candle, which was fixed by clay to his borrowed miner's hat, cast no light below, and, as he glanced down, when his leading foot found no rung to rest on, he saw only tiny flickering points of light from the candles of the miners descending before him, a long drop below him. He reached with his foot again and touched a sound rung and moved slowly down.

Above him he heard steps on the ladder drawing near. He called up the black shaft, "Careful! I'm just below."

" 'Tis all right, booy," a voice boomed down to him. "Just you yell if I do tread on you."

By slow steps from platform to platform Robert descended the stages of the ladderway. The first part of the descent had been perpendicular, but then the shaft had been driven at an angle to follow the lode. It seemed, from the echo, to be wide and spacious but the candlelight penetrated only a shiver into the gloom. Robert was engulfed by a velvet blackness, so thick, he thought, that if he were rash enough to let go the ladder and reach out a hand he could have felt it.

He paused to take breath. At the start the shaft had been cold and drafty, but here, at what must already be six hundred feet underground, the air was clammy and his heavy clothes stuck uncomfortably to him. The exertion of the descent and the closeness of the air made breathing difficult and when he reached the next sollar he stopped to rest. The man above joined him.

"Sorry you came, doctor?" he asked. Robert recognized Captain William Henry Hosking, brother to "Brimstone" and, like him, a noted lay preacher.

"I'll survive," said Buchan. "Give me a moment here."

They sat together on the narrow wooden platform. They could hear below them the distant voices of the rescue party descending further into the lower levels of the mine.

"It's a different world down here," Robert said and his voice echoed in the cavernous drive.

"A hard, hard world. A man's world," said Hosking. "Only the hardest get through and not always them. We've another hundred fathom or so to go. All right, doctor?"

"All right, cap'n," Robert Buchan replied giving a Cornish intonation to his reply.

"Off you go then." The mine captain's voice held a warmth of response.

Robert began to move with more ease. Though his clothes still clung to him and the air was close and oppressive, his feet and hands moved in a rhythm only occasionally interrupted by a missing ladder stave. They made steady progress and in a while became aware of the nearness of the party below.

"Hold at the next level, doctor. You wait here while I go down along to see it's safe. I'll be back directly."

Hosking moved away along the drive. The roof dipped abruptly so that he had to stoop to get through. Soon the flicker of his candle flame disappeared and Robert was left sitting beside the shaft, alone with his thoughts, thoughts that took him above ground to the warm body of Ellen.

He could hear a meaningless jumble of voices muffled by the intervening rocks, then there came a sudden alarmed shout and immediately upon it a thundering cascade of sound, a bass roaring echo through the rock, a shake of the earth around, and a thrust of air out of the drive that buffeted him against the rock and doused his candle flame. He sat, astonished, deafened and afraid. Silence for a long moment was about him, then from the drive came voices, steps running, faltering in the dark. He bellowed into the void. "Hold on! Doctor Buchan here!"

"Thank God, doctor," a voice said. "Strike a lucifer somebody."

There was a spurt of flame and then the gradual clearing of the deepness of the dark as candle after candle was lit. Buchan saw four miners standing there.

"Where's Captain Hosking?" he asked.

"We'll go back and look directly," said one of the men. "But if you don't mind, doctor, we'll sit for a moment and get our senses back."

"What happened?" Buchan was impatient, anxious to get along the level to the rockfall, do his job and get safely back to grass.

"We'd got to where the first fall had been when Cap'n Hosking joined us. The timbers of the stull had cracked and the roof had caved in. It closed off the level. I reckon there's no hope for the lads buried beneath it. There's not a sign of them and there's tons fallen. 'Twill take days to clear, and more." He paused and one of the other men said into the silence that followed, "Joe Treglown and his two boys and his old uncle."

"Then . . . ?" prompted Robert.

"We was examining the timbers when Cap'n Hosking joined us. He must have seen something for he shouted a warning. Then he was caught and two men with him. I do reckon the cap'n's a goner. But time it's chanced to clear, we'll go and look. You wait here, doctor."

"I'll come with you."

"You don't belong to do that. There's nothing you can do yet awhile."

"I'll see for myself."

"Then if you're coming, doctor, follow me. Tread warily, there's maybe more rock to come."

Robert stooped to follow the miner into the passage. The drive, rough-hewn, was wide enough to permit a hand barrow to be dragged along. Rocks jutted dangerously from sides and roof, so that Robert was glad of the hard miner's hat he had been given.

"Here we are, doctor," said the leading miner, holding his candle aloft. The narrow drive had opened into a gunnis, a large cavern from which the lode had been worked. The overhanging rock had been propped with timbers of pitch pine, nearly two feet square, solid and huge to form a firm support, but ahead even these massive struts lay broken, piteously inadequate to bear the weight of rock. Great veined heaps of boulders closed the drive, wetly glistening in the candle glimmer.

" 'Tis hopeless," said one of the men, echoing Robert's own thinking.

"No, 'tis not," said another. "They'm over to there, at the side. The fall's not so bad there. The timbers might have held."

They moved cautiously, aware that a slip of a foot might bring another fall, another crack of timbers and the collapse of the stull and the roof upon them. They spoke in whispers as if a loud word might bring disaster. The leading miner crawled to the new fall and cupped his hands about his mouth to call, quietly, into the rock.

"Cap'n! Cap'n Hosking?" They held their breath.

"Cap'n Hosking?" he repeated and, to their surprised delight, a voice, strong and deep, came in answer.

"Ay. That you, Tom?"

"Iss, cap'n. And the doctor's here."

"I'll have need of him, maybe. But there's a weight of rock about."

"Are you hurt, cap'n?"

There was silence for a moment and then a short laugh. "I'm in one piece, more or less, but I cannot speak for young Aaron and his father."

"We'm here, cap'n," said a slow voice, breathless almost. "But 'tis not comfortable." There was a faint chuckle and then a gasp as if pain had struck.

"I'll come to you," said Robert.

The miner, Tom, looked at him and shook his head as if questioning the doctor's sanity.

"I'll stay with you," he said. "But you lads," turning to his companions, "go up along for more help. We'll need more men to shift this heap. There'll be plenty willing."

Robert crept along, with slow caution, under the jutting beams and jagged rock.

"Hold it, doctor," he heard Tom's voice behind. He lay, motionless, and listened to the fall of pebbles and the groaning of timbers.

" 'Tis nothing," said Tom and Robert began again his slow crawl. He touched a foot and felt his hand along a leg.

"Who's that?" a voice said.

"I'm the bal surgeon."

"Please God," said the voice. "It cannot be. I do be mazed with pain. 'Tis black herein, dead, deadly black." The voice went on, a rasping coarse voice, an unreal disembodied sound from within the fall. Then the words stopped and were replaced by an intermittent mumbling.

"Is that you, Aaron?" came the voice of Captain Hosking.

There was no reply.

Robert Buchan slid back from under the rock to Tom. They looked at each other.

" 'Tis bad, doctor?"

"I can ease the pain at any rate." He shook his head in an attempt to bring himself to reality. The flickering candlelight, the gaunt shadows curling on the dark walls, the gray shape of his companion, and the vast bulk of the tumbled rock, all was unreal. He was dreaming, surely, and would wake to find himself in bed.

In bed, with Ellen beside him.

Then he heard Tom's voice and knew that reality was here in this cavern, with an infinite weight of rock above and about them. A whimpering came from within the heap and Robert was recalled to duty. He took a syringe of morphine and crawled back to the man he had found. From the side where Hosking lay his voice was raised in the hymn "Rock of Ages Cleft For Me." The singing, vigorous at first, gradually petered out.

"That's as much as I can do," Robert said, crawling back to Tom.

"Then," said the miner, " 'tis well to go back along, out of harm's way, till help comes."

"I'll stay," said Buchan. "I can bring some cheer to Captain Hosking in the meantime."

Tom moved back along the level while Robert moved cautiously to the corner where Hosking lay, face visible, but shoulders trapped beneath the weight of rock.

"I'd get out from under if I were you, doctor," said Hosking. " 'Tis not like a bal surgeon to linger below ground."

Robert did not answer and for a long while there was silence, broken only by the dripping of water from the walls, and a rasping breath from within the heap.

"You'm a stubborn bugger," said Hosking at last. "But then you'm a Scot." He paused for breath. "What brought a Scot to Cornwall?"

"Luck," said Robert.

"Good or bad?"

"Good, so far."

"Let's pray it hasn't changed," said Hosking. His voice was strained now, as if he was talking against pain.

"Are you married, doctor?"

"No," answered Robert. "Not yet awhile." He thought of Ellen sleeping safely where he had left her and smiled at the memory. Yesterday, from start to finish, had been a total delight. It had been natural and proper they should be together like that. It had been, from the moment of their meeting at Redruth station to the last tender moments of their lovemaking, a wholly satisfactory day.

"Not yet," he repeated. "But maybe soon," and was surprised to hear himself say it.

There was silence again for so long that Robert began to wonder if Captain Hosking had fallen into unconsciousness, but then his voice came again, slow and careful, as if breath were almost too precious to part with in speech.

"A Scottish girl, your intended?"

"No. Cornish. From a miner's family." Again he wondered at himself. Could the passion of one night so change his life? He heard steps and voices from the direction of the shaft. "There's help coming," he said. "I can hear them."

There was no answer for a moment then again the thin tune of a hymn came from within the mound of rock and timber.

Robert turned to the voices. There seemed to be a good number in the rescue party. First to emerge was Matthew Rowe, the underground captain, whom Robert knew. He spoke gruffly to Robert.

"Maybe you'll be of use, doctor, when we've done our job, so you're welcome, but you'll be best off, and so will we, if you keep out of the way back along. We'll tell you when we need you but 'tis miners' work now."

Rowe turned away and, in the light of a new and plentiful supply of good, clean-burning Palmer's candles, he began to survey the lie of the rock. When Robert failed to move, he gestured impatiently to him and Robert, seeing the wisdom of his bidding, went back along the level to the shaft, where he was thankful to find a fresher flow of air. His clothes were sticking to him and he followed the example of the miners and stripped to the waist. He put his jacket at his back to protect his shoulders against the rock and then, in spite of his determination to remain alert, he fell asleep, to dream wild, terrifying and confusing images of death—by drowning, in falls from mountainsides, in quicksands, image rapidly succeeding to image, so that death never came but, worse, continually threatened.

IV

ELLEN had slept heavily. She woke, at the sound of movement about the house, to find herself in a strange bed, surrounded by objects of an opulence she could not have imagined. She was startled and then, with a flush of pleasure, she recalled the evening before. She was warm, relaxed, content. The doubts of last night were gone. She stretched her limbs and sighed and turned to greet her lover.

She was alone. Where he had been there now remained only a sheet turned back, an empty pillow. She raised herself to her elbows to look around. He had gone, but she was not disturbed. She thought it would have been pleasurable to reach for him, feel his smooth soft skin, to close herself against him. A wave of tenderness for him swept over her and she lay back. Ready to close her eyes and sleep and dream of him until he returned to her.

A knock came at the door and she smiled to herself.

The door opened and in came, not Robert, but his house-keeper. Ellen was sharply aware of her nakedness under the bedclothes and dared not move for fear of revealing it.

"Your things," the housekeeper said with distaste. "Here they are. They're dry." She put Ellen's clothes disdainfully at the foot of the bed then added harshly, "You'd better get up and get going. You can have something to eat before you go, if you want."

"Doctor Buchan?" Ellen asked.

"The doctor? He's gone. He's got work to attend to. You don't imagine he could wait for the likes of you. You'd better be gone before he comes back." She stared pointedly and her eyes showed, Ellen felt, an awareness of her nakedness under the blankets.

"Did he leave any message?" Ellen forced herself to ask.

"Why should he?" the housekeeper answered and, with a contemptuous lift of the head, swept from the room.

Ellen lay for a moment unable to accept Robert's neglect of her. The warm recollection of the night before was there still but slowly it was being replaced by a growing sense of shame. She rose from the bed and, naked as she was, went to the washstand. There was water in the ewer and she poured some into the basin. There was soap too, a smooth and scented extravagance, and a towel, thick and soft. She put her hands to the soap but pride made her hesitate, pride and anger at the humiliation forced on her by Mrs. Honeychurch's manner. She wanted to go to the door, stride downstairs in her nakedness and confront the harridan, brazenly declaring herself the doctor's chosen lover.

But why was he not here? Why had he left no message? How could he have abandoned her to face that woman's scorn by herself? How could delight turn so sour?

Where was he? She looked around the room to seek there some echo of his feeling for her, some evidence of his affection, a note perhaps? A flower? Some token.

There was nothing.

She looked down at herself, suddenly ashamed of her nakedness. She dressed hastily. Her clothes were dry, but her boots were heavy with mud. She scuffed it off and let it lie, where it fell, on the golden carpet.

She wished she could as easily brush away her sense of uncleanness. Yesterday she had experienced a sensation of pleasure unfathomable in its delight; now she was plunged into an abyss of feeling—pain, remorse, disgust—she could not define the bitterness that mounted. It fought within her at the joy which had overcome her before. She closed her eyes to summon up the image of Robert to her, but he would no more come to her in imagination than in reality. She could see only a white heat of anger.

She looked about her at the rich furnishings and her anger heightened. She had been betrayed by this semblance of solidity. She had allowed herself to be bemused and corrupted by this show of wealth. Such a world held nothing for her but humiliation. She looked into the long mirror to make certain she showed to the outside world none of the shame she felt inside. She drew herself up to look proudly at herself, and saw not rage but bewilderment that Robert had forsaken her. Had it meant nothing to him, the ecstasy they had created for each other?

She put the thought from her, then, as she turned from the mirror, she saw the bed where they had lain, the stained sheet, and she was caught with recollection again. She refused to yield to it, drew herself up and turned her back on the room. As she stood on the landing she heard, somewhere in the house below, women's voices. She went slowly down, wondering if she should leave a message for Robert, ignoring his neglect of her.

As she stood at the foot of the stairs, hesitating, she heard the voice of the housekeeper, spiteful, strident, suddenly clear, talking to a companion, saying "some young baggage, some trollop he's brought from the streets. You know what men are."

Ellen opened the front door and fled from the house.

V

Robert woke shuddering, not from cold for the air was close and warm, but from fear. His candle had guttered out and he woke to a thick and encompassing dark. In his confusion he thought he must still be asleep and was appalled at the reality of the nightmare. He felt rock hard against his back.

Then he recalled where he was and dared not move for he had a vivid memory of the deep shaft somewhere beside him. A wrong step might lead to his plunging, as in his dream, down the narrow hole into the furthest depths of the mine.

He stayed where he was, breathing shallowly, trying to thrust panic from him by thinking with painstaking detail of his home, his drawing room, the fireplace, the sofa, and in careful reconstruction of the patterns of the wallpaper. His breathing became deeper and slower and, as he opened his eyes again, he thought he could begin to distinguish shapes moving grayly toward him.

"Doctor?"

"Aye."

"There's need of you now, we're thinking."

They moved back to the gunnis, where Captain Rowe was guiding the rescue party in their slow and careful labors.

"What is the time?"

"Three o'clock in the afternoon, doctor. You've been below for nigh on twelve hours."

A thin wavering voice came from within the jumble of timbers: Hosking singing again, not a Methodist hymn this time, but a miners' bawdy song.

> Bal maidens here, bal maidens there,
> Bal maidens'll buck you any old where.

Rowe laughed. "I don't know if his sperrits be picking up, or if he's in delirium, but 'tis a good job his brother isn't here to listen to that. All right, cap'n?" he called.

"All right, cap'n," the answer came.

"The doctor's coming in to talk to you, Will'm Henry."

"Tell him to wipe his feet first," answered Hosking.

In the hours that followed Robert was hardly aware of the

passing of time. Down here, more than two hundred fathoms deep in the candlelight, there was a dreamlike quality to his surroundings, for him at any rate, who could only watch and wait until his services were needed. Not so for the miners, for they, in slow painful shifts, strained every muscle, sweat pouring from them as freely as the runnels of water poured down the rock walls. But Robert, as he sat back, saw the figures moving as phantoms, slow and solemn. He slept at times, so that reality merged into dream and back again. From time to time he was called to help Hosking in his pain, but there was little he could do save speak encouragingly. And all the time he was himself fearful of the weight of rock poised precariously above.

They brought Aaron Jenkin out first, bound him to a stretcher and took him back along the drive to the ladderway, while Robert remained to tend to Hosking. Aaron's father still lay hidden beneath the fallen rock.

Hosking was no longer conscious.

" 'Tis as well," said Rowe. "He'd see the danger." The captain gestured at the timbers and rock. " 'Twill take prayer as well as skill to prize him from that. . . ." He stood silent, his miner's judgment quietly assessing the chances.

"Take a breather, doctor," he said. "Go up to grass. We'll send for you when we need you next."

"I don't think I could climb the ladderway as I feel now."

"You'll have to sometime."

"I'll bide here."

Robert wondered at his own obstinacy as he looked around him. This was not his world; it belonged to the Bryants and their like. These subterranean caverns and channels, these stopes and drives, winzes and rises, were familiar ground to his miner friends. Now he saw them as they must: hot, oppressive, close and threatening.

His arm was being shaken. He roused himself with difficulty and stared unseeingly at the miner stooping over him.

"Cap'n Rowe says 'tis time to wake you. We're near to freeing Cap'n Will'm Henry."

Robert rose stiffly and moved over to the rock fall. A place had been cleared around Hosking and all but his right shoulder and arm were free from the weight of rock. His clothes were stained with blood and mud, and torn by the jagged rock, but when Robert crawled to him and examined him he was reassured to find the damage to his lower limbs was not serious. But Robert feared it would not be so for his arm and shoulder, where the rock had fallen heavy and direct upon him and pinned him firmly beneath. He was still unconscious.

Robert turned and nodded to Rowe. The mine captain took a last careful look over the heap of rock and timbers, signaled to his miners.

Robert, kneeling beside Hosking, heard the creak of a lever, a timber prop, heard the gasped breathing of the men, heard a rattle of pebbles, then, as the rock moved an inch, two inches, more, from Hosking's crushed shoulder, he slid, snake-like, beside the injured man, until he too was beneath the creaking groaning mass. He put his arms beneath Hosking's body and slowly, gently dragged him forth. His back jarred against the rock above and he heard a sharp word of warning from Rowe. But he was indifferent now to all but the need to succor the man in his arms, the need to protect his shoulder from further injury in the moving, and yet the need to get him quickly out of danger.

"We cannot hold it much longer," said Rowe.

A miner came to take the weight of Hosking's legs and, together, they moved him out.

"All clear," said Robert quietly, suddenly aware again of the danger about him. "All clear."

Rowe urged his men to be as careful in the lowering of the rock as they had been in the raising. The timbers creaked, the rocks shifted, pebbles rolled again and, to a sigh of relief from the miners, the rocks settled to silence.

"We'd be wise to delay no longer," the mine captain said. "The rock looks steady enough at the moment, but it'll not hold for long."

They lifted Hosking to a stretcher and Robert, with a gentle skill summoned from somewhere within his weary mind, bound his shoulder and then his whole body to the stretcher. Still moving with caution the party left the gunnis. Robert paused to look at the jagged fall of boulders.

"And Aaron Jenkin's father?" said Robert.

Rowe spoke behind him. " 'Tis as good a burial ground as many a miner gets."

"That's no consolation for their families."

"They're not alone in their grief. There are more widows than wives hereabouts."

"That's a hard view."

"It's a hard life," answered Rowe.

They left it to the miners to get Captain Hosking up the long ascent of the ladderway while they slowly followed, Robert hardly able to raise one foot after the other. From above, as they climbed, came a faint melody: it was Hosking, once more singing a hymn as he was borne aloft. "Nearer my God to Thee," came the distant words.

"He's a right one, William Henry," said Rowe. "Not like his brother Able, Brimstone as is. I don't know if we'd have had so many willing to risk their necks for him."

He stopped, put his hand to Robert's arm. "Listen."

There was a soft rustle, a shift of the air, and from the workings they had left came a deep rumbling roar. A gust of dust-laden air thrust past them out of the level to be lost in the shaft.

"God rest them," said Rowe. "There'll be no getting back to them now."

They climbed slowly up and Robert became aware of the change of air, from the close and clammy sweltering of below, to the crisp, fresh and piercing here above. He realized he was stripped to the waist and that he had left his jacket and shirt below. His trousers were mud-stained and torn; his hands, trunk and face were thick with the dust of the mine; his hard hat was a miner's hat, so that he knew he must seem, to the men at the head of the shaft, to be one of them, a miner.

His legs almost folded under him as he stepped from the shaft. Captain Rowe put out a hand to steady him.

"You'll do well to get home, to a long sleep," he said.

"I'll see Hosking to hospital."

"You'll not. They'll have done that already. We're used to these things. You'll get off home."

Robert was too exhausted to argue and by now the biting air snatched at his breath and seized his lungs. A figure approached and looked uncertainly at him.

"Doctor? Doctor Buchan?"

He recognized the miner who had brought him here, last night? The night before? When?

"Aye," he answered. "That's who I am."

"I stabled your pony here. I'll harness it to your trap and drive you home." He was dressed neatly in dark clothes, with a white high collar. His face was scrubbed clean and his hair tidily brushed. He helped the doctor onto the trap, wrapped the traveling rug around him and took hold of the reins.

"I'll get you there in no time, doctor."

As they drove away Robert was aware of the incongruity of the neat, tidy miner driving the trap, and himself, dirty, huddled, half naked. It was an inglorious way to be brought home, but he was too tired to care, too tired to think, too weary to notice the Sunday-best-dressed people assembling for worship. Before they reached his home the clip-clop of the pony's hooves had lulled him to sleep.

Chapter Nine

I

ELLEN had no peace within her. She felt betrayed, and betraying—of herself and of James. She had not intended to love Buchan and could not say now why she had. And what was this love? Was it love that had drawn her to his arms, that had made her body yield to his, welcome him? The tenderness of the moment could still, she knew, deceive her. She tried to deny it a place in her memory, but there was too much to be suppressed, the touch of him, the passion in his voice, the sigh of his contentment at their moment of union. All that was not so easily erased.

But over his voice she heard that of Mrs. Honeychurch, cold, hateful and contemptuous, and she heard the implication of her phrase, "You know what men are," and Ellen felt the surge of shame again, making her flesh creep uncomfortably.

She had washed herself down at home with the rough carbolic soap that served for all cleaning purposes. She had evaded Julia's half-questions about her absence overnight.

"I didn't say anything to Granny," Julia said, clearly hoping for enlightenment herself.

"How is she?" Ellen asked.

"Poorly. She wants to see you."

Ellen went up the narrow stairway. The room in which her Granny lay had two windows, one looking into Pitti-Patti Lane, the other giving a view over the valley. She stood for a moment looking out over Trehaddle, making out the path which wound between high hedges to the ford. She had walked there with James. They had held hands, and they had kissed. That was so long ago.

She heard a movement from her grandmother and turned to see her trying to lift herself up the bed. Above the bed-head was a scriptural text "The Lord maketh poor, and maketh rich. He bringeth low and lifteth up." Under the window stood a chest, upon it a basin and ewer, and next to them a Bible.

"Ellen?" Her grandmother's voice was barely audible.

Ellen moved to help her grandmother, putting her strong arms around the frail shoulders to ease her up. There was no weight to her, no substance, only spirit.

"Ellen," she repeated, as if the name gave her some comfort. Her eyes, pale and faded, seemed to frame a plea. Ellen stooped and kissed her brow. It was smooth, the dry skin stretched taut; her thin gray hair straggled untidily; her cheeks were sunken. Ellen took a cloth and wiped her grandmother's face, and gently combed her hair.

"The valley," said the old lady. "How does it look?"

Ellen gazed out. The trees were almost in full leaf, save for a tall ash on the other bank of the stream.

"Beautiful," she said. "As always."

"The ash?" her grandmother said after a while.

"There's some green showing," said Ellen and wondered if it was her imagination at work that saw the faint burgeoning against the boughs.

" 'Twas there," said Alice Pascoe. She stopped as if unable to summon strength to describe her memories of the ash. "He was tall, and tender, and strong."

Ellen took her hand. There was no flesh to it, but there was still a sinewy strength, or seemed to be at first, until the clasp loosened.

Alice Pascoe sighed. "A miner," she breathed. "Proud.

Stubborn." Ellen looked at her grandmother and smiled. What a union it must have been with a proud and stubborn miner married to this obstinate stiff-necked woman. She bent down again to kiss the old lady's cheek.

" 'Tis needful," said her grandmother.

"What?"

"To be proud."

Ellen looked about her at the bare furnishings, the humble room. Her grandmother caught her glance.

"To be proud of yourself," she said and her voice faded as if the effort had been too much for her.

"Tell me," she said at last, "tell me about him."

"Who?" Ellen was surprised. For a moment her mind was full of Robert.

"Your man."

"My man?"

"Your James. D'you think I don't know?" She put her hand out to touch Ellen's arm. "I'm not blind." She sighed and her thoughts seemed to turn inward. "He was tall, and tender, and strong," she breathed again, almost without voice.

"Tall and tender and strong," Ellen echoed and looked out again on the countryside where the ash raised its elegant arms to the sky.

"Time for chapel," said her grandmother suddenly and moved weakly on the pillow as if she would get up and go.

"Shall I read to you?" asked Ellen.

The old lady glanced at the Bible and then at Ellen as if suspicious of her granddaughter's intentions.

"No," she said. "Tell me. Your man." Ellen was confused. She tried to think of James, but it was Robert who came to her mind. "Where is he?" said her grandmother. "He doesn't come."

He never will, thought Ellen. He wants no more of me and I want no more of him. It is finished.

"Who?" she said.

"James. Where is he?" Her grandmother's voice was querulous now. "I want him. Bring him here." She raised herself from the pillow and said, with sudden sharpness, "Do as I tell you, girl. Bring him here," and then, exhausted with the sudden flash of spirit, she sank back to her pillow and closed her eyes.

Ellen crept from the room.

"I wish I could," she said to herself, and was not sure if it was of James or Robert she spoke.

II

THE visit by Buchan to James had taken long to have an effect but at last it began to work on James, to remind him of the world outside. Though the cell, the long corridors, the dull routine, were present reality, another reality existed outside. Buchan had been proof of it. James did not know why, but he resented Buchan. He had no cause to, for without his past aid he would be even more crippled than he was. Nevertheless he resented the fact that it was Buchan who had brought a breath of the outside to him; he would have preferred another savior.

Gradually he began to think in terms of release. It would come someday, if he could survive, and survive he would, he told himself. He would remain James Bryant to the end of his term and he would come out of the gates of the jail still himself, the James Bryant he was and had always been.

He began to question who and what he was. Before his imprisonment he had had no self-doubts, but now he asked of himself, What am I? A prisoner, but still a man, a man who had to protest against injustice, however futile that protest seemed. He recognized now the futility of the fire raising at Wheal Busy, but it was better to protest than to submit. What else could he have done? he asked himself in his long and lonely hours. Methuselah gave no answer, nor did his other friends, Samson and Noah. They were silent, they kept their counsel.

Reason told him that he should have attempted to persuade his comrades to join in a union to protect their interests by reasoned argument with the mine companies. But what use was reasoned argument when power of dismissal and engagement rested solely in the hands of the companies? When men were so in debt that they were virtually in thrall to the mine? When the workhouse threatened? He could not resolve the issues for himself. He only recognized that if he were faced with the same choices again, he would very likely behave in the same way again, doomed though such behavior was.

Though he thought of that night at Wheal Busy often it was to Ellen his thoughts returned. He had fought against this at first, but it was no use. He called upon her to come to him, whispering her name into the dank air of his cell. She came and he introduced her to his friend Methuselah and the others, but when he reached out his hands to touch her, she vanished, and he was left alone, fingers clutching the empty air.

He did not cease to call her in the night, pleading with her, and she came, but never close enough, and he would fold his arms about his shoulders, trying to imagine it was her holding him. There were times when he reviled her for holding herself from him. Annie Rowe would not be so unwilling, he told himself, but he did not say Annie's name aloud, for he was afraid Ellen might hear and despise him for his inconstancy.

The gray light of morning seemed to bring sanity of a sort. He chided himself for the fancies that came to him, but Ellen's presence in the cell seemed real—at times more real than his own.

But if it was Ellen who came to him in the night it was the hated image of Brimstone Hosking he saw in the daytime, in the prison staff who berated him, even in some of his fellow prisoners. Hosking. It was Hosking he blamed for his ill fortune, Hosking, whose harsh authority at the mine had forced him to rebel, Hosking alone who was responsible for the sabotage attempt.

But through his fantasies, his self-pity, he retained some pride, some sense of self. "I am a hard-rock miner, skilled in my craft," he would tell himself. "They cannot rob me of that, however long they keep me here."

Gradually the despair which had cloaked him began to lift. He sought contact with his fellow prisoners and found the discipline of the jail not so harsh as to deny him this companionship. And he remembered the Methodist minister, Abraham Luke, who had come to visit him in the early days of his sentence. He asked to see him and some weeks later, when the minister arrived, James gave him a message for his father.

"And, sir," he said. "There be a young maid nearby. I'd be grateful for a word of comfort to her too."

The minister smiled and nodded in approval.

"Her name?" he asked.

"Ellen Bray," James said and, enjoying the sound, repeated the name again and again. "Ellen, Ellen, Ellen Bray."

"I'll see she knows," said Abraham Luke.

III

ELLEN had little time to herself now that she had sole responsibility for looking after her grandmother, with Julia working at the candle factory. At times Granny Pascoe showed an alert and critical interest in her surroundings; more often she was filled with maudlin regrets for a lost past. Ellen found this distressing for even in the days when she thought she disliked the old woman she had admired her spirit, her refusal to submit.

Fight it, she wanted to say. Fight it. But she kept quiet, comforted the old lady and discovered resources of understanding in herself that she had never suspected.

"I'll call a doctor," she said once, in one of Granny's lucid moments.

" 'Tis not worth a candle," said her grandmother. " 'Twould be a waste. What could he do you can't?"

And it was true. The care and companionship which Ellen gave was all that was needful. She thought, nonetheless, she would ask Robert when he came with papers for Richard to have a look at the old woman.

But he did not come.

He did not come, and the suspicion arose within her that he had used her. She was one of many. That alone could explain why he ignored her so, why he had left her without a message, a token.

There had been silence.

She nursed her sense of grievance until she began to imagine she had yielded to him against her will. But it had not been so, she knew it. At the thought of that evening she could not suppress the return of a sense of delight. She knew she should feel shame, but she recollected pleasure. She tried to convince herself of the sinfulness of her behavior, but there had been none on her part. Her surrender had come from love.

And his? Surely his tenderness and passion could only come from the same deep affection that stirred her.

But . . . the doubts would not vanish. She heard his housekeeper's voice, saw the contempt in her eyes, the sneer on her lips and felt shame then, shame and anger that she should have been subjected to such treatment. She wanted to confront Robert and challenge him, but a stubborn pride made her pretend indifference to him.

"Ellen," she heard her grandmother's weak voice calling and went to answer her.

The following morning, after Julia had left for work, Ellen went upstairs to make sure the old lady was comfortable. She was asleep, breathing lightly, her pale face hollow-eyed, shadowed, skull-like. She felt the need to get away, to speak to someone, and there was no one but Jane. She would not tell her what had happened—she could not disclose that even to Jane—but her friend was a woman of experience in love and the simulation of love. She was worldly-wise, and Ellen felt it was that sort of wisdom she needed.

She walked into Redruth and could not resist the urge to go past Robert's house. She paused on the pavement opposite, and her eyes went to the window of the room where she had lain with Robert. As she stood she saw a carriage draw up to the house, a frock-coated man step down and proceed up the drive. The door was opened to him, and Ellen caught a glimpse of Mrs. Honeychurch. Her sour face reminded Ellen strongly of the flight from the house and she walked rapidly away.

She hurried past the station to the Rose Tavern and turned to the linny at the back. The door opened and she was confronted by Reuben Menear. He stared at her and reddened. "I was in Redruth," he explained needlessly. "I thought I'd call." He brushed past her before she could speak and hastened away. Ellen turned into the room. Jane was in bed, leaning on the pillow, blanket drawn up to her bare shoulders.

"I'm sorry," said Ellen, though she did not know what it was she was sorry for.

"Nothing to be sorry about. He'd finished," Jane said and picked up a florin from the pillow and tossed it in the air. "He's generous, that Reuben. Twice the usual—always."

"Always?"

"Well. . . ." said Jane and explained no more.

"Let's go and spend this," she said, flourishing the florin between finger and thumb.

"You'll have need of it," said Ellen.

"Easy come, easy go," said her friend and began to dress.

"Why?" asked Ellen, though she knew the answer.

"I have to live," Jane said. "And there are worse ways of earning a living. I pick and choose. I don't take any old sod. Coming?"

She had painted her lips and pinned her hair so that her ringlets framed her round face. With practiced artifice she had colored her once naturally rosy cheeks.

"Will I do?" she said and offered herself for Ellen's approval.

Ellen smiled but there was something in her smile that made Jane look closely at her.

"What is it?" she said.

"Nothing," said Ellen, not yet ready to confess her feelings, even to her friend.

"There's something," said Jane. "A man!" she said. " 'Tis that, there's no doubting." She reached out a hand to touch Ellen's cheek. "I do know the signs," she said. "Too well."

Ellen shook her head as if to deny the suggestion, but Jane smiled, in the certainty of her understanding.

"A man," she said. "Who?"

It was pointless to deny. She had to tell someone about her frailty and it could only be Jane.

"Robert Buchan," she whispered, and then more loudly, "Doctor Buchan."

Jane nodded as if it came as no surprise.

"You love him?"

"Love? What's that? Can you tell me?"

Jane shrugged her shoulders, then laughed, but with little humor.

"Love? I ought to know, I suppose. I've had my share. Panting in the grass, under the trees, groping against a hedge, being bounced in a hotel bedroom, even. What's love? It's the feeling of him, the wanting him, the longing to see him, the knowing he's away, beyond you, maybe thinking of another. It's wanting his child, having his child maybe." She looked sharply at Ellen. "Is that it, my love?"

"No!" Ellen denied. "Not that." It could not be, she thought. She would know, surely, would have known from the moment of conception. "No," she repeated. "Not that."

But she wondered.

Jane was studying herself in the mirror, pursing her lips. She turned from it to Ellen.

" 'Tis not just the thinking of love," she said. "He's taken you. I can see it in your eyes, my lover. There's no reason to be shamed."

Ellen was silent.

"You feel shame?" Jane persisted.

"No," Ellen asserted. "No . . ." Her voice faded. "He's ignored me since. I'm nothing to him."

Jane shrugged her shoulders. "Maybe 'tis so. Forget him. He's a hero now, you know, talked of in the papers. Reuben . . ."

"A hero? Tell me," Ellen interrupted. "Tell me!"

" 'Tis said he spent hours below ground at Uny, after a rock fall helping the rescue. Several were lost, 'tis said, and but for him 'twould have been more. He was took ill when he came to grass. They do say he was near to dying himself."

Ellen stood from the bed. She must go to him. There was no fault to him, none at all. He would have sought her out if he could.

"When was it?"

Jane was not sure. "Some three weeks since, I reckon."

"I'll go to him," said Ellen. "I must." She opened the door to leave but Jane detained her.

"Be certain, my love," she said.

Ellen turned away. I am certain, she said to herself. I am certain.

Ellen turned from Jane, her friend forgotten, her mind conscious only of Robert. She would go to him. She understood now why he had not sought her out. He could not. It was she who must go to him, she who must declare her love, bring him back to health, comfort him.

She stood again on the pavement opposite the house. Where was he? Which was his room? She saw a figure moving in an upper window. It was Mrs. Honeychurch. There was no mistaking her witchlike appearance. She pitied Robert that he should be left to the mercy of that woman.

She strode up to the front door and raised her hand to the knocker. It was wrapped in cloth to soften the sound. She hesitated at that, but determination to be with Robert was strong. She knocked once and again. The muffled sound was enough, for almost before she had taken her hand from the knocker the door opened. A maid stood there, prim in her uniform and her manner.

"Well?" she asked.

"Doctor Buchan," Ellen demanded.

Footsteps approached from within the house.

"Who is it, Mary?"

"A young woman, Ma'am."

"Tell her to go to Dr. Angove. He's taking the doctor's patients." The housekeeper looked over the maid's shoulder and saw Ellen. "Oh, it's you," she said. "I'll deal with this, Mary." She gestured to the maid to leave them.

"Well," she said, standing astride the threshold. "There's nothing for you here."

"I want to see him," Ellen said.

Mrs. Honeychurch laughed, a short, scornful snort. "Who are you to see Doctor Buchan?"

Ellen could not answer. Was she to say, "We are lovers"? "I want to see him," she repeated obstinately.

"A man like him? Why should he want to see the likes of you?" the housekeeper answered and moved to close the door. Ellen thrust her arm forward and held the door open.

"I shall see him," she said.

"You shall not."

They stood confronting each other, neither willing to yield, then Mrs. Honeychurch said, "I'll tell him you're here." Ellen drew back her arm and the door closed. She heard a chain being fastened.

She waited, listening for movement inside the house. She imagined she heard voices, perhaps Robert's voice, but she could not be sure. She stood away from the door and looked up to the window of the room where, she imagined, Robert was lying. She could see nothing.

The door opened a mere inch or two, held by the chain, and Mrs. Honeychurch peered through.

"He won't see you."

"I don't believe you."

"He wants nothing to do with you."

She is lying, Ellen thought; she must be.

"Go away. You'll get nothing here."

I've asked for nothing, Ellen said to herself, for nothing but a word with him, a sight of him.

"It's no use waiting there. He'll not see you." The housekeeper closed the door, and there was nothing Ellen could do. She stood helplessly facing the hostile house, empty of any feeling but puzzlement. Then rage seized her, so that she stepped to the door and raised her fists to beat upon it, but, as quickly as rage had risen, it subsided. She was not defeated, but she was not one to beg. If Robert had no wish to see her, then she could wipe him from her thoughts as easily as he had dismissed her. But it was not he who had dismissed her, it was Mrs. Honeychurch. She still carried within her a belief, or at least a hope, that Robert had not understood her message. He had not meant to reject her.

She took heart in the thought, but doubts lingered and discomfited her.

IV

ROBERT Buchan had often argued that conditions in the mines were injurious to health; the evidence was all around, in the pallid complexions of the miners, the early deaths, the shallow and painful breathing that came from years underground. Buchan argued that though risk was natural to the work it was aggravated by the neglect of men and managers. The mining men he spoke to nodded sagely, agreed and did nothing to change things.

He had expressed special concern over the contrast between the hot clammy conditions of the levels and the cold damp air the miner met when he came to grass. Most of the mines had poor changing facilities, the men coming up to a changing house which was little more than a long unheated shed exposed to wind and rain. Now he was proof himself of the justice of his charges. He had returned from Wheal Uny feverish and exhausted, shivering at the cold. He was barely aware of reaching his house, of the concern of Mrs. Honeychurch and the arrival of one of his colleagues from another part of town, Dr. Angove. He did not recall how he got to his bed but now, as he lay at rest between the cool prim sheets, he knew how ill he was.

Angove was not noted for his professional skills, but Robert, in his weakness, was happy to hand himself over to him. Angove put his condition down to exhaustion. "Needless," he chided. "There's never any point in us going below ground to them. But, don't worry, you'll be as right as rain in a few days.

Good beef and broth. Nothing to worry about. He'll be up in a day or two," he assured Mrs. Honeychurch.

In a few days Robert was worse, so that Mrs. Honeychurch herself, from his high fever, his rapid breathing, the bluish tinge to his cheeks, was sure it was pneumonia. Angove confirmed her fears and prescribed drafts of Dr. James's powder to bring down the fever. He arranged for a woman to come in to help with nursing his colleague and visited him daily until the crisis.

It was Robert's robust constitution rather than the fly blisters, powders, potions and leeches prescribed by Angove, that brought him through. The day after the crisis had passed, when he woke from a long, deep and revitalizing sleep, he seemed unaware of the danger he had been in. He had an unusual feeling of contentment; he was weak, but it was a weakness that was, in a sense, reassuring, for he knew he had a reason, a good reason, for lying reposeful in bed. He was grateful when Mrs. Honeychurch and her helper Mrs. Blight, lifted him to a chair and changed the disturbed sheet of his sickbed. He was glad to return to bed and lie cool and quiet, untroubled by the wild images of his delirium. His mind seemed to have been swept clean by the tempest of his fever, for it was empty of thought, of concern. He was content to allow impression to soak in, to savor the rich colors of the curtaining, the convolutions of the wallpaper design, to follow the elaborate carving on the wardrobe, and lose himself in the reflections within the shiny brass knobs of the bedposts.

He wondered at his taking delight in such simple familiar things. He guessed it was because he had been so near to losing them. For the moment he had no thought of what lay outside his room, of people or things beyond his immediate touch. He lay propped on the heaped pillows and, not wanting even to read, took with uncommon placidity the beef broth and porter jelly fed to him by an anxious Mrs. Honeychurch, and relaxed in unworried acceptance of circumstance.

Mrs. Honeychurch knew this was too good to last. She could not keep the outside world away altogether. Her first surrender was to Captain William Henry Hosking. He had been waiting for news of the young doctor and, as soon as word came that Robert was fit to be visited, he presented himself.

With slow fragile steps Robert had managed to move down-stairs to his drawing room and here, warmed by a blazing coal fire, he lay on the sofa, his thoughts idly drifting, untethered to any fixed point. Even his previous last moments in the draw-ing room, when he had sat at Ellen's feet, were lost to him. The past was distant and the present was mistily unclear.

When Hosking came in it seemed to Robert that, of the two of them, it was he himself who had suffered most from their sojourn underground. Hosking, though his right arm was bound in a tight bandage, looked cheerfully robust. His jacket hung loosely over his shoulders. He touched the dangling right sleeve.

"It will be filled soon. You see I kept it after all, but I'm told it won't be much use to me." He drew up a chair to face Buchan. "I wanted to thank you."

"For what?" said Robert with an effort. "Doing my job?"

" 'Twas more than that. I do remember so clearly those hours every minute it seems, the close heavy blackness of it, the very taste of rock on my tongue, and the smell of it in my nostrils. I've never been buried afore, and I don't want to be buried again. Not before my time anyhow. 'Twas a long time there below, in the dark void." He frowned. "I saw more of myself then than I've done for years back. Strange. But I knew I'd come out of it all right. Do you know why?" He paused and looked inquiringly at Robert, who merely shook his head. "You were the reason. A lifeline. Your voice, so calm, so quiet, so real. The only light in the dark was your voice."

Robert was too listless to protest, but he thought Hosking had overvalued his part.

Hosking looked hard at the doctor.

"Do you remember what we talked about there below?"

"All manner of things, I imagine," Robert answered.

They were interrupted by Mrs. Honeychurch bringing a decanter of Madeira wine, two glasses and some biscuits. She poured a glass of wine for each of them before leaving. Hosking raised his glass and looked at Robert through the amber-brown liquid.

"Yes, all manner of things. I mind them all. I'd time to think then and I've had time since."

"It's not very clear to me," said Robert. "Not yet. I'm still. . . ."

"You'm still mazed," Hosking said, lapsing into Cornish dialect. " 'Tis not to be wondered at. Do you mind what you told me of marrying?"

Robert looked at the mine captain in surprise, at his glowing cheeks reflecting the fire's heat. How indecently healthy he looked in spite of his ordeal and his injury.

"Do you remember?" Hosking prompted.

The effort to recall was too much for Robert. The present was enough for him to support. Hosking passed the glass of wine to him.

"You spoke of marriage—to a Cornish girl, a miner's family, you said."

Robert's hold on the glass tightened and the liquid shook. His mind flooded with memory, recollection overwhelmed him, and he shut his eyes to enclose the thoughts within him. Where was she? Ellen! Where had she been during the last weeks? Why had there been no word from her? Or had there been word, and had Mrs. Honeychurch turned her away?

"Doctor." He heard distantly the deep voice of the mine captain and reluctantly opened his eyes. He had been about to recapture something, some soft, gentle, reassuring tenderness of feeling. He focused unwillingly on the figure in front of him.

The mine captain went on, " 'Tis a narrow world hereabouts, narrow and narrowing. I feel tied myself, watched and worried, gossiped about and picked over. I married a foreigner you see, not just a foreigner from up-country, but from oversea, and a Catholic what's more. My brother Abel's not forgiven me yet."

What is he trying to say? wondered Buchan.

"To get on, you need to marry someone local people can accept and approve." Hosking looked reflectively at Buchan. He went to the fire and stirred the coals. The flames leaped up.

" 'Tis cold out," he said, "and wet and cheerless. You need a woman's warmth here, not just a housekeeper's. Yes. Get wed. That's all you need to make you at home here. I've heard talk. You're well regarded enough, but a good Cornish wife, from a mining family, yes, she'd help you. You're in good standing, your name's well known, and the Uny business will bring credit to you. I'll see to that. They'll be looking for a new Member of Parliament when Reid has sense enough to give in to his ill health." He stood with his back to the fire, swaying as he spoke.

"They'll not need to look further than you. You're well thought of by the mine lords. Langarth sings your praises. All you need now is a Cornish wife to set you to rights."

Robert became inattentive again, his mind drifting. The warmth of the fire, the wine and the companionship of Hosking were soothing. His thoughts spread lazily about him. His hands felt the plush velvet of the sofa and the touch recalled Ellen to him. A coal fell in the grate, a flame spurted, and he saw with astonishing clarity the features of Ellen before him, the dark sweep of her hair, and felt the touch of her work-roughened hands. He caught his breath at the vividness of the recollection. He wanted her beside him, to comfort him, to be comforted, to be cherished.

"What?" he said, conscious that Hosking had spoken.

"I'm sorry. I'm tiring you."

Robert was hardly aware when Hosking left. He was alone now with his sudden sharp memory of Ellen. He turned to the door at a sound, half-expecting to see her, as she had been, clad in that ridiculous black garment of his housekeeper. But it was Mrs. Honeychurch herself who stood there.

"You'll be off to bed now," she commanded. His illness had given her an authority she was reluctant to relinquish.

"I'm going out," he said. She looked at him in astonishment. "Have the trap brought around. I'll be dressed by then."

"I'll do no such thing," she answered.

He stood up and pretended a strength he did not feel.

"I'm going out." Mrs. Honeychurch looked as if she would bar his way but he said firmly, "Have the trap brought around in ten minutes. I'll be ready."

"You'll wrap up warmly," she said and watched solicitously as he found his way to the stairs.

He was not fit to drive to Sunny Corner, he knew, but he could not deny the impulse. During his fever he had remembered nothing clearly and, with his convalescence, he had been too indolent to think of anything but the pleasure of recuperation. That idle, meaningless content had gone, shattered by the thought of Ellen. He dressed carelessly and rapidly and before going downstairs went into the guest bedroom as if she might still be there—or some impression of her. But there was nothing. She was not here. She was at Sunny Corner and it was there he would go to find her. He had things to say.

Mrs. Honeychurch watched him anxiously as he climbed into the trap and took the reins.

"You don't belong to do this," she admonished. " 'Tis a cold wind."

He was surprised. He felt no chill and was indeed indifferent to the weather.

"Where are you going?" asked the housekeeper, but he did not answer, snapped the reins and stirred the pony to life.

V

ELLEN was concerned at having left her grandmother for so long. She had been wrong to leave her and foolish to confide in Jane, she thought. She had got precious little comfort from that. And she had got none from her visit to Robert's. Her love for Robert was meaningless to him and so to her.

And yet? Was his housekeeper to be trusted? Perhaps she had not spoken to him about her visit? Ellen could not believe any woman could be guilty of such deceit. And yet how could she believe that Robert had no wish to see her? That was even harder to accept. She hastened out of the town and turned off the road to cross the moors by the tracks which led from working to working, past the mine called Wheal Bloody Nose.

She hurried, guilt at leaving her grandmother making her break into a run. She should not have left her. The old lady's mind had wandered more and more to the past in recent weeks. She would ask if there was any news of Matthew, her dead husband, and she talked to Ellen as if she were someone else —a sister maybe. She wondered what would happen to them when Granny died. The cottage was held on a three-lives lease, and Granny Pascoe was the sole survivor of the names listed. The house would revert to the landowner and they would be homeless. Where then could she go?

She knew what Julia's fate would be, her sister had already declared it: she was going to live with Mark, to look after him and his father. Julia would not need for a home. But what of her? She paused for breath and realized she had come to the point where, once before, she had stood with Jane to look over the village of Carharrack, and had seen the miners marching, her father at their head. She recalled the pride she had felt at the sight.

There was a group of people at the edge of the village, too distant to be identified. Someone seemed to be injured or sick, for she saw two men lifting a figure down from the seat of a trap and carrying it into a nearby house. She was unconcerned, for anxiety for her grandmother blinded her to others' troubles. It had nothing to do with her in any case. She hurried along, skirting the village and made her way across Cusgarne Downs to home.

In the cottage there was no movement. Ellen prepared some warm milk with bread and took it upstairs to her grandmother.

"Here you are, Granny," she said and stooped to wake the old lady.

Alice Pascoe opened her eyes. "What ails thee?" she said.

"Nothing," said Ellen.

"I can see. I'm not blind. You're troubled. Troubled. . . ." Her voice faded but her shrewd eyes focused on Ellen for a moment and then drifted toward the window.

Ellen crept from the room and, as soon as Julia returned from work, went to see Richard. Here was friendship and true love, she thought. Between them, the old miner and herself the bal maiden, was an understanding that no other relationship could rival. They had grown closer over the years as she had read to him, had argued at times, had resolved their differences, and had now reached a sympathy with each other that needed no words to declare itself.

She went and sat on the floor beside his chair, her hand resting on his knee. She looked up at him and studied the scarred cheeks, the grizzled hair, the firm mouth. In him was a quality her father had had, a pride that went with his craft, a craft that had come from his forefathers. He was a miner still, even though his blindness cut him off from the drives, the levels and the stopes.

Her thoughts turned briefly to James, but she could not let them stay long with him. He was lost to her. She had made sure of that by her surrender to Robert. Even if he thought of her still it was a different Ellen he knew. She was no longer the young innocent girl he had charmed with his swift smile, his flashing eye; she was a woman, with the knowledge of a man within her.

And as the weeks passed—still with no word from Robert—she realized that there was within her not just the recollection of their lovemaking. She was pregnant. She had become certain of it. It showed itself not merely in the queasiness of the early day, but in her vulnerability to emotion, the ease with which she was moved to tears.

Now when she read to Richard—*Nicholas Nickleby* again in the absence of papers from Robert—it was she who wept, so that she could not continue to read, and Richard, moved to tears also, urged, "No, no, my lover, 'tis not real, 'tis imagined," as if it was the tragedy of Smike that moved her and not the sorrow of her own situation.

She returned one evening from Richard's, fraught with emotion, to find Julia and Mark lying together, naked it seemed, beneath the blankets on the bed which she and Julia shared. She turned hurriedly away and went upstairs.

Her grandmother was lying as she had been when Ellen had left her earlier, but her bed cover had slipped aside.

"Granny," Ellen said softly, not wishing to wake her too suddenly.

She reached out a hand to straighten the bed quilt, but withdrew it sharply. Then, slowly, gently, she touched the old lady's hand where it lay as if she herself had reached to draw the quilt up.

"Granny," said Ellen again, but she knew her granny was no longer there. This was no longer the fiery indomitable Alice Pascoe; she had fled and only a shell remained.

Ellen lifted her eyes from the bed to the text on the wall. "He bringeth low and lifteth up." She went to the window to look out upon the valley, to where the ash tree, now fresh and green with life, stretched its sheltering arms. She stood there for minutes and when within her she heard her grandmother's whispered "He was tall, and tender, and strong," the tears came at last, tears for Alice Pascoe, tears for herself, and tears for the child she carried within her.

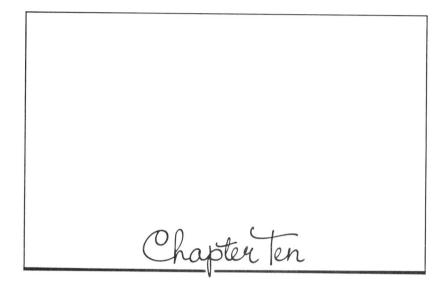

Chapter Ten

I

ROBERT had been brought home from Carharrack and his attempted drive to Sunny Corner in a state of collapse. He was unable to explain what he had been doing there, for he was no longer sure himself. He had driven in a haze, pursuing a shape which, phantomlike, evaded grasp. The name of the vision eluded him and as he lay in uneasy delirium for several days he was haunted by a feeling of desperate disappointment.

Gradually he returned to sense, the images cleared and memory recalled Ellen to him. Now, however, it was an Ellen distanced somehow by his weeks of illness. She had not come to him. She had not even called to inquire. He had asked Mrs. Honeychurch and she had listed all those who had called with good wishes: many patients, the Hoskings and other acquaintances and a messenger from the Langarths, but no Ellen Bray.

He took warning from his collapse at Carharrack to allow himself longer to recover. His practice was being shared by Angove and another doctor, Trethewey; knowing them he was confident his patients would welcome his return, but he felt no compulsion to hurry about it.

He had newspapers brought to him and read avidly the small items of local news in the *West Briton*, but there was never any mention of her. There hardly would be. What would an unemployed bal maiden do that could be worthy of comment?

I am mad, he told himself. She has no interest in me, why should I have any concern for her? He thought of sending a message to her by one of his servants, but pride forbade him.

She was brought vividly to his mind on the occasion when a deputation of Liberals, led by Abel Hosking, came to call. He was still not wholly fit and when he rose to meet them Hosking bade him be seated.

" 'Tis better to take care," Hosking said. "We want a fit man, a sensible one."

"A brave one," said another.

"A man of principle," said a third.

"A man of good standing," said a fourth.

"Who deserves our good opinion," said Hosking.

Buchan looked in surprise at his visitors.

"Mr. Langarth has empowered me to express his approval of your candidature," said one of the men, whom Buchan recognized as Tredinnick, a lawyer and Langarth's agent.

"Not that that's needful," said Hosking.

"But desirable," said someone.

"I don't follow," said Buchan.

"Reid is dying, poor fellow," said Hosking, lowering his voice lugubriously. "Our Member of Parliament. Can't hold out much longer." He hesitated, closed his eyes and put his fingertips together as if sending up a silent prayer. "We're looking for a man who understands our interests but is not too closely allied to the mines, someone who is popular with the new voters, can command their support, someone with the right instincts. We think you're the man. No," he added as Robert opened his mouth to protest, "we know you're not Cornish, but we're not so narrow that we can't see good in a foreigner like yourself. You've shown yourself one of us. The men in the mines admire you and that's important now. Your behavior in going down Uny and saving that young brother of mine has been noted. You saw the *West Briton* after the accident?"

Buchan shook his head.

"You became a hero. We'll trade on that." He looked at

his companions and they nodded in agreement. "You accept? You'll allow us to put your name forward?"

"The Langarths will be very disappointed if you refuse," said Tredinnick.

"No need to answer now," Hosking said. "But give it thought—and don't be too long about it." He gestured to the others and after each had shaken Buchan by the hand they left. Hosking remained, standing solid and portentous, with his back to the fire.

"You're not a Methodist?" he said, regretfully.

"Brought up a Presbyterian," Robert answered.

Hosking brightened. "Next best thing. Now, to other matters. You need a wife. Young William Henry told me your plans. To marry a Cornish girl. 'Tis a good idea. And of mining stock, he said, which is better still. Has she accepted you? There's no time to lose. Get it out of the way before the election."

Robert did not know what to answer.

"You have asked her?" Hosking said doubtfully.

"Not yet."

"Get on with it, then. Who is she? Perhaps I can have a word—with the family, that is. Make sure there's no opposition there. Who is she? What's her name?"

"Ellen. Ellen Bray," Robert slowly answered, reluctant to parade his love for approval.

"Bray. Cornish name. That's good. I don't know her. What are her parents?"

"Dead, I believe."

"Ah. No opposition there, then." Hosking seemed satisfied. "She's got money of her own, no doubt."

Suddenly Robert laughed, an impulse he could not control.

"Not a penny!" he said.

Hosking was silent.

"She's a bal maiden."

"What!"

"A bal maiden. Or was. She's out of work."

"What did you say she's called?"

"Ellen Bray."

"Bray. I've heard the name. Ellen Bray. My God!" He leaned toward Buchan. "You're not serious?"

"I am, but I don't know if she . . ."

Hosking did not let him finish. "You're not intending to marry her—a bal maiden! It won't do. It won't do at all. Take her to bed by all means provided you're discreet about it, but marry her! That's insane. I don't think you'd find us willing to overlook a marriage of that kind. And besides, you need a woman of substance, and one who won't disgrace you in company, one fit to take her place in society, one you wouldn't be ashamed to introduce to your friends. No, Robert—I may call you Robert?—I'm old enough to be your father and to advise you. I've seen the world. I *am* the world hereabouts and I tell you a marriage of this sort would ruin you, end any idea of your becoming an MP, even end your practice too. A bal maiden! I can't believe it. And a known unionist and trouble-maker." He turned from the fire and began to pace up and down. Robert was silent. He did not know what to say. He was not robust enough yet to argue with Hosking.

"Robert. Here's my advice. Set her up quietly somewhere. Not locally. Plymouth or St. Ives—or London itself. That's it, London. Your wife here need never know, nor anyone else hereabouts. You'll need money, of course, a wife who's complaisant and well endowed." He stopped and turned. "I know the very one." He waited for Robert to react but when no reply came he went on. "Leave it with me. I've a young niece, a Hosking, a silly girl but nice enough and there's a tidy sum to be settled on her. Leave it with me."

Robert wanted to protest, but he was anxious for Hosking to go. He was tired; his mind was buffeted by Hosking's blustering and he had hardly followed his last remarks.

"Well?" said Hosking, smiling with relief at the solution he had elaborated. "That's a happy outcome."

He reached down and shook Robert's hand as if a compact had been sealed.

"We need men like you at Westminster," he said as he left. "I'm glad we see eye to eye."

II

ELLEN was unprepared for the distress her grandmother's death brought. She had grown to admire the old lady but had not realized how much she loved her. She hid her tears from Julia and tried to keep her grief to herself; but Richard knew. She did not know how, but he knew. He could not see the sadness in her eyes, but he heard in her voice an emotion she could not conceal. She wondered how much else of her he read. She dreaded his discovery of her pregnancy, for she could not risk forfeiting his respect.

She accused herself of shamelessness. But it had not been like that; she had felt no shame in taking Robert to her, only a deep desire to hold him, a longing to caress him, to be caressed and held by him. The longing was still there, a bodily urge that she could not deny. And more, her heart leaped at the very thought of him. Pride—resentment at the humiliation she had suffered at the hands of his servant—told her to forget him, but it was no use. She could not forget him, now or ever, for she had within her a reminder of her love for him, her surrender.

She decided she would go to him. She would not tell him of her state, not until she had seen him and known his love for her. She would outface the woman Mrs. Honeychurch, ignore her, demand to see Robert. It was her right.

She prepared herself carefully for the meeting, brushing her hair, her chief glory, until it shone. She peered into the speckled looking glass until she was satisfied. She remembered the mirrors in Robert's home and recalled with a sharp and precise vision the view of herself, naked, as she had moved to douse the light. And with that recollection came a flood of memories, details from the evening, the warmth of the fire, the rich softness of the carpet beneath her feet, the gentle searching touch of Robert's fingers and the hard maleness of him. He would see her, acknowledge her, his love for her was real, she was certain of it. She set off, her spirits uplifted, confident in her lover.

Resolution faltered as she drew near his house. Why had he not sought her out? Surely he should be taking the initiative. She asked herself why she should be humbling herself to come here. But pride weakened before her love and her need to see him. She went up the steps and knocked at the door, hesitantly and then with more firmness. She stood holding her head high as she heard steps coming to the door.

"The doctor's still not seeing any patients," said the maid who came to the door. She seemed to recognize Ellen and be wary of her.

"I'm not a patient, I'm a friend," Ellen asserted.

The maid looked her up and down and took no pains to hide her incredulity.

"He's not seeing anyone. He's got someone with him anyway."

"I'll wait," said Ellen and, before the maid could prevent her, she had stepped across the threshold.

She could hear voices in the drawing room. One voice was brusque, authoritative, a voice she knew and hated, the voice of Brimstone Hosking; the other was quiet, softly breathed, a voice which stirred her heart. It was that voice, the voice of Robert, which somehow frightened her. How could she bear it if he were to deny her? She had been foolish to come. She was conscious of the solid comfort here and thought of the bare rooms in her Granny's cottage. Her world and that of Robert had no meeting. She did not belong here. She could not wait.

She turned to go, but the door into the drawing room opened and she saw Abel Hosking stretch out a hand to someone inside the room.

"We need men like you at Westminster," he said. "I'm glad we see eye to eye."

He passed Ellen without a glance and the maid, still hovering uncertainly, opened the door for him.

Ellen's mood changed again. I'm here, she thought, and here I'll stay till I've seen him. The door into the drawing room was open and she could hear movement inside. She walked toward it, but the maid caught hold of her.

"You can't go in there," she said indignantly. "You'd better go or I'll call Mrs. Honeychurch."

Ellen looked at the girl. "Call her then," she said defiantly.

"Who's there?" came Robert's voice, mildly curious.

"A young woman," called the maid. "I'll see to her," and Ellen felt the maid's hand again on her arm. She shrugged it off and stepped toward the door. "No!" said the girl in horror at Ellen's temerity. Ellen stopped at the door, for Robert appeared, drawn forth by the noise. He stared at her, as if unable to believe she was there. She could not read the expression in his eyes, for his face was in shadow. She wanted to see there the love that she was sure was in hers, but there was nothing, nothing she could be certain of.

"That's all right, Mary," he said, dismissing the maid. "I'll see to Miss Bray." He stepped aside and gestured to Ellen to go into the drawing room.

She turned to face him as he closed the door behind her. She could still not interpret the look in his eyes. She wanted to draw close to him, to reach out a hand to touch him. He looked pale, and she wanted to chide him for self-neglect, she wanted to tease him, say childlike things to him, murmur confidences, share secrets with him, *the* secret. But he stood there, surveying her, studying her, appraising her.

"What is it?" she said and was aware her voice carried doubt.

He smiled and her heart lurched at the sight. She made a move to him, a small move, a hint of a move merely, but it was enough. He came to her and put his hands to her face to hold her there as if he wanted to convince himself of the reality of her presence. Their eyes held each other and she saw a tenderness in his that comforted her and drew her to him. She reached up to kiss him but, at that moment, a knock came at the door, and Robert hurriedly stepped away from her.

"Yes?" he said impatiently.

The door opened and in came the black-gowned Mrs. Honeychurch. She looked from the doctor to Ellen.

"I'll see to the young woman, doctor. We'll find her some work to do in the kitchen. She looks strong enough for that." Her mouth contorted in the pretense of a smile. "Come along, miss."

There was a moment's silence before Robert spoke. "No," he said awkwardly. "There's no need, Mrs. Honeychurch. I'll see to Miss Bray. I know what she's come for."

Do you? Ellen wanted to say, but she kept silent. The sense of humiliation returned to her. What was it about this woman? Why could Robert not declare his love there and then? Why could he not take her by the hand and say to his housekeeper, "This is my wife-to-be"?

Ellen had no sooner framed the question in her mind than

she realized how foolish she was to think in such terms. Who was she that she could hope to become the wife of a doctor? She turned to the mirror and saw herself, a working girl, a bal maiden, built for labor at the bench, not for the niceties of polite society.

She had been wrong to come here. She had demeaned herself in doing so.

She heard Mrs. Honeychurch leave the room and the door close. She turned to Robert, intending to say good-bye, but she could not. He was standing with his back to the door, as if he had divined her intention to leave and was determined to prevent her. He was smiling, as if there was something in Mrs. Honeychurch's intervention that had amused him. He came toward her and held out his hands to her. She took them in hers and her wish to leave vanished at his touch. He drew her to the sofa and sat beside her, not at her feet as he had that other time. She wanted to reach out a hand, as she had then, and stroke his hair, but she controlled her impulse and, uneasily aware of the presence nearby of Robert's servants, sat stiffly, unmoving.

Silence lay between them as if they had either nothing to say to each other or too much. How could she speak of her secret? I have your child within me, she wanted to say, and I do not know how to tell you. She gazed at him, hoping some remark of his might unloose her emotions, make speech easy for her, but he was not looking at her. He was staring thoughtfully into the fire.

"You saw who was with me?" he inquired, without turning to her.

"Brimstone Hosking," she answered, unable to keep the loathing from her voice.

He seemed unaware of her feelings. "He came to me to talk about my selection as candidate. I'm likely to be the next Member of Parliament for the Mining Division." At last he turned to look at her and she saw the proud light in his eyes, the pleasure at the esteem he enjoyed. He seemed to be waiting for her to acknowledge his self-importance in some way. She could not respond as he seemed to wish. The prize he spoke of was remote, beyond her understanding. She knew what an MP was, but how did it match with Robert, the bal surgeon, this man, this lover of hers?

He kept his eyes on her.

"Well?" he said.

"You're pleased?"

He raised his eyebrows at the question. "Can you doubt it? I can do so much. And there's so much to be done." He paused and turned to look into the fire again, as if dreams were easier to see there. "So much to be done," he repeated. "So many injustices to be righted. So much to be fought for."

She looked at him as he sat gazing into the flames. The firelight turned the paleness of his hair to gold.

"I . . ." she began.

"What?" he said, but there was no real interest in what she had to say. He glanced at her and for a moment she thought he was about to speak—of her and her place in his life, but if the impulse was there he suppressed it.

"It will bring changes," he said.

"Of course." She hoped the disappointment she felt did not show in her voice.

He glanced at her again, with a speculative look in his eyes. She waited.

"I shall have to live in London," he said. "I shall miss my friends here. An MP is not paid, of course, and if I give up my practice here I shall have to find other sources of income, some way of supporting myself."

What is this to me? she thought. I want only to hear one thing, and you talk of money, of income. Her impatience burst out. She stood to look down on him.

"That's not what I want to hear," she said.

He looked at her in surprise.

"Have you nothing to say to me?" she demanded.

His eyes opened wider.

"I came here, expecting, hoping—" She stopped. What had she hoped? That he would declare his love for her? She had not expected this talk of parliament, of London, of money. Why had she come? Not to plead. Her pride would not allow that. It was her pride, anger at her abasement, that made her speak now.

He opened his mouth to speak but she was quicker.

"You left me . . . that night . . . alone, to face your servants, your Mrs. Honeychurch. You did not think to ask of me, to leave me a token, a message, a word?"

He tried to interrupt but she would not be stopped.

"You brought me here, took me to your bed and . . . abandoned me. What am I to you? A strumpet? A cheap whore, a trollop from the streets?" She could go no further. She could hear Mrs. Honeychurch's voice clearly in her mind. She wanted to ask how many others he had brought home before her.

He stared open-mouthed at her, voiceless, astonished—or guilt-struck, she thought—at her outburst. Then, "I . . . you did not . . ." he began, but as he spoke a knock came at the door and Mrs. Honeychurch entered.

"Miss Veronica Langarth, sir," she announced and stepped aside to admit the suave, elegantly dressed daughter of the mine lord.

Ellen looked at the young woman. She had seen her before, with Robert, when he had come to Jane. She was a woman from another world, Robert's world maybe.

Ellen turned her back on Robert and strode to the door. "Miss Bray," he said.

"Yes, Dr. Buchan," she said coolly and turned to face him.

He shrugged his shoulders. He looked pale, tired, defeated, and for a moment she had the urge to go to him and comfort him but Mrs. Honeychurch, a smile on her thin lips, held the door open for her, and Ellen marched past her into the hall and to the front door. She heard Robert say "Miss Bray" again. She ignored it. The "Miss Bray" angered her and, in a way, humiliated her as much as the housekeeper's treatment of her.

He has denied me, she said to herself, as she swept down the steps. He has denied me; now I know him for what he is.

III

ROBERT Buchan stared at the door. It had closed upon Ellen and he did not know how that had happened. Physical weakness seized him and he had to lean against the wall until his strength returned. He had not realized the toll his sickness had taken of him. He had been buoyed up by the visit of the selection committee and their obvious approval of him, but now this seemed worthless. He was confused.

Set her up in London, Hosking had advised. He had meant to speak to Ellen about it, tell her his future had a place for her, but it seemed she was in no mood to listen and he was glad now he had not mentioned it.

"Robert." Veronica's voice was concerned. "Come and sit down. You have been doing too much." He felt her hand on his arm and allowed himself to be led back into the drawing room. "You shouldn't be seeing patients."

"She's not a patient."

"I recognized her. The bal maiden."

He nodded. He had energy for little more. He wondered why Veronica had called and wished she would leave so that he could sort out the perplexities that threaded in and out of his mind.

"Mama is getting her way," said Veronica. "Father has persuaded the Liberal committee to support you."

"I had a visit," he said, and his spirits revived a little.

"You must concentrate on getting fit. Make yourself known —even more than you are. Speak out on issues that concern us." She had the courtly air of a patroness. "Have you thought what issues are of most concern to you?"

He did not answer. Issues? What were they? The hunger that he saw in the homes of Redruth, the despair of the mother, the hopelessness of the man in the house, the indifference of the well-to-do? Were these issues? Was it on account of these that Hosking and his friends wanted him as their represent-ative? Was this why Rebecca Langarth had marked him out for preferment? This the reason Veronica was here?

"Well?" she said.

"I have thought," he answered.

"Women's rights," she said. "Do they enter into it? Votes for women. Mr. Mill's campaign failed last time around, but another chance will come. It *must* come sooner or later. I've been in touch with friends in Bristol. They've started a society for women's suffrage there."

His mind was wandering. What had he said or done to anger Ellen? He had hoped for her sympathy and under-standing, but she had turned from him.

"Are you listening?" Veronica said. "Have I been talking to myself?"

Slowly his mind cleared. "Women's suffrage," he said. "Yes, I heard."

"A cause worth fighting for."

"Among others."

"Women, asking for justice. Do you not support us?"

"Of course," he answered, but it was not a cause which stirred him in the way that he was moved by the poverty in the streets of Redruth.

"We can work together for it, Robert." Her eyes blazed with conviction, her heavy brows frowned in concentration and for a moment, he thought she looked almost beautiful in the intensity and commitment of her expression.

"Together?" he said.

"You and I. Shall we agree? I'll work for your selection and you'll speak for the cause. A voice like yours, once you're a member of Parliament, would carry weight." She put out a hand to his shoulder. He was sitting on the sofa, physically tired but once again mentally alert, wakened by ambition, by the thought that with the support of the Langarths—and especially of their daughter Veronica—he was destined for political fortune. "What did Hosking have to say?"

What had he said? Something about setting Ellen up as his mistress in London. He hesitated then smiled and said, "We talked of a marriage into a local family."

"Oh."

"I have no money of my own," he explained.

"And Hosking's solution?"

"A niece of his. It's a wealthy family."

"You can do better than that." She tapped him on the shoulder, playfully. "Have you thought? Don't look so surprised, Robert. I'm not my mother's daughter for nothing. Think of it. Now I must go. I've agreed to hold meetings in Truro and Camborne to explain the issues of women's rights. When you're fit you can speak for us." She bent down and lightly touched his forehead with her lips. "Mrs. Honeychurch," he heard her call and was aware that he was alone.

I am dreaming, he thought. I am delirious still. In fact he felt hot and weak and strangely excited.

Mrs. Honeychurch came to him. "Miss Langarth gave me instructions to take great care of you." She was beaming with good will, basking in the honor of a word from one of the great family.

IV

ELLEN turned away from Robert's house, indignation seething within her, but fearful of the effect this might have upon her unborn child she controlled it. She walked on rapidly to the bottom of the town and realizing she was not far from Jane's home, decided to visit her friend. There she would find warmth and affection, even love.

The door to the linny was open and Jane was standing on the threshold, as if waiting for someone. Behind her two bundles of clothes were stacked.

"I'm leaving," she announced cheerfully.

Ellen felt a tremor of fear, but Jane was quick to reassure her.

"I'm going to Reuben, to Stithians. To live on the farm." Her eyes showed uncertainty.

Ellen took her friend's arm. "You'll make a good farmer's wife," she said.

"I wonder," said Jane.

"He's a good man," said Ellen.

"I know he is," said Jane. "It's me I'm not sure of."

Is there a solution like that for me? Ellen wondered, but could see none.

"You'll be welcome," said Jane. "I can say that, because Reuben's said it himself. He's a big man, in all sorts of ways." She sniggered. "Big in heart too. You need have no fear. Your granny's cottage?" She left the question unfinished.

"We've three weeks before the lease is up."

"You'll be welcome." Jane took her friend's hand. "You'll need help. Come to me when you do."

"I must find work. Julia cannot keep me."

She walked slowly back to Cusgarne, past mine workings and dressing sheds. Perhaps work was to be had there, perhaps she could give a false name. But her face was too well known; word had spread: she was a troublemaker and no one in the mines would employ her. She began to realize the desperation of her position: she would be without a roof when the lease on her granny's cottage expired; she had a child within her and no man to support her. Her sister Julia would be all right— she would live with Mark and Richard, and they would survive.

She passed Wheal Jenny, its entrance barred now against intruders, its shafts and drives closed, its engines sold, the engine houses gaunt and empty. She paused for a moment, remembering the father and brother who had lost their lives there, and sorrow for them and pity for herself made her weep as she stood.

She realized she was not alone. A man leading a horse had paused too.

"A grievous sight," he commented. She turned aside to hide her tears. "And cause for private grief?" he added.

She wanted no comfort from a minister, but his voice was kindly and she could not offend. She turned to him.

"A father and a brother," she said.

He looked closely at her as if he recognized her. She knew him. He was the Methodist minister Abraham Luke, who had once brought news of James to Richard. She thought to question him but he anticipated her.

"Miss Bray?"

She nodded.

"I have a message for you. The young man, Bryant, in Bodmin Jail."

"I believed he'd forgotten me. I'd heard nothing."

"I'm sorry not to have seen you before. Some time since he asked me to seek you out and bring you comfort."

"And can you?"

"He's surviving. He sometimes weakens. He'll be a changed man. But within those walls even to survive is something." He sadly shook his head as if seeing before him the darkness of a cell. "He's a young man of courage—physical courage, of course, he's a miner. But courage of the spirit, that's a harder thing to hold to."

"His leg?" In her mind she saw James hobbling toward his captors.

"He walks awkwardly. But that's of small account." He looked at Ellen. "He would welcome a word from you, I know. I could take a message."

"Tell him . . ." What am I going to say? she thought, and hesitated.

The minister watched her. "A cell's a dark and lonely place. Outside has no reality save when a word from a loved one comes to bring hope."

"I can write," she said at last. "I'll write him a letter."

A lone magpie tumbled about the derelict engine house and Ellen remembered her mother repeating the nursery legend. "One for sorrow, two for mirth, three for a wedding, four for a birth."

One for sorrow. She nodded to the minister and turned for home.

She tried to write that evening, but her thoughts were too much in turmoil from the encounter with Robert. She went to see Richard and, in response to his urging, read to him, from a broadsheet folded among the books. Her voice, soft at the outset, rose with passion as she went on. The words suited her mood.

We're low, we're low, we're very very low,
As low as low can be;
The rich are high, for we make them so,
And a miserable lot are we!
And a miserable lot are we! Are we!
And a miserable lot are we!

Down, down we go—we're so very very low—
To the hell of deep sunk mines.
But we gather the proudest gems that glow
When the crown of a despot shines;
And whenever he lacks, upon our backs,
Fresh loads he deigns to lay.
We're far too low to vote the tax,
But we're not too low to pay.

Richard, familiar with the words, repeated the chorus and, at the end, said, "There's more meaning in your voice than in the verse. What ails you, my love? Thoughts of James?"

She wished she could tell him. It would take so little to

make her unburden herself, but as she looked across the fire-light and studied his scarred forehead and pitted cheeks, she rejected the thought. She could not bear to hurt him by con-fession.

"Reverend Luke brought news of him."

"I know," she said. "He spoke to me."

" 'Tis that oppresses you?" When she did not answer he went on. "Don't you fret yourself about where to live. There's room for you and Julia both."

"I must find work—somewhere where my face isn't known. Truro. That's the answer. 'Tis a lively place, I'm told."

"There are no mines thereabouts now," said Richard.

"There must be need for girls—in the smelting works." She became hopeful as the idea of going to Truro took hold of her. It was far enough away for her not to be recognized. Perhaps she could, if she found work, settle there, have her baby there, make a new life there.

"Truro," she announced firmly. "I'll try there."

She inquired in the village and discovered that Penrose, the carpenter and coffin maker in the village, was taking his wagon to Truro the following week to collect timber. She begged a lift from him and he agreed to take her to the town.

Work was not to be had. She did not think her notoriety had preceded her, for the overseer at the Carvedras smelting works seemed sympathetic, but shook his head sadly. She re-turned to the quayside and sat for a while watching the boats loading and unloading. Then she strolled along to the bridge at the foot of Lemon Street. It was market day and the town was busy with farmers and their wives from the surrounding countryside. She felt at ease in the crowds and mingled with them, gazing like them into the shop windows, admiring the stylish goods. Outside the Royal Hotel her attention was at-tracted to a notice advertising a meeting to be held there "This Day, Wednesday, at 3:30, to discuss the Issue of Women's Suf-frage."

Ellen saw a number of soberly-dressed women standing together inside the entrance and, yielding to impulse, she walked up the steps toward them. A hotel porter eyed her suspiciously but shrugged his shoulders as, with set determination, she marched into the hotel. The women turned toward her and one came forward, eyes alight with interest. Ellen saw she was

Veronica Langarth, Robert's friend, and suddenly regretted her temerity.

"Miss Bray, isn't it?" the woman said.

Ellen nodded, surprised at being recognized.

"I'm so glad you've come. I'm afraid there aren't many of us yet." She took Ellen by the hand. "In the room along there. You'll find one or two others."

Ellen went into the room, where half a dozen women sat, separately, self-conscious, ill at ease. Ellen felt their eyes following her as she went to the rear of the room. She was painfully conscious of her worn clothes. These others were not working women, though one had the red cheeks and country manners that suggested she might be a farmer's wife. She gave Ellen a friendly nod and was about to say something when the women who had been waiting in the hall of the hotel were led into the room by Veronica Langarth.

Ellen was intensely moved by the meeting. It was not that the speaker—from Bristol—was passionate in her statement; she argued coolly, seeking to convince by reason rather than emotion. But it was the first time that Ellen had heard the case for women's rights and it seemed so to match her own inner thoughts that she felt a slow access of strength, a feeling of rightness about her, and, to her astonishment, a feeling of power. Women together could work miracles; she was convinced of that. How could anyone deny them their rights when the case was so clear? How could the injustice of their treatment survive against such a barrage of good sense? She did not know if the others were as stirred as she, but at the end they applauded as heartily.

"Now," said Veronica, "there aren't many of us, but there's enough to begin. We want a small committee here in Truro and I expect you'll all want to help, so let me have your names and addresses and we'll start from here. The Truro Committee for Women's Suffrage." She smiled at the women, assuming their agreement. "And Miss Bray," she said. "I shall need your help in Redruth. I think that's where you rightly belong?"

Ellen nodded. She could not speak, fearing if she did that she would sob with the force of emotion that filled her.

Veronica Langarth smiled. She was used to her words being greeted by awed submission. "Wait until I've finished with these Truro ladies and then we'll talk about Redruth."

Ellen waited. Penrose would have left by now. He had said he would be ready to return at four. It must be well past that. She did not care. In her present mood of exaltation she could walk to Penzance and back if it served the women's cause.

"Right, Miss Bray," Veronica said. "I'll expect to see you in Redruth tomorrow. Tabb's Hotel. Three-thirty. Bring any other women who might help. I'll see you then." She turned away and Ellen, bemused at the shift of events, sat for a moment before leaving the hotel.

There was no sign of Penrose at Lemon Quay so, without hesitation, Ellen set off to walk the seven miles home with the echoes of the speech ringing in her mind, raising new thoughts, giving her new courage. Perhaps life was not so desperate an affair after all. Where women could gather together hope sprang. Her step lightened and, in spite of the growing burden of the child within her, she strode confidently on.

V

THAT night she remembered her promise to Abraham Luke that she would write to James. Now she felt she had something to tell him, something of encouragement. She did not pause to think that he, as a man, might find her feelings difficult to grasp; she only knew she had to tell someone, and who better than James? She took pen and ink, hesitating over how to begin. She could not reveal all the truth about herself. Nevertheless, when she began to write words came easily, as if they had been building up inside her, waiting for release.

"My James," she wrote and tried to make the world outside his cell real for him.

> Sunny Corner is still as pretty as ever and the valley below. Autumn is here, with the bryony berries and even some blackberries still along the lane. I saw the badger the other day, the old boar, and was reminded by his grizzled look of the man who preached at Sunny Corner Chapel that day I went with you. Do you remember? It is all waiting for you—the hedgerows and the gorse and the heather. . . .

She stopped there and thought, But I shall not be waiting. I shall have gone—somewhere—I don't know where. I shall have gone. But she did not write it.

> Julia and Mark are in love. He is a good-looking boy and reminds me of you. Your father is well and goes about the countryside almost as easily as any of us. He walks down to the village and up to Pulla Cross and everyone stops to talk to him along the way. And in the evening I read to him and we talk endlessly about the world and the way of things.
> He has meant so much to me. Through him I have found out so much about myself. . . .

It was true. It was not only the meeting in Truro which had revealed her beliefs to her: they had been nurtured by Richard and her father before him, ideas of justice, the need to fight for one's rights. It was becoming clearer to her as she wrote. She had not consciously thought it all out before, but it was true; she knew now what she believed in and what she had to do.

> He has told me of their old struggles—him and my father—to get justice for the men, to change conditions for the miners so that they could get a fair living. And I know they were right, right to persuade the men to band together to protect each other. It seems a hard job here among the tributers, but up-country it is happening. William has written from Lancashire to say the colliers there are feeling their strength.
> So my father and Richard have shown me the way. But there is something else I feel.

Here she hesitated, for what she had to say now seemed very personal to her. He might not understand, but she had to say it.

> There is more. I am a woman and I feel as a woman, but as a woman I am despised. When I lost my job trying to stand up for the rights of the bal maidens, nobody thought much of what I did. I was forgotten the week afterward. If I'd been a man there

would have been other men surely to back me up. But because I was "only" a woman it did not matter that I was blacklisted.

I have rights as a woman to be heard. I don't know how, but I have as much right as any of God's creatures. I think of my grandmother—she is dead now and got little out of life except, at the end, my love. All her life, I think, she lived for others and that, it seems, is the lot of women. Well, if this is so—that I have to live for others—let it be for others like me, women who are treated unjustly, women who are disregarded, women who are abandoned by their men to face the harsh world alone.

I don't know how I shall work in this way but work I shall, wherever I am.

I have been very serious, but I expect that is something you will understand.

Will he? she wondered, or is he still the rash young man I knew? Surely, imprisoned as he has been, he cannot have remained the same, but she could not know what changes had come to him.

She put her pen down and let her mind wander to their time together. She remembered best how she had lain by his side in the hut at Wheal Busy, how she had reached out to him, drawn his hand to her so that it touched her naked breast. She shuddered at the memory. She had been innocent then, she had loved James with a purity of spirit that seemed to have gone forever.

She picked up her pen and tried to write of her love for him, but it would mean nothing if she wrote it. What was the love she felt for him, anyway? She knew it was both less and more than that she still felt for Robert.

"Think of me," she concluded and signed "Ellen," then sat, drained by her outpourings and near to tears.

VI

THE meeting in Redruth seemed an anticlimax after the meeting in Truro. There were only three women present beside

Veronica Langarth and Ellen. Miss Langarth did not seem disheartened.

"We've enough for a committee," she said, but the three other women demurred at the notion they should be involved, expressed vague support for the idea of votes for women, and left shaking their heads.

"Well," said Veronica. "It's just you and me." She had to look up to Ellen for she was five or six inches shorter.

"Now," Veronica said. "To work. Can you write?"

Ellen nodded.

"Can you speak? You know what I mean—deliver a speech, argue a case, persuade others?"

Ellen shrugged. She had never tried but in her new mood of conviction she thought she might be able to.

"You're a fighter," said Veronica. "I know that. I saw you once, at Wheal Busy, leading the women there. That's the spirit we want." She looked Ellen up and down and then raised her eyes to Ellen's. "Where can I find you when I need you?"

Where shall I be? wondered Ellen. Who can tell?

"I'll find you," she answered, "if you tell me where."

"I'm taking a house in Camborne," Veronica said. "Father has helped—poor man, he's not sure he approves but he can't deny me. It's to be my headquarters. You can come there as my assistant. At a wage of course."

She had the arrangements clear in her mind, brooked no refusal and insisted on Ellen making a note of the address.

VII

ELLEN'S way home from the meeting took her near her old working place of Pednandrea mine. Near it she observed a crowd of women, wearing their bonnets and hessian aprons, fresh from the dressing sheds. It was the end of their shift. They seemed in angry mood as they, seeing her, stopped and harangued her.

"You were right," said one, Polly Richards, a dark gypsylike woman. "You were right when you told us to band together. That bugger Carkeek and the cap'ns, they care naught for us."

"What's the matter?"

"A cut in wages that's what," said Bessie Rule, whom Ellen

remembered as a woman of slow speech and steady habits, not one to be easily roused to anger. She was angry now, her voice shrill.

"What are you going to do?" Ellen asked.

"We'll not go back till they give us back our penny a day," said Polly Richards.

The other women had gathered around.

"We heard what you did at Busy," said Bessie Rule. "We were proper proud it was you."

"You can do the same for us," said Polly Richards. "You've a way with words. You can tell 'em what's what."

"We thought a meeting . . ." Bessie said. "The bal maidens at Wheal Bassett, Dolcoath and Carn Brea feel like us. They'd come out if we could talk to 'em."

"Talk to them then," said Ellen. She remembered, with a sour flavor, how indifferent her workmates at Busy had seemed when she was dismissed.

"Talk for us, Ellen love. Talk for us." This was from Meg Clemens who had worked at the bench longer than most. She was a neat, self-contained woman who had always distanced herself from the bawdy gossip of the others. Ellen had liked and respected her.

"Talk for us, Ellen," the others echoed.

"Like father, like daughter," said someone and Ellen was pleased that her father was remembered.

"Aye. He was a fighter too," said Meg Clemens quietly.

Ellen needed no more persuasion and went at the head of the women to the gates of Carn Brea mine. Word had spread before them and a crowd of bal maidens had gathered there. A cheer arose as the women from Pednandrea appeared. A crate was dragged forward for Meg Clemens to stand on. Meg drew Ellen up with her.

Ellen looked about her and saw, instead of the forty or so women she had expected, two or three hundred, dusty from their work, aprons still about them.

"They've come from Uny and Bassett as well," said Meg. She raised her hand and silence fell.

Afterward Ellen could not recall what she had said. She only knew that after the first uncertain moments she had spoken with fire of the bal maidens' case so that by the end of her speech the women could not contain their fervor and marched in a body to the company office at Carn Brea.

Ellen refused to go with them as their spokeswoman. "I'm condemned as a troublemaker," she said. "It won't do you any good to have me along."

So as the women moved away she was left alone, awed at the power to move that her voice possessed. Veronica Langarth had asked her if she could speak. Now she could answer.

Julia was waiting for her at the cottage. She had collected her few private things together in readiness to move in with Mark and Richard.

" 'Tis fixed for three weeks' time—our marrying," she announced to Ellen. She was brimful of content and for a moment Ellen felt envious. As she stood on the threshold looking in on the near-empty room, she heard a step on the road. It was Richard.

"Ellen?" he said and as she moved into the cottage he followed her and stood listening to the echoes.

" 'Tis comfortless here. I do wish you would come to us when the lease goes."

She did not reply.

"Where will you go?"

She diverted his attention from her by telling him of the meeting at Carn Brea. He expressed no surprise that the bal maidens had chosen Ellen to speak to them, and talked long beyond dark of the struggles of Ellen's father and himself to persuade men to unite in a society. When he had gone, Ellen sat for a long while. Where *would* she go? The time for her confinement was still some months away, but she could not pretend to ignore it. She had been unable to hide her condition from Julia, though she had resolutely refused to tell her the name of the man responsible. Nor would she give in to Julia's pleas that she should live with them. That she could not do; perhaps Richard would understand, would not reproach her, but she dare not risk it. She could not bear to forfeit his respect. He must know one day, she supposed, but not yet.

There was only one thing to do. She would go to Jane. She would leave without fuss after the wedding and write later to Richard and Julia to explain.

And after the ceremony at Gwennap Church, when the few guests—cousins of Mark from the village of Frogpool and three friends of Julia from the candle factory—moved with Richard and the bride and groom to the Fox and Hounds at Comford, Ellen slipped back to the cottage, left a brief note to say she had gone inquiring after work, then walked across country to Reuben's farm.

Jane was in the farm kitchen, baking. Ellen wondered at the transformation. Jane looked healthy and cheerful and opened her floury arms to her friend in welcome.

"I knew you'd come," she said and took Ellen's bundle. "What else is there? Reuben will bring it."

"Nothing worth going for," said Ellen. She had been mildly doubtful of Jane's reception of her and was reassured, and when Reuben came in from the fields at midday, she found his welcome no less warm. Here was understanding, sympathy, friendship. She would be content.

Chapter Eleven

ROBERT Buchan had taken Veronica's words to heart. "Concentrate on getting fit. Make yourself known," she had said. Getting fully well took time but he spared himself as much as he could, only gradually assuming full responsibility for his practice and paying more attention to his middle-class patients and their less demanding needs than to those in the teeming hovels of Redruth's backlets.

To make himself better known he began to write letters to the local papers on matters with which he was familiar, on the health of miners and on the dangers of some of their habits. His letters were well received by the mining community; they were moderately phrased and reflected a general concern; he made no criticism of any identifiable mine and his readers could always assure themselves—and did—that "they were not as other men."

Abel Hosking visited Buchan frequently. He commented on the letters with qualified approval.

"Raise general issues," he advised, "not particular ones. Concentrate on the follies of government in interfering with those who know best. Protect local interests—the mining community. They're the ones you have to win. The men in London, they're your target. They know nothing."

Robert nodded agreement. He had begun to see an ally in Hosking. He had his good will and did not mean to lose it. Ambition had, like a slowly advancing cataract, begun to blind him to Hosking's narrowness of mind.

"And," Hosking went on. "What of your plans—to marry? I'll bring my niece to meet you." He looked closely at Robert. "You've not got any foolish notions about that other young woman, I trust?"

Robert shook his head. "If you mean the bal maiden, no."

But he could not dismiss her so easily from his mind. In the evenings sometimes, as he sat in the drawing room before the fire he would recall the evening when she had appeared at the door in that ridiculous black gown of his housekeeper's. Once he went up to the bedroom where he had lain with her and stood at the door looking at the bed as if by that he could re-create the wonder of those moments. But there was no calling her back. There was emptiness there in the room, as there was in his spirit, without her.

He would see her once more, and if she still refused to listen to him, he would forget her, put her out of his mind, form his plans for the future without thought for her.

The afternoon of the following day he rode out of town and across country toward Cusgarne. As he topped a rise near Carharrack he saw spreading before him the old copper field of Gwennap, a scarred and pitted landscape. This was the mining division which he hoped one day to represent. He had no difficulty in believing what Hosking had told him: that Gwennap had yielded more copper than any other part of the world. The signs were there to see, the vast heaps of dead rock, spoil from a thousand shafts, the dozens of engine houses straggling the seams, the derelict mine buildings. He thought of the two sorts of men who had shared in the search for the earth's riches: the Hoskings, prosperous, secure, powerful, the masters; and the Bryants, laborers, drivers, diggers, the men of craft, the hard-rock miners.

He turned from the scene to ride to Sunny Corner, not hurrying his horse, suddenly uneasy at the approaching meeting with Ellen, unsure of what he would say to her, unsure of what he wanted to say. He half-rejected the impulse that had brought him here but he rode on along the lanes, his thoughts becoming turbulent, almost as restless as in the days of his delirium.

He dismounted at Richard Bryant's door. He would call to see Richard and get news of Ellen there. He could pretend he had come to see the old miner. It would not seem strange for him to do that. Ellen's sister Julia met him at the door. It was odd, thought Robert, how little there was of her sister in Julia. The girl was cheerful, uncomplicated, placid. She welcomed Robert with a friendly smile.

"Your friend Doctor Buchan is here," she called to Richard.

Richard came out of the kitchen, with hand outstretched, as if sighted.

"You look well," said Robert as they sat on either side of the hearth.

" 'Tis this young maid's doing," said Richard. " 'Tis Julia's doing. She do be living with us now her granny's dead."

"And Ellen?" said Robert carelessly.

There was a moment's silence before Richard answered, "She's gone to find work."

"Where?" asked Robert.

"Up-country. Up along to Plymouth maybe. She'll write and tell us, she says. She'll not forget us."

Robert looked to Julia for further explanation but she offered none.

She's gone, he thought, and there's no knowing where. She has turned away from me, put me out of her mind. Perhaps it is better that way.

He returned to Redruth morose and dissatisfied, telling himself life was simpler now.

Chapter Twelve

I

ELLEN was content enough. Here, with Jane and Reuben, there was no talk of mines or mining; there were no books, they had no newspaper and it was only on rare visits to Redruth market that they seemed to recognize a world existed beyond the farm. Ellen kept busy in the fields or the farm kitchen and ended the day satisfactorily tired. She tried not to think of Richard, for when she did guilt assailed her. She knew how much her company had meant to him, how her reading and their talks together had livened his days. He would miss her and she missed him. She wrote to Julia asking her to tell Richard she was well and would come to see him when she could. But she did not tell them where she was living out of fear he would somehow seek her out and discover her secret.

When her time arrived the first warning came in the shippon. She had not known what to expect and was certain the contractions she felt would result in the birth of her child there on the straw. But she had time to get back to the farmhouse, time to think she had imagined the onset of her labor. Jane, coming in muddy from the potato field, knew better and called

Reuben to go for Mother Trethewey, the village midwife, and calmly took charge.

It was eight hours before her labor was through, eight hours before Ellen held in her arms the daughter she had given birth to. Holding her, looking in wonder at her, pain now only a memory, she wanted to cry to Robert to come to her, to share in the miracle. She slept then and when she woke, remembering her desire to see Robert, felt shame at her weakness. She cradled the child to her breast and murmured, "You are mine, my child, my daughter, my Alice." For she had decided to name the child after her grandmother, hoping in so doing to give her some of the qualities of the old woman, to endow her with independence and a pride in herself.

The child was fair with a tinge of auburn to her hair and Ellen knew, though she tried to deny it, that there was a likeness to Robert in her. She pushed the notion from her. You are a Bray, she told the baby, a Bray through and through. It was now that she felt the need of a family; she wanted Julia to admire the baby, and the family she wanted encompassed Richard; he was family to her and more. He had taken the place of a father and had a right, surely, to share in the joy she felt over her child. It would be wrong to hide Alice from those others whom she loved. There was no shame to the child—only delight.

She made up her mind to take Alice to Cusgarne and show her to Richard. He could only love the child. And when Alice was twelve weeks old and already with a personality all her own, Ellen set off early one morning to walk the few miles, excited at the thought of seeing Julia, no longer fearful of telling her news to Richard.

It was early April and primroses dotted the banks. The Downs were golden with gorse, as almost always. She remembered the saying, "Only kiss a maid when the gorse be in bloom." There was never a time when the gorse was bare. There was always a flower to be found and a maid to be kissed, she supposed, if a man looked hard enough. She smiled at her fancy. In spite of the child in her arms her step was light, her heart carefree, spirits uplifted by the thought that once again she would see Richard, talk with him, read to him, share her deep feelings about Alice with him. She had no doubts now that he would understand; she had been wrong to think otherwise.

She saw the cottage ahead, a thin plume of smoke rising

from the chimney. Her pace quickened and Alice, who had been sleeping, woke and whimpered.

"There, my love," she crooned and held the child up, showing her as if she would understand why they had come.

There was a quiet about the cottage. The door was open and Ellen stood for a moment looking in at the room. It was empty. Somewhere from above a voice came to her, a man's voice, familiar and yet, because it was unexpected, startling.

It was James. She had not realized his time for release was near, and surely it was not. What was he doing here?

There was another voice, too low to be distinguished, but it was there certainly, for James was talking quietly, uttering a phrase, then waiting for an answer. It must be his father, it must be Richard above. Why was he not downstairs sitting in his accustomed place before the fire? She felt a tremor of anxiety and went, with Alice in her arms, to the foot of the stairs and called softly up.

"Richard?"

Above the conversation ceased.

"Richard?" she called again. "James?"

A figure appeared at the head of the stairs: James. A dark shadow above, but James; she could not fail to recognize him. He was there, tall and slender, but she could not see his face, could not know if his mouth still had that curling smile, his eyes that swift, challenging look.

"James?" she said as if she were uncertain it was he, but she knew there was no mistake. James had returned.

"Ellen?" He too seemed unsure. He came downstairs, moving slowly from step to step, his right leg dragging awkwardly. "Ellen?" he repeated when he reached her and looked, without surprise it seemed, at the child in her arms. She wanted to explain but could not find the words.

"Alice. My daughter," she said simply. Now she saw him clearly, she saw the curl of the lips had gone; lines were etched in the gray sunken cheeks, so that there was little of the reckless youth left to see. "Oh, James," she said. "What have they done to you?"

He smiled then, and for an instant she saw the man she had known, then his mouth set again in lines drawn, she knew, by long years of loneliness.

"He's been asking for you. For you—no one else. It seems strange. You're not one of us." She wondered at the bitterness suggested, but again a slow, almost unwilling smile robbed the words of hurt. "I mean," he said, "you're not a Bryant."

Not quite, she thought, but Richard means as much to me as anyone could.

"He's ill?" she said anxiously.

He did not reply but stood aside and gestured to her to go to see for herself. She mounted the narrow stairs reluctantly, cradling Alice to her. The child was sleeping again, her round cheeks flushed. She paused at the door of the bedroom. Richard was propped up against the bedhead, a bolster at his back. He lay still, with not a flicker of movement, but as she stood silent on the threshold he became aware of her, with that eerie knowledge of her presence he always had.

"Ellen?" He turned his head toward her. His face was brown and windburned like a farm worker's.

"Richard," she said, regretting the past months of separation, the sense of shame which had kept her away, but which, she now knew, had no place between them.

"There is someone with you," he said. "I can hear."

"My child," she answered and went forward and put Alice in his lap.

He was silent, but put his fingers delicately to be guided by Ellen to Alice's soft cheeks.

"A boy or girl?" he asked.

"A daughter—Alice."

The baby stirred as if to wake and then began to whimper.

"She needs feeding," said Richard. "I recognize the signs." His voice, which had been faltering, seemed to be gathering strength. "See," he said, "she's hungry," for Alice's lips had turned to his finger and were opening to it.

Ellen took the baby and, unloosening her blouse, fed her nipple to the baby's eager mouth.

" 'Tis a lovely sound," Richard said and sighed, as if recalling his own Jessica and the days of his young manhood.

"She's beautiful, I know," he said. "Like you."

The old miner was breathing shallowly, as if he had not strength for more. Ellen heard a movement behind her and half-turned carefully so not to disturb Alice. It was James. He shook his head, signaling her to ignore his presence. Richard was asleep, lulled by Alice's contented suckling. There was a smile on his lips. James crept out.

Ellen sat until Alice had finished, then slowly and carefully she moved to the door and down the stairs, still holding the baby to her breast. James was sitting by the hearth, facing his father's empty chair, gazing into the fire. She stood for a moment looking down on him. There were gray threads in his close-cropped hair.

"He's dying," he said. "It was Reverend Luke who brought the news. They set me free for that. They shut me away from him when I could share life with him. Now he's at the end they set me loose." He looked up at her. "I should be grateful, I suppose. I have one last chance to make amends."

"Make amends?"

"For my neglect of him and his teaching. If I'd listened to him these years would not have been lost."

"He doesn't blame you," she said.

"There's no need. I blame myself. I have blamed myself these long years. I have thought days and nights about it, wondering. I told Methuselah." He stopped.

"Methuselah?"

"You wouldn't understand." He nodded toward Alice. "She's a pretty one." He stared thoughtfully at the child. Julia must have told him, Ellen thought. He wants to ask me who the father is but dare not. I would not tell him, for the father is irrelevant. She is my child.

Alice was asleep but still clung to the breast. Ellen prized the nipple, swollen from the sucking, from the lips and buttoned her blouse, then she put Alice across her shoulder and gently winded her. James met her eyes and she tried to read the meaning in his look—contempt?—anger that she had borne another's child? There was no telling. But then he looked at the baby again and a smile broke at the sight of her, rosy with sleep and contentment. At least Alice was accepted.

"How long has he been ill?"

"A month or more I gather, but worse the last days."

She was angry that she had kept away. She could surely have helped.

"Where's Mark?"

"At the mine. He'll hurry back after core. Julia wrote to William. There'll be nothing he can do in time."

"Where is Julia?"

"Gone for the doctor. Let me hold her," he said and reached for Alice. She settled the baby in his arms and went back to Richard.

He was still sleeping, a slight movement showing his breathing. She wanted to hold him, spare him some of the boundless strength which coursed through her. Why could it not be shared with him? Could she not bring life to him, as he had once brought hope to her? Yet she could do nothing but sit beside him and watch. Beside his bed was a small roughly made set of shelves. A candlestick was placed on it, to give light to whoever watched in the night by the bedside. On the shelf below was a book—read by the watcher? Or kept there by Richard to finger and remember the days when he could see to read himself?

She picked it up. It was a copy of the Bible, well thumbed.

"Ellen?" The movement had disturbed him. His voice was barely audible.

"I'm here," she said and knelt beside the bed so that she could be nearer to him. She took hold of his hand and pressed it to her lips.

"You should have stayed," he said.

"I know now."

They did not need to speak to convey their feelings but Richard seemed to want to say something. He seemed to be trying to gather strength. "James," he said and paused. "Is he the same?"

"Sadder and wiser," she said.

"But a miner still," said Richard. He seemed to want some reassurance.

Where would James find work as a miner now? He was an outcast like herself, a troublemaker. There was no place for him in Cornwall, no place for either of them.

"A miner," Richard sighed. She knew he wanted to talk, as he had so often in the past, of the days before his blinding, of the craft he so cherished. He would have liked now to talk of the men, the mines he had known, but he no longer had the strength.

She talked for him: of her father and brother, their hopes, their skill, the hopes of those miners who had urged their fellows to combine, and, failing, had gone overseas to work. But she talked mostly of his sons, the Bryants, Mark and William and James, heirs to his craft. Of James—and as she talked she wondered what her feelings were for him. He was a good man, in spite of his follies; he had been a passionate man and, in the past, she had returned that passion. They had both changed now, he through confinement, and she too, she thought with wry humor, through confinement but of a different sort. How strange that one word should relate to two such different things.

She realized she had fallen silent and that Richard was silent too; his grasp on her hand had loosened and his eyes were closed. For a moment she thought life had fled from him, but a light breathing stirred him. She kissed his forehead. He felt cold, and again she wanted to lie beside him, embracing him to give him warmth, the warmth of her love, but she merely drew the blanket up to cover his shoulders.

She turned and saw James at the door, holding Alice and watching her. He moved downstairs in front of her and handed Alice to her. The child came between them—in more ways than one. He looked at her over Alice's head as Ellen took the baby from him. He wants to know, she thought, I cannot tell him. It is a thought private to me, important only for me.

There was a sound at the door and they turned together to look around, standing closely, almost intimately.

Robert Buchan stood there and behind him Julia. He had stopped in surprise at the sight of them there, making, it would seem a family group.

"Well?" he said brusquely. "Upstairs?"

James nodded and Buchan went swiftly to the stairs.

Ellen felt a hollowness, as if the breath had been knocked out of her. She wondered if James was aware of her response to Buchan's appearance. She sat down suddenly, afraid her knees would fold under her. The suddenness of the movement startled Alice and woke her. She raised her voice in a sharp wail. Ellen drew her close to comfort her. The baby quieted and lay looking up at her mother, mouth puckered. For a moment Ellen had an absurd fear that Robert might claim her and she held the baby protectively to her.

She heard movement on the stairs and turned to watch,

anxiety for Richard overcoming her. James and Julia stood beside her, all waiting for Buchan to appear. He paused as he reached the foot of the stairs. His eyes moved rapidly past Ellen toward James. He was frowning broodingly.

They waited. He seemed to shake thoughts from him, as if they had nothing to do with the situation here. He addressed his remarks to James alone.

"There's little time left. You can do nothing for him but offer comfort—if words can be of comfort." He paused and glanced beyond James to the open door which gave onto the garden. The spring sun shone warmly on the cottage walls. "A brave, honest man. Go to him," he said to James. "It's company he needs. Even when he seems to be sleeping, he'll be conscious of those near. Go to him."

James went slowly up the stairs, and Julia followed him. Ellen moved to go with them, but Robert put a hand out to prevent her.

"There are people enough up there," he said. He looked searchingly at her and glanced at the child. He raised his eyes from the babe to Ellen; there was a question in them, but she stared back at him, unwilling to reveal anything, closing her mind to him. Outside, his horse whinnied and with a sudden impatient gesture Robert moved away to the door. He turned there and was about to speak when Julia appeared at the foot of the stairs.

"Richard wants you, Ellen," she said, and held out her arms for Alice.

In that moment Robert had gone. Ellen kissed her sister, held Alice out to her and went upstairs.

Richard was sitting up, supported by James. Slow tears coursed down James's cheeks. When he looked at Ellen she saw that his grief was almost beyond control. She moved to take his place and as her arm replaced his around Richard's shoulders, James moved away to stand at the window.

Richard lay in Ellen's arms, his head falling against her breast. She had held him like this once before, when he had been brought back, scarred and blinded, from the mine. She held his head against her, holding back her own tears, calming herself, giving her strength to the comfort of her friend, holding him gently, her hand against his cheek.

She was unaware of the passing of time. It meant nothing

here. She was unaware of the moment when Richard died. It did not matter when. But at last she gently lowered Richard's head to the pillow and let the tears come.

II

BUCHAN paused outside the cottage for a moment before mounting his horse. Maybe he should have stayed with his old friend until the end came, but he could not remain in the house with James Bryant and Ellen on such intimate terms as they seemed. There was nothing he could do for Richard now that they could not. He was distressed that he had been unaware of Richard's decline and angry that his own affairs had led him to neglect Richard. He had lost sight of his old friend in the cultivation of the new—the men of influence—and he was ashamed. He could never forgive himself.

He rode over the Downs, in his grief almost unaware of his surroundings, then, as he came to the entrance of the old Wheal Jenny, he was reminded. He drew his horse up sharp. The workings were deserted, the machinery gone, the engine houses mere shells. It was here he had first met Richard, bleeding and powder-burned from the accident which had blinded him. He had been brought here by Ellen, a mere girl at the time; he had noticed her even then. His mind had not been free of her since.

It is free of her now, he told himself, for she has no thought for me. The sight of her with the man Bryant had stirred him with a primitive emotion, intense dislike for Bryant and anger at Ellen: jealousy. He rode on toward Redruth, leaving the mines behind him, telling himself that he no longer had reason for visiting Sunny Corner; that world was no longer part of his. As he rode, he thought of the baby he had seen. So intimately close had Bryant and Ellen seemed with the babe in her arms, that he had supposed it to belong to James. But that could not be; the man had only lately been released from jail. Perhaps the child was not Ellen's, but her sister's. That could not be either: Ellen's pose revealed motherhood, in her look of pride, her tenderness, her protective shielding of the child. It was Ellen's, he could have no doubt.

There was something about the child that set him thinking.

He began to calculate, and as he did so his memories of that night with Ellen returned vividly before him. He wished the child could be his, the result of that evening of magic, but it could not be; Ellen would not have been so unfeeling as to hide his own child from him. The child was another's. He did not know whose and he told himself he did not care. That part of his life was behind him. Ellen had no concern for him and he must deny he had any for her.

He arrived home dispirited, conscious of a feeling of loss. He put it down to grief over Richard, but it was more than that; a dream that had lingered with him since he had admitted to himself his love for Ellen was dispelled for good.

His housekeeper was waiting for him, bustling and eager with news of a visitor who had come moments ago. Buchan was in no mood to be hospitable, but surprised to learn the visitor was Langarth shook off his depression and greeted the man warmly. He liked Langarth for he had an honesty that cut through the intrigues of his wife and daughter; he preferred to come to the point, to let people know where he stood.

"I hope you have no objection to my calling on you without warning. I was in the neighborhood."

"I am delighted that you should," said Buchan. "Not a call on my professional services, I trust."

Langarth, robust with health, smiled. "I have my own man if I need him, which is rare. No, not that. It's about Reid. I've had words with him. Told him it won't do to hold onto his seat in Parliament when he's often too ill to leave his bed. Got his promise to resign at the end of the next Parliamentary session. Thought I'd let you know. Gives you a few months to get your-self organized. A different life, Buchan. No more ministering to the needs of the sick and the poor—just the needs of the nation. Of the mining interest. That's where your attention is needed."

"I'm gratified," said Buchan, "and astonished."

"Reid's a stubborn fellow, but we'll keep him to his prom-ise." Langarth hurried away then, to the disappointment of Mrs. Honeychurch who had arrived with a decanter of whisky. She stood for a moment after his departure expecting her employer to reveal the purpose of the visit, but when Buchan remained silent she retreated.

The mood of despair which had accompanied Robert from

Sunny Corner had lifted. He still felt a deep sadness at the coming death of Richard, but the news Langarth had brought drove other thoughts from his mind. The Liberal Committee had already half-pledged themselves to him and the patronage of the Langarths was enough to clinch his selection as candidate. And once chosen he was unlikely to be defeated at the polls. He was liked and respected, he knew, not merely by the mine captains, the agents, the pursers, the merchants, but also by the working miner, many of whom now had the right to vote. He would be a popular candidate.

And, he assured himself, he would be a good MP. He had ideas; he had an understanding of ordinary people and their troubles and he could help to remedy their condition. And there was an obstinate streak which would stand him in good stead in the struggle for change.

He smiled and preened himself at the thought of being Robert Buchan, MP. But there were problems. He had no in-dependent means. He thought of Abel Hosking's niece, Bella, a dull and complaisant woman; marriage to her would provide financial support, but little else. How could he reconcile himself to that when love was absent? Love? Ellen arose in his mind, provoking him with her beauty, her fire, her power to move. He tried to thrust the image away, but it was too real. It is useless to think of her, he told himself. She has no thought for me. That episode is closed, an aberration, best forgotten. But to forget her was not within his power. As his desire for her reawoke, his jealousy was kindled again at the thought that she had betrayed him. She had turned from him to James—he was sure that was the significance of their presence together at Rich-ard's. She is not worth my thinking of her, he told himself, but reason had no influence on him.

He was distracted by a summons to a mine accident, to which he arrived when the injured man, leg broken in a fall from the ladderway, had already been brought to grass and treated by his workmates. But Robert was glad he had re-sponded to the call. He had a reputation to protect. That was important now.

The following day he was visited by Veronica. She knew of Reid's promise to her father.

"The campaign properly begins," she said to him.

"What campaign?"

"For your return as a Member of Parliament."

"There are obstacles to be overcome first, things to be done." He wondered if she would understand.

"A marriage?" she said, understanding him very well. "A marriage of convenience? It could be a marriage between like souls, a compact of mutual benefit."

He did not reply.

"We each have causes to fight for. One cause we could both agree on. Do agree on, I'm sure."

"Women's suffrage?"

"You do support it?" She was quick to read hesitation in him.

"Of course. Common justice demands it."

"Then?"

He smiled at the rapidity of her challenge. "There are other injustices to be remedied—poverty, ignorance, the right of working men to organize freely."

She brushed his objections aside. "They are as nothing to this major human grievance. Besides, secure the one and the others will follow." She looked closely at him. "Are we agreed?" she asked.

"We are agreed," he conceded, wondering what she meant by a "compact." Did it extend to marriage? Was that what she was hinting? If so, such an idea had attractions. She was a lively and intelligent woman whose influence could be useful. During the last months they had seen a great deal of each other. They had become close, but he felt no great love for her—regard, affection, respect, but not that passionate stirring of the blood. . . . He thrust from him the picture of Ellen that the idea evoked.

"There are still obstacles," she said, smiling. "My parents."

"I thought . . ." he began.

"Oh, they approve of you as an aspiring politician, but not, I think, as a suitor for my hand."

He shrugged his shoulders. What then has this talk of compacts been for? he wondered.

"Leave them to me, Robert. I am not my mother's daughter for nothing."

She departed without a touch or gesture of affection, save a smile—a knowing smile, he thought afterward. He knew he was being used, manipulated; the Langarth womenfolk were accomplished at that. What need had they of the vote? he asked himself. They wielded power by other means.

Chapter Thirteen

I

ELLEN returned to the farm and tried to settle back into the routine, but the death of Richard, the return of James and the sight of Robert had all disturbed her. She was in turmoil. With the loss of Richard came a return of the grief she had felt at the death of her father and brother, and even more keenly felt than that for her emotions were, in other ways, at full stretch. The chores of farm life, in the milking shed and in the fields, had comforted her before but gave her no solace now. It was not her element, the steady change of seasons, the slow pace of nature. Her temperament demanded action, struggle. Only concern for Alice kept her at the farm; but for her daughter she would have left, left Cornwall, even perhaps turned her back on England and made a life for herself in the Colonies.

She thought of James frequently, and fondly. But he no longer had the power to stir her as he once had. He was a good man, she told herself, and would make a good father—he had shown a tenderness toward Alice which moved her—and it was tempting to think of him as a husband, but it would not do. She turned from the idea without clearly knowing why. She recalled how she had written to James with fervor about the beliefs which had become clear to her. She had written of what she had then thought her destiny; where were her good intentions now? Surely love and concern for her daughter need not prevent her being true to her own self. She remembered Miss Langarth's invitation to join her at her headquarters in Camborne. "You can come as my assistant," she had said. Ellen's spirits revived, and one morning some weeks after Richard's death she left Alice to Jane's loving care and went to Camborne.

She found the house, an imposing granite mansion, at the end of a long shrub-bordered drive. A neatly dressed maid opened the door to her and showed her into a room where a flustered Miss Langarth sat behind a desk. She looked up as the maid announced "Miss Ellen Bray." It took a moment for the name to register, then she stood and said, "It's taken you long enough to find me."

"I had something else on my mind," said Ellen.

"Well. You're here now, thank God. Not too soon." She moved from behind the desk and gestured to the chair. "Here you are."

Ellen shook her head. "I don't know," she said. "I'm not used to that sort of work."

"No more am I," said Veronica. "You can tell, can't you?" The desk was cluttered with papers, pamphlets, cuttings from newspapers.

"Anyway, I'm no longer alone," said Veronica. "Women here are spineless creatures, willing victims. I have no patience with them." She studied Ellen closely until Ellen began to resent the inspection. "Yes," she said finally. "You'll do very well, but if you're to make an impression when you speak, you'll need something else to wear. I'll have my dressmaker see to you. Something simple, black, respectable."

Ellen began to regret the impulse that had brought her here. What had dress to do with such weighty matters as women's suffrage? She looked down at herself. She had dressed as respectably as she could to come here. Her dress was shabby: black and simple but worn and frayed. She looked what she was, a working woman, and she felt no shame in it. Why should she be expected to dress and posture and pretend to be something she was not?

"I'm very well as I am, thank you," she said.

"Ah yes," said Veronica. "I know, but appearances are important—to some people. Plans," she added in a businesslike way. "We've made some progress in Truro, none here and none in Redruth. I was beginning to feel disillusioned. Alone. Now there are two of us. We're both fighters I know that—in our different ways of course." She drew a diary out from among the papers on the desk. "Meetings in Penzance. St. Erth. Helston. I can't possibly cover them all. You'll have to learn to speak, get up the case. There's the *Women's Suffrage Journal* over there. That'll help."

Ellen started to protest but Veronica continued.

"You'll live here, of course. It will be so much easier. Rachel will see to you."

This time Ellen managed to speak. "I have a child."

Veronica was silent. She is offended, thought Ellen, but she had misjudged her.

"There's room for a nursery. We'll get some woman in to look after it."

"No," said Ellen, aware that her life was being directed by this woman, decisions taken for her in a way that offended all her being. "No," she repeated.

Veronica looked in surprise at her.

"I want no one else having anything to do with her." She was reminded that Jane was looking after her now. But Jane was different. "Not a stranger," she said.

"But if you're to be of any use to me—to the cause," Veronica amended, "you will have little time for the child."

"Then I'll get back to her now," said Ellen and moved toward the door.

"Please, Miss Bray. Ellen. We'll work something out. It can be done. It must be done. That's the difficulty with women—their divided loyalties."

Loyalties, thought Ellen. What a strange word to describe the complex bonds that tied her to Alice.

II

VERONICA worked something out and Ellen found it difficult to resist the other's authority. She might have resented it but for the fact that in accepting it she was serving the cause of women's suffrage. To Jane's disappointment she brought Alice to Camborne and together they settled in the house under Veronica's protection. Ellen would have been more at ease had she been treated as a servant, eating in the kitchen and living with the domestic staff on the top floor. But Veronica would have none of it. Ellen was to be her companion in the cause and was to be treated as such; and Ellen learned, from careful observation of Veronica, to behave appropriately to her new status. Gradually she accepted the changes forced upon her, occupying a spacious bedroom with her daughter, being attended by servants, not having to bend her back to manual work, but she could not feel this style of living to be natural to her. She accepted it, but did not enjoy it.

There were many visitors to Veronica's house, drawn more by Veronica's connections, Ellen felt, than by support for her campaign. Robert Buchan was a frequent caller. When he had first seen her in the office he had seemed surprised, but now he regarded her presence there as normal and took her for granted. Ellen could not take him for granted; she hoped he would speak to her—of the past—and every now and then he would look at her as if about to say something. Words, however, rarely came, and then were mere polite phrases without significance. But at least they were able to speak to each other without apparent embarrassment or hurt. It was as if their acquaintanceship had only just begun, as if the Ellen and Robert of the years past had been two other people.

Ellen worked hard on the papers in the office, sifting reports for Veronica, sorting clippings from newspapers, compiling material from all sorts of sources on the conditions of women. She was, as ever, glad that her father had insisted on her learning to read and write, and especially grateful for the years spent reading to Richard: those years had broadened her mind and sharpened her intellect so that, she knew, she was Veronica's match in presenting the women's case. Veronica acknowledged this and recognized that Ellen often spoke more persuasively, in an idiom that was the listener's own.

It was uphill work, nevertheless. Meetings were poorly attended and, though the listeners seemed convinced by Ellen's reasoning, interest faded when she asked them to work for the cause. One in Penzance was a depressing experience. There were only a dozen or so present and they were concerned with more material problems than the right to vote. The discussion afterward concentrated on the poverty of the area.

"What'll your women's suffrage do for that?" said one sad-eyed woman. "Our children go near-naked to school for want of clothes. They go empty-bellied too. What will you do for they?"

She understood their hopelessness and felt she had no word of ease for it. There was a Cornish Distress Fund which was supposed to help but she made no mention of it, for the people here wanted work, not charity.

Ellen was impatient, wanting action, wanting a scene where her passionate nature could express itself. She knew now she could speak. She had, in the past, moved Richard by her readings, she had stirred the bal maidens with her oratory, now she felt, given the occasion, she could hold an audience in thrall. She was beginning to feel a power in herself that she had not suspected. The fire showed itself occasionally at her meetings, more especially when there was opposition; she was at her best then: she needed the steel of confrontation to strike sparks.

No reports of their activities appeared in the press. There seemed a calculated indifference to what they were trying to do. Veronica was particularly galled by the fact that in the north—as reported in the *Women's Suffrage Journal*—meetings were well attended and enthusiastically supported.

"We are appealing to the wrong people," Veronica said to Ellen. "We need to convince the men of influence."

"And who are they?"

"The mine captains, the agents, the lawyers, the ministers and the Members of Parliament—or those who hope to be," said Veronica. "I'll take a leaf from my mother's book, hold a reception. I'll draw them in. I know them all. They'll come to my summoning, never fear. Then we'll show them."

She was confident with the ease that came to one of her class. Ellen was amused at her assurance but had little hope herself that support would be found among these smug merchants and their matrons. But it was worth trying.

She was surprised when Veronica said that the case for women's suffrage should be put to the guests by Ellen herself.

"I think not," she protested.

"Indeed it should. A Cornish voice will please them. And you speak with such sense of purpose. They regard me as slightly eccentric in my opinions. We want them to see the demand for women's rights as something natural and proper. I'm sure you will present the case perfectly."

Ellen allowed herself to be persuaded, and she and Veronica sat to draw up the list of those to be invited. "The Hoskings, of course, the whole brood," said Veronica. "The Thomases of Dolcoath, the Daniells of Truro. I suppose William Teague of Illogan." Ellen wrote the names. They were men of substance in the mining community. She remembered Abel Hosking well. Would he remember her? She had no reason for thinking him likely to be won over, but it would please her to try. She was no longer a bal maiden employed by him, to be dismissed at a nod.

"I shall enjoy this," she said with relish.

"The Vivyans of Camborne, Walter Pike, and, of course, Doctor Robert Buchan."

"Robert Buchan?"

"Of course," said Veronica. "He's likely to be the next Member of Parliament, as soon as Reid does the decent thing and dies, or resigns."

Robert Buchan, wrote Ellen, but her hand shook and the pleasure she had foreseen in the occasion vanished. His presence there would unsettle her. To meet him as a casual visitor to the house was one thing; to stand before him and declare her principles was another. Then, she thought, how can I be afraid to declare my principles? I am his equal, a proponent of a cause that declares me the equal of any man.

III

ELLEN began to have doubts about her part in the reception. What notice would these men of affairs take of her, a bal maiden? She was of the lowest of the low, a working woman to be used and cast aside, a woman of no consequence. Veronica smiled at her objections.

Veronica herself set out to impress. Refreshments, with wines and spirits, were to be provided in abundance. "I'll not have them compare me, to my disadvantage, with my mother. They'll remember this evening."

So shall I, thought Ellen. She was irritated by the lavish

display, angered at the expense, annoyed that the support of men should have to be intrigued for in this way.

Ellen prepared herself carefully for the occasion. She had little choice of clothing other than the simple black respectable dress bought for her by Veronica. She arranged her hair to fall about her shoulders, held by a black ribbon from straying too freely. She had no jewelry to adorn her, nor did she wish it. She would leave it to Veronica to impress with style and ostentation. She had been on edge at the thought of speaking in Robert's presence. Now that nervousness was absorbed in the larger fear that overtook her at the thought of speaking to these men of property and influence, men who, by the nature of things, took women to be their handmaidens, subservient and submissive. She drew herself up proudly, looked at herself in the mirror, smoothed her dress and went downstairs, ready to meet anyone, ready to face Robert too.

The guests had begun to assemble, men of Camborne, Redruth and beyond, the men who were to be persuaded to support the women's cause. Their eyes turned to her as she came down the stairs into the wide hall and, nodding distantly to them, passed into the main reception room where Veronica was regally receiving the guests.

"Come and stand by me, Ellen," she commanded. "I will present you to each in turn." She looked what she was, a woman with authority stamped on her by generations of prerogative. "Captain Josiah Thomas," she was saying. "How good of you to come. Meet my friend, Miss Ellen Bray."

Ellen greeted the gray-bearded sharp-eyed mine captain.

"Captain Hosking. I hoped you wouldn't ignore us," said Veronica. "Do you know Miss Bray?"

Brimstone Hosking paused in front of Ellen. He looked closely at her, smiled and said, "No. I've not had the pleasure."

Am I so different? thought Ellen. Is it just that I'm not wearing my apron, or that my hair is no longer covered by a bonnet? Is that all that's changed? She was tempted to remind Hosking of their past meeting but Veronica was already calling the next guest to her attention.

"Of course you know Miss Bray, don't you Robert?"

There he was, tall and broad, bulky almost. In the bright lights from the glittering chandelier his eyes seemed a paler blue than she remembered, his hair more tinged with red. He stood before her, smiling, nodding as the others had done, with, it seemed, no more feeling than they. He was one of them, one of the "men of influence," absorbed by them into their company.

She acknowledged him with the same inclination of the head as to other guests. But he was not satisfied. He held out his hand to take hers and old emotions were awakened at the touch. He said nothing, but looked into her eyes. She tried to read meaning into the look but there was no telling, and then, in the moment before she turned away to meet another guest, she saw desire. It disturbed her.

"Ellen." She heard Veronica at her elbow. "It's time we began. I think everyone's here, everyone who matters."

There was a hum of chatter among the assembled men. They looked at Veronica with curiosity and some looked at Ellen with the same questioning: what can these women have brought us here for? What can two women want with us?

"Gentlemen," Veronica said. "You have been so good as to accept my invitation to come and there is such expectation in your eyes that I cannot hold out any longer. I have to declare why I have chosen you to hear our message. You are men of substance, of influence in the world." She flattered them with accomplished ease. "Who better than you to show Cornwall the way forward? But it's not for me to tell you the reason for this assembly. It is for my friend, Miss Ellen Bray, to win your support. She is a Cornish woman. I doubt if any of you will be able to resist the power and passion of her advocacy of Women's Suffrage."

"Women's Suffrage?" exclaimed a thick-set red-faced man.

"Yes, Captain Teague. Women's Suffrage." In the moment of silence that followed Veronica said, "Ellen. They are ready for you."

"Woman's Suffrage!" said Teague again, this time scornfully.

"The right of women to cast a vote," said Ellen. "The right of women to influence affairs, the right of women to speak their minds." She glared at Captain Teague, as if defying him to challenge her further. "Women's suffrage," she repeated. "That's what we stand for. That's why we've invited you here to listen to the case, to persuade you to use your influence to remedy an injustice that's reigned too long." They were silent, these men of influence, excited perhaps by curiosity to hear more, perhaps even willing to be convinced, she thought as she looked around at them. Some were staring open-mouthed at her, lost in admiration maybe, or just astonished at her eloquence; others were frowning, angry at having been lured into hearing an argument for a cause that was contrary to nature; others looked bewildered, glancing at their neighbors, hoping for guidance as to how they should react. Ellen smiled within herself. These men were no different from others she had met at her meetings; they had the same prejudices, the same suspicions, the same arrogant male assurance. She would show them.

She raised her voice slightly, for a soft mutter had begun among the group near Abel Hosking. Ellen, undeterred, spoke calmly, presenting her case persuasively, arguing with conviction and reason. The muttering continued and then grew louder and suddenly erupted with a cry from Hosking himself: "By God, I know her now! She's a bal maiden, nothing but a bal maiden! Who's she to tell us what to think? I got rid of her as a troublemaker. I'll not listen to her now."

Ellen tried to ignore him but the men around him began to snigger among themselves, to talk loudly with deliberate offense, to shuffle their feet and nudge each other, creating such uproar that Ellen realized it was useless to persist. She found herself reddening with anger at the humiliation they were subjecting her to. The arrogance of these men was unshakable; they were indifferent to logic, to reason, to justice. She stood on the low dais Veronica had provided, surveying the room. Disorder had spread and arguments had developed between men who seemed interested in the case and those, Hosking and the majority, who were noisily hostile. She raised her voice further so that it cut, strident, through the babble.

"You will listen," she said. "Maybe not now, but one day you will listen, to me and the millions like me. Then you will tremble in your shoes, as you have never done before. Your wives and daughters—how long do you think they will put up with your strutting airs, your bluster and your insolent manners?"

Veronica was at her elbow, urging her to control her temper, but Ellen would not, could not, listen.

"I despise you," she said. "And what you stand for. I despise your arrogance and the ignorance it stems from. Men of influence! You are worthless!"

She stepped from the dais and walked toward them. They were silent now and parted as she approached and let her pass through to the stairs. But behind her the hubbub rose, angry, violent, abusive. She had seen Robert in the group near Abel Hosking. What had he done to help her? Nothing. He had remained silent while Hosking insulted and shamed her. He was as bad as the rest. She flung open the door into her bedroom and strode to the window to get a breath of clean air. Carriages were assembled outside, the coachmen gathered in groups waiting for their masters. As she watched she saw Abel Hosking emerge with his toadying admirers. They clapped him on the back, laughing with him. She turned from the window in disgust.

"I shall go back," she said aloud. "I shall go back to Stithians, to the farm, work there at honest tasks." But she knew she could not go back, for that would signify retreat. It was here among these mindless opponents that the case had to be made, fought, and won.

There was a knock on the door and Veronica came in. Ellen began an apology, but there was no need. Her friend was smiling.

"Come down," she said.

"Have they gone?"

"Most of them. It's our friends who are left—those who favor the cause. They want to meet you."

"I haven't frightened them off?"

"Come and see."

Ellen followed Veronica downstairs to the room where she had spoken her mind. There were four or five men left. She did not recognize any of them. Now she did not want to meet them. Her blaze of fury had left her exhausted, and all she wanted to do was rest. Veronica introduced her to the men. Robert was not among them.

"I'm proud to know you," said one called Rabling, smiling. "'Tis a long time since I've heard so fiery a speaker outside chapel, and never by a woman. It did my heart good. I wish my Sarah could have been here." He turned to Veronica. "You should have invited wives as well, Miss Langarth. It would have curbed their ill manners. And I must apologize for them, Miss Bray. We're not all so rough and uncouth here along."

"Are you the only ones interested in our case?" she asked.

"No indeed. But it takes a lot of independence to stand against Brimstone Hosking when he's in a fighting mood," said Rabling.

Or courage, thought Ellen.

Veronica seemed pleased with the evening's work. "They can't ignore us," she said to Ellen when they were alone. "Never again."

IV

BUCHAN had been tempted to stay behind when Hosking and his friends had swept out, but he felt he needed to be alone, to allow his emotion to subside. He had been intensely moved by Ellen's appearance and by her defiance of the oafs who had vilified her. She had been magnificent, fit to stand beside Veronica Langarth as an equal. Indeed she had been the more impressive of the two, the more handsome, the more passionate. He had wanted to protest at Hosking's treatment of her and did not know why he had remained silent. It was, he felt, that he had been overwhelmed by the force of Ellen's personality, dumbfounded. He was under its influence still. He must return to the house and tell her how moved he had been by her words and her pride.

He felt a hand at his elbow and turned to see Hosking. The mine captain drew him aside. Buchan controlled his urge to attack the man for his discourtesy to Ellen.

"Buchan." Hosking spoke softly, looking around to make certain they were not overheard. "Is that the woman? The one you spoke of?"

Buchan nodded.

"Take her away. Hide her in London. If you're seen together here, she'll finish you. Be warned. Take her to London. Or better still get her out of your mind." He walked away before Buchan could answer.

Get her out of his mind? That was easier said than done. He was aware of her presence with him wherever he turned. And it was Ellen he needed with him, not Veronica. Yet he needed Veronica too; without her, hopes of a political career were doomed. There seemed no way out, save that suggested by Hosking. "Hide her in London. Hide her in London." The counsel reverberated until it began to seem a proper solution, indeed the only solution possible. Veronica need never know: theirs was a political understanding, with a political purpose; no emotion was involved. He persuaded himself that the only obstacle to the plan was his own reluctance to propose it to Ellen.

The child—what of her? Again he wondered. It might well be his, though he found it difficult to understand why Ellen should conceal it from him. He would demand the truth of her and, if the child was his (and he was gradually convincing himself it was) that would give him the right to approach Ellen with his—Hosking's—suggestion.

Most of the carriages had gone. He hesitated about returning to the house but he saw Hosking was watching him. It would not do to offend him and when he saw Ellen again he wanted her by herself. What he had to say was for her ears alone. He would choose a time when Veronica was away. She need not, must not, know his mind in this. He knew she was to spend some days in Bristol soon, and he made a note of the opportunity that would give him.

Chapter Fourteen

I

"THEY are ignoring us," said Ellen. "We have made no headway. We are going about things in the wrong way. I have searched the papers, every dreary column, for mention of us and there is none. There might be no one who believes in women's suffrage for all the attention we get. We are going about things in the wrong way. Trying to persuade those thick-skinned, brute-brained 'men of influence' as you call them, is useless. We need to go to the working man and woman."

Veronica did not agree. "What use are those who have no power? What can they do?"

"There will be no hope if we don't convince them," said Ellen. "And I am doing no good here."

"Indeed you are," Veronica protested. "Those men who stayed after the reception were persuaded of the case. And Robert—Robert Buchan—though he did not stay behind, supports us. He has assured me. He will be a tower of strength."

Ellen was silent. She recalled the way Buchan had clung to the company of Hosking and wondered at Veronica's confidence in him.

"I'm to spend a few days in Bristol, discussing policy," Veronica said. "Take things easily while I'm away. You have been working too hard. Give your mind to Alice for a couple of days."

She was grateful for the respite. On the first morning of Veronica's absence she spent time in the nursery instead of the office, and walked Alice in her bassinet through the streets of the town and out into open country. She returned and had just put Alice down when there was a knock on the door and Rachel appeared.

"Doctor Buchan is here to see you, ma'am. I hope Alice is not ill."

Ellen reassured her. "What does he want?"

"He's here, ma'am." She opened the door for Robert and returned downstairs.

"Well?" Ellen said, with as distant a manner as she could.

He ignored her, went over to where Alice was playing and stared down at her. Ellen moved to intervene. He looked from the child to her.

"Why did you not tell me?"

"You were interested?" she said with disbelief. "You made no effort to reach me."

"I came to find you as soon as I could. It was too late."

"It's too late now."

"No," he denied. "Why should it be too late? Did it mean nothing to you? Does it mean nothing to you now? The child. What's her name?" His voice was soft, pleading.

"Alice," she said as softly.

"Alice," he repeated. "She's my child, is she not?"

"If you mean you had a part in her beginning, yes. But you have no part in her now."

"You cannot deny me."

"I can and will."

"The birth certificate?"

"It states 'father unknown.' "

She was not sure what emotion was shown in his face.

"Ellen." He drew closer to her. "Look at me."

She raised her eyes to his and saw again the desire in them. She tried to make her own gaze indifferent but felt there was no hiding the feelings stirring within her. She had loved him, made love to him, been possessed by him, and she was moved now by the nearness of him. She was excited by it, and as he put out his arms to draw her close his touch kindled something within her. She wanted to yield to him, but something else, some pride, a lingering resentment, held her back.

He took hold of her and pressed himself upon her, so that she felt his strength, the male power of him. She smelled the cigar smoke clinging to his clothes, saw the purplish veins in his cheeks, the reddish hairs of his Dundreary whiskers, and the darkness in his open mouth as he leaned to kiss her.

She turned her face away so that his mouth touched her cheek only. He forced her around to meet him and pressed his lips against hers, but, when he realized her determination not to respond, he dropped his arms and stood back, glowering at her.

"Have you no feeling left for me?" he said.

She did not answer. She could not lie to him. She had wanted to give way to him and wondered how she could have resisted him. He needed only to speak to her with affection, to say a word of love and she would have confessed her longing to be held by him. He had said nothing of love. His feeling for her was expressed in demand, in pressure upon her, in the desire in his eyes; there had been nothing of tenderness.

"What are you?" he said, looking at her. "A mere worker for a cause? A suffragist and nothing else?"

"Is that not enough?"

"Of course it's not enough. A woman isn't calm cold reason. She's flesh and blood and emotion. What are you?"

She was tempted to laugh. Could he not see she was compounded of all those things?

"I thought, that night of the reception, that you were inspired by passion. I was proud of you."

She did laugh then, a laugh of disbelief. "You showed no signs of it, when I was abused." He sought to interrupt but she went on. "What do you want now?"

"I came to ask you . . ." He hesitated. "It is no use."

"To ask me what?"

"I wanted to do something for you and the child."

"We want no charity from you." She turned angrily from him.

"Not charity. I would set up a home for you and Alice." She was not sure she had heard aright.

"A home," he said. "Not so grand as this, but a home. Yours."

She turned back to him, unbelieving, and searched his face, anxious to see there a sign of the love his words suggested. He waited for her to respond.

"A home," he repeated, when she remained silent.

She reached up a hand to touch his face. Doubts vanished. He bent down to her and kissed her, almost bruising her with the force of him. She breathed his warm male breath, the desire which she had so long suppressed overwhelmed her, so that, even here, in Alice's room, and in her presence, she wanted to take him, to be taken. His desire was evident too, as he held her to him and his lips moved from her mouth to her nose, her chin, and down to her neck. She was aware that uncontrolled, uncontrollable noises issued from her as the happiness within welled up. She wanted to shout her love, declare it to the world, but she only whispered to him, between the urgency of her breathing, "I love you, Robert, my love."

She became aware of movement in the house below and held her head away from him to listen.

"This is no place," he said. "Come back with me." Then he seemed to recall something. "No, we must wait. There is time."

"Time?"

"To set up a home for you—and Alice."

She felt her heart beating and took his hand to hold it to her so that he could feel it too, to know the depth of her longing for him.

"A home," she echoed and wondered why they had wasted so much time, why he had not been near her to take Alice to him, to be father to his daughter, and husband to her.

He smiled down at her. "A home for you. Where I could visit you."

"Visit?"

"Whenever I could. Discreetly, of course."

"Discreetly? What need is there of discretion?"

"Well, of course," he said, as if there could be no argument, "we wouldn't want gossip. It would do neither of us any good. It would be best in London, when I'm elected. You would like that, I'm sure. There'd be less likelihood of discovery there."

She stared at him. She knew now what he was proposing and was astonished at it.

"A kept woman," she said tonelessly.

He smiled. "I'd make sure you wanted for nothing." She felt his hand, under hers, move against her breast. She snatched it from her and moved away from him, turning her back to him, to conceal her hurt. She had not misjudged him, after all. There was never anything but humiliation for her in his treatment of her. "We're low, so low, so very very low," the words from the broadsheet poem came loudly to her.

She felt his hand at her shoulder but shrugged it off. She wanted to turn and face him with contempt but she was afraid she would show her pain, and pride forced her to conceal it.

"You'll see the good of it, I know," she heard him say.

"What of my work here, for the cause?" she said, covering up her anguish, wanting him to go, but hoping desperately for a word of affection from him.

His voice showed surprise. "There'd be no call for you to be involved, not with a home to look after, and your daughter. And me, from time to time."

She did not reply. She was conscious of the physical warmth emanating from him. He was close to her and if she turned she would be in his arms again. She moved to Alice, picked her up and stood facing him, in control of herself again.

"I'll leave you to think about it," he said. "I'll see you again in a day or two."

She let him go and stood, holding Alice to her; she was stunned by the enormity of his suggestion. She could not deny the attractions it held, the opportunity to live in comfort with Alice, in London, near the center of things, making a home where Robert could visit. She banished the thought immediately, angry for being tempted even for a moment by an arrangement which would keep her discreetly hidden, out of the way, a creature too humble to be allowed to share a man's whole life.

He is blind, she said to herself, blinded by ambition, corrupted by flattery and the society he keeps. If he, or anyone, wants me, they will have me on my terms, and I will be known for what I am, a companion fit for a man, a lover giving all, given all, sharing life and work. I know this is not what is expected of me. It is not what is expected of any of us, even of a wife. Our "exalted duty" is to serve man, she recalled an article in a newspaper she had read recently. And what of a mistress? she asked herself—exalted duty of a different kind—the submission of body, of will, the dependence on the generosity of a man—were the two roles so different?

Alice stirred in her arms. Ellen looked at her daughter and said, "Will it be different for you, my love?"

II

SHE could not remain in Camborne waiting for him to reappear. When he came for his answer she would not be there, and that would be answer enough. She left a message for Veronica saying she was going to return to Cusgarne for some days; she would go from there to the meeting that had been arranged in Redruth.

Julia was delighted to welcome them. She announced she was pregnant, with a pride that suggested only that was needed to make her life complete. She took Alice from Ellen and crooned over her.

"You'll have room for us for a few days?" Ellen asked.

"As long as you like. Mark and I still sleep downstairs in the linny. You can have Richard's room."

"And James?"

"In the little room beyond Richard's."

Ellen remembered. It was part of the bedroom really, separated only by a thin partition.

"You'll be happy here, I'm certain," Julia said, taking Alice with her into the kitchen.

Ellen knew Alice would thrive in Julia's care. At sixteen months she was a friendly child, interested in everything, toddling about the cottage, exploring this new world. And Ellen was happy too to spend a few days recapturing the magic that Sunny Corner had always held for her. It was especially at this time of year, when the first blossom began to show on the blackthorn, that its enchantment was strongest, with new growth abounding everywhere along the lanes. She discovered again the delights of the valley, with the cattle from the Manor Farm contentedly grazing by the stream as it meandered through the pastures.

She spent the first three days refreshing herself with the peace of the countryside, leaving Alice in the secure love of her aunt. And she spent those days in the company of James and as she did, some of her old feeling for him returned, not with the intensity she had experienced before but with a calm acceptance of him as he was, with all his faults.

She was saddened by the changes prison had wrought. The fire had been doused, the energy sapped. He was watchful and wary as if he could not even now believe he was free and his own man again. She encouraged him to talk, for his long years of silence had made him hesitant, and as they walked along the valley his manner eased and he spoke again of his vision of America. But now the dream seemed more unreal even than before. He was unable to find work, blacklisted as he was, and could see no hope of raising the money for his passage. He was a defeated, sadly old young man, and she felt pity for him.

She thought at times of her former love for him. Love was there still, but transmuted. Desire—physical desire—seemed to have no part in it, but she longed to comfort him, help him to regain his will. He needed her, she felt, and there were times when she wanted to give herself to him and by her own vigor to re-create the James she had once known.

She did not speak of this to him in their walks together and he gave no inkling of how he felt toward her. He seemed unsure of himself, anxious not to offend, a different man altogether from the James who had led his fellows in the attack on the mine.

Ellen's stay at the cottage was broken into by the need to attend the meeting in Redruth. There had been no message from Veronica and Ellen assumed she was still in Bristol. Ellen walked to Scorrier, caught the train to Redruth and found two of her supporters waiting for her at the station. One was dressed in black, a widow, wearing a mourning ring, heavy with jet. The other bore a marked resemblance to her. They were Mrs. and Miss Burroughs, mother and daughter.

They seemed uneasy. "We're not sure how many we'll get," said the older woman. "Or what sort they'll be."

"It's an open air meeting," said Miss Burroughs. "We hope you don't mind. We've put posters up advertising it, with your name, but someone's torn them down."

"It's not easy," said her mother.

"No," said Ellen. "It never is, but I like it better that way. The harder the fight, the more satisfying is the winning."

The women led her down Fore Street to the bottom of the town and turned along the Portreath Road. "There's a bit of common here along. It's well lit there," said Mrs. Burroughs. "Miss Tangye's waiting. She'll have a box for you to stand on and there'll be other friends." She sounded nervous and looked at Ellen as if afraid she would resent the simplicity of the arrangements.

There were four women waiting on the common, a small triangle of spare land not far from the Rose Tavern. The streets were empty and quiet, save for a sudden sound of raucous laughter from the inn. It was followed by a cheer and a burst of song.

"Well," Ellen said. "Let's to it." She stood on the box and looked at the half-dozen women. "We'll have to do better than this if we're to get anywhere," she said, but smiled to show her criticism was not aimed at these women.

"It's not the hour yet," said one. "We said eight o'clock on the posters. The town clock's not yet struck."

They waited in the balm of the evening for the clock to strike. A couple, arm in arm, passed and turned back to them, curious at the group. A few hundred yards away, at the crossroads, a number of men and women stood watching, perhaps waiting for them to begin before they ventured near. Another hoot of mirth came from the tavern.

The town clock began to strike the hour. Ellen waited until the last chime, raised her arm and began. This was her world, she felt, a world numbed with hardship, but one she was capable of restoring to feeling. She saw that the men and women at the crossroads moved toward her, and others, as if magnetized, followed them from somewhere. Soon her audience had grown from the faithful half-dozen women to a satisfying thirty. She looked at them as she spoke, noting with her practiced eye the sober clothes, the alert and earnest gaze. These were her people, honest solid working men and women; these were the ones she had to convince, not the "men of influence" of Veronica's circle. None of the women had the vote, and perhaps few of the men, but these were the ones who mattered. She spoke fluently, co-

gently, passionately and she saw her audience was held, persuaded by her argument, moved by her oratory. Her voice
carried along the road and others came to join them so that
the crowd grew to fifty or so. She saw pride in the eyes of the
women who had organized the meeting and was glad for their
sakes that they had been rewarded by a good turnout. She drew
her speech to a close. The women at the front applauded enthusiastically and the remainder joined in.

At that moment, from behind the crowd, a jeering laugh
erupted. A group of men, red-faced, slobber-mouthed arrived
from the doors of the tavern. They stood for a moment on the
edge of the crowd, laughing among themselves, then one shouted
an obscenity that made the women draw in their breaths. A
man in the audience turned to rebuke the drunkards. It was
no use. Ellen stood on the box, silent, as the men at the back
jeered and yelled and then, with a sudden concerted movement,
broke through the audience toward her.

"Get 'er, lads," shouted one man, less drunk than the rest,
in control of himself, and, it seemed, in control of the mob.

She recognized him. Carkeek, the overseer from the sheds
at Pednandrea. She recognized his sleek dark hair, his sallow
skin, and she saw malevolence in his eyes.

"Get her!" he shouted again, and the men hurled themselves toward her. Mrs. Burroughs and her friends were pushed,
screaming, aside. One woman started to belabor the men with
her fists, shouting oaths as frightful as the men's, scratching
wildly at one red-haired man and beating him into retreat; but
the others came forward.

Ellen stood her ground and, hands on hips, glared defiantly at them. They hesitated, but Carkeek, behind them,
shouted, with stark ferocity, "She's the one. Grab her. Let her
have it."

The leading man thrust at her and Ellen struck out at him,
swinging her fist at his face, halting him for a moment. Then
she saw from the corner of her eye some missile flying at her
and raised an arm to deflect it, but it hit her on the temple; a
man reached for her legs and tried to drag her from the box.
She felt her skirt tear, saw a hand lifted to strike her, averted
her face and felt a blow on the shoulder that knocked her to
the ground. There was a hand at her hair, another at her blouse;

she knew cloth had torn; she heard screaming, whether from herself or one of the other women she did not know. She felt blood in her mouth, warm and salty. She struck out wildly, determined to drive off the attack upon her. She smelled sweat and alcohol and tobacco and fear. She tried to get to her feet but the weight of men was upon her, holding her down. She did not know what was happening, only that the world about her was dark. The soft evening light had gone and only a terrifying blackness was left.

A shout penetrated her mind and shook her from the stupor that had threatened. There was something about the voice she knew. It rose again, savage and furious. One of the men attacking her was dragged away. She heard a male cry of anguish and then a sound of retching. She took into her mind all the details around: a flash of light, another sharp cry of pain, a crack of bone, the rush of feet as another of her attackers fled.

Then she was freed of fear, of the sour smell of her assailants. They had gone and she lay sprawled on the grass with a man kneeling beside her, supporting her in his arms. She felt a cloth at her nose, staunching the blood which poured from it, or from another wound near it.

"Ellen," the voice said. "We must go. They'll be coming back."

She tried to move. She knew she ought to. The voice told her to and she must do as it said, but it hurt to move and the hurt seemed to be everywhere. She smiled to herself. It had been a good meeting, she thought. "The harder the fight, the more satisfying the winning." She had said that somewhere, she remembered.

"It was a hard fight," she said to the voice.

"It's not over yet," the voice replied and added, "We must get her away from here."

She felt arms raising her. She relaxed in them and allowed herself to be carried away. She could hear nothing now but the clop of a pony's hooves, the turn of wheels; there were no angry shouts, no jeers.

She was dreaming a wild dream, or rather a nightmare, for she had a sudden moment of fear as the arm was taken away from her.

"Help me," she said and felt the arm return to hold her. Then reason left her, sound and touch receded and there was nothing.

III

It was as if time had slipped back. She was here again. She recognized the room, the great bed with its white sheets, the rich red curtains, the mirror in the large wardrobe.

She tried to sit up but pain struck her. There came back to her then the taste of terror, recollection of the meeting in Redruth, the uproar of it. And she remembered the voice and calm returned to her, the deep Scots voice, the voice that had roared angrily and had then, close and gentle, cosseted and comforted her.

She lay, head on the soft pillow, relaxed in warm content in spite of her aches. He had come to her defense, saved her from Carkeek's roughs and brought her here. Here—she recalled her last stay in this room. For a moment she saw the sharp features of his housekeeper and resentment returned, but it was dispelled by the memory of his voice and its concern for her. He had brought her here and she was glad of it.

She moved, warily because of her aches, stretching her arms and legs. It hurt, but not acutely. There was nothing wrong with her that rest would not heal, she thought, but her head ached and she put up a hand to it to discover a bandage around her forehead.

She moved her legs to the edge of the bed to sit up but as she did the door opened and Robert appeared. He frowned when he saw her.

"You'll not move from there," he said. "I need to keep you under observation yet awhile." He reached to her legs, lifted them and put them under the bedclothes again. She lay back while he examined the wound at her temple and replaced the bandage, treating her with a gentleness and concern that moved her.

"Miss Langarth's below," he said. "I let her know what happened yesterday."

"Yesterday?" She was surprised.

"You spent the night here."

Again! she thought, but how differently.

"I happened to be passing the meeting. I saw the trouble and brought you here."

He seemed pleased that she was there, dependent upon him, and she could not help responding to his concern for her. It was warm and safe here, with someone else to take decisions for her. This was how it could be if she let herself accept his offer to find a home for Alice and her. This was how it could be, a comfortable home with every material need provided, and a man to come, from time to time.

From time to time, to visit, whenever he could, discreetly. Was that enough?

"I'll send Mrs. Honeychurch with something for you to eat," he said and, smiling tenderly upon her, he left her.

She watched him go to the door, where he turned to look at her again, a smile on his lips and a look of satisfaction in his eyes. He had taken her for granted, she realized. He had assumed she was happy to accept his proposal. For a second she lay unmoving then she recalled he had said he would send Mrs. Honeychurch. Her loathing for the housekeeper revived and with it a sense of shame that she had come near to considering Robert's proposal seriously. She must get away before the insidious trap of these surroundings closed on her, before the comfort of this house robbed her of the pride which sustained her. In spite of her stiffness she struggled into her clothes. I must get back to Alice, she told herself. She needs me. I must keep her to me.

She went to the door and opened it with difficulty, for she felt slack with weakness. She closed it behind her and went to the stairs. Voices came from below, Robert talking to his housekeeper. She looked down and saw him and stood still, afraid he might look up to see her, but he went into his drawing room and she heard Veronica's crisp tones questioning him.

She crept slowly downstairs, conscious of her aching limbs and throbbing head. She had crept from this house before, with the sounds of the housekeeper's contempt ringing in her ears. Now it was the voice of Veronica she could hear coming from the half-open door.

Ellen paused at the foot of the stairs to take breath.

"Well, Robert," she heard Veronica say, "the time has come to take the plunge. My father will raise no objection. It's my mother we have to concern ourselves with."

"I thought she regarded me with favor," said Robert.

Veronica laughed. "Of course, my dear, as a political hopeful, but not as a son-in-law. We shall have to work hard at that."

Ellen started. She wanted to move, to leave the house, but she could not.

"Now that you're becoming a man of affairs she will see reason. I'll make sure of that," Veronica went on. "A mere doctor is one thing; a Member of Parliament with a bright future is quite another."

There was silence and Ellen wondered what intimacy it covered.

"We can both serve our purposes," Veronica said. "You have no reservations?"

There was a further silence, then Robert answered, "None."

Ellen tiptoed past the door and had reached the front door when behind her, from the kitchens, she heard steps. She turned to see a maid, with a tray, moving to the stairs. Hurriedly she opened the front door and left the house now almost unaware of the pain in her body for the anguish in her mind.

She had thought of yielding to Robert, of becoming his kept woman; she had been tempted to think of being his secret "wife"—what harm was there in that? But now she saw it as a shameful betrayal, of Veronica, but mostly of herself. She was afraid the maid might have seen her and that Robert would pursue her, and when she saw a growler at the curbside she had it take her to the station. The cabby looked with curiosity at the bandage at her forehead and she pulled her hat brim down to try to hide it. She took the train from Redruth back to Scorrier and saw nothing of the journey for she was blinded by anger at Robert's perfidy.

How could he—how *could* he? she said to herself over and over again.

Chapter Fifteen

I

THE following day, leaving Alice with Julia, she returned to Camborne. She would tell Veronica that she could no longer live there; she would make as her excuse the need for Alice to grow up in the care of a family—and there was truth in that. But the real reason, which she could not hide from herself, was that she could not bear to live under a roof with Robert's wife-to-be and knowing how close she had come to betraying her. Yet she needed to continue her work for women's suffrage, and the money which Veronica paid her would be welcome to Julia.

Veronica was alarmed when she heard her decision.

"But that surely does not mean you'll stop working for the cause? You're needed here, don't you see?"

"I can come by train—" Ellen began.

"No, I'll arrange for a carriage to collect you each morning and return you to Cusgarne in the evening." Veronica was insistent and Ellen yielded.

"I'm so glad," said Veronica. "I have so much to do, so

many plans." She looked at Ellen as if anxious to confide in her. "Reid has resigned at last."

"Then," said Ellen, trying to keep expression from her voice. "Robert Buchan, MP."

"Yes. He will have to give up his practice here, of course." Veronica seemed infected with gaiety, an excitement no longer to be suppressed. "He needs the support of a woman of wealth. A bride. Someone who can steer him into office, provide an entrée into the right circles—where power resides. . . . Well," she said, when Ellen did not speak. "Will I fill the bill, do you think?"

Ellen was still silent.

"I thought you might have guessed. We've planned it for some time. Robert's making a formal approach to my father at this very moment. My mother can't object now. It might offend her if I were to marry a mere doctor, but he promises to be so much more than that. And I . . ."

"The power behind the throne?"

"Of course, my dear Ellen. Do you disapprove?"

"Not in the slightest if that's what you want."

"We'll live in London, of course, near the heart of things. I can do so much more there."

And I, thought Ellen, will work among my own people, speaking, organizing, persuading, making a little progress here, suffering a setback there.

"Yes," she said to Veronica. "You will be well suited there using your charm on the men of influence."

"I'll keep this house of course, and you will still use it as your headquarters."

There was work to do here still, and Ellen settled down to it. She had notes to write for a women's group in Helston and she sat at her desk to concentrate upon them. She heard Veronica's carriage leaving—she had gone to her parent's house, Ellen supposed. She gathered her notes together.

She did not hear the door open but became aware that someone was there. She looked up expecting to see Rachel, but it was not. It was Robert. He was smartly dressed, in a high-buttoned frock coat. He had come from paying his call at Trevorrow, she guessed. This was his suitor's costume, not that of his workaday round.

"You heard of Reid's resignation?" he asked.

"Veronica told me," she said. "She's not here."

"I know," he said.

"She told me something else. Did her parents agree?"

His face clouded and he turned away from her. "Oh yes," he said. "They see no objection now, though they're none too pleased."

"And you?" Ellen asked.

"Do you mind?"

"You can marry who you will. It makes no difference to me."

He came to her and put his hands on her shoulders as she sat at the desk.

"Why did you leave so hurriedly yesterday? I was concerned for you." He gently touched the bruise on her cheek, not as a doctor would, but as a lover. She flinched, but not from pain. His hands then touched her neck, his fingers running up it into her hair. They were strong fingers and for a moment she found the feel of them pleasant. She jerked her head away, pushed the chair back and stood to face him.

"So, you'll be off to London then?"

"Soon, when my selection is confirmed. To arrange things. It won't take long. Then you can turn your back on all this."

He had taken her agreement for granted, Ellen thought with astonishment. He had no doubts about her. He did not know her. He took hold of her by the elbows and held her to look at him.

"It will be a quiet life for you," he said. "Humdrum maybe. And I don't suppose I'll be able to see you as often as I would like, but you'll be there for me to come to. In the background. Secret. Private. In our own world. Hidden." The idea of secrecy seemed to intrigue him.

She eyed him with disbelief but he seemed unconcerned at her reaction. "Veronica," she said.

"What of her? She'll not know."

"Indeed?"

"Ours will be a marriage of political convenience. She wants my influence. I need her wealth. We understand each other. But don't let's talk of Veronica," he went on. "She has no part in this."

"Save that it would be her money, would it not?"

He sensed at last the coldness in her voice. "Does that make a difference?"

"No difference at all, to me."

He seemed slightly reassured. "I'll find a home for you in London. It will only take a month or two."

"What do I want with a home in London? What should take me there when everything I need is here?"

"What do you mean?" he asked. "We'll be happy together, I promise you. Whenever I can get away. Here in Cornwall if you like but we should have to be so much more careful."

"Tucked away in a corner, concealed, not to be spoken of?"

"It can be no other way, Ellen. What would you have me do?"

"I would have you do nothing. Take your seat in Parliament, marry your woman of wealth, set up some woman as your paramour, live as many secret lives as you wish, but don't expect me to share one of them with you."

"You do not understand."

"I understand only too well. I am to be a bedfellow, a domestic companion, a . . ."

"A lover," he interrupted.

"Is that what you mean by a lover?" she said. "A woman to be hidden from the world, to share only a part of life with you, fit for sport in bed, but . . ."

He seized hold of her by the shoulders and shook her. She winced, with pain this time, for he had gripped her where Carkeek's men had bruised her.

"I want you," he said. "Do you not see? I need you."

"I have no need of you," she said. "Nor love for you. Nor feeling for you, save contempt."

He let his hands fall and moved away from her and went to the window.

"Robert Buchan, MP," she said. "That should be enough for you."

"Come with me, Ellen," he turned to say.

"I expect you will do well," she said, "with Veronica to help. She is a woman of mettle. She knows what she wants."

"And you?"

"I know what I want too, Robert," she said, but she did not know.

"The man Bryant?" he said, his brows lowering.

"He would have me as I am, would not want to hide me from view, would let me share . . ."

But she did not finish for he had left her. She heard the door slam. She went to the window and watched him as he mounted his horse, jerking angrily at the reins. She saw him halt at the gates to the drive and stop to raise his hat to someone there, playing the part. He was a public man now and she was pleased for him and pleased too that she had purged herself of him.

II

ROBERT Buchan rode away, trying to control his emotions, but anger had hold of him in such a way that though his actions were rational his mind was disordered with rage. Bryant, Ellen, Veronica—there seemed to be no precise origin of his feelings of fury; they were all despicable, objects of his loathing. They had all contributed to a state of mind that was near insanity.

Bryant—he had never liked the man; he was reckless, impetuous, a wild rebel, a destroyer: he regretted the help he had given him at Wheal Busy. And yet, he admired the man; had he not been a rival he would have found cause to approve his independence of spirit; and James Bryant, in spite of the pressures upon him, had never revealed the names of those who had helped him. Buchan's anger against James eased.

It was Ellen, not Bryant, who deserved his contempt. She had led him on, set her cap at him, bewitched him until he had been willing to humiliate himself by offering her a home, a home which she had cruelly spurned. And yet, he remembered the passion and the pride with which she had rejected him and he wondered at it. It moved him, for it was that very strength of mind which had drawn him to her in the first place, the fact that she was herself, a woman who fitted no pattern, a woman without equal. Ellen was not at fault.

It was Veronica. She had corrupted him. She and her

mother had manipulated and molded him. What he was now was their creation. It was Veronica.

He had ridden out of the town and was now riding along a ridge, looking down over the Red River. He could see children working in the tin streams and wondered at the way the law was defied, with impunity it seemed, but he did not give the matter more than a passing thought.

Veronica was to blame.

He pulled his horse up and shook his head in amazement at himself. The blinding red fury had gone. He could think rationally again.

Why was he blaming everyone but himself? He could not lay any charge at Bryant's door, nor at Veronica's, nor at Ellen's—save that of being herself.

And at his own door? Was he himself? Was he true to his destiny? Whence came his ambition?

He had been flattered by the interest the Langarths had taken in him. Rebecca Langarth had given him her patronage and he had accepted it, played the game according to her rules, cultivated her good will and that of the "men of influence." In so doing he had persuaded himself he could keep faith with his radical principles and could hold to his opinions without voicing them. Once in Parliament, he told himself, he could speak and vote as his conscience directed. In the meantime he could keep to himself those views which were unwelcome to the mining interest (such as his belief in the right of working miners to organize in self-protection).

He tried to close his eyes to the self-loathing which mounted within him, but it was not to be hidden. He looked around him. From where he sat, astride his horse, he could see vast distances, over the sparkling sea to the north, around to the ruins of Carn Brea and the multiplicity of mine workings, to the roofs of the town of Redruth.

What was he doing here when there was work to be done there? There was present reality, with scarlet fever rife in the hovels of the town. There, in the practice of his profession, was a role he could play without self-doubt.

During the next days he threw himself into his work in Redruth, seeking by his efforts to confine the disease. The close conditions in which the families lived made it impossible to prevent the spread of the infection but Buchan refused to admit

he was helpless; nor was he entirely powerless, for his minis-
trations eased the pain of the sufferers, soothed the anguish of
the parents and, in the end, did restrict the scourge to a small
area of the town.

He ended his days tired but in a way content. He had been
trained for this; he knew his job and was good at it. He put his
political ambitions to the back of his mind for the moment and
he tried, by the same devotion to his practice, to put Ellen out
of his mind altogether.

It was not to be.

III

ELLEN soon got used to the new routine; Veronica's carriage
called for her in the mornings and returned her to Sunny Corner in the evenings. She could not live in the Camborne house
but she was not at ease in the cottage, for she was constantly
aware of the presence of James. It was impossible to be unaware
of him.

He would sit in the chair that had once been his father's,
staring into the flames, but at a move from her he would look
up anxiously as if hoping for a sign, some indication—of what?
What did life hold for him? She wished she could move to him,
to offer him some hope, and almost put out a hand to him. She
refrained; she feared that touching him would release something, something explosive, destructive maybe. Hope seemed
to have deserted him. He no longer spoke of America; even
that dream had vanished.

Then she returned one late afternoon and at Alice's insistence took her along the lane for a walk. They had not gone
far when they met James coming up the hill from the village,
arms laden with pieces of timber. He was whistling gaily as he
had so long ago.

"What is it?" she asked.

"Wood," he said. "For a sea-chest. Penrose let me have it."

"A sea-chest?"

"America," he said. "I'm bound for the new world. Mr.
Luke has found money for my passage somehow."

She turned and went with him back to the cottage, Alice
at her side.

"I'll miss her," he said, nodding to the child. There was no need to ask who else he would miss. His eyes showed her plainly that a word of encouragement would bring him to her.

"When do you go?" she said.

He did not answer and she thought he had been hoping for something different from her. When they reached the cottage she went inside and gave Alice her tea and put her to bed. When she came downstairs she heard outside the sound of wood being sawn. The sea-chest was begun. Later, as dark fell, James came in and joined her. There was a heavy silence between them, and Ellen was glad when Julia and Mark came in, for she was afraid if she were left alone with James for long she would, from sympathy and affection, lead him to declare himself. She was safe in company and James was safe from her. When she got up to go to join Alice in bed she knew his eyes followed her movements; she resisted the impulse to glance back at him.

"Good night," she said without turning and went upstairs to lie beside Alice. But she could not sleep. She was hiding something from herself she felt. She needed love, the love that James could give maybe. Yet whenever she closed her eyes it was not James who came to mind. She saw the fair hair, the blue eyes, the strong, determined features of Robert. It was he who was with her, who would remain with her every living moment. I must free myself of him she told herself. But she could not free herself through James. That would be a betrayal of him.

She heard James come to bed, heard the boards give as he lay back. She held her breath, fearing wildly that he would hear her thoughts, they were so close lying there, a thin boarding all between them.

She heard a whisper.

"Ellen." So faint as to be almost nothing but a sigh. "Ellen," came again from behind the partition. "I love you, Ellen." It was said so softly that the avowal might have been the product of her imagination.

"Are you there?" he said.

"I'm here," she answered.

"Do you hear me?"

"I heard."

"I dared not tell you."

"You have told me," she answered.

"Come to me, Ellen."

She did not answer. She did not know how.

"Come to me. Please." There was, in the whispered voice, a hint of desperation, a poignancy that clutched at her. He is alone there, she thought, and soon he will be more alone, venturing into the dark mysteries of America.

"I'm coming," she said and rose quietly from Alice's side and moved out of her room to his.

She stooped at the door and stood just inside the room. His bed, a wooden bench set against the wall, almost filled the room. He was sitting on it, knees bent, his arms clasped around them, his shoulders hunched. He did not look up when she came in. He seemed to be talking to himself, though the words were meant for her. "I love you, Ellen," he was muttering. "Come to me, please."

She stepped to him, knelt beside the bed and reached a hand to touch him. He started with surprise and turned and looked at her with glazed eyes.

"You're here," he said. "I called and you came." There was astonishment and wonder in his voice, as at a miracle. He looked around him and put out a hand to touch the wall. "I thought . . ." Then, in disbelief, he shook his head. "I was there, in my cell. I felt the stones, the cold damp stones. But I am here," he said. "With you." His voice ended in a catch of breath and, without warning, he buried his head in her breast and wept.

She clutched him to her, stroking his hair, murmuring sounds of consolation, of pity, of understanding. She could feel the tears coursing down his cheeks and the moistness of them on her breasts. She held him close, hoping the shuddering would stop, that in her comfort of him he might forget the dark terrors of his cell. Slowly the sobbing ceased and he lay there, motionless, his face buried between her breasts. Then he moved and she felt his mouth against her, moving down to find a nipple, to rest there, tongue to the tip, his lips moving gently, sucking.

She could not refuse him. Pity for him moved her so that she wanted to suckle him, to hold him safe. "James," she said. "My love." And she felt love for him, love for a bewildered defenseless child.

But, with the movement of his tongue against her nipple, sensation of a different kind reached to her; desire stirred; her own need rose in demand; she let her hands slip from his head to his shoulders, wanting to touch his flesh as he was touching hers, wanting him, to lie with him, breast to breast, belly to belly, thigh to thigh. She moved from her kneeling position to lie alongside him.

There was still, in a remote corner of her mind, a faint echo of reason, a voice urging her to caution, but the physical urgency of her desire would not let her listen. Then as she lay beside him, letting her hands seek him out, she heard, but refused to heed, a soft whimper. It came again, rising more insistently, a cry for her.

"Mammy, mammy."

Her hands ceased their exploration and instead took hold of his, holding them, preventing them from probing, touching, sapping her will.

"Mammy, mammy." Alice's voice began to rise in anxiety. "Mammy."

"I'm coming," she called and though James put out a hand to stop her she slipped from him and ran next door.

"There, my love," she said and bent to Alice, hugging her child to her. But desire was still on her, blood racing. She covered Alice with kisses and fondled her until the child was reassured and asleep again. Ellen lay beside her daughter then turned her eyes to the door. James stood there, in his shirt, a shadow merely.

"No," she said softly, "I'm sorry but it cannot be." She wondered how she had found the strength to deny him when the memory of her need was so fresh. "No, James, no," she said again as he moved toward her. She sat up and pulled the bed cover up to her shoulders.

"You'll not come with me?" he said. "To America, to share my life?"

"I cannot," she said, surprised at the firmness in her voice.

"When do you go?" she said softly, as Alice stirred.

"Next Friday."

"So soon?"

She was dismayed. Her feelings for him—though she had refused him—were deep, unfathomably so. She could hold him here maybe, if she spoke lovingly. One word would seal it.

"I shall miss you," she said, rejecting the temptation.

He turned and left her.

Chapter Sixteen

THE men who gathered at Hosking's invitation for the purpose, as Hosking said, "of clearing the ground for your acceptance by the Liberal committee," were men of the mines, stubborn men, bound by tradition, hard men, who prided themselves on their knowledge of rock, were contemptuous of the outsider, resented central government, vaunted their Cornishness. Buchan was continually surprised and gratified that in spite of this they welcomed him.

"There are a few doubters who say we need a local man," Hosking told him. "I've said there's no one understands the mining community better than you."

"I'm flattered," said Buchan. They are all suspicious of one another, he thought. I'm a neutral, neither agent, mine lord, smelter nor merchant. But he recognized it was Langarth's advocacy that was the main factor in his advancement.

The men gathered there did not after all discuss his selection as candidate. They had other matters on their minds. A new Factory Act was proposed which, said Hosking, was going to cut through practice in the mines and ruin Cornwall.

"They're going to make it impossible for us to hire juvenile labor," said Hosking belligerently. "D'you realize, Buchan, they're telling us we can't employ youngsters fulltime. No night work, no overtime, no Saturday afternoon work. They'll be telling us how to blow our noses next. What does Whitehall know about Cornish mining? It's a man's business. What does a quill-pushing government inspector know about that?"

Robert listened to the catalog of complaints against government interference.

"We need boys to work," said Hosking, and the company echoed their agreement. "Without them the mines can't survive, not in these days. And the families need the work too. How would they get by without what the lads bring home? And what will happen to Cornish mining if boys stop learning their trade at an early age? Pick and gad, not pencil and slate is what they need to be busy with." He looked to his fellows for approval. "These men from Whitehall," he added, "what do they know of us and ours?"

"We need men of our own at Westminster to tell them the truth. Men who know the mines," said Josiah Thomas. He looked at Buchan. "What do you think, doctor?"

"He's one of us," said Hosking. "One of us."

Was he one of them? Robert had listened to them in silence, wondering what motive drove these men. For the most part they were solid, thoughtful citizens, pillars of the community, devout attenders at church or chapel. They might, like Abel Hosking, have human failings, but they were discreet in pandering to them. Yet these men, kindly and charitable in one part of their lives, were blind to injustices they themselves created.

Was he one of them? Was he to live according to their standards?

The following afternoon he was visiting a patient in a village outside Redruth when he was summoned to Wheal Uny.

"A young boy," he was told. "Fell down the ladderway. We brought him up. We heard you were near at hand. We thought we'd better get you though 'tis not likely to be much use."

It was no use. The boy was dead. He had been taken into the miners' changing shed. A group of men and boys stood around him. Buchan knelt beside the lad. His body was distorted, bones broken in the fall, but his face was unmarked. It was the face of a child, unspoiled by time, a round face, lips slightly parted, eyes closed. Buchan looked at the group surrounding him. There were other faces like this boy's among them.

"How old are you?" he asked one dark, lively eyed youngster.

"Ten, sir."

"Why aren't you at school?" said Buchan.

The lad turned away and a man in the group drew him aside.

"How old was he?" Buchan gestured to the body.

A man knelt beside Buchan and took the boy's head in his hands. "My brother's son, he is."

"How old?" repeated Buchan.

"Ten—eleven, what does it matter now?"

"What's his name?" said Buchan as he helped to raise the body onto a cart.

"Jem Eathorne," said the man.

Robert knew the family. The father had lost his hand in a mining accident and seldom found work. He turned away, angry at his inability to help. As he left the mine he saw more children, two boys and three girls, none as old as ten, he reckoned, by the buddles where the ore was washed. They had been drawn from their work by the accident. When a man shouted angrily at them they hurried back to their tasks.

Robert found it difficult to control his feelings. What hope was there for a people so careless of childhood? He mounted his horse and rode from the mine, the image of the dead boy clouding his mind.

Was it true that the mines could not survive without the use of children? What could a child do that could not be done better in some other way? One of the girls he had seen had been no older than eight. She was barely out of infancy. How could this be, in the 1870s?

He rode to the Eathornes to prepare them for the arrival of Jem's body. They received the news with resignation. There was a fortitude about these people that he had to admire. He noticed that there was something about Jem's mother that reminded him of Ellen. It was nothing physical—though her hair was dark, perhaps once richly dark as Ellen's—it was the woman's spirit, something proud and unyielding about her; perhaps all the women of miners had to have this quality; he had seen it before.

He left the Eathornes and returned to his home, desperately tired, forgetting that Veronica had said she would visit him that evening. He was irritated to see her carriage at his house. The day had left images in his mind that could not be dislodged. He felt he had been wounded and needed salve to heal him.

He got none from Veronica. She was all business and intrigue, and burst into talk the moment she saw him.

"My dear Robert. It's going so well now. I had heard rumors that some of the committee wanted a local man, Henry Tremayne."

Buchan knew Tremayne. "A good man," he commented.

"Really, Robert," Veronica said impatiently, "you cannot afford to speak kindly of your rivals. Anyway your support of the mining interest has convinced them."

"My support?"

"Your promise to oppose the Factory Act. To oppose the government's efforts to change Cornish practice."

Had he promised? He had said nothing, but his silence on the issue must have been taken as support.

She noticed his abstracted air. "What is it?"

He was seeing the body of the young boy, Jem Eathorne. It was boys of his age they were talking about.

"Perhaps . . ." he began.

She looked at him, uneasy at his tone.

"Perhaps it's time customs did change."

"You cannot say that. Not at the moment. What would the selection committee think?"

"Be damned to the committee."

"You cannot be damned to them at this stage, Robert. You must do nothing to upset your chances."

"Keep my mouth shut, you mean?"

"Of course, if that's necessary to ensure your selection. What harm is there in that? You can begin to speak your mind when you are in the House."

He was silent. He had been so often silent lately.

"Well?" She spoke sharply, her voice clipped, imperious.

"I was called to a mine today. I was too late. A boy was

killed. He was ten." He stared at her, seeing not her, but the wasted life. He remembered another occasion long since, when he had been moved by the death of three young children, and had spoken of it to Richard—and to Ellen. He remembered how Ellen, a girl then, had been sensitive to his feelings, had encouraged him to unburden himself, and had comforted him by her understanding.

He looked at Veronica. She had no understanding, felt no sympathy. She was anxious only about his selection, concerned only with her maneuverings.

"Well?" she said again.

"I cannot approve the use of children in the mines," he said. "I have seen children of eight, nine, ten."

She was silent for a moment, studying him.

"You must not be so foolish as to voice such an opinion at the moment." It was a statement rather than a question. "It will offend the mining interest, you realize?" she went on.

"Abel Hosking and his friends?"

"They are powerful men."

He did not answer. He had no energy left to confront her.

She smiled at his silence. "I can count on you, Robert. I know that."

He let her go, then took himself to bed, hoping desperately there would be no call to disturb him in the night.

II

ELLEN found it more and more difficult to work with Veronica now that she knew of the understanding between her and Robert. She suppressed her feelings, for the work she was doing was important to her and Veronica's support was needful. She felt she was beginning to be known—not among the "men of influence"; these she ignored—but among the working women of Camborne, the women of Maynes Row and Straypark Lane, the women whose men, so often, had left them to seek work abroad or up-country, women who stoically faced a hostile world, and survived, alone.

Veronica did not care about these women. Since they had no political influence they were valueless to her. Ellen sometimes wondered why Veronica bothered with her. After all, she was one of them.

She returned from a visit into town to their headquarters.

"Is that you, Ellen?" she heard Veronica call from the study. Ellen joined her. She was looking flushed, mildly angry.

"I do not understand him," she said. "Robert Buchan," she added. Ellen was silent and moved to depart for home. "I do not understand him," Veronica repeated. "He has discovered that Hosking and Thomas and other mine captains are allowing boys of eleven to be employed below ground."

"I know of younger ones than that," said Ellen.

Veronica ignored her. "He's blind. He forgets his adoption as candidate depends on his standing with men like Hosking and Thomas. Without them even my family's support will be useless."

"Does it matter?" Ellen asked, indifferent to Veronica's political intrigues.

"How can you say that? Another voice at Westminster speaking for women's suffrage? Is it not worth sacrificing his principles for that?"

"If he can sacrifice one principle, he can sacrifice them all."

"He'll come around." Veronica smiled. "He'll see where his interest lies."

Yes, thought Ellen, I have no doubt he will, but she had glimpsed in his brief protest to Veronica something of the Robert she had once known.

She asked the coachman to drop her on the Downs. It was a clear evening and though she was impatient to get home to Alice, she needed the solitude to think. She had rejected Robert—there was no going back on that. She knew she only had to extend her hand to James and he would take her and Alice and make them his.

She stood at the crossroads, hesitating. She had paused here often in the past, had stood here with Jane, had kept tryst with James. A few hundred yards away was the little Sunny Corner chapel, where Richard and his family had worshipped and where once she had gone for the sake of a moment with James. He had meant so much to her in the past, until—until his imprisonment. That had changed him, and it was in that time that she had become linked with Robert. She swept the name from her mind. Robert had no hold on her. James, for all his faults, was honest and loyal. He was incapable of double-dealing; he was direct, open, and he was in love with her.

She walked slowly between the high hedges, listening to the wind as it stirred the leaves of the trees overhanging the lane. Here she had walked with James, had held hands, and as she came to a farm gate she remembered how once they had gone into a field to embrace and been discovered by Mark and William. They were days of innocence, but innocence was gone. Memories of the past stirred her and woke feelings of deep affection, for Richard, for all the Bryants, and for James. He had meant so much to her then, could he not mean the same now? It was easy to think so.

He was playing with Alice when she arrived, sitting on the floor with her, laughing with her, and she was deeply moved by it. He did not see her until Alice called "Mammy." Then he glanced up, and seeing the look in her eyes stood to face her and showed, without any possibility of doubt, the depth of his own feelings for her.

Without thinking she reached to him and held his face between her hands and kissed him. The touch of her seemed to release something in him. He sighed deeply and responded to her kiss with mouth open. She moved her hands from his face and gently stroked his head, anxious not to deceive him as to her feelings.

"Mammy!"

They looked down. Alice was sitting at their feet, holding her arms high to be picked up.

"My love, my lover," crooned Ellen to her child, and James stood beside them, wanting to share their belonging.

Julia was moving in the kitchen and Ellen, with Alice in her arms, joined her. Her sister was big with child and was bearing her pregnancy well. She was content in her love for Mark, had never doubted that love.

Ellen was conscious of James at her back. He let his hand rest gently on her neck, not possessively, as Robert had, but hesitantly. She wished she could turn to him, declare her love for him, but it was not there to declare, not as he wanted it. She busied herself with Alice, took her upstairs and ignoring the unspoken demands of James upon her sang to her child until she slept.

The next morning she watched as he put the finishing

touches to his sea-chest and printed his name, JAS BRYANT TO
AMERICA. With the naming of the destination the parting grew
nearer and with it the feeling of loss.

She helped him to gather his possessions together. There
were not many, but the books which had belonged to Richard
were now his. Ellen handled them with love for they reminded
her of the past when there seemed no complications to press
on her, as now.

She was not so handy with a needle as her sister but she
made herself responsible for mending and patching his shirts.
It was a labor which she enjoyed and she wondered at herself.
As she sat, the thread to her teeth to bite it short, she was aware
that James was watching her. She would not raise her eyes to
meet his for she was afraid her resolution would weaken and
allow the affection she felt for him to masquerade as love.

"There," she said. "All ready," and handed the shirt to
him.

Chapter Seventeen

ROBERT Buchan saw that all the major men of mining had been drawn to the meeting. In every voice he heard about him there was indignation, a determination to show the men at Westminster how strong their feelings were. They greeted Buchan as a friend, a man of the establishment, one of them. Like them he was frock-coated, well dressed, sleek and comfortable. He did not know why he had been so careful with his attire. He should have come straight from the homes of the poor, the diseased, the Eathornes, with the odor of disinfectant about him; but he had changed, pomaded his hair, and now like the rest was the very picture of respectability. Within him there was, however, a growing unease, a self-disgust, a feeling of distaste for his companions and their arrogant assumption that they had his support.

Teague, of Illogan, nodded to him over the heads of the others and forced his way through the crowd. "I've got a resolution," he said, "protesting against the new Act forbidding the use of children." He prodded Buchan with his forefinger. "You know, Buchan, the old Act lets us employ children fifty-four hours a week. No harm's ever come to a boy by that, you take my word."

He turned away to greet another acquaintance before Buchan could protest. I cannot stay here and put myself through this charade, Buchan thought. I cannot sit still while men like Teague proclaim their self-interest is motivated by concern for the child. He moved back toward the door, intending to plead the need to attend a patient if he were challenged. His absence for reasons of that kind would not be held against him. There would be no need for him to declare in public his support of these men.

He successfully evaded questioning and reached the steps of the Royal Institution. There he paused a moment on the steps looking out on the gas-lit street. Rain was falling. A child stood at the foot of the steps and ran out to hold a horse as a brougham stopped, and held out a hand for a reward to the man who descended.

It was Abel Hosking. He ignored the boy and, seeing Buchan, greeted him effusively. "Ah, my dear Robert. You've come to give us your backing. Good man. It will do you no harm to speak. You're not a mining man, but it's as well to let 'em know you've the interests of the mines at heart." He took Robert by the arm and led him back into the hall.

So, thought Robert. There is no escape. I shall have to speak.

II

ELLEN could not bear to be at Sunny Corner to see the departure of James. She left early in the morning with a brief good-bye and went to Camborne, determined to bury herself in work so that she might forget the significance of the day. She found Veronica in an angry mood.

"He has done it," she said. "He has spoken out. There was a meeting last night in Truro. He could have kept quiet but he chose not to." She glared at Ellen as if she were to blame. "Robert Buchan," Veronica went on. "I put my trust in him and now he betrays it. I doubt if even I can undo the damage he's done."

"What has he done?"

"He announced in public that he supported any Act that would restrict the employment of children in the mines." She could not hide her indignation.

"And do you approve the employment of children in the mines?" said Ellen.

"In a limited way, of course I do. How else could families survive?"

"Perhaps better pay for their fathers might help."

Veronica was not to be halted. "He's almost ruined any hope of being chosen as the Liberal candidate. Hosking won't have him and in that case my mother will abandon Robert too. Read that." She handed Ellen a newspaper and Ellen read the passage Veronica indicated. Captain Abel Hosking had spoken against any interference from Westminster in the working of the mines. He stated, it was reported, that "the Metalliferous Mines Act of a few years earlier had allowed children between the ages of eight and twelve years of age to work on an average fifty-four hours a week. He did not think any violence was done to children by this. He argued that if children were to be taught the use of the implements by which they were to earn their livelihood in after life, the sooner they took them in hand the better." The report then commented briefly on "an intervention by a Dr. Buchan, more notable for its vehemence than its logic, stating his intention, were he to be elected a Member of Parliament, to seek legislation to change what he called this sorry state of affairs. We ask ourselves who is likely to support the claims of such a man to represent the Mining Division? There are other, better informed, men only too willing to succeed the retiring member."

"You see?" said Veronica. "How can I rescue him from follies such as that? He seems determined to ruin his chances. I thought him a safe man, not prey to his emotions, one I could work with, shape to my purposes."

"I had not thought of Robert Buchan as a man to be molded to shape. He seems to me too strong for that."

"Too stubborn maybe. We shall see. We shall see how he takes to my ultimatum."

"Your ultimatum?"

"I have no intention of tying myself in marriage to a country doctor. A man of affairs, yes, I could accept that. But a doctor? No!"

Ellen turned to her work. She had no wish to hear how Veronica was to deal with Robert. They deserved each other with their "marriage of convenience," but she felt a reluctant admiration for Robert's outspokenness on the employment of children. Perhaps at last he had found a cause he could not abandon, whatever the risks it held.

She returned to Cusgarne that evening sensitive to the gap left by James's departure.

During the night a wild storm erupted; a wind rose suddenly from the southeast, howling into the valley, tearing at the trees, and making the slates rattle and tumble slitheringly down the roof. Alice woke and cried with terror at the sound, and soon the whole uneasy household gathered in the main room of the cottage and huddled together, while outside the wind shrieked and wailed.

" 'Tis a rough old night," said Julia, drawing her blanket to her.

"God help the sailors on a night like this," said Mark unthinkingly, and they were reminded of James.

"They'll not put to sea in this," said Julia. But the storm had come without warning and the *John Gray* had been due to sail on the afternoon tide. By now it would be off the Manacles.

The storm ceased as suddenly as it had risen. There followed a stillness so complete that Ellen thought she had been deafened until Alice again began to cry. She put her daughter to bed, and after Mark and Julia had also gone to bed sat by the empty hearth, unable to settle her mind, anxious about James. She tried to assure herself no harm would come to him, but she knew how dangerous a southeasterly was to ships in Falmouth Bay.

On the way to Camborne the next morning the wildness of the night was evident in the broken boughs which strewed the lanes. In the town itself slates littered the pavements and chimney stacks leaned dangerously. There were rumors of ships lost in the storm, of boats at anchor wrecked in Falmouth harbor. Ellen went into town to see what she could discover of the fate of the *John Gray*, but there was no news of substance.

She returned to the house to find storm of another kind. Veronica was pacing up and down the office, almost too angry to speak.

"I told you," she burst out as soon as Ellen stepped into the room. "They'll not have Buchan. There was a meeting last night at which they agreed on Henry Tremayne instead. Why did he behave so?"

"Perhaps it was important to him."

"Of course it was important to him. But why did he not hold his tongue until his position was secure? No one would have thought any the worse of him. Well, he's burned his boats now. So that's that. We shall have to get to work on Tremayne. He's not unsympathetic to our cause, I fancy."

"And Buchan?"

Veronica sighed. "I had high hopes for him. Perhaps in time he'll regain his reputation. All that good will thrown away—on a matter of principle as he calls it!"

A matter of principle, Ellen reflected, and how long will that last? He is a man of inconstancy. I have proof of that.

"It's too late now," said Veronica. "I've summoned him here to tell him so."

Ellen smiled. Robert would not have taken kindly to that sort of behavior. Yes they deserved each other, these two.

Chapter Eighteen

I

ROBERT Buchan had not been surprised at the insults heaped on him by his former friends. Friends? He realized that he had not had friends among these people. They had been using him, and he had been using them. Now that he had shown himself in his true colors they had every right to reject him. He had no tinge of regret about his decision to speak against the Hoskings and the Teagues, no regret that by his decision he would forfeit the good will of the Langarths.

And Veronica. They had never pretended love for each other. The end of his political career would mean the end of their marriage plans, of that he was certain; and he breathed with relief that he no longer had need of her money to support his ambition. He had been freed of a burden. He was his own man. He had seen the truth of it in the last days, in the alleyways of Redruth, in the home of Sampson Eathorne, on the workings at Wheal Uny.

His thoughts swung to Wheal Uny, to the time when he had stayed underground there, keeping the hopes of William Henry Hosking alive. It was then, somehow, that things had begun to go wrong. Before that . . . before that there had been Ellen. He recalled her then, as she had come to him, shy, uncertain, yet totally accepting, totally his, and himself totally hers. Now with the abandonment of his ambition and the finding of himself, came a sharp awareness of her, not as she had been then, but as she was now, proud, independent, a woman of dignity. And he had offered this woman a place as his "kept woman," offered her a home, discreet and hidden, out of the public gaze, as if there was something in her to be ashamed of.

He wondered at his thinking such a woman as Ellen could have considered so humiliating a proposal. He had been blind. Now he had to face her. He had to face Veronica too, clear the air. But it was Ellen he had to see, to confess his shame to her; maybe he had nothing to hope from her—he did not deserve hope—she had indicated her feelings for the man Bryant. He could have no hope himself, but he could not let Ellen think the man she had seen in the months past was the real Robert Buchan. At least he could plead for her forgiveness. She could not deny him that.

And Veronica had summoned him to meet her. He smiled at the prospect. He would swallow his pride and let her anger wash over him. He would be glad to be free of her and her machinations.

II

BUCHAN took the train to Camborne and arrived late in the afternoon. Veronica, angry at being kept waiting, assailed him as he crossed the threshold.

"You are aware of what's happened?"

Robert stared at her, apparently unconcerned at the frustration boiling within her. Ellen, sitting at her desk, saw him glance in her direction. She bent to her work.

"You've heard of the decision?" Veronica said coldly.

"I know they've chosen Tremayne as candidate. He'll suit them well." His voice showed no regret. It was as if the choice of Tremayne had come as a relief rather than a disappointment.

"You realize what this means?" Veronica said.

"That I've lost your parents' support? Yes. And yours?" His inquiry was cool, as if he was indifferent to the answer.

"What can you expect?"

"Then we're free of each other?" Buchan said. Ellen wished she could have closed the study door to exclude the quarrel, but it was too late now. She began to wonder if Buchan were staging it for her benefit. What difference did it make to her what these two decided to do with their lives?

"Free of each other?" said Veronica. "There's been no formal announcement so of course we're free. I've no intention of settling in Redruth as the wife of a bal surgeon."

"A bal surgeon? I doubt if my contract as a bal surgeon will be renewed. I'll be a mere town doctor, going my humble way about Redruth, attempting the impossible. Fortunately it's a job I know. And I know my place, too—at last."

"We had high hopes of you." There was regret as well as anger in Veronica's voice.

"I had high hopes myself. I still have. But not in the same way," Robert said.

Ellen glanced up, unable to control her curiosity. He was standing at the door, looking in at her.

"I still have hope," he repeated. "But not of the kind you mean," he said over his shoulder to Veronica.

"The carriage is here for you, Miss Bray," Rachel announced. Ellen was glad to move and rose from the desk. As Robert went to the door with her Veronica said sharply, "You will be here promptly on Monday, Ellen. We have a busy week ahead. We must invite Tremayne to meet us." She ignored Buchan. "We shall have to work hard on him."

"I shall be here," said Ellen.

She walked to the front door followed by Buchan, very conscious of the nearness of him. His hands took her elbow as she stepped to the carriage. She would have shrugged him off but decided that was to make an issue of something of no consequence. She was aware of his fingers holding her and tried to ignore the feeling that ran from his touch to her every nerve. He gave orders to the coachman to drive to Redruth and to her surprise he got into the carriage with her.

"You don't object?" he said with a diffidence foreign to him. "I have something I must say. I must speak with you. I could say nothing there. That house of Veronica's stifles me."

"You spoke there once," she said, making no effort to hide her disdain.

"I am ashamed that I could have thought so little of you."
He had turned his head away from her as if to look at her would
shame him more. His voice was low, almost as if he were speaking not to her but to himself. She had to concentrate to catch
his meaning.

"That night . . . that whole day. Does it mean anything to
you, I wonder, that memory? Did it mean something to you
then? I believed so. To me, that night meant everything." He
paused, for a moment only, in recollection and then words
tumbled from him. "I cannot forget it, nor any part of it, from
the beginning to the end. I was called from your side, tore
myself away from you, left you there, where. . . . Those terrible
weeks that followed, the waiting for you, waiting, hoping. I
remember it so clearly now." He leaned over to her and she
allowed him to take her hands in his. "I hoped every day for
a word from you, hoped you would come."

"I came."

"Only to reject me. You went away, kept my child from
me. No, don't speak," he said as she opened her mouth to
protest. "Hear me out. Even if it changes nothing, hear me out.
Some madness overcame me. Forgive me if you can. I cannot
bear you to think that the Robert Buchan you have seen of late
is me. It was not me you saw fawning on those men of influence.
It was another, blinded with ambition, flattered and deceived
so as to deny himself. I am not the lapdog of the Langarths, a
puppet to jerk and posture at Veronica's will. I am my own
man, the man you once knew. Why did you turn from me?"
he suddenly asked.

She hesitated, moved by his confession, then, "You had
ignored me, refused to see me. I thought you had used me,
that I was one of many. Your housekeeper . . ."

"What of her?" he interrupted. "What has she to do with
it?"

She told him of the hurt she had suffered and the woman's
refusal to admit her to see him. "I thought she spoke for you."

"Ellen!" His voice was anguished with longing. "I have lost
you. And deservedly so. But do not think ill of me. That I could
not bear."

The carriage slowed in the traffic of Redruth, turned into
the road leading to Robert's house and drew to a halt at the
entrance to his drive.

He released hold of her. "Can you forgive me?" he asked.

She could not answer. Not yet. He had said so much that her world, which had seemed so settled—and empty—before was once again in turmoil.

"What of you?" he inquired, but hesitantly as if he recognized he had no right to an answer. "You'll marry Bryant?"

"James? He sailed for America yesterday."

"Yesterday?" His voice was sharp.

"On the *John Gray*."

"Come inside," he said and to the coachman, "Wait here. Come inside, Ellen, please."

"I ought not."

"There's no ought or ought not between us. You'll come in." His voice held concern. "It is for your sake. There is something I have to tell you."

"The *John Gray*?" she said. He nodded.

She allowed him to take her into the house; indeed there was nothing she could do to resist, for will had left her; she was emptied of sensation, preparing herself for the news he had to give. He took her into the drawing room. She had been there before, but it did not seem to matter. Her mind was clear of memories; thoughts of James were all she could hold. She felt a glass put in her hand. She looked up. Robert was there.

"Brandy," he said. "Sip it."

She did as she was told. The fire in the alcohol startled her and she came to her senses.

"Tell me," she said.

"The *John Gray* has foundered," he said. "Driven onto the Manacles. Feared lost with all hands."

"Feared? It's not certain?"

"There's little hope. None."

"You said there's little hope. That means there's some, however small."

He shook his head.

"How can you be certain?" She looked about her and was suddenly conscious of the room, its reminders of the past. "I must go," she said.

"Where?" he asked.

"Wherever there may be news. Falmouth. Coverack. Wherever is nearest to the place it sank."

"What good will it do?"

"I must know."

"There may be more news tomorrow. I'll take you there if you still wish to go." He took the glass from her and stood looking down on her, with tenderness and sympathy. "I'm sorry," he said. "I wish it had not been me to bring the news."

He helped her into the carriage. She wanted him to keep hold of her hand. She needed his strength and concern to help her over the next days. She needed his love, she knew it now, and wished she could confess it to him. She turned to watch him as the carriage drove away, wanting to tell the driver to turn back, but not daring to

III

THEY came to the little cove in the early afternoon of the next day. From the cliffs above they could see the upturned hull of the *John Gray* beyond the rock called the Minstrel. In the church of St. Keverne, a mile inland, lay three corpses washed ashore earlier, two seamen and a woman.

Ellen, with Buchan beside her, stood on the beach watching the men and boys who lined the water's edge, dragging wood and other flotsam from the sea. One pair rushed into the waves to reach a pale figure, floating, drifting, receding a little, then drawing near again. She went down to look, though Robert tried to hold her back.

It was a woman the men dragged to the beach, a woman, near-naked, clothes stripped from her by the seas, a woman, young and comely once no doubt and bright with hope, but lifeless now, flesh scarred and livid, hair lank with seaweed. The men carried the body up the beach and Ellen waited, watching the waves curling, mildly now, along the shore.

"Ellen," she heard Robert say. "There's no hope."

"I know," she said. "I know, but I owe it to him to wait."

"Owe it to him? We owe it to the living, not the dead."

"I know that too. It can do no harm to wait a little longer."

"He may not come ashore here," he said. "He may never come ashore."

"I might have been with him," she said. She gestured to the corpse being carried by the men up the cliff path to the village. "That might well have been me."

"Thank God it's not," said Robert.

"He wanted me to go with him," she said. "I only had to put my hands out to him for him to take me with him."

The waves crept further up the beach. Wooden wreckage was heaped safely on the rocks beyond the tide. Gulls screamed and mewed about the cliffs. Robert had turned to her, understanding she had refused James, but not daring yet to believe it.

"You would not go with him?" he said at last.

"I could not," she said. "He was a friend, a deep, deep friend and in some manner we belonged together, shaped in the same fire, sharing the past that made us."

"The future?"

"For him the future lay in America and now . . ." She could not hold back the tears, though she tried. A sob burst from her and Robert took her to him, holding her against him, until slowly the shuddering stopped.

She stood for a moment, letting his strength comfort her. She looked up at him and he gently wiped the tears from her cheeks.

"I loved him in a way," she said.

"In a way?" He looked into her eyes.

"There are many ways of loving," she said.

"I know of only one."

"And that way?" she asked. As they stood, in close embrace, they were unaware of the men dashing to and forth dragging debris up the beach.

He was silent. His hands began to fondle her hair.

"I am ashamed," he said at last. "Ashamed that I could ever have thought of hiding my love for you from the world."

He has spoken at last of love, she thought.

She released herself from his hold and turned her back on him to look out to the rocks, Minstrel and the Manacles, rising dangerously from the sea. There was a scuffle among the crowd on the beach. The waves had brought a pile of wreckage near to where Ellen and Robert were standing, timbers, wooden boxes, broken spars.

"Go on, Matt. You were there first," a man shouted to a youngster. "Hold it boy. Hold it. I'll be with you."

The man leaped into the waves and hauled out a chest, bringing it almost to Ellen's feet.

"Sorry, lady," said the boy Matt. " 'Tis fine takings, this."

He sees only delight, not sadness, in this, she thought. She looked at the wooden chest he was guarding. It was crudely made, but the paint on it was still fresh and bright. It read JAS BRYANT TO AMERICA.

"Poor bugger," said a man. " 'Tis no use to him now."

Ellen moved to protest as Matt began to prize the lid open. What did it matter? 'Tis no use to James now, she agreed.

The lid was raised. She stared in at the sodden articles and wanted to weep again for the drowned hopes. It was no use weeping. Robert was right, the living not the dead had need of her.

Robert took her elbow. "What's in there is the past," he said. "There is another chest to be opened now. The future." He hesitated. "The future together, you and I, and our daughter, Alice."

She felt Robert's hand take hers and draw her back from the lapping waves. The men quarreled over their spoils, drawing from the chest a patched shirt and some sodden papers. Then they dashed into the sea as another body, floating gently in the shallow sea, drifted forward and back. She moved to it, into the water, heedless of the men about her and the smell of the brine, the mewing of the gulls and the sighing of the sea, heedless of all but the body lifting and dipping to the tide.

She reached James first but it was Robert who, with two of the villagers, drew him to dry land. His eyes were open, his mouth had the curl to his lips that had so enchanted, but his skin was bluish with the taint of death. She knelt beside him as if, by holding him now, she could convey to him what she had felt for him, but he was beyond the telling. He knows, she thought; he could not help but know that between us there was something that was ours alone.

"We'll take him up along," she heard a villager say. They had brought a hurdle and now they put James on it and, with four men to carry it, bore their burden to the church in the village.

"To set off three thousand miles and end up here, twelve miles from port," said one of the men, shaking his head. He turned to Ellen who was walking beside them, stumbling on the narrow path. " 'Twas bound for America, that sad wreck," he said.

"I know," she answered and thought of the lure of that dream, of the dangers that faced men on the way there, and none so threatening as the rocks of the Cornish coast.

She watched them lay James's body close to those of the other victims. In the gloom of the church their shapes were indistinct. They were mere dead flesh, men and women no longer.

He has gone, she said to herself, and turned aside to keep her tears hidden.

Robert was there, a few feet away, watching and waiting.

"We'll have him taken home," said Robert.

Home: a plot in a country burial ground near to the grave of his father, under the bright Cornish sky, with the taste of gorse in the air.

They left the village and Ellen did not look back to the sea and the rock where the *John Gray* had foundered. She did not want, any longer, to look back. There was the future to face, to hold to, to shape maybe; she would not be tossed by circumstance, to be cast ashore, finished with, hopes wrecked; she would make her future for herself, and if there were tempests on the way she would survive them, she and her daughter Alice.

She felt Robert's hand reach for hers. She let him hold it. He had declared his love. Perhaps then he too would be involved in that future. Perhaps they would share what lay ahead.

She turned her head to him and saw in his clear blue eyes what she had longed to see before—not mere desire, but tenderness, understanding and love.